ng an innocent had transformed more than one merry bachelor into a far less merry husband.

At *once*. That meant *immediately*, or *right now*, as in *this very second*.

She pushed against his chest again, harder this time.

Bloody, bloody, bloody hell.

His innocent temptress was determined to escape him. She writhed and flailed and tried to twist off his lap. She'd flee as soon as he released her, that much was certain. She'd flee and he'd never get a close look at her. He'd never know who she was and he wouldn't be able to find her again.

Unthinkable. Find her he would, innocent or not.

Robyn tightened his arms around her. He had to know who she was.

Then he'd let her go.

PRAISE FOR *A WICKED WAY TO WIN AN EARL*

"A delightfully delicious debut that grips readers with the very first scene and doesn't let go . . . Watch for this new-comer to become a fan favorite." —*RT Book Reviews*

Unbearable desire . . .

He'd better stop at once, as kissing and fondlin

A

Season of Ruin

ANNA BRADLEY

BERKLEY SENSATION, NEW YORK

**BERKLEY
SENSATION**

**An imprint of Penguin Random House LLC
375 Hudson Street, New York, New York 10014**

A SEASON OF RUIN

A Berkley Sensation Book / published by arrangement with Katherine M. Jackson

ISBN: 9780425282649

PUBLISHING HISTORY
Berkley Sensation mass-market edition / August 2016

PRINTED IN THE UNITED STATES OF AMERICA

10 9 8 7 6 5 4 3 2 1

Cover art by Gregg Gulbronson.
Cover design by George Long.
Interior text design by Kristin del Rosario.

Penguin
Random
House

To my Portland ladies,
and the many red threads that connect us.

I'm so glad we all found each other.

My deepest thanks to my agent, Marlene Stringer, my editor Kristine Schwartz, and my publicists Nancy Berland and Kim Rozzell-Miller. I'm so thankful to have an opportunity to work with such a talented, creative, and enthusiastic team.

A special thanks to the readers who have welcomed me into their reading lives.

Chapter One

A high, thin voice floated on the air, audible even through the closed door. The music had begun. Pleyel. Of course. The *Scottish Airs*. What else?

Good God—musical evenings. Of all the bloody dull entertainments the *ton* inflicted on the gentlemen of London, the musical evening was the bloodiest. One stood about in a stifling room and waited for the music to start, then one squeezed one's arse onto a miniature chair and pretended to appreciate the efforts of a screeching soprano. Wait, stand, squeeze, listen, pretend. It was damned tedious.

Robyn rolled his shoulders inside his tight coat. He had no intention of escorting his sisters all over London this season. That is, unless they wished to forgo their card parties, routs, and balls in favor of a visit to the gaming hells, or a frolic with the Cyprians in Covent Garden.

He tried to imagine his sister Eleanor at a hazard table, her long, elegant fingers wrapped around a pair of dice as every rogue in London breathed down her neck. Or his sister

Charlotte, engaged in a debate with the whores at the Slippery Eel over how low was *too* low when it came to low-cut bodices.

No, he couldn't picture it. Shame, too, because it would have been amusing.

Robyn pressed his ear close to the door and listened. Not to Pleyel, but for the soft shuffle of a lady's slippers creeping down the hallway. He preferred petite, dark-haired ladies, especially those of an accommodating nature, to Pleyel.

Ah, dear old London. Wickedness lurked everywhere, even in the unlikeliest places. Another reason to love the old girl.

Where the devil was she? He tapped his foot, his eyes fixed on the door handle, willing it to turn.

It shouldn't be long now.

"Which do you think the handsomest?" Charlotte tapped Lily's wrist with her fan and nodded her head toward the center of the drawing room.

One couldn't take a step in any direction without tripping over one elegant nobleman or another, but there could be no doubt which group of gentlemen Charlotte referred to. Lily had noticed more than one feminine eyelash batting in that direction.

"My goodness," Eleanor interrupted. "Is Lord Pelkey wearing a pink waistcoat?" She peered over Lily's shoulder at the gentleman in question. "Oh, dear. It *is* pink, with green embroidered butterflies. That leaves him out. No gentleman who wears a pink waistcoat with green butterflies can be considered handsome."

The ladies tittered.

"Better to ask which is the wickedest," said Miss Thurston, a sour young lady with a head full of dull brown frizz and a perpetually peeved expression. Her maid had clearly taken pains with her hair, but what had no doubt begun as fashionable ringlets had long since succumbed to the heat of the room. Poor Miss Thurston looked as if she wore a brown, fuzzy animal of some sort on her head.

"One of them is as wicked as the next," she declared.

Perhaps the loss of her curls had curdled her temper.

"Mr. Robert Sutherland is the handsomest." As far as Lily was concerned, there was no question. It wasn't that he was so tall or so remarkably well formed, though he was both. It wasn't even his thick dark hair or heavily lashed black eyes.

No, it was his smile. His mouth was just a shade too wide. In another man, that mouth might have been a flaw, but Robyn had a slow, suggestive smile, and he wielded it like a pickax. That smile could crack the ice around the coldest feminine heart.

"And the wickedest," put in Frizzle-Hair.

Charlotte sighed. "Poor Robyn. How awful, to be the wickedest gentleman in the wickedest city in England."

Lily just stopped herself from rolling her eyes. If she believed half the tales and dire warnings about the wickedness of London, she'd refuse to leave her bedchamber at the Sutherlands' Mayfair town house.

When they first arrived in town, she'd expected to find cutthroats wielding knives in broad daylight, a pickpocket's fingers forever in her reticule, and leering rakes on every street corner. She'd kept a keen eye out for the rakes, as she didn't wish to be caught unawares, but to her knowledge she'd not yet seen one, leering or otherwise, and she'd been here for nearly six weeks already.

It was true she hadn't been out in society much since her arrival. She'd spent most of her time helping her sister Delia prepare for her wedding to Alec Sutherland, but Delia hadn't been Lady Carlisle for more than a few days before Eleanor and Charlotte Sutherland, Alec's younger sisters, had whisked Lily off her feet and into London's social whirl. Their mother, Lady Catherine, had graciously offered to sponsor Lily, and all three young ladies anticipated a lively season.

Leering rakes, indeed. Handsome, fashionable gentlemen abounded, each more scrupulously polite than the last. Lily had rarely seen such a concentration of impeccable manners. The only thing that had given her a moment's concern was the price of hats on Bond Street.

She was fond of hats.

No matter what Charlotte said, Lily hadn't seen any real evidence of Robyn's wickedness. She prided herself on her fair-mindedness, and she wouldn't dream of condemning a man without evidence.

"What about that one?" Lily gestured with her chin at a tall, golden-haired gentleman. "I can't like the look of him. He has cold eyes."

All four heads swiveled to assess the golden-haired gentleman.

Charlotte craned her neck to see over a large woman wearing a towering purple turban adorned with tall peacock feathers. "Ah," she murmured with a significant look at Lily. "*That* is Lord Atherton."

Lily met Charlotte's eyes. "It is, indeed?"

Well, then. That changed everything. Perhaps she *could* like the look of him, after all. It would help if she did, as she intended to be married to him by the end of the season.

She glanced back over at the group of gentlemen. Lord Atherton stood just at the edges of it, his back a bit rigid and his air abstracted, as if he were only half listening to their conversation. He wasn't as tall as Robyn, but he was certainly tall enough to satisfy Lily.

Charlotte, who loved a matchmaking caper more than anything, rubbed her hands together in anticipation. "Yes. We'll have Robyn introduce you, and—"

Miss Thurston interrupted her. "He does *not* have cold eyes! Why, how unfair you are!" She looked as though she'd like to slap Lily with her fan. "Lord Atherton is the very model of a refined English gentleman. He has a spotless reputation."

Lily didn't argue this point. His spotlessness wasn't in question. If it had been, she and Charlotte would never have settled upon him, after prolonged discussion, as Lily's perfect mate and the potential future father of her children.

Charlotte didn't entirely agree with Lily's choice. In fact, she'd insisted Lord Atherton was "as dull as a stick of wood." She'd attempted to steer Lily toward a more exciting young gentleman, but Lily wouldn't hear of it.

Excitement wasn't part of her plan.

Perhaps Frizzle-Hair had set her cap for Lord Atherton? If so, Lily feared she was destined for disappointment, for that spotless and refined model of English manhood hadn't looked her way once tonight. He hadn't looked Lily's way, either, but he would before the soprano had sung her last note this evening.

"Didn't you just say one of them is as wicked as the next?" Lily asked, turning to Frizzle-Hair.

That young lady gave a worldly sniff. "You're from the country, aren't you, Miss Somerset? Perhaps you aren't familiar enough with town gentlemen to venture an opinion, and should defer to those with more knowledge on the subject."

"Perhaps," Lily agreed, all politeness, though she was tempted to laugh aloud at the idea that Frizzle-Hair was an expert on gentlemen of either the town or the country variety.

Charlotte gave Lily a sly wink. "How, Miss Thurston, do you judge the degree of a gentleman's wickedness?"

"Well, one does hear things about Mr. Sutherland, you know. Scandalous things." Miss Thurston clamped her lips shut as if to prevent any of these scandalous things from emerging.

Charlotte gasped. "Why, Miss Thurston! Surely you don't rely on gossip to make your determinations?"

"Well, I . . ." Miss Thurston faltered. Her face flushed. "That is, of course not."

Charlotte took a deep breath and patted her chest with the tips of her fingers. "Oh, I'm *so* relieved to hear it, for the gentleman who escapes gossip's vicious tongue may simply hide his debauchery with greater cunning. That would make him *wickeder* than the others, not less so. Wouldn't it, Miss Thurston?"

Miss Thurston's fountain of wisdom on the vagaries of the English gentleman appeared to have run dry, however. She looked from Eleanor to Charlotte, then from Charlotte to Lily, dipped into a shallow curtsy, and hurried away without another word.

Charlotte watched her scurry off, frizzy curls flying, then snapped open her fan with a quick flick of her wrist. "I enjoyed that."

Lily stifled a giggle. "You're the wicked one, Charlotte."

Charlotte gave her fan a vigorous wave. "Robyn is every bit as bad as Miss Thurston says, but I can't have her say so right to my face, can I? He *is* my brother, after all."

Lily glanced back over at the group of gentlemen, but Robyn was no longer there. She scanned the room for a dark head towering over the rest of the party, but he seemed to have disappeared. "Where did he—"

"Come, let's find a seat," Ellie said. "They're going to start."

Miss Sophia Licari, the soprano, had taken her place at the front of the room.

Lily gathered her skirts in her hand. "Save my seat, won't you? I need to visit the ladies' retiring room. My sash is twisted."

Ellie frowned. "Can't it wait?"

Lily fingered the tiny fold in the green satin sash at her

waist. No, it couldn't wait. She couldn't abide a twisted sash under any circumstances.

"Shall I accompany you?" Charlotte asked. "The house is rather confusing—"

"No, no. Just point me in the right direction. I'll find it."

Charlotte made a vague gesture toward the door. "To the right, just there. Down the hallway, the last door on the left. Hurry now, Lily, or you'll miss the best part."

Damn it, his ear had begun to ache from being squashed against the door. If Alicia thought he'd wait all night for her—

A faint sound came from the hallway, just outside the door.

Robyn froze, breath held. *At last.*

A moment later the handle twisted, the door opened a crack, and a dainty, white-gloved hand appeared. He seized her wrist and nearly jerked her off her feet in his haste to get her through the door.

He'd waited long enough.

"What—" she squeaked.

He placed his lips against her ear with a low chuckle. "What took you so long? I was just wondering the same thing myself."

He eased her backward against the door, leaned his body into hers, and released her wrist. He let his fingers brush against her hip as he reached behind her to twist the lock. The bolt slid home with a sharp click.

God, she smelled incredible. He buried his nose in her neck and inhaled. Odd, but he'd never noticed her scent before, and a man didn't often come across a woman who smelled like a meadow. Fresh, like grass warmed by the sun, or like a daisy would smell if it had a scent. He'd have expected a more sophisticated perfume from Alicia, something sweeter, heavier. Less subtle. What a pleasant surprise, this scent. He nuzzled her neck and suppressed a sudden, absurd urge to growl.

Two unsteady hands came up to grasp the lapels of his coat. He expected to feel her arms slide around his neck, but instead she pushed against his chest. "I don't—"

"Of course you do." *Otherwise she wouldn't be here.*

Robyn had no interest in a polite chat, and he'd long since learned the best way to keep a woman quiet was to give her something else to do with her mouth. He dropped a brief kiss on her warm, scented neck but resisted the urge to bury his face in her hair.

A man *should* linger over a scent like hers, but Lord Barrow's study wasn't the place to do it. He could easily be carried away by that scent, and before he knew it, he'd have Alicia flat on her back on what was undoubtedly a very fine carpet.

It wouldn't do to muss his lordship's carpet. It wasn't gentlemanly.

Then again, there was a settee. *Blast*—he should have tested it while he waited for her. But no matter. He'd noticed a desk, as well. A wide, empty desk. Lord Barrow, bless him, was quite tidy. Robyn would have to remember to send the old boy a fine bottle of brandy to show his gratitude.

Alicia's hands tightened on his lapels. "Please—"

Ah, so eager. He did enjoy it when they begged. "No worries, pet. I'll take care of you."

He lowered his head and crushed his lips against hers. He could have tried for at least a modicum of finesse, but this was by no means Alicia's first time alone in a dark, deserted library with an amorous gentleman. She knew what was coming.

But instead of devouring him as he'd expected, a strangled whimper escaped her and she jerked back, away from him. There was no place for her to go, of course, as she was trapped between the door and his body, but she squirmed to break contact with his mouth.

Alicia, a shy virgin? That was doing it a bit brown, but if she wanted to play games, he'd act the part of the lustful rake to her chaste, innocent young lady. He placed his palms on either side of her face to hold her still and ran his tongue across the dry, closed seam of her lips.

She didn't open them. Robyn swept his tongue insistently against her mouth, but the delectable lips remained closed. What was Alicia playing at? She'd been keen enough to get him in here, and he'd been keen to come in part because he'd expected to get his tongue inside her mouth.

He swept it across her lips again. No luck, but all the same, Robyn felt a flutter of desire tickle low in his belly. The moment she denied him the pleasures of her mouth, he found he could think of nothing but how to get his tongue between her lips to surge into her slick heat.

It was something new anyway.

He didn't often have to make an effort to get inside a woman, her mouth or any other part of her. Women made no secret of their attraction to him, and Robyn felt it was impolite to refuse their advances. He took his pleasure where it was offered. Widows, actresses, opera singers, a mistress here and there—they were all delightful diversions in much the same way a visit to Tattersall's or a jaunt down Rotten Row diverted.

Predictable. Simple. Fleeting.

But challenging? No. Women weren't challenging, and hadn't been since he'd been a randy fifteen-year-old lad agonizing over a saucy, buxom maid at his family's seat in Kent. She'd given him a merry chase until at last she'd led him to a remote part of the rose garden. He'd pinned her against a stone wall and taken her right there, his breeches around his ankles, the sun on his back, his head swimming with the scent of roses. He couldn't recall her name now, but to this day the scent of roses and the texture of rough stone still made him hard.

The maid had been the first in a succession of ladies who'd fallen into his arms like pins hitting the turf on a bowling green. Alicia, however, showed not the slightest inclination to hit the turf. She remained stubbornly, temptingly upright.

Christ, he was jaded. Jaded and debauched, because the idea of overcoming her token resistance aroused him. He would *make* her open for him. He would coax her, render her so dizzy with passion she would have no choice but welcome him into her mouth. The flutter of desire in his belly unfurled and grew until it became a conflagration.

Robyn slid his tongue away from the seam of her lips. He'd have it inside her before they left this room, but he could take his time getting there. His teased his mouth across hers, nibbling at one corner, then the other. He slipped his tongue deftly across the perfect curve of her lower lip to tease her, then he discovered the faint bow of her upper lip. He darted the tip of his tongue into the tiny gap again and again, until he thought he'd go mad if she didn't open her lips.

She made some small sound then, some faint whisper of . . . surrender? He burned with anticipation, but her lips remained closed. Her hands still clutched at his coat, but with each soft touch of his mouth, he felt the tension ease from her, one vertebra at a time, until her back relaxed against the door.

Robyn slid his hands between the door and her body to stroke the arch of her lower back, right where it swelled into what promised to be a luscious backside. After a few moments her fists opened and she laid her hands flat on his chest.

Yes. That was it. He smiled against her mouth.

He would not have believed a practiced siren like Alicia could work him into such a frenzy. He'd had dozens of women just like her before. She was no innocent, but damned if she didn't have him imagining she was. He was wild to get into her mouth and find out if she tasted as perfect as she felt. Would she be sweet, like honey, or rich, like new cream?

He'd thought only to have a frolic with her, but perhaps a more permanent arrangement was in order? She was married, of course, but that made no difference to him. He'd had married lovers before.

For God's sake. He hadn't even kissed her properly yet.

He laid his hand against her neck and pressed light, feathery kisses against her cheeks, then another on the tip of her nose. They were gentle, playful kisses—not at all the kind of kisses he'd normally share with a woman like Alicia. Or *any* woman, come to that, since the women he favored were all different versions of her.

At some point he'd begun to pretend it wasn't Alicia at all. Not very gallant of him, but it kept the illusion intact. The innocence of her lips under his, feigned though it was, touched him somehow. He was almost reluctant to end the moment at all.

Almost.

Then, without warning, as if she sensed a change in him, she wrapped her arms around his neck. Robyn froze, afraid she'd retreat again, but then she gave a low, breathy sigh and melted into him. The blood pounded through his body. He wanted to crush her against him and take her mouth roughly then, but he held himself back and instead let just the tip of his tongue graze her lush bottom lip.

Once.

Her lips opened.

Robyn had the strangest urge to sink to his knees, but if he did he'd take her down to the floor with him, and they no longer had time for *that*. But *this*—he'd been wild to get inside her mouth since she'd opened the door and he'd seen her white-gloved hand.

White gloves? Robyn stilled as he conjured an image of Alicia as she'd looked from across the drawing room. Petite but curvy, dark hair swept on top of her head, catlike gray eyes aglow with wanton invitation. A dark blue gown and long black gloves fit tightly to her slender arms. Hadn't she had a diamond bauble of some sort on her wrist?

Well, maybe she'd worn the diamond bracelet on the other wrist? The one that hadn't opened the door? Yes, that must be it. And perhaps she'd simply changed into white gloves on her way to meet him in the study? Yes. Yes, of course, she'd want to change her gloves on her way to an illicit assignation.

He was still trying to convince himself this was a perfectly reasonable explanation when a hesitant tongue brushed against his. With that one shy stroke, every thought fled Robyn's head but one.

She tastes like wild strawberries.

"Delicious," he murmured, his voice as rough as a cat's tongue, and so husky he hardly recognized it. He stroked the soft skin of her jaw as his tongue twined with hers, then slipped two fingers under her chin to tilt her mouth up to his to deepen the kiss.

A low, pained groan broke from his chest when at last he was able to take her mouth fully. His tongue touched her everywhere, lost in her sweet, tart taste. She met each glide and stroke and thrust, and he wanted to roar with triumph.

Maybe they did have time for *that*, after all.

He swept her into his arms and backed away from the door. He'd intended to lay her across Lord Barrow's desk, but he only made it as far as the settee. He dropped down onto it, his lips still joined with hers, and dragged her on top of him, across his lap, his throat dry, pulse jumping in his neck, ready to devour her.

Jesus. It's just a kiss. A kiss, like any other kiss he'd shared with countless other women.

But it wasn't the same, and somewhere in his passion-fogged brain Robyn recognized it. This kiss was different. He hadn't lost control with a woman since he'd turned sixteen, but now his body shook with the need to get inside her.

He cupped her cheek to urge her mouth closer to his and dragged his palm down the front of her neck and over the smooth, warm skin left bare by her low-cut gown. He traced his fingertips to the very edge of the neckline, where the smooth silk met the soft skin of the tops of her breasts.

Oh, God. Such a light touch, but he could feel the faintest throb of her heart under his fingers.

Her pert little backside pressed against his groin, his tongue twined with hers, and he was about to fill his hand with her soft breast. Had this not been the case, Robyn might have noticed it when she stilled on his lap. He might have felt just the merest whisper of a retreat.

As it was, he didn't notice a thing until she withdrew her tongue from his mouth, and then every part of his body howled with the loss. He couldn't fail to notice when she went stiff and unyielding on top of him and began to struggle in earnest to get away. It cooled his ardor just enough to enable him to think clearly.

Damn it. Something was wrong.

The white gloves. He was certain Alicia had been wearing black gloves and a high-necked gown. He'd noted the style because it was an unusual choice for Alicia, whose breasts were forever spilling from her bodices. There was something else, as well. Just now, when he'd swept her into his arms, her head had rested under his chin. Alicia was petite; her head wouldn't have reached farther than his shoulder.

Well, *someone's* head had rested there, for he'd buried his face in her hair to draw in as much as he could of her intoxicating scent. He was damn sure he'd just run his fingertips over the bare skin of *someone's* neck and bosom, as well. Even the finest silk wasn't that soft and supple. Or that warm. And her scent—that grass in the sun, daisies in a meadow scent. Alicia was charming in her way, but no woman of her experience could manufacture a scent like that, a scent of pure, distilled innocence.

He really *wasn't* kissing Alicia. The shyness, the hesitation, the reticence—it wasn't feigned. He hadn't the faintest idea whom he *was* kissing, but he was quite sure she was an innocent. A responsive, eager, passionate innocent, but an innocent nonetheless.

He'd better stop at once, as kissing and fondling an innocent had transformed more than one merry bachelor into a far less merry husband.

At once. That meant *immediately*, or *right now*, as in *this very second*.

She pushed against his chest again, harder this time.

Bloody, bloody, bloody hell.

His innocent temptress was determined to escape him. She writhed and flailed and tried to twist off his lap. She'd flee as soon as he released her, that much was certain. She'd flee and he'd never get a close look at her. He'd never know who she was and he wouldn't be able to find her again.

Unthinkable. Find her he would, innocent or not.

Robyn tightened his arms around her. He had to know who she was.

Then he'd let her go.

Chapter Two

Robyn Sutherland was trying to put his tongue inside her mouth.

She knew something was amiss as soon as she felt the strong fingers wrap around her wrist. This wasn't the ladies' retiring room, and these fingers didn't belong to a lady. They belonged to Robyn Sutherland, and if the fingers were his, then it stood to reason the tongue sweeping across the seam of her lips was Robyn's, as well.

She'd mistaken the room. Robyn, who'd just thrown the bolt on the door behind her, had mistaken the lady. He was eager, impassioned, and quite obviously waiting for someone else.

Someone who *wanted* his tongue inside her mouth.

Goodness gracious. She'd never heard of such a thing. Was this how gentlemen kissed in London? Or was this just how Robyn kissed?

The wickedest gentleman in the wickedest city in England.

She thought the statement utter nonsense not ten minutes ago, but that was before she discovered what a determined tongue he had.

Well. She had far more to contribute to a discussion of his wickedness *now*. It didn't speak well of him that he was hiding in a dark room, lying in wait for some female of questionable virtue, right in the middle of Lord and Lady Barrow's musicale. Not well at all.

"What—" she began.

He chuckled. "What took you so long? I was just wondering the same thing myself."

She knew that chuckle, that voice. This particular gentleman hadn't ever spoken to *her* in such a low, husky murmur, but she couldn't mistake that teasing drawl.

"I don't—" she tried again, but she wasn't sure quite what she'd say. *I don't think this is the ladies' retiring room? I don't have time to be accosted tonight? I don't think you should put your tongue there?*

He brushed his mouth against her neck. "Of course you do."

Lily took a deep breath and warned herself not to panic, even when he pressed against her and she realized she was trapped between his warm, eager body and the hard wooden door at her back. Being accosted by an amorous gentleman was not part of her plan this evening, but she must not fall into maidenly hysterics, especially over a simple case of mistaken identity. It was easily set to rights.

Hysterics would cause a scene, and Lily detested scenes. They were messy.

She turned her head to the side in an attempt to break contact with his mouth, but he followed the movement as if he were a horse and she'd hidden a lump of sugar under her tongue.

She wished he'd stop, for at the moment she had other things to worry about than avoiding his lips. She needed to work out if she should be *more* worried Robyn was the rake

in question, or *less* so. It did complicate matters. If he suc-
ceeded in getting his tongue in her mouth, she'd never be
able to look him in the eye again.

So there was that.

She'd much prefer to escape this room before he realized
who she was, but short of rendering him unconscious, she
couldn't see how she'd manage it. She couldn't simply explain herself. It was a miracle he hadn't already recognized
her voice, though admittedly the antics with his tongue must
take a great deal of concentration.

Besides, one had to open one's mouth to offer an explanation, and under the circumstances, that seemed risky.

She needed a new plan, one with an escape route. If only
she had a bit of paper, she might be able to work it out . . .

Lily's eyes widened as the hot tongue swept against her
mouth again, but she kept her lips sealed. Robyn was a
gentleman. She was safe with him as long as she remained
unwilling, and a lady communicated her unwillingness by
keeping her lips *closed*.

Robyn would never bestow his attentions on an unwilling
recipient. Would he? He couldn't be as wicked as his sisters
claimed he was. Charlotte in particular was so apt to dra-
matize, Lily had begun to suspect the wicked London Rake
was as much a fiction as wicked London itself.

Now she wasn't so sure.

Robyn made one more foray against her mouth with his
tongue, but she kept her lips as resolutely closed as a rosebud
in the depths of winter. Surely he'd give up now and release
her? Then she had only to find a way to escape before he
saw her face, and it would be as if this little adventure had
never happened.

It wasn't that she hadn't wondered how it would feel to
kiss Robyn. She had, more than once. She'd imagined it,
even—kissing him, wrapping her arms around his neck. It
was impossible to know Robyn and *not* wonder. He was so
handsome, so charming, and there was that smile. Lily was

after all a woman, and as susceptible as any to a charming smile.

Besides, it was safe enough to *imagine* kissing Robyn. Truly kissing him was less so, for any number of reasons. For one, until recently he'd been wildly enamored of her sister, Delia. Lily and Delia looked very much alike, and, well, no woman wanted to feel as if a gentleman would rather kiss her sister than kiss her.

Or worse, pretend he *was* kissing her sister *while* he kissed her.

That was the trouble with Robyn. One just never knew with him. He might still be besotted with Delia. Or not. Maybe he'd come in here for an illicit liaison, or maybe he simply hadn't been in the mood for music tonight.

Or maybe she was just a coward.

So be it. Cowards didn't get into scrapes. Lily didn't like surprises, and Robyn was unpredictable.

For one, he was far more persistent than she'd imagined he'd be, for he hadn't released her when she refused to open her lips to him. No, he'd begun to nibble at her as if she were a pastry, first at one corner of her mouth, then the other. He didn't touch the seam of her lips now, but let the tip of his tongue brush lightly over her bottom lip, tasting her there before he moved up to trace her upper lip. There he stayed. He traced it again and again, as if he'd found something there that fascinated him.

Oh, my. It was soft, coaxing. Lily's back went boneless and she melted against the door behind her. This felt . . . different; so much nicer than an insistent tongue trying to batter its way into her mouth.

He shifted and slid his hands around her so they rested on her lower back. His slow caress should have soothed her, but instead it made the room tilt and sway so she had to place her hands flat against his chest to steady herself. His satin waistcoat was smooth and slick under her fingertips, his heart pounding through the fine fabric.

She felt his lips move against hers, felt the corners of his mouth turn up.

He was smiling.

Some sound escaped her, a sound she'd meant as denial that emerged instead as a breathless sigh. A sigh of pleasure. Of encouragement.

Oh, dear. There was a reason she'd vowed not to open her lips.

She didn't like surprises.

Robyn dropped little kisses against her cheeks, soft as a butterfly's wing, and then he did something that astonished her. He kissed the tip of her nose. The gesture was so sweet, so tender and unexpected, Lily's arms stole around his shoulders.

He went motionless when he felt her hands at the back of his neck, as if he waited for something else. Something more. His tongue, the tongue she'd tried so desperately to avoid, now felt necessary to her, as if she would stop breathing if she couldn't taste it.

Lily opened her lips.

Robyn surged inside as if he'd waited an eternity to be there, and this time his demanding, insistent tongue felt so sweet inside her mouth that her knees buckled beneath her. Without thinking, Lily matched his ardor. She twined her tongue with his and returned each of his teasing strokes with one of her own.

"Delicious," he whispered hoarsely, and his voice was at once both Robyn's voice and not his voice at all. The lips against hers were his and not his, and dazed as Lily was, she knew, she knew even then this kiss would change everything. They couldn't go back to what they had been before. Not after a kiss like this.

She didn't want that, did she? Perhaps it wasn't too late to set it right again. If they stopped right now, maybe . . .

The floor disappeared from beneath her feet as Robyn swept her into his arms. He buried his face in her hair and then he was sitting, and he'd pulled her onto his lap. She felt his thighs under her bottom and his breath coming hard and fast against her neck. His chest rose and fell under her hands.

He dragged a warm palm down the front of her neck, and before she could take another breath, she felt his finger against the neckline of her gown. Just one finger, a slow, teasing caress. He barely touched her, just drifted his fingertip over the narrow band of silk where her gown touched the skin at the top of her breast, but his touch felt like a trail of fire against her flesh.

Oh, dear God. He'd thrust his tongue into her mouth and now he'd put a finger on her breast. She wasn't sure what came next, exactly. His entire hand? They'd already gone too far, and it felt too good to be in his arms—so good she couldn't trust herself to stop him from taking it farther.

She tried to draw away but he held her fast against him. Even when she began to struggle in earnest, he only tightened his arms around her. She had to get away from him. Now, before he touched her again and she no longer wanted to escape at all . . .

Crack!

Her palm landed on Robyn's cheek with enough force to make his head snap sideways. Lily stared down at her hand in disbelief. She didn't realize she had such a spectacular slap hidden in her palm. How thrilling to find it there! But as gratifying a slap as it was, it didn't deliver the desired result.

The confounded man still held on to her.

Why hadn't he released her? Perhaps young ladies slapped his face so often he'd grown accustomed to it? She'd intended to flee faster than she'd ever flown, before he could get a good look at her, but Robyn was wilier than she expected, and quicker. She twisted and flailed like a fish on a hook, but he held on like a champion angler.

He rose from the settee with her dangling from his arms as if she were a sack of flour. Her feet touched the ground, but one of his arms clamped around her midsection before she could get any traction.

"Release me this *instant*—"

But she wasn't going anywhere until he decided she could.

"The devil I will. I think I've a right to see your face, given you've just slapped mine."

He followed this declaration with a long string of curses and hauled her along with him toward the lamp in the opposite corner of the room.

Lily wanted to sink to the ground in mortification, but it was too late for a swoon. Robyn snatched the lamp off the table and raised it so the muted light shone fully on her face. She closed her eyes and waited, breath held.

His fingers tightened at her waist, but he didn't say a word. Lily opened one eye and peeked at him, but shadows hid half his face and she couldn't read his expression.

Perhaps *he'd* fallen into a swoon?

"Damnation," he muttered after what felt like an eternity of silence. He released her, and his arms fell to his sides.

Lily didn't approve of profanity, but the word did seem appropriate, given the circumstances.

Damnation, indeed.

Chapter Three

His shy, chaste young virgin, his meadow-scented innocent with her dainty, delicate hands—hands that had lain against his chest so sweetly only moments before—had just delivered a blow so powerful, his brain wobbled like a jelly inside his skull.

And that was the least of it.

His shy, chaste young virgin was none other than Lily Somerset. Lily, his sisters' dearest friend, and a guest in his mother's home. Lily, his sister-in-law. Lily, the one woman in London irrevocably off-limits to him, and perhaps the only woman in London he didn't care to despoil of her virtue.

At least, he hadn't cared to despoil her before tonight, before he'd discovered straitlaced, proper Lily hid the softest lips he'd ever kissed and the most tempting curves he'd ever laid a finger on under her starchy exterior. He hadn't even needed *all* of his fingers to tell that her breasts were . . .

Stop it! Never mind her lips or her breasts. Robyn closed his eyes for a moment and concentrated instead on what would happen if his brother Alec ever found out about this particular incident. Robyn didn't like his chances of keeping his head attached to his neck if Alec did.

He opened his eyes to find Lily looking up at him as if she dreaded what he'd say next.

"If you wanted to kiss me, Lily, you could have just asked. You needn't have gone to all this trouble."

Her mouth dropped open, then she crossed her arms over her chest. "If you wanted me to slap your face, Robyn, I would have been delighted to oblige, even without the kiss."

He grinned. "You didn't have to slap me at all, you know. I would have let you go. I only wanted to see your face before I did."

So I could find you again. And ruin you.

Alas, there would be no ruination *now*. He'd never find another woman in London with her taste and scent, either. Wild strawberries, a meadow on a sunny day . . . good God. He was going to have to move to the country.

She ran a hand over her hair to smooth the curls he'd disarranged. "Well, I didn't know that, and I didn't know it was *you*. I thought it far more likely to be one of those conscienceless seducers London is infamous for."

"Or else you *did* know, and you just wanted to slap me."

Her face flooded with color. "I—I didn't know. I didn't kn-know it was *you* I'd slapped," she said, as if she could barely get the words out.

Robyn moved a step closer. "I didn't know it was *you* I'd kissed. If I let you slap me again, may I kiss you once more?"

He grabbed her hand and held it against his smarting cheek, unable to resist teasing her a little. What did a prim, proper young lady do when a rake teased her? This would be his only chance to find out, for once they left this room, he'd never touch or tease her again.

Anything that might happen between them while they were still here didn't count, did it?

Lily didn't seem to share that logic. She tugged at her hand until he released her. "I have a better idea. I'll slap you again, only harder, and you'll let me go as you should have done the first time. I'll hurry back to your sisters and you can get on with kissing whomever you're lying in wait for."

Lying in wait? Surely he wasn't as predatory as all that? After all, he'd been invited here. Not in so many words, perhaps, but invited nonetheless. That made him the prey, not the predator.

But somehow he didn't think Lily would see it that way.

Admit nothing. He blinked at her and tried to look innocent. "What makes you think I'm lying in wait for someone?"

Lily expelled an impatient breath. "Why else would you be in here alone, lurking right by the door, watching it so closely I'd scarcely set a toe across the threshold before you whisked me off my feet and into the room? Then you locked the door behind me."

He laughed. "That proves nothing, except I have great presence of mind in seizing an opportunity."

Lily pursed her lips. "It wasn't precisely an *opportunity* you seized. Or did you mean you'd seize anyone who happened to walk through the door?"

"I'd lurk by the door forever for another chance to seize you," he said, surprised to hear the words leave his mouth. He'd never had any inclination to seize Lily before, yet even now he itched to close his hands around her waist.

Robyn shook himself. Why all the bloody honesty all of a sudden?

Admit nothing.

"Let that be a lesson to you," he added when she remained silent. "Anything can happen when you follow a gentleman into a dark room."

"Follow? Don't be absurd. I never followed you. I hadn't any idea you were in here. I thought this was the ladies' retiring room."

Robyn raised an eyebrow. "You mean to say you're perceptive enough to notice a gentleman lying in wait by the door, but not perceptive enough to realize this isn't the ladies' retiring room?"

"I did realize it! Only it was too late to do anything about it by then."

He took a step closer. "Ah, yes. I forgot. You were all atremble by then, in fear for your virtue, certain you were in the arms of a conscienceless seducer."

She bit her bottom lip nervously. "Wasn't I?"

Robyn's gaze drifted down to her lips. "Perhaps you were. The kiss was far more devastating than the slap, you know."

Damn it. More confounded honesty.

"You're only teasing me—"

He shook his head. "No. Even more devastating after I knew it was you."

Christ. *Admit nothing.* Was that so difficult?

Admit nothing, especially if it's true.

The truth was that before tonight, before he'd kissed her, he'd hardly even noticed Lily. Oh, she was beautiful, just like her sister Delia, with the same thick golden brown hair and those famously blue, blue eyes.

But Lily . . . well, she was too *neat.* Too proper. She was buttoned, laced, smoothed, and groomed to perfection. There wasn't a stray curl to finger or a hint of ankle to admire. Any lust he might have felt for her was overwhelmed by an urge to wrinkle her gown or pull every pin from her hair, then shove it back in, upside down and backward.

He'd met Delia and Lily at a country ball in Surrey when he'd come from Kent to escort Charlotte and Ellie home from a visit with their aunt Mathilda, who lived near Maidstone. On their last night in Surrey, his sisters had teased and cajoled until he'd agreed to attend a country ball and meet their new friends, Delia and Lily Somerset.

Robyn hadn't anticipated much pleasure in the evening, but he'd had nothing better to do, so he'd gone and been stunned to discover either of Charlotte and Ellie's new friends could rival London's most celebrated belles. He'd never imagined such lovely young ladies were hidden away in the depths of Surrey, or he would long since have taken up farming. Or fox hunting.

Or whatever it was gentlemen did in the country.

The ball had been made up mostly of families from the surrounding neighborhood, but one young matron had brought guests who were on a visit from London. Robyn had been standing by when these fashionable young ladies were introduced to Lily and Delia.

"Oh, yes," one of them had said, looking down her long nose at the two sisters. "I believe I recall the name *Somerset*. Your mother was quite famous when she debuted, wasn't she?"

"Infamous, you mean," the other young lady put in with a smirk.

Millicent Somerset, or Millicent Chase as she'd been known before her marriage, had been a famous jilt. The *ton* still spat shards of glass over Millicent Chase's story, for she'd been one of their own, and she'd betrayed them all by marrying some nobody without family or fortune, and then she'd had the gall to move to the country, bear five beautiful daughters, and live in a state of unrepentant happiness until her sudden death a year ago.

Delia had looked the first young lady right in the eye. "It's odd, isn't it, Lily, how often London visitors make that very same comment? I can't account for it, unless every lady in London stands around the same ballroom night after night, exchanging the same vicious gossip."

Delia had drawn breath to deliver another scathing set-down, and he'd been wild with impatience to hear what she'd say next, but then Lily had laid a hand on her sister's shoulder, and Delia had fallen silent. Lily herself hadn't said one word, and not a flicker of emotion had crossed her face. If he hadn't known otherwise, Robyn would have believed she hadn't heard the sarcastic comment at all.

He'd been fascinated with Delia after that. Briefly anyway. His infatuations never lasted long. He'd spent the better part of his mother's recent house party at Bellwood sniffing after Delia like a hound on a fresh scent, but he'd lost interest even before they all returned to London.

Just as well, too, since Delia had married his brother, Alec, six weeks ago, at the start of the London season, and not a moment too soon. More than one high-minded dowager would be counting the weeks between the wedding and the birth the minute their child arrived.

As for Lily, he'd dismissed her out of hand. He liked women with spirit, and he'd concluded from this episode that she hadn't any. Even worse, she was a scold.

Had that been it? Or had Delia simply been wearing the lower-cut gown of the two of them? He was a man, after all, and not a terribly complicated one.

Perhaps he'd been a bit hasty in his determinations. Lily kept it well hidden under that prim exterior, but she did have spirit, and it took only a few stolen kisses and one finger to a breast to unleash it in full force. His cheek still smarted.

Not that it mattered. Spirit or no spirit, the rules were clear. Robyn didn't generally bother with rules, but debauching his sister-in-law was a bit much even for him. It would be more than a bit much for Alec, who'd strangle Robyn with his own cravat if he found out Robyn had laid a finger on Delia's sister.

It was quite simple, really. *Don't touch Lily.*

If he wasn't permitted to touch her, then . . . "We'd better return to the drawing room. Charlotte and Eleanor will be looking for you."

Lily gave him a meaningful glance. When he failed to move, she made a twirling gesture with her fingers to indicate he should turn around. "Yes, very well. But I need a moment first."

"Whatever for?"

A blush stained her cheeks. "I can't go back to the drawing room looking like *this*."

The fragile neckline of the gown, low-cut to begin with, had succumbed to the struggle with him. He supposed he couldn't let her skip back into the drawing room looking like *that*—as if she'd just been kissed and then tumbled in a meadow of warm grass and daisies.

"Of course." Robyn tried not to devour the sight of her bosom and failed miserably. When had she started wearing such low-cut gowns? "I noticed the same thing myself."

He hadn't. But then he was accustomed to seeing women in various stages of undress.

She turned away from him and made some mysterious adjustments to her gown only another female would understand. When she turned back, he couldn't help but notice her repairs hadn't been entirely successful.

Robyn choked back a laugh. "Can I help you?"

She glared at her bodice, then glared at him. "I think not."

He held up his hands in an innocent shrug. "I'm not looking."

He was.

She tried to smooth the neckline to cover her breasts. His mouth went dry as he watched her pat at the fabric.

"I'm ready," she announced.

He leaned a hip against the door. "No, you're not. Your sash is twisted."

She mumbled something about "dratted ribbons" and tried to smooth the wrinkle out of the sash, but it was no good.

Robyn crossed his legs at the ankles and grinned at her. If she wanted perfect ribbons, she'd have to remove her sash. While he watched. Then she'd likely need his help to tie it again.

So. Just how badly did Lily want perfect ribbons? Badly enough to practically undress in front of him? At least, that was how she'd see it. He'd find it less thrilling, of course, as he routinely stripped women of far more than their sashes.

With his teeth.

She bit her lip, then reached around to untie the sash.

Robyn felt his grin widen. *Ah-ha.* The high price of perfection.

He watched, more intrigued than he should be, as she pulled the bow loose and the green ribbon fell away from her waist.

Thrilling enough, though.

She ran the twisted end of the satin through her fingers to smooth it. She held it in place against her front, hesitated, then turned her back to him. "If you wouldn't mind?"

Mind? He was jealous of a length of ribbon. "Not at all."

He took the ends of the ribbon in his fingers and pulled the sash firmly around her. He let his knuckles brush against her slim waist as he tied the bow.

She turned around to face him. "There. Is that satisfactory?"

He looked her over. Smooth ribbons. Every hair in place. Breasts covered. This was the Lily he recognized. "I liked it better before."

She gave a haughty little sniff and turned back toward the door. "You *would.*"

He hooked a finger around her sash and drew her back again. "You can't just wander out into the hallway as if you're picking flowers in a meadow, you know."

Funny, the way that particular image kept coming up.

He opened the door a crack and scanned the hallway. "Let me at least look first. If there's no one about, you can return to the drawing room. I'll follow after a few minutes so it doesn't look like we've been off somewhere alone together, for you may as well go back to Surrey tomorrow if you're seen leaving a dark room with me—*Christ!*"

The door jerked out of Robyn's hand. A petite brunette wearing a dark blue gown dashed through it, straight into his arms.

"You waited for me," she breathed in low, husky tones as she wound her black-gloved arms around his neck. "It took me an eternity to get away, and all the while I could think of nothing but this."

She sank her fingers into the hair at the back of his neck and pressed her lips passionately against his.

Alicia had finally arrived.

Lily stood there, white-faced, as Robyn seized his second opportunity of the evening.

He did have great presence of mind, just as he'd claimed, for he kicked the door shut behind the woman. To be fair, he didn't precisely *seize* her, though his hands closed around her waist. "Alicia! Give me a moment, pet," he said, trying to hold her away from him.

"Don't tease me, Robyn," the woman whispered, still oblivious to Lily's presence. She pressed light kisses against his mouth with her heavily rouged red lips. "There isn't time."

"Alicia," Robyn said, still holding her waist. "We have company." He jerked his head in Lily's direction.

We have company. And just like that, Lily felt like *she'd* intruded on *them*.

The woman ceased her attack on Robyn long enough to notice Lily's presence. Her eyes widened with shock, then narrowed as they swept over Lily's gown, which remained disheveled, despite her efforts to right it.

Lily supposed the woman was pretty, if you liked her sort. The sort that wore paint on her mouth, that is. She had abundant dark hair, very fine pale skin, and thickly lashed gray eyes with a feline tilt at the corners.

"Why, Robyn," the woman purred at last. "I know you're

a man of strong appetites, but it never occurred to me you'd find another woman to replace me if I were delayed."

Lily stiffened, but Robyn spoke before she could say a word. "Who could replace you, Alicia? It's a simple misunderstanding."

"Is it?" The woman studied Robyn's face. A faint palm print was now visible where Lily had slapped him. "Very well. But you're extremely rude, Robyn. Aren't you going to introduce me to your friend?"

Robyn shrugged. "No. She's on her way back to the drawing room."

"Oh, but wait. There's no need for an introduction," the woman said, clapping her hands together as if delighted. Her voice was pleasant enough, but the gray eyes were cold as they settled on Lily. "Miss Somerset, isn't it? We were introduced at Lady Fenton's soiree just last evening."

Lily stared at the woman and felt a cold shiver dart down her spine. They *had* been introduced. She remembered now. This was Lady Downes. Lily's eyes darted to Robyn's face, but he didn't look in the least ashamed. He gazed back at her, his eyes glinting with deviltry.

Lily dipped into a stiff curtsy. "Lady Downes."

She knew all along Robyn intended to meet a woman here, despite his protestations to the contrary. It hadn't occurred to her to wonder who the woman might be, however. She'd had vague notions of widows. Or opera dancers, though now she thought of it, she wondered how she could imagine that to be the case, for opera dancers wouldn't be welcome at Lord and Lady Barrow's musical evening.

But Lady Downes! She wasn't a widow—not unless Lord Downes had just dropped dead in the card room, for Lily had seen him there not an hour ago. An illicit liaison was wicked enough, but an illicit liaison with a married woman while her husband played whist down the hall, less than thirty paces away?

The wickedest gentleman in the wickedest city in England.

Lily hadn't believed it. Robyn was unreliable. Careless, even. At worst, reckless. But willfully, deliberately wicked? This was far worse than anything she'd imagined.

She knew she hadn't any right to, but she felt as if he'd tricked her. She glanced at him again. His wide mouth twitched with suppressed laughter, as if he found the situation amusing, but he only said, "Go back to the drawing room, Lily."

She didn't answer. She didn't speak at all. She walked out of the room without a backward glance.

"Why, Lily," Charlotte asked when Lily slipped into the seat beside her. "Wherever have you been? Did you get lost?"

Lily felt as if she'd been gone for days, but it had been less than twenty minutes. "Yes. I'm sorry, Charlotte. I ended up in the wrong place."

She had, in every sense of the word.

Charlotte gazed at her in concern. "You look pale. Do you have the headache?" She nudged Eleanor, who took one look at Lily's white face and rose from her seat.

Charlotte took Lily's arm and led her to the back of the room. "Let's find Robyn and have him escort us home."

Robyn reappeared in the drawing room after another ten minutes, which was just long enough for Lily to wonder how many of Lady Downes's body parts he'd managed to seize in that time. Had they finished what he and Lily had begun? Or had they set up an assignation for later this evening?

"There you are, Robyn," Eleanor said. "Will you call the carriage? Lily's ill."

Robyn's dark eyes took in Lily's pallor. He raised an eyebrow, but made no argument.

The carriage ride home was silent. Charlotte and Ellie thought Lily had the headache, and they remained quiet. Robyn never spoke a word, but lounged across from her, long legs sprawled in front of him and an arm flung across the back of his seat, as relaxed as if he carried on an illicit liaison with a married woman every night.

Perhaps he did.

Lily stared out the window. She and Robyn had become friends after a fashion during the Sutherlands' house party, and she'd hoped they'd remain so, especially since they'd be under the same roof for the whole of this season, but whenever she looked at him now, she knew she'd picture his laughing, too-wide mouth stained with Lady Downes's lip rouge.

Her heart sank and settled like an anchor in her stomach, cold and heavy.

She didn't know if she was angrier at Robyn for being as wicked as his sisters said he was, or at the odious, frizzle-haired Miss Thurston, for being right about him all along.

Chapter Four

The trouble with delicious lips was once you'd tasted them, you couldn't *un-taste* them. The same was true of a spectacular kiss, or an especially lovely pair of breasts, or a captivating scent. A man couldn't un-kiss a woman, or un-touch her breasts, or un-inhale her scent. Once he'd tasted, touched, and inhaled, the horse was well and truly out of the barn. No use slamming the door now.

Robyn stumbled from his bedchamber and made his way down the stairs to the breakfast room. He hadn't even *seen* Lily's breasts last night. He hadn't even laid a finger on them. Oh, very well, damn it. He'd laid one finger on *one* of them. Not even a handful, and hardly enough to fall into a frenzy of lust, but still he'd been awake most of the night, imagining what it would have felt like to lay *two* fingers on them.

Or more. Perhaps even an entire palm.

"Good morning," he mumbled to his sisters, both of whom sat in the breakfast room drinking their morning chocolate. Lily was nowhere to be seen. Just as well. After his lurid dreams last night, he was sure to ogle her breasts over his toast and coffee.

Neither of his sisters replied to his greeting. Robyn didn't take any notice of this until he seated himself and lifted his coffee dish to his lips, only to find both his sisters glaring daggers at him over the rim.

"What?"

Damn it, he sounded guilty already, and neither of them had said a word yet. He made it a policy never to feel guilty for any of his sins, as it was a short step from guilt to confession.

"Well, well, well. Robyn," Eleanor said. "You're up late this morning. Had a busy night, did you?"

"No later than usual, I think, and no busier than usual."

"Indeed?" Charlotte placed her teacup in her saucer. "Well, Ellie, we do have to concede that point, for it's all part of an evening's entertainment for Robyn to ruin a young lady's reputation."

Robyn kept his face neutral. His sisters had found out about the scrape with Lily, then. "Whom have I ruined this time?"

"I think you know," Eleanor said. She tossed a paper across the table toward him.

Charlotte snatched the paper up and tapped a finger at a story on the front page. "Go ahead. Read it." She thrust it at him.

He didn't have to look far to see what had his sisters in such a froth, for it was right there on the front page, complete with a crude sketch of a young lady slapping the face of a leering gentleman.

Prepare yourselves for something very shocking, dear readers! Your devoted Mrs. Tittleton has discovered from an unimpeachable source that London's favorite rake, Mr. R-b—t S—-r—d, who arrived back in town from his family's seat in Kent just six weeks ago, is up

*to his usual scandalous antics! Mr. S. was seen at Lord
and Lady B——'s musical evening last night, but the
notorious rogue seemed to find the music far less engag-
ing than he did the person of one Miss L—y S—r—t,
with whom he spent an intimate half-hour alone in Lord
Barrow's study. Mrs. Tittleton doesn't doubt the lovely
and innocent Miss LS and Mr. RS were simply discussing a mutual interest in Pleyel's Scottish Airs, but one
does hope the newly minted Lady C——le will offer her
young sibling some wise counsel about the wickedness
of certain fashionable London gentlemen.*

A mutual interest in the *Scottish Airs*? He looked up from
the paper but stifled the urge to laugh when he saw the grim
look on his sisters' faces.

"It's true, isn't it?" Eleanor said. "That's why Lily was
so pale and quiet when she returned to the drawing room
last night. How could you, Robyn?"

He hadn't. Not in the way the scandal sheet claimed anyway. "Did you consider even for a moment, Eleanor, that it
isn't true?"

She looked so taken aback, Robyn instantly had his answer. It hadn't occurred to either of his sisters to doubt the
story. *Good Lord*. Between the gaming, the bordellos, the
carriage races, and the mistresses, he'd become less credible
even than Mrs. Tittleton.

"But if it's not true, how would such a story get about?"
Charlotte asked. "You must have been up to some kind of
mischief. Mrs. Tittleton is hardly a reputable journalist, but
even she couldn't have conjured such a tale out of nothing."

But it *had* been nothing. Or nearly nothing. Very close
to nothing.

Admit nothing.

Sometime during the night, however, when he hadn't
been dreaming of Lily's breasts, a conscience must have
sprouted in the barren soil of his brain.

Very well. It hadn't *quite* been nothing, then. But how had Mrs. Tittleton gotten ahold of it? The only people who knew were—

"Alicia." Of course. It made perfect sense. She'd been ready to spit with ire when she found him in Lord Barrow's study with Lily.

"Alicia? Not Lady Downes?" Charlotte asked. "What's she got to do with it?"

Bloody hell. He'd have to confess the whole story. "I arranged to meet Alicia in Lord Barrow's study, but Lily mistook the study for the ladies' retiring room, and, well—"

"You didn't bother to verify the identity of the lady who entered the room, but pounced on Lily," Charlotte finished for him, as if this were exactly what she'd expect of him. "How on earth could you confuse Lily with a worn-out seductress like Lady Downes?"

"It was dark."

His protest was halfhearted at best. At some point he'd realized it wasn't Alicia in his arms, but he'd carried on anyway. He'd been so intent on getting his tongue in his siren's mouth, he hadn't given a damn who she was. If he'd known it was Lily, he'd have stopped. Of course he would have. He very probably would have.

Eventually.

"For goodness' sake, Robyn, I hope you aren't contemplating an affair with Lady Downes!" Ellie said. "She's more vicious than a nest of vipers."

"I'm not contemplating a thing with her, aside from possibly wringing her lovely neck."

That much, at least, was true. Any fleeting interest he'd had in Alicia had evaporated after he'd kissed Lily. Alicia had seen at once how things were, and she'd reacted the way any woman who believes herself irresistible to men *does* react as soon as one resists her.

She'd flown into a fury, and then she'd got her revenge, the vindictive shrew.

"Good morning." Lily entered the room and took a seat at the table.

Robyn studied her as she signaled the footman for a cup of tea. She'd scraped her hair back from her face, the heavy locks held prisoner with what must have been dozens of pins. The delectable bosom he'd fantasized about last night was hidden under a layer of heavy, dark blue fabric and what looked to him like ten layers of fussy lace.

She was trussed up like a Christmas goose.

Last night she'd been an alluring temptress, but this morning—well, she was back to being dull, perfect Lily. Even her gown fell in careful folds around her, like an obedient dog commanded to sit and stay at his mistress's feet.

"Good morning, Lily," Charlotte and Ellie replied in unison. Their voices rang with false cheer.

Lily took one look at them and lowered her teacup to her saucer. "What's happened?"

"Happened?" Eleanor asked, her eyes wide and innocent. "What makes you think anything's happened?"

"Ellie," Lily warned. "Is it Delia? Where's Lady Catherine?"

Charlotte sighed with resignation. "Delia is fine, only nauseous again. Mother left early this morning to see to her. Alec is frantic. We thought perhaps you'd gone with Mother. You're rather late to breakfast this morning."

"I, ah, couldn't sleep," Lily said. She focused all of her attention on her teacup. "I sent a note round to Delia that I'd see her this afternoon."

Robyn perked up at this. She couldn't sleep? *Good.* Why should she enjoy the sleep of the innocent when he'd tossed and turned all night?

Because she is innocent, and you're guilty.

Bloody inconvenient thing, a conscience.

Charlotte's fingers edged toward the scandal sheet during this exchange and closed on the corner of the paper. She was about to whisk Mrs. Tittleton and her damning account out of Lily's sight when Robyn slammed his hand down on the paper to stop her.

Lily's eyes flew toward him. Color rushed into her cheeks when her eyes met his and Robyn felt a thrill of satisfaction. If he couldn't ignore her, then he'd make damn sure she couldn't ignore him, either.

"Robyn!" Eleanor cried. "What do you think you're doing?"

Robyn fixed his eyes on Lily. "You can't hide it from her. She'll find out one way or another. Why not now?"

"Hide what?" Lily asked. "Find out what?"

Ellie glared at Robyn, her face flushed with annoyance. "We didn't intend to hide it from her. We'd just rather she be spared having to read *that*."

Lily's gaze followed Eleanor's accusing finger to the scandal sheet under Robyn's fist. "May I see that, please?"

"Certainly." Robyn snatched the paper away from Charlotte and handed it over to Lily. Charlotte scowled at him, one corner of the ripped page still clutched in her fingers.

Lily's eyes moved over the page, her face growing ever paler with each line she read. None of this was her fault. Robyn knew that, and he did feel a twinge of regret that she'd managed to get tangled up in one of his scandals. Yet at the same time he was curious to see what she'd do when she found herself at the mercy of some sordid gossip's vicious pen.

By the time she'd finished, however, she was so dead white, he'd begun to question the wisdom of letting her read the paper in the first place. If she swooned, there'd be no end of uproar, and his breakfast would be spoiled.

Lily folded the paper into neat thirds and placed it carefully next to her plate. "Oh. Oh, no."

"Now, it's not as bad as all that," Charlotte began in soothing tones. "It's not *The Times*, you know. It's only Mrs. Tittleton. No one will take any notice of her nonsense. Why, I'm sure very few people even saw this at all."

"They did see it." Ellie's voice was grim. "They did take notice."

Charlotte glanced anxiously at Lily. "What do you mean, Eleanor? How do you know that?"

Ellie sighed. "A few nights ago at the Fentons' ball I managed to wheedle a promise from Lady Jersey that she'd give Lily a guest voucher to Almack's, but I've had a note from her this morning with her regrets and apologies. She *claims* she forgot she'd promised the ticket to Lady Fenton's niece, but I don't believe it for a minute. She's obviously read Mrs. Tittleton and decided to bar Lily from Almack's."

Was that all? Robyn lifted a forkful of eggs to his mouth. "After last season I swore I'd never set foot in the place again. Nothing but dry cake and watery lemonade. Consider yourself lucky you're no longer obliged to go."

"Don't be dim, Robyn," Charlotte snapped. "Almack's sets the tone. Everyone else will follow their lead. If Lily is barred from Almack's, she won't be invited anywhere else for the rest of the season."

Lily patted the corners of her mouth with her napkin, set it aside, then rose and walked to the door. "I'll send another note to Delia and begin packing."

Robyn took a bite of his toast. "Packing? What nonsense. You'd let Mrs. Tittleton chase you out of London over a trifle like this?"

Lily's fingers twisted nervously in the lace at her neck, but she didn't avoid his gaze. "You said yourself if anyone knew I'd been alone in a room with you, I may as well return to Surrey immediately." She waved a hand at the scandal sheet. "They've seen. They know. Every single one of them."

Robyn rolled his eyes. "You can't mean to say you took me seriously. For God's sake, who gives a toss what the *ton* thinks? Surely there's a way around it, in any case."

Charlotte shook her head. "I can't think how. Oh, Lily!

What about Lord Atherton? This will upset all our plans. Why, he may be married by next season!"

Robyn looked from Lily to Charlotte and back again, and this time he didn't bother to stifle his laugh. "Atherton? You can't be serious."

Charlotte glared at him. "What's wrong with Lord Atherton?"

Robyn smirked at his sister. "*Wrong?* Why, he's perfect. He's a saint among men. A paragon of virtue. The epitome of the proper English gentleman. *That's* what's wrong with him."

That, and he was the dullest man alive, at least on the surface. Robyn was convinced something unspeakable lurked underneath all that perfection.

Lily turned as red as a beet, but she ignored his teasing. "There's no way around it. If I stay in London, it will spoil Charlotte's and Ellie's seasons, as well. They'll have to go everywhere without me, or else stay home themselves. I won't allow it," she added when she saw Charlotte open her mouth to protest.

"Unless . . ." Ellie said.

Every head at the table turned toward her.

"What, Eleanor?" Charlotte asked. "Unless what?"

"I have an idea," Eleanor said. "But the success of it depends entirely on Robyn."

Now every head turned in his direction. Robyn put his fork down on his plate. It depended entirely on him? *Christ.* He didn't like the sound of that.

"The *ton* will expect one of two things, now Mrs. Tittleton has tattled Lily's business all over town. You can leave London under a cloud of shame, in which case it will be assumed you are guilty of an indiscretion and the Sutherlands acknowledge your guilt, or—"

"We acknowledge nothing of the sort!" Charlotte interrupted. "Alec will never agree to see Lily or Delia humiliated in such a way. Why, he's liable to go mad if he sees Delia's name has been mentioned in such a scandalous, libelous—"

"Or," Eleanor continued, speaking over her sister, "Lily can be seen all over London with her excessively attentive, correct, very proper escort."

Lily stared at Eleanor. "*What* excessively proper escort?"

Eleanor smiled. "Why, Robyn, of course."

Robyn choked on a swallow of coffee and Charlotte had to raise her voice to be heard above his sputters and gasps. "Robyn! Have you lost your wits, Eleanor?"

"Not at all. Don't you see? If he'd truly compromised Lily, he'd either have to marry her, or—oh, for goodness' sake, Robyn!" Eleanor broke off, annoyed. "Don't look so appalled. I'm not suggesting you actually marry. I'd never wish such a rogue as you on Lily."

Robyn pounded on his chest with a fist to clear his windpipe. "Wise of you."

"Either he'd marry her," Ellie continued, "or else she'd drop out of sight for good and leave all the dowagers to shake their heads over her corrupted virtue. The *ton* will never expect to see something else entirely."

Charlotte was smiling now. "You mean, a notorious rake escorting a debutante all over London?"

"Exactly," Eleanor said. "He isn't marrying her, so he can't have compromised her. He isn't avoiding her, and she hasn't fallen from the face of the earth, so he can't have compromised her. However one looks at it, he can't have compromised her."

Charlotte clapped her hands in glee. "Oh, Ellie, you're brilliant! It's even better because Robyn *is* such a notorious rake. The *ton* won't know what to make of it."

Ellie nodded with satisfaction. "He'll escort her all over London with the full approval of the Sutherland family. We'll simply brazen it out until the gossip dies down. It soon will, with nothing to feed it."

"It will slow things down with Lord Atherton," Charlotte

said to Lily, "for he's bound to think Robyn is courting you.
Then again, a little competition may be just what we want.
After all, Lord Atherton doesn't know you regard Robyn as
a brother."

A brother? Oh, certainly, if a sister was in the habit of
sticking her tongue in her brother's mouth and practically
shoving her breasts under his fingers.

So he was expected to sacrifice his own pleasures in
order for Lily to snag Atherton? If he agreed to this scheme,
he'd never have a moment's peace.

Robyn glanced at Lily. Her face betrayed nothing, but he
imagined she thought any solution that depended upon him
was an appallingly bad idea.

Well, it *was* a bad idea. Ridiculous, to cast him as the
heroic knight of London society when he was far more likely
to puncture himself with his sword or drop Lily from the
white horse than rescue her.

So he'd involved her in one of his scandals. What of it?
It was a simple accident, nothing more. Perhaps she did have
a right to expect him to help her out of it, but what difference
did that make to him? Other people had made the mistake
of expecting things from him, and he never troubled himself
much about any of *them*. This was no different, and anyway,
Charlotte and Eleanor exaggerated the matter. The *ton*
would move on to more promising gossip quickly enough,
with or without him.

And Lily—if he agreed to help her, she'd expect far more
than he had any intention of delivering. She was the type of
woman who did. The type he avoided, as if they carried
some contagious disease. He sought out women like Alicia
for a reason. They didn't ask for a thing from him except
sensual pleasure. He could give them that, and they were
never disappointed. It saved a great deal of fuss and bother
if no one expected much more from him.

But not Lily. She looked like she was about to take orders
at the nearest convent in her severe blue gown. He could

hardly believe she was the same woman who'd kissed him with such sweet passion last night.

Maybe she and Atherton would suit, after all.

"What about Almack's?" Charlotte asked. "We still don't have a voucher for Lily."

"I'll get the voucher," Robyn heard himself say.

Once again, every head turned in his direction. Eleanor's eyebrows rose. "How will—"

"Never mind *how*. I said I'll get the blasted voucher, and I will."

It happened he could get the elusive voucher with very little inconvenience to himself, as he knew just the scoundrel who could lay his hands on one. It was an easy enough promise to make, and though it may have escaped his sisters' attention, he hadn't promised another damn thing. He'd get the voucher, fulfill his obligation to Lily, and then he'd be free to wash his hands of the whole affair.

Eleanor and Charlotte lapsed into a happy silence. They didn't seem to notice that Lily hadn't said a word.

Chapter Five

It was midafternoon before Lily arrived at Alec and Delia's town house in Grosvenor Street. To her surprise, she was taken to Delia's bedchamber instead of her private sitting room. She found her sister stretched out on the bed.

Lady Catherine hovered over Delia with a cool cloth. "Oh, Lily. I'm glad you've come." She kissed Delia's cheek and rose from her place at the side of the bed. "I'm not sure if I should worry more about Delia, or Alec," Lady Catherine murmured to Lily.

The shades were drawn to keep the glare out, but even in the dim room Lily could see Delia looked pale and exhausted. "It's all right, isn't it?"

"Oh, yes. It's a good sign she's so ill, as it means the child is strong. That's little enough comfort to her now, though, I'm sure. It wasn't a comfort to me when I carried Robyn."

"Robyn behaved abominably *even in the womb*? That is, I mean to say, Robyn made you ill?"

Blast it.

Lady Catherine didn't seem to notice Lily's gaffe. "Oh, dear me, yes! I felt quite miserable, I'm afraid, and my husband wasn't ever there to . . ." She trailed off, as if not sure how to finish the sentence.

Lily jumped in to cover the silence. "I saw Alec downstairs. He looks exhausted. Delia says he's so worried for her and the child, he doesn't sleep well."

Lady Catherine smiled proudly. "Alec is going to make a fine father, and as long as Delia can keep a little food and water down, she'll be fine, as well."

"I'll stay with her for the afternoon if you like." Lily held out her hand for the cloth.

Lady Catherine handed it to her and crossed over to the bed to pat Delia's hand. "I must be off. Feel better, dear."

On her way out the door, Lady Catherine stopped and laid a hand on Lily's cheek. "You're a good girl, Lily. I know you want everything to be well, but this takes time and patience. Promise me you won't wear yourself out with worry over it."

Lily smiled at her. Over the past few months Lady Catherine had become almost a mother to her, and like all mothers, she saw everything. "No, my lady. I won't."

"Good." Lady Catherine kissed her cheek and disappeared through the door, leaving the two sisters alone.

Lily hurried to the side of the bed and took her sister's cold, clammy hand. She could see a fine sheen of sweat on Delia's brow. "Oh, dear. You do look ill, Delia."

Delia gave a weak nod. "If I look as awful as I feel, I must look like death itself. I've heard of ladies who suffer thus in the early months of pregnancy, but I never imagined it would be so dreadful."

Lily squeezed her hand. "Well, perhaps it's a good sign you're so ill, for it likely means you're carrying the heir."

Delia had closed her eyes, but at this she opened them again. "Indeed? Why do you think so?"

Lily stood up and wandered around the room. She picked

up Delia's hairbrush, studied it, and set it back down again. "It must be a boy. Only a man could cause so much misery."

Delia raised her head from the pillows. "My goodness, Lily. What a cynical thing to say."

Lily didn't answer. She crossed the room to the settee, gathered the pillows there, and placed them behind Delia. "There. That's better."

Delia leaned back with a sigh. "Thank you. Now, is there anything in particular you'd like to talk about?"

Lily wandered over to Delia's dressing table and began to rearrange the items scattered across it so they lined up evenly. If she changed the subject now, she knew Delia wouldn't press her. She always told her sister everything, but then she'd never had much to tell before. Now she hesitated, and the worst of it was, she didn't know *why*, for she was desperate to unburden herself.

She supposed she was embarrassed. Perhaps if she led up to it slowly—

"Robyn kissed me!"

Lily snapped her mouth shut, horrified. She'd intended it as a confession of sorts, but it sounded more like an accusation, as if she were telling tales on Robyn.

For pity's sake. She was worse than Mrs. Tittleton.

But if Delia was shocked, she gave no sign of it. She settled herself more comfortably against her pillows. "Well? Did you enjoy it?"

Lily's mouth fell open again. "Delia! What kind of question is that?"

Delia chuckled. "A rhetorical one, for there's no need for you to answer. I can see you did."

"I never—I most certainly didn't—that is, what do you mean, you can see I did?"

What an awful thought. If Delia could see through her so easily, Robyn likely could, as well. He might even now be boasting to his friends about how soundly he'd kissed her and how her knees had quivered under her skirts.

How dare he?

Delia sat up against the pillows. "I can tell because you're in a fuss about it. No woman fusses over a kiss she didn't enjoy."

A fuss, indeed. What nonsense. She never fussed about anything. Whether or not she'd enjoyed the kiss was hardly the point. It was irrelevant, in fact.

Lily frowned down at a bottle of scent in her hand. *Had* she enjoyed it?

She'd certainly felt it everywhere, not just her lips. Did that mean she'd *enjoyed* it? It didn't seem like the right word to describe how she felt about that kiss.

It had been more like being on the back of a runaway horse, soaring over hills and galloping through streams and flying over logs in one spectacular jump after another, heart pounding and hair flying, breathless and terrified. When the horse slowed at last to a walk, one didn't think to oneself, *What a* lovely *ride. I* enjoyed *it.*

She'd never been run away with before, and she didn't intend to start now.

Lily dropped the crystal stopper back into the bottle of scent. Oh, what did it matter anyway? It was the first and last kiss she'd ever share with Robyn Sutherland. She hadn't *enjoyed* enjoying it, which was reason enough not to repeat the experience.

"He didn't *mean* to kiss me," she said, as if this made all the difference.

"Robyn kissed you by accident?" Delia asked. "How would such a thing happen? Did his lips bump into yours somehow?"

Lily scowled. "I'm glad you find this so amusing, Delia. No, his lips didn't bump into mine. It was dark, and he thought he was kissing someone else."

Delia's eyes went wide. "This *is* getting interesting. How did you end up in a dark room alone with Robyn, and who did he think he was kissing?"

Lily sighed. She'd come this far. She may as well just tell the whole story and be done with it. She needed to put the fiasco with Robyn out of her mind and rethink her plan, especially as she'd missed her chance to be introduced to Lord Atherton last night.

"It happened at Lord and Lady Barrow's musicale. I mistook Lord Barrow's study for the ladies' retiring room, and—"

"Why would you go off to the ladies' retiring room alone if you don't know the house? You know how easy it is to get lost in these grand London town houses. Why not take Charlotte or Ellie with you?"

"The music was about to start and I didn't like for them to miss it. But my sash was twisted, and—"

Delia laughed. "Oh, Lily. Not the ribbons again!"

Lily smoothed her hands over her skirts. "You know I can't abide twisted ribbons, but you've always said I'm too fastidious, and now I suppose I've gotten what I deserve."

"Surely it's not all that bad. What happened then? Did you kiss him back?"

Lily hesitated. She *had* kissed him back, and worse, she'd known very well it was *him* she was kissing. At least he had an excuse. He'd thought he was kissing Lady Downes.

Oh, it was mortifying.

"Well, you see, I went into the wrong room, and what do you think? Robyn was in there, in the dark, alone, waiting for Lady Downes."

Delia's brow wrinkled. "Lady Downes? I don't think I know her."

"She has dark hair and wears quite a lot of red paint on her mouth and very low-cut gowns." It wasn't the most charitable description, but, well, Lady Downes *did* wear paint and low-cut gowns.

Lily couldn't imagine what Robyn saw in her in the first place, unless it was the low-cut gowns. He'd seemed preoccupied with Lily's low-cut gown when they'd been locked in the study together. She thought of the tip of his finger against her breast and smothered a shiver.

She never should have let Charlotte talk her into the revealing bodices.

Delia shrugged. "That could be any number of ladies."

"Yes, well, it doesn't matter what she looks like. What matters is she's *married*, Delia, and Lord Downes was at the musicale as well, and not three rooms away from Lord Barrow's study at the time!"

"Ah." Delia nodded, beginning to understand. "So Robyn had planned to, ah, *entertain* a married woman right under her husband's nose? My goodness. He is rather wicked, isn't he?"

"Yes!" Lily cried, relieved Delia had at last arrived at the obvious conclusion. "Charlotte says he's the wickedest gentleman in the wickedest city in England, and I'm afraid I must agree with her, for—Delia! What are you laughing at?"

"The wickedest gentleman in the wickedest city in England? That's a bit much, isn't it? Robyn's wild, yes, and I confess I hope Alec doesn't hear of this latest escapade. But young, fashionable gentlemen like Robyn must have their fun, and the *ton* turns a blind eye to it."

Lily's mouth tightened to a thin, prim line. "I don't see why they should. It only encourages them, and—"

"This isn't Surrey, Lily. Everything is different in London; it's really another world entirely than what we're accustomed to."

It *was* a different world, one where gentlemen had liaisons with married women, and ladies painted their lips, and the *ton* devoured scandal along with their morning chocolate. This world had a great many twists and turns and jagged edges, just like—

Lily froze as a memory tugged at her consciousness.

Dear God. It was the puzzle maze all over again.

London society was as incomprehensible to her as the

puzzle maze she'd been lost in as a child. Here were the same twisted pathways and blank hedges that had terrified her then, except now instead of enormous topiaries and leering statues, it was Mrs. Tittleton who hid in the shrubs, and Lily had no more idea which way to turn now than she had then.

Five-year-old Lily had run through that maze in a blind panic, her gasps echoing in her ears as she stumbled down one gravel path after the next. At the time she'd thought being lost was the worst thing that could ever happen to her.

It wasn't. She knew that now.

She'd never found her way out of that maze. Her parents had to come in and rescue her. But this time she hadn't any parents to come search for her, and that . . .

That was the worst thing that could ever happen. To her, or to anyone.

"What does Robyn's liaison with Lady Downes have to do with his kissing you?" Delia asked. "There's more to this than you've told me."

There was. Much more, and much worse. Lily hesitated. Perhaps she shouldn't tell Delia about Mrs. Tittleton, after all? She didn't want to send her sister into a swoon.

"Don't think to hide the worst of it from me, Lily."

"Oh, very well." Lily rose, fetched her reticule, and pulled the pernicious Mrs. Tittleton from its depths. She handed the sheet to Delia. "This is the worst of it."

She half expected Delia to brush off Mrs. Tittleton as she had Robyn's liaison with Lady Downes, but by the time Delia finished reading the scandal sheet, her face had gone as tight as a fist. "Oh, Lily. This is dreadful."

Lily wrung her hands. "It's not as bad as all that, is it? You've just told me London is more permissive than the country—"

"For the *gentlemen*, yes. For married ladies. For young unmarried girls, it's just as restrictive as Surrey. More so, even, for the *ton* is addicted to gossip, and while they care little about what happens behind closed doors, they are particular indeed about appearances."

For goodness' sake. Lily cared about appearances, too, but it didn't do for one to become so preoccupied with her gown, she forgot to put on her drawers. Surely what was underneath counted, as well?

Delia crushed the paper as if she had Mrs. Tittleton's neck between her hands. "Whatever will we do?"

She looked so agitated, Lily grew alarmed. "Ellie had an idea." Honesty compelled her to add, "But I'm not sure it will work."

Delia patted a space on the bed. Lily settled down next to her and explained Ellie's plan to have Robyn act as her escort until the scandal blew over.

Before she'd even finished, Delia was nodding her approval. "Ellie is wonderfully clever, is she not? Her plan is just the thing. The *ton* can't focus on one scandal for long, and something new is sure to come along. I don't think I even need mention this to Alec at all."

"Won't he hear of it on his own?" Lily asked.

"I doubt it. He never reads the scandal sheets. I suppose one of his acquaintances might hear of it, but none of them will like to call Alec's attention to it, for it might make him furious enough to throttle the messenger."

Lily bit her lip. "Hadn't *you* better tell him? He won't throttle *you*."

Delia stared at her. "*Me?* Certainly not. I'd much rather he never find out at all. He's worn out with worry as it is."

"But if Alec doesn't know, who will see to it Robyn fulfills his obligation in this?"

Delia raised her eyebrows. "Robyn, of course."

Lily fiddled with the tassel on one of Delia's pillows. "Any plan that relies on Robyn is doomed to failure. He's far more likely to be off rolling dice at the gaming hells or chasing Lady Downes around Lord Barrow's study than acting the proper escort. Besides, he didn't precisely agree to Ellie's plan."

"I can't believe Robyn would leave you to the mercy of the *ton*. What if we have his promise?"

"Oh, he'll promise easily enough, and just as easily break it. He's forever breaking promises to his sisters."

Delia considered Lily for a moment. "Robyn breaks promises because no one expects any better from him. You underestimate him, Lily. Everyone does, even Robyn himself. Give him a chance, won't you? Doesn't he deserve at least that much?"

Lily wound an uneven thread tightly around her finger and yanked it out of the tassel. "I haven't much choice in the matter, do I? We haven't any other plan, and Charlotte thinks Lord Atherton will marry this season."

Delia frowned. "You're still set on Lord Atherton, then?"

"Of course, though Mrs. Tittleton has set me back a good deal. I gather Lord Atherton is rather fussy about decorum. This scandal with Robyn comes at the worst possible time."

Delia hesitated. "I don't know Lord Atherton well, and I don't think you do, either, Lily."

Lily dismissed this with a wave of her hand. "I know everything I need to know about him. He's the very soul of propriety. Charlotte called him the most dependable gentleman in London. I believe she was poking fun at him, but dependability is no laughing matter to *me*. He'll make an ideal husband."

"Dependability is all very well, but there are other desirable qualities in a husband, like tenderness, and passion. How do you know he possesses either?"

Lily began to yank more loose threads out of the tassel, one by one. Passion caused that weak in the knees, butterflies in the belly feeling. She'd felt passion when Robyn kissed her, and now look at what a mess she was in.

Last night's passion was today's unmitigated disaster.

She didn't want butterflies, and she didn't want a man who made her forget herself so entirely, she'd slap his face. "I don't want passion. It hasn't any place in a marriage."

Delia made an odd choking sound and laid her hand on her belly. "Wherever did you get that idea?"

"Oh, you know what I mean. It's a serious business, contracting an advantageous match. Think of the doors that will open for our sisters if I marry as well as you have."

Their three younger sisters had come for Delia's wedding, but had returned to Surrey immediately afterward to close up the cottage and prepare for their permanent move to London. They'd join Delia and Lily here next month. Iris, who was eighteen, would debut at the start of next season, and Violet and Hyacinth would soon follow.

A brief silence fell, then Delia tugged the tassel out of Lily's hand. "Dear, I want to speak with you about something, but I don't want to upset you."

Something in Delia's face made Lily uneasy. She tried to smile. "Upset? Do you think I would shout at my pregnant, ill sister?"

Delia didn't smile back. "No. I know you won't shout. You never do. You rarely raise your voice at all. Don't you ever *want* to shout, or fall into a rage, or hurl something across a room?"

Lily's heart gave an anxious thump. Even if she had an urge to throw something, she wouldn't indulge it. Hysterics led to chaos, and she couldn't bear chaos. She avoided it at all costs.

Delia put her hand over Lily's. "Remember those dolls you had when you were a child? You'd play with them for hours, and when you weren't playing with them, you'd arrange them on your bed, from the smallest to the tallest, sitting straight up against the pillows, their hair smooth and dresses tidily tucked around their legs. I always adored that about you, Lily—you take such wonderful care of the things you love."

Lily nodded but didn't speak. For some reason her throat had gone tight.

"But ever since Father and Mother died . . ."

Delia took her sister's hand and curled Lily's fingers into her palm, then she covered Lily's hand with both of hers and squeezed, gently at first, then harder, so Lily's fingernails began to dig into her skin.

Delia looked down at Lily's fist, trapped between her hands. "It may seem safe to live this way, but it's exhausting, keeping everything in orderly rows. It's tight, like a fist. Hard. It hurts, and nothing can get in or out."

Lily stared down at her fist clenched between her sister's fingers. Her heart felt as tight as that fist, but she meant to keep it that way; otherwise she'd fall back into the yawning chasm that had opened beneath her after her parents' carriage accident.

Delia didn't understand.

Lily had never been a daring sort—even as a child she'd been careful. Cautious. But ever since her parents' sudden deaths, she felt as if she teetered on the head of a pin, and a breath in any direction would tip her over into the dark, bottomless abyss. The only way she could keep her balance was not to breathe too deeply, or move or feel too much. If she could only stay in control and behave as a proper young lady should, nothing awful would happen.

Proper young ladies didn't end up in the scandal sheets. They weren't shunned by the *ton* or barred from Almack's. They didn't wander into dark rooms or slap gentlemen's faces, and they didn't let notorious rakes kiss them senseless.

Delia loosened her hands, uncurled Lily's fingers, and pressed her sister's palm against her own. "You can't arrange your life like you arranged those dolls, Lily. You can't line people up in neat rows. If you stay closed and tight, it will become harder and harder to open your heart with every day that passes, and after a while you won't remember how to open it at all. Do you see?"

Lily nodded, but she didn't trust herself to speak. She had an overwhelming urge to put her head in Delia's lap and sob. She might have succumbed to it had Alec not walked into the room at that moment.

He went straight to Delia. "How do you feel, love?" He lay a tender hand against her cheek.

Delia put her hand over his and turned her head to kiss his palm. She smiled up at him. "I feel so much better. Lily has kept me company."

The tension around Alec's mouth eased a little. "Has she?" He smiled affectionately at Lily, but he dragged a weary hand through his hair, and Lily noticed there were dark circles under his eyes.

Delia was right. She couldn't burden Alec with this business between her and Robyn. She'd have to make the best of it without Alec's help.

Chapter Six

If one considered a fist to the face an improvement, Robyn's
day improved once he escaped the family breakfast table,
and he made it a point to do nothing of any use to anyone
for the remainder of the day.

He pummeled the daylights out of Pelkey at their usual
Thursday afternoon bout at Gentleman Jackson's. Pelkey
was a big, meaty chap, and it was damned good entertainment pummeling him, rather like pounding on a side of beef.
Robyn had the advantage, being quick and deadly accurate
with his fists. Pelkey rarely landed a punch, but when he
did, he sent Robyn sprawling, and this afternoon Robyn had
been just distracted enough for Pelkey's huge fist to connect
with his face.

He flinched as he ran careful fingers over the dark purple
bruise that shadowed his left eye. It hurt like the very devil,
but he'd gladly take a fist to the other eye rather than sit
through another interrogation by his sisters, or endure more
of Lily's reproachful silences.

After Pelkey had scraped him up off the floor at Jackson's, they'd dallied at Tattersall's all afternoon, then gone to White's for supper. Lord Archibald had met them there and the three of them had wandered off to the theater to see Miss Bannister play Viola in *Twelfth Night*.

As soon as they were seated, Pelkey nudged Robyn in the ribs. "Louise Bannister is a saucy little piece, eh?"

She was. A brunette, too. Robyn had recently decided he preferred brunettes. "Talented, as well."

He watched Miss Bannister's hips sway in her tight costume as she sashayed across the stage. Saucy, indeed, and no doubt easy to please, both in bed and out of it. He needed a good, hard ride. So why not saddle up Louise Bannister?

Pelkey chortled. "You can be sure her talents aren't displayed to best advantage on the stage, Sutherland."

Her assets were, however, especially in her eunuch's costume, which clung to those assets like a second skin. Plump, lush assets they were, too. "What say you, Archie?"

Lord Archibald, whose family seat bordered the Sutherlands' seat in Kent, was one of Robyn's oldest and closest friends.

"I'd say the theater manager has taken some shocking liberties with Shakespeare."

Robyn rolled his eyes. "About the lady, I mean."

Archie surveyed Miss Bannister, his face a mask of indifference. "She's all yours. I prefer fair-haired women, with blue eyes."

"The insipid blond, white-skinned English rose, eh? That's not very imaginative of you."

Archie turned to him with a smirk. "Really? But I'm sure I just read somewhere you like blondes well enough, Robyn."

Robyn stretched his long legs out in front of him and leaned back more comfortably in his chair. "No good ever came of *reading*, Archie. Best avoid it, especially the scandal sheets."

Archie shrugged and turned his attention back to the

stage, where Miss Bannister was on her knees, pleading with her Orsino, her breeches pulled tight across her thighs.

Archie cleared his throat. "On second thought, Sutherland, perhaps Miss Bannister isn't a bad choice, after all, since you find yourself with an insatiable appetite for brunettes all of a sudden. She looks to be, ah . . . a *fit* enough specimen."

Robyn's eyes wandered over her arse. She did look fit, for any number of wicked things. So why wasn't he the least bit interested in fitting her with a saddle and grabbing the nearest riding crop?

"Come now, gentlemen," Pelkey said. "Cool blondes, sultry brunettes, red-haired vixens—why limit yourself to just one? Or even to one at a time? Lovely ladies of every color, size, and skill await us at the Slippery Eel. Shall we?"

Archie offered no objection, and it seemed as good an idea as any to Robyn. Once they arrived at the Eel, however, he found none of the ladies on offer there pleased him any more than Louise Bannister had.

It was a trifle worrying. His eel was usually so accommodating.

Pelkey, more eager than he was discriminating, had chosen a somewhat battle-weary brown-haired wench. Archie waved off a petite blonde in favor of a bottle of whiskey and a lonely seat on a settee, and there he sat, swilling his drink and smirking at Robyn. "What's the matter, Sutherland? Can't find a brunette to your taste this evening?"

Pelkey snagged the arm of a slender dark-haired woman as she walked by, and gave her a little push toward Robyn. "What's wrong with this one?"

Robyn studied the woman's face. She was pretty enough, but the area beneath his falls remained stubbornly unresponsive, and *not*, he was sure, because the woman wouldn't taste of wild strawberries. He'd never known a whore who did.

Or any woman who did, for that matter.

Except one.

He shook his head. "Not tonight, sweetheart."

Archie took a long pull from his bottle, not bothering with a glass. "Don't tell me you've developed more refined tastes, Sutherland. Worst thing that can happen to a man. Innocence has a certain appeal, though, doesn't it?"

Pelkey snorted. "Innocence? You're in the wrong place for that, Sutherland. Better settle for the brunette. She looks as though she could wring some life into you."

Robyn ignored this. He watched Archie raise the bottle to his lips again. "What would you know about innocents anyway, Archie?"

Archie laughed. "Not much, though I do know if you despoil one, someone is damn well going to make sure you do something about it. So what do *you* plan to do about your most recent mess?"

Robyn raised an eyebrow. "*Do?*"

"What mess?" Pelkey searched the floor at Robyn's feet, a puzzled expression on his face.

Archie gave Pelkey a disgusted look. "You can't just walk away from it this time, Sutherland. She's not one of your doxies."

Pelkey looked from one to the other of them. "Who? The brunette? Certainly she's a doxy. Not Sutherland's doxy, though. She never even touched him."

No, Lily wasn't a doxy, and she wasn't *his*. He was hers, though, at least according to his sisters. He was trapped right in the palm of her dainty little hand, and if his sisters had their way, there he'd stay for as long as it took to remove the stain on her reputation.

No matter how hard she squeezed.

He grabbed one of the empty glasses on the table and thrust it at Archie. "Of course she's not a doxy, and no one will believe she is, no matter what they read in the scandal sheets. I can't see what all the fuss is about."

Archie poured a hefty measure of whiskey into the glass and handed it back to Robyn. "My, you are naïve, at least when it's convenient for you to be so. It doesn't matter one whit if they *believe* it, just as it doesn't matter if it's true. Scandal is scandal, and the *ton* devours scandal like a jungle full of starving savages."

"Savages with short, feeble memories. It will be over before it ever takes hold. You'll see, Archie."

Archie shook his head. "You may not take it seriously, Robyn, but the *ton* will. It isn't going to go away, and it will be Lily who suffers for it."

What bollocks. But Robyn didn't want to argue with Archie, and he was wasting his time at the Eel, since he remained uninterested in any slippery frolics with the ladies on offer this evening.

He finished the rest of his whiskey in one swallow. "I believe I've had enough fun for one night, gentlemen. Enjoy your evening."

"You're leaving *now*?" Pelkey began. "But you haven't even—"

Robyn let the door slam shut behind him before he could hear the rest of Pelkey's objection.

It was early yet. Not even midnight, and he was in no hurry to get home. Perhaps he'd walk to Mayfair. The cool air would clear his head. Or perhaps a footpad would attack him. He'd quite enjoy a brawl with a footpad.

He began a determined whistling, for that was what a gentlemen did when he'd had a pleasant day. He whistled.

So he'd faced an inquisition from his sisters and been set to the torture for his sins, the torture in this case a sentence to attend balls at Almack's. Then Pelkey had thrown him across the room and blacked his eye, and Archie had scolded him as if Robyn were a naughty child.

Now here he was walking home, unsatisfied and wondering why he hadn't felt even a twitch of interest in the brunette.

All very pleasant.

His hopes for a brawl faded as he neared Mayfair without

any sign of a footpad or even an obliging cutthroat. Good God, what had London come to when a single gentleman remained unmolested on the streets at night?

He'd reached the iron gates surrounding the back garden when he noticed a fine black carriage rolling down the street. It came to a silent halt in front of the Sutherland town house. The footman placed the stairs and a young lady stepped gracefully down onto the pavement.

Lily. There was no mistaking that lithe figure. He'd know it anywhere. He'd know *her* anywhere, even without the gleam of the gaslight on her hair.

Damn it. There was the twitch he'd looked for earlier.

Shouldn't Lily be tucked safely into her bed at this hour, dreaming pure white dreams, like all the other respectable virgins in London?

A gentleman alighted from the carriage after her. A tall, well-formed gentleman who took her arm to escort her to the front door. They passed into the foyer and the door closed behind them.

Out alone with a gentleman at midnight? How shocking. If *she* hadn't a care for her reputation, he saw no reason why *he* should.

Robyn had the most absurd urge to creep up to the window and peek into the foyer to see what Lily and her mysterious gentleman were doing. He could easily scale the low iron railing around the garden, and it was mere steps to the window from there . . .

He'd taken a few steps forward before he realized what he was doing and a wave of disgust engulfed him. *Christ.* Was he actually contemplating creeping through the shrubbery and peeking through a window?

Damn it. Not even a twitch of interest for Miss Bannister, in *breeches*, no less. Not a twinge at the Eel, but now here he was about to leap over a railing and skulk through the bushes so he could spy on Lily?

He was going through the front door, just as he would if

he *hadn't* lost his mind. He forced himself to walk calmly up the path and through the door.

Lily stood in the foyer saying good night to her tall, handsome, solicitous gentleman.

Alec. *Of course.* Who else would it be? Lord Atherton? Even Lily wasn't that efficient.

Both of them stared at him. Alec had a sort of detached amusement on his face, but Lily looked horrified. She covered her mouth with her hand. "Robyn! Oh, what did you do?"

He scowled at her. What the devil did she mean by that? He hadn't done it, whatever it was.

Alec gestured to Robyn's eye. "Did one of your indiscretions finally catch up with you?"

Robyn reached up to touch his face and winced. Oh. Right. He'd forgotten the black eye. "Pelkey," he said with a shrug.

Alec nodded. "Ah. Finally landed a punch, did he? His hands are the size of two roast beefs. Like getting kicked in the eye by a horse, I imagine."

"Something like that." Robyn's gaze narrowed on his brother's face. "I hope you don't mind my saying this, brother, but you look as bad as I do."

Alec grinned. "Not that bad, I hope." He turned to Lily and kissed her check. "Thank you for staying tonight."

Lily squeezed his hand. "Of course. Good night, Alec."

"Best put something on that eye," Alec said to Robyn before he disappeared out the door.

Robyn and Lily were left standing alone together in the foyer. She looked as though she'd rather be anywhere else, and it occurred to him they hadn't been alone together since their passionate interlude in Lord Barrow's study.

If he took just one step closer to her, he'd be able to catch her scent. Unable to help himself, he moved forward and drew in a deep breath. Oh, God—there it was. Hot sun on meadow grasses. Daisies.

And there *it* was—another twitch. Not just a twitch, actually. More like a surge.

"Does it hurt?" Lily asked.

Does it hurt? Was she joking? "Er, not yet, but it will if I don't do something about it. Soon."

"What can you do for it? Put ice on it? It might take the swelling down."

Robyn blanched. *Ice?* That didn't sound like a good idea. Downright painful, actually—

Oh. Right. She meant his *eye.*

Lily regarded him warily for a moment. "I suppose I could help you with it, if you like."

Robyn closed his eyes to better imagine what it would feel like to have Lily help him with his pressing problem. His nether regions, so stubbornly resistant earlier, were quite enthusiastic about *that* idea. His problem was growing larger by the second.

You're behaving like a child. Still, he couldn't help but indulge in the innuendo, made even more salacious because Lily remained oblivious to it. "Did you say you'll help me? I'd be delighted to have an extra hand to help soothe the, ah, pain."

"Yes. It will be difficult for you to do it yourself. You can't see it very well."

On the contrary, it was making itself quite visible. He felt a grin spread over his face. "I have done it myself before, on occasion." On countless occasions, if the truth were told.

Lily looked puzzled. "How many black eyes have you had?"

Robyn's brain registered the reference to his eye, but his cock, which had gone from a twitch, to a surge, to leaping in anticipation, remained unconvinced. He'd completely forgotten about the throbbing in his *eye.*

She turned toward the kitchens. "I think cook has some salve in the stillroom."

At that point, nothing could have stopped him from

following her. He did take off his coat to hold it in front of him, a nod, at least, to propriety. Surely she wouldn't notice the state he was in? She was an innocent. How much could she possibly know about the male anatomy?

"Sit here," she said when they reached the stillroom. Robyn sat obediently on a stool while she fiddled with some jars in a cupboard. "Ah, here it is. Betsy gave me this when I cut my leg on some thorns in the rose garden."

Robyn adjusted his coat to cover more of his lap. *Do not think about Lily rubbing salve on her bare leg . . .*

Her fingers, slippery with the salve, gently touched his eye. She moved closer to get a better look until she was standing almost between his legs, her breasts displayed temptingly under his chin.

He kept his gaze straight ahead. Perhaps this hadn't been such a wise idea, after all.

She wasn't trying to tease him. She hadn't any idea his body grew more desperate with every stroke of her fingers against his face. She was so close, yet he couldn't touch her. She touched him, but so lightly, with just her fingertips, and only on his face. His hands were mere inches from her waist. The slightest tilt would bring his head against her neck.

He'd engaged in every kind of debauchery, but he'd never experienced anything more erotic.

Ah, God. It was torture of the most exquisite kind to sit here, surrounded by her scent while her soft fingers stroked him. He opened his knees a bit wider before he lost control and snapped them closed so she was caught between them.

Almack's wasn't his punishment. *This was.*

"Why did Lord Pelkey hit you?" She dipped back into the salve and he felt her fingertips against the swollen skin under his eye.

Robyn sat as still as he could and tried not to pant. "He didn't—he was—"

String a sentence together, you fool.

"We were boxing. At Gentleman Jackson's."

Lily's brow furrowed with distaste. "Boxing? I can't understand why boxing appeals to gentlemen. It's so uncivilized."

Uncivilized? She had no idea. He was on the verge of downright savagery. "Men *are* uncivilized. Even gentlemen. That's the very reason it appeals."

Her delicious pale pink lips settled into a tight, disapproving line, but instead of cooling his ardor as they should have, those severe lips made him want to kiss her. Kiss her until they softened, and opened, and he could slip inside.

"Speaking of savagery," he said, though they hadn't been, "what did Alec say when you told him about Mrs. Tittleton? I'm surprised he didn't black my other eye."

Her blue eyes met his for an instant before she went back to her ministrations. "I didn't tell him. He doesn't know anything about it."

Ah. So she thought to appeal to his honorable side, did she? Her mistake. He didn't have one. "I'm shocked at you, Lily. However will you make sure I behave myself and do the proper thing *now*?"

He tried not to notice the way her fingers brushed close to his ear as she tended to the outer edges of the bruise. Bloody Pelkey. He did have fists the size of roast beefs. It felt as if Lily were touching him everywhere.

She cocked her head to one side, considering this. "Why don't you just do the proper thing anyway, and leave Alec out of it?"

Robyn snorted. "What fun would that be?"

She'd begun to work on the inside corner of his eye, but her hand stilled at his mocking tone. "I don't see why you'd draw the line at disappointing Alec, in any case. You don't hesitate to disappoint your sisters. What's the difference?"

Well, then. She knew him better than he thought.

In truth, there *was* no difference. He broke promises. He disappointed his sisters. He disappointed Alec. He disappointed his mother. God knew he'd done nothing *but* disappoint his father.

He shrugged. "Alec holds my purse strings. I wish I could claim some more honorable reason, but there it is."

"Yes, well, as you said, men are uncivilized."

He couldn't take any more of her stroking without leaping on her. He grasped her wrist and jerked her hand away from his face. Her pulse leapt against his thumb, and he couldn't stop himself from pressing his lips against the soft skin there, just for a moment, before he released her. "Ladies, too, on occasion. After all, it was *you* who struck *me* last night, if you remember."

Color surged into her face. "I remember you deserved it."

Ah, he did love to tease her. He didn't know any other woman who blushed so delightfully. Or blushed at all, come to think of it. "I remember it was worth it."

She placed the stopper in the jar of salve, pushed it down tightly, and set it back in the cupboard, each movement calm and deliberate, then gave him a reproving look. "Perhaps it would be best if we both forgot it entirely."

She turned on her heel, but before she could make her grand exit, he stopped her with a low chuckle. "Oh, love. It's far too late for that."

Chapter Seven

The lemonade at Almack's did taste like water. Lily hadn't tried the cake, but she knew it would crumble to dust in her mouth, even if it wasn't as dry and stale as rumor claimed.

"You look lovely tonight, Lily," Lady Catherine said for the third time. She patted Lily's hand. "That color brings out your eyes."

Lily smoothed a fold of her pale blue gown between cold fingers. "Thank you, my lady."

She'd blushed to the roots of her hair when she'd caught sight of her reflection in the looking glass this evening, but Charlotte only laughed and insisted she wear the gown so the gentlemen could admire her "devastating bosom."

Well, Charlotte needn't have bothered. Devastating bosom or not, Lily had spent the entire night languishing on the side of the room with Lady Catherine while Charlotte and Eleanor danced.

Her very first ball in London, at Almack's no less, and she was a wallflower.

Poor Lady Catherine looked rather puzzled, as if she couldn't understand why Lily hadn't yet been asked to dance. Evidently Lady Catherine hadn't read the scandal sheet. She was the only person in the room who hadn't. For all their sophistication, it seemed the *ton* wasn't above a peek at Mrs. Tittleton.

Voucher or not, Lily was being soundly shunned.

Frizzle-haired Miss Thurston stood not ten paces away, but she hadn't acknowledged Lily with so much as a word or a nod the entire evening. She whispered and giggled to her friend behind her fan. The friend darted appraising glances at Lily, whispered back to Miss Thurston, then both young ladies erupted into malicious laugher.

Lily turned away. She ran a careful finger over the fan clutched in her hand and wondered how she'd ever thought she could manage in London society.

"I can't imagine where Robyn is," Lady Catherine fretted. "It's so provoking!"

"He must be delayed," Lily said for the sixth time in less than two hours.

It had become quite the theme of the evening, trying to imagine where Robyn was. For everyone except Lily, who did her best *not* to imagine where he was. He wasn't *here*, so what did it matter?

"I'm certain he'll turn up any minute," she added, though in truth she thought it far more likely they wouldn't see Robyn for days.

She should have known he'd never appear tonight. She'd suspected as much, but to suspect a thing and truly *believe* it . . . well, if they were the same thing, she wouldn't be choking on bitter disappointment with each sip of weak lemonade.

For all his carelessness, she hadn't really believed Robyn would toss her to the *ton* like a lamb to ravenous wolves.

A guest voucher, or "stranger's ticket," had appeared for Lily at the town house late that morning. Charlotte and

Eleanor amused themselves for quite some time with speculations about how Robyn had managed to secure it.

Lily had been stunned silent when the voucher arrived. Was it possible Robyn would turn up to escort her tonight, after all? Perhaps Delia was right. Perhaps they did all underestimate him.

She'd lingered over her looking glass for quite some time that evening while Betsy, Charlotte's lady's maid, brushed her hair until it shone. Betsy had pinned the heavy waves to the back of Lily's head and nestled a thin silver band in the gleaming locks to hold it away from her face.

None of these efforts were on Robyn's behalf, of course. She wasn't such a fool as to primp and preen for a capricious man like *him*. She knew better than that, which was why her heart *hadn't* sunk into her slippers when she finished her toilette and came downstairs to find only Rylands, the butler, standing guard in an otherwise empty foyer.

Lady Catherine, Ellie, and Charlotte came down the stairs after Lily. "Have you seen Robyn, Rylands?" Lady Catherine asked. "Is he waiting in the carriage?"

Rylands gave a stiff bow. "No, my lady. Mr. Sutherland left early this morning for his club and hasn't yet returned."

"Oh, no," Charlotte moaned. "He's gone to White's? Why, he could be there for the rest of the night! Or anywhere in London, come to that."

He could be locked in a dark room with Lady Downes, sampling the charms he'd had to forgo the other night. Or sampling the charms of any willing female in London, come to *that*. Wherever he was, his plans didn't appear to include a ball at Almack's.

"He *did* get the voucher, Charlotte," Ellie reminded her sister. "He promised he'd be here."

Lily stood quietly, but under cover of her skirts, her hands clenched into fists. He hadn't promised anything of the sort. He'd been very careful *not* to promise, in fact. He'd said he'd procure the voucher and he'd done so, and that was the last of the miracles they'd witness tonight.

Blast the man. It infuriated Lily to stand there and look at Ellie's hopeful face and know Robyn wouldn't come.

"Surely we can wait another few minutes?" Eleanor said. "I'm certain he'll be along."

They did wait, for another twenty minutes. Lily tried not to squirm in her satin slippers as they all waited for Eleanor to get tired of standing in the foyer with her eyes fixed on the door.

"Oh, bother!" Ellie exclaimed at last, throwing her hands up in the air. "Shall we send a note round to White's and hope for the best?"

The chances that Robyn was still at White's were slim, indeed, and all of them knew it.

Lily gathered her skirts into her hands and started toward the door. She'd had quite enough of this. "Send the note, by all means, but we needn't wait for a reply. We'll go without him."

Eleanor and Charlotte exchanged glances. "Are you sure you wouldn't rather wait?" Eleanor asked, fixing Lily with a meaningful look. "Robyn *particularly* wished to escort you to your first ball at Almack's."

Lily shrugged with a carelessness she couldn't quite feel. She had no wish to brave the *ton* without an escort after Mrs. Tittleton's perfidy, but neither would she allow Ellie's and Charlotte's evening to be spoiled, and she couldn't bear to wait here another minute.

"So he will. He's sure to arrive at Almack's in no time." She met Ellie's eyes with a look that asked: *How bad can it be?*

Eleanor's return glare looked rather forbidding. *Quite bad, indeed.*

Lily hadn't any opportunity to change her mind, however, for Lady Catherine spoke up then. "Of course Lily's right.

He may even be there now," she added, with the confidence only a fond mother could feel.

Eleanor gave Lady Catherine a skeptical look, as though she wondered if her mother had actually *met* Robyn. "Very well."

Off to Almack's they went, and now they were there with no possibility of escape, Lily began to see how right Ellie was. As bad as it could be was quite bad, indeed.

"I can't understand it." Lady Catherine flapped her fan to and fro. "I thought for certain he'd be here by the time we arrived."

Lily's head began to throb. She didn't want to think about Robyn anymore, and she'd rather chew glass than spend the rest of the evening discussing him. She gestured to the dancers, hoping to distract Lady Catherine. "Look, my lady. Charlotte and Lord Atherton dance beautifully together."

They did. They looked well together, too. Perhaps Charlotte would marry him.

Someone should.

A half hour earlier, Lord Atherton had set out across the ballroom, his eyes fixed on their corner of the room. Lily held her breath and did her best not to look too eager when it became clear he was headed in her direction.

Perhaps he hadn't read Mrs. Tittleton? Proper gentlemen didn't pay attention to gossip, did they? Surely Lord Atherton wouldn't believe such vicious—

He stopped in front of them and bowed correctly. "Good evening, Miss Sutherland."

Charlotte curtsied. "Lord Atherton. This is my dear friend, Miss Lily Somerset."

Well, that was the introduction out of the way, at least, and now perhaps—

"Miss Somerset." Lord Atherton bowed. His cool blue eyes swept over her and then as quickly dismissed her. He turned back to Charlotte before Lily had a chance to say a word, and held out his hand. "Miss Sutherland, will you favor me with a dance?"

And just like that, all of Lily's hopes burned to ashes.

He hadn't been precisely rude to her, but he'd looked right through her, as if she were one of Almack's gilt mirrors.

It seemed proper gentlemen did read the scandal sheets, after all.

Charlotte's face colored angrily, but Lily gave her a tiny frown and made a subtle gesture with her chin toward the dance floor to indicate Charlotte should dance with him. She could hardly refuse him, after all. It wasn't proper.

The evening had gone from bad to worse after that. The other gentlemen followed Lord Atherton's example, and Lily hadn't left Lady Catherine's side all night.

Just then Eleanor's partner delivered her back to Lady Catherine and ambled off to fetch her a glass of lemonade, leaving the three ladies alone.

Ellie's eyes sparkled and her cheeks were pink from her exertions on the dance floor. "My goodness! It's very warm in here, isn't it?"

Lily ran her hands up and down her bare arms. "Is it warm?"

The sparkle in Ellie's dark eyes dimmed. "Robyn hasn't arrived." It was a statement, not a question.

Lady Catherine shook her head. "No, he hasn't, and it's nearly ten o'clock."

Eleanor wrung her hands. "The doors at Almack's close at eleven. No one, not even the Duke of Wellington himself, is permitted to enter the ballroom once the doors are closed."

Lily jerked her chin a notch higher. She didn't need the Duke of Wellington, and she didn't need Robyn Sutherland, either.

He could spend the rest of the season chasing Lady Downes around every desk in every study in every town house in London. Delia had asked her to give Robyn a chance and she'd done so, just as she promised she would.

Now she was free to pursue her own ends. She needed a new plan, and once she got through this miserable evening, she'd devise one guaranteed to deliver the desired result.

One that didn't include Robyn Sutherland.

"Damn it, Sutherland! Hold 'er steady, will you?"

"She's as steady as she's going to get." The trouble was the rest of the room had gone atilt. "Stop blathering, Pelkey, and take your turn, or give someone else a go."

Lord Pelkey placed the end of his cravat between his teeth and leaned over the barmaid who squirmed in Robyn's lap, one of her plump legs extended, her skirts pulled to mid-thigh.

Pelkey took his time perfecting his position, for despite Robyn's threat, Archie wasn't in any condition to take a turn. He hadn't yet surrendered to unconsciousness, but it was a near thing. His lay with his head on the table, his eyes fixed on the barmaid's lifted skirts. He didn't seem to be aware of much else.

"Come now, sweetheart," Lord Pelkey coaxed through a mouthful of starched linen. "Stay still, won't you?"

The barmaid gave a shrill laugh. "Go on, then, guv. Do it!"

It was both disturbing and fascinating, watching Pelkey twist this way and that in an effort to wrap the whole length of the cravat around the barmaid's leg with just his teeth. At one point his head was entirely engulfed by her skirts.

Which was rather the point, Robyn supposed.

Finally Pelkey crawled out from underneath the barmaid. He slapped the girl on her fleshy thigh. "Got it! You owe me five guineas, Sutherland."

Robyn would gladly have paid Pelkey the five guineas just to get the barmaid off his lap. Mary's generous bulk didn't do a thing for him, aside from cut off the blood circulating to his legs.

Or was her name Molly? He couldn't remember.

He also couldn't remember quite what he was doing in London's west end, drinking himself into a stupor with Pelkey. He hadn't intended to end up here; that much was certain. They'd started at White's, hadn't they?

Lord Pelkey dropped into a chair, grasped the barmaid's hand, and drew her off Robyn's lap and onto his own. "Can't think why you'd want the damn voucher to Almack's, Sutherland. Nothing but debutantes there."

Ah, now he remembered. Of course. Almack's. London's great monument to vanity and social ambition. He'd promised to get Lily a voucher to Almack's.

Well, he'd got the voucher, and now he'd be rewarded for his good deed with another evening of watching Pelkey grope some giggling barmaid. Even bloody Almack's would be more entertaining than this.

Pelkey ran a hand comfortably up Mary's calf and under her skirts. "Debutantes and chastity, that is." He shuddered, as if *chastity* were a filthy word.

Robyn watched in distaste as Pelkey's other hand settled on Molly's arse. "Perhaps I find chastity titillating."

Why not? He'd tried everything else.

Pelkey snorted. "Doubtful. What's the real reason, Sutherland? Thinking of marrying, are you? Want to inspect this season's goods?"

"The voucher isn't for *me*."

"Who then? One of your mistresses? Be funny, that, a bird of paradise flaunting her feathers at Almack's. I'd even turn up there myself to see it." Pelkey guffawed with such feeling, Molly nearly toppled off his lap.

Robyn sighed. Pelkey was a revolting enough specimen, but he had his uses. One couldn't beg, borrow, or steal a voucher to Almack's, but one could extort one, and Pelkey was handy when it came to extortion. As usual, gossip proved more powerful than gold. The dragons who guarded the keep to Almack's had secrets to hide, much as everyone else in London did.

Robyn couldn't fathom why, but the ladies were fond of Pelkey. Maybe it was the roast-beef-sized hands. They gave the ladies lurid ideas. Lurid ideas led to secrets, and Pelkey was a deep, dark, and dirty one. The worthy dragon in question would do anything to keep her younger sister's liaison with Pelkey from meeting the light of day, even fix her signature to a voucher for Almack's.

Archie raised his head off the table. "S'not for his mistress."

Pelkey wrapped an arm around Mary's waist and guffawed again. "What's that, Archie? Did you say something?"

Archie frowned and tried again. "Voucher," he said, more clearly this time. "It's for Miss Somerset."

Damn it. Of course Archie *would* regain consciousness just in time to drop that little morsel into Pelkey's lap. Now Robyn would have to explain the whole bloody mess to Pelkey, whose wit was such he'd never understand it on the first go.

They could be there all night.

"Somerset?" Pelkey asked. "You mean the blue-eyed chit who just married Carlisle?"

Even Archie, who was by no means lucid, shook his head at this. "Why would Lady Carlisle need a voucher to Almack's? It's for her younger sister. Miss *Lily* Somerset."

Robyn raised an eyebrow. "You seem to know a great deal about Lily's business. How is that, Archie?"

Archie swiped with his coat sleeve at the part of his face that had been glued to the table. "I called on Lily and your sisters this afternoon and Ellie told me all about it. She also said you were escorting Lily to Almack's tonight." He glanced around him at the sticky tables and the barmaid enthroned on Pelkey's lap. "Does this look like Almack's to you, Sutherland?"

Robyn shrugged. "Similar company."

Archie didn't look amused. "If you're here, who is Lily's escort tonight? Don't tell me you sent her off to Almack's alone after the Mrs. Tittleton debacle?"

He looked so horrified, Robyn was taken aback. It wasn't as bad as all that. There might be a few whispers, yes, and a little lukewarm gossip. An old dowager or two would shake their heads over Lily, but that would be it.

"Badly done, Robyn," Archie said. "The *ton* will eat her alive and pick her bones clean. No need to settle for stale cake tonight."

Robyn opened his mouth to reply, but Pelkey, who was still trying to make sense of this recent astonishing information, interrupted him. "What? There's two blue-eyed chits?"

"There's *five* of them." Archie had met the three youngest Somerset sisters at Delia and Alec's wedding. "And each one of them a blue-eyed temptress."

For God's sake. Archie was worse than a gossiping old woman. Maybe *he* was Mrs. Tittleton.

Robyn hadn't intended to offer any information about Lily's sisters to Pelkey, who was the worst kind of lecher. Alec wouldn't like it, and besides, Robyn would rather *not* see Pelkey's eyes fall out of his head and into Mary's bodice.

Or was it Molly?

Archie only grinned at Robyn's dark look. "Beauty runs like a stallion with a burr under his saddle though that family."

"But Sutherland wanted the other blue-eyed chit," Pelkey insisted. "The first one. He went on and on about her one night, nearly bored us all to death, he did."

Archie belched. "Well, that one married his brother, didn't she?"

Pelkey pinched Molly's ribs. "Well, never mind, Sutherland. One's the same as the next, eh?"

Mary squawked, either at the pinch or the sentiment. Robyn wasn't sure which.

"One of them is as beautiful as the next," Archie said.

Robyn drummed his fingers against the table. Archie had prostrated himself before Lily every day for a fortnight during the Sutherlands' recent house party, with no success. You'd think a few weeks of rejection would cure him, but it seemed Archie's admiration hadn't faded.

Pelkey leered. "What does she look like?"

Archie raised his glass in a drunken toast. "Like her elder sister. Enough said."

Robyn leaned back in his chair and crossed one leg over his knee. "She's too . . . tidy."

Archie stared. "You're blind, Sutherland. I can't think of anyone this season to equal her, aside from your sisters."

"Now Sutherland's sisters . . ." Pelkey began slyly.

Normally hearing either of his sister's names on Pelkey's lecherous lips would be cause for a brawl, but this time Robyn wasn't even listening.

Tidy or not, Lily had opened her mouth so sweetly under his when he'd kissed her the other night. That kiss—that slap to the face? She might look the perfect, proper lady, but he had only to recall the way her tongue felt inside his mouth to suspect her prim exterior hid a bounty of wanton delights.

All that passion, wasted on a dullard like Atherton. All that spirit, writhing in that luscious body, left untapped. Someone had to help Lily loosen her stays, and as Robyn was the only man who'd ever breached the bodice of her gown, he practically had an obligation to do it.

She didn't really want Atherton, and even if she did, she'd never catch him. Tempting as she was, she was still Millicent Chase's daughter. A staid, upright stick like Atherton would never overlook that fact. Why, Robyn would be doing her a service if he kept her from wasting her time on the man.

He hadn't any other plans for the season aside from the usual debaucheries, and they'd grown rather dull of late. It would be far more amusing to tease Lily and watch that blush flood her cheeks, and anyway, it would please his sisters. If Lily took to wearing her low-cut gowns again, it would please him, as well, for then he could watch that blush steal over her neck and throat and tinge her bosom with the most delicate pink . . .

Besides, what if Archie was right? A picture rose in his mind of Lily, standing alone at Almack's, choking on stale cake while everyone around her whispered and stared. No matter what Archie claimed, even Robyn wasn't so hopeless he could dismiss that image.

He got to his feet and gave Archie's chair a shove with his toe. "Come on, then."

"Where are we going?"

"Almack's. *Now.* It's nearly half ten."

Archie smiled and stood up. "That's the way, Sutherland."

"I'm coming, too." Pelkey jumped to his feet so quickly, Molly tumbled off his lap. "Want to see this new blue-eyed chit of Sutherland's."

Mary landed unceremoniously on her arse on the dirty floor. "Oi, guv, ye' dropped summat, didn't you?" she screeched, shaking her fist at Pelkey.

"Never worry, sweetheart," Pelkey said over his shoulder as he walked toward the door. "I may return for you later this evening."

"Ye show yer face in here again and I'll slice off yer—"

Pelkey slammed the door shut, cutting off the last of Mary's threat. "I suppose I'll never get my cravat back *now*."

Chapter Eight

The conversation continued to float around Lily, but as she'd long since given the evening up for lost, she paid no attention. She kept her head up and her eyes straight ahead. Had it not been for Miss Thurston's gasp, she'd have spent the rest of the evening staring at Lady Sutton's enormous yellow turban.

It was a quiet gasp, subdued, but audible enough to catch Lily's attention. Her gaze flew toward the entrance just in time to see Robyn stride through the door of Almack's.

Blast the man. He even made a black eye look enticing.

As soon as he entered, there was a decided lull in the conversation, then a buzz of excited voices as the entire company began to speak at once. They sounded like a swarm of greedy bees about to devour a particularly succulent flower.

Lily yanked at a tiny wrinkle in her glove, her lips tight. It was just like Robyn to appear *now*, when the company

had at last ceased whispering about her. They'd all but forgotten her, but now every head turned toward her again and
a wave of anticipation rippled through the ballroom.

Lord Archibald and Lord Pelkey followed on Robyn's
heels. Lily was happy to see Archie, but how in the name
of heaven had Lord Pelkey managed to cross Almack's sa-
cred threshold without a cravat? The *ton* had humiliated her
all evening simply because she'd mistaken Lord Barrow's
study for the ladies' retiring room, for pity's sake. Why
should she be punished and Lord Pelkey allowed to stroll
about and violate every rule of proper dress?

Lady Catherine laid a hand on Lily's arm. "Oh, thank
goodness. You'll soon have a partner, dear. Robyn's here."

Eleanor didn't look quite as ready to forgive Robyn as
her mother did. "Cut it a bit close, hasn't he? He's arrived
just in time to save his skin."

Lady Catherine clearly wished to put the entire incident
behind them. "Perhaps, Eleanor, but we won't discuss it here.
Besides, no real harm's been done."

"That's by no means certain," Eleanor muttered to Lily.
"*I* may still harm *him*."

A gentleman appeared at Eleanor's elbow just then to
claim his dance. "Robyn is looking for you, Lily," Ellie
muttered in her ear before her partner could sweep her away.
"I'm sure you'd much rather tear his hair out than dance
with him *now*, but you must if we wish to discredit Mrs.
Tittleton. Do feel free to stomp on his feet, though."

Eleanor disappeared in a whirl of midnight blue skirts
before Lily could say a word.

Dance with him? All that twirling about this evening
must have addled Ellie's brain.

Mrs. Tittleton could fly through Almack's window, flap
around like a monstrous black crow and squawk her lies to
the entire ballroom, and Lily would *still* refuse to dance
with Robyn Sutherland.

He did appear to be looking for her, or for someone, at any rate. He glanced over the couples as they whirled around the ballroom. She supposed it hadn't even occurred to him she wouldn't be invited to dance this evening.

He scanned the room again, a puzzled expression on his face, then she saw Archie gesture toward her and murmur something to him, and at last Robyn's eyes caught hers.

She intended to crush him with one righteous glare, but such a strange look passed over his face when he saw her that she became disoriented. He looked . . . as if he weren't sure whether to be amused or furious.

Before she could decipher his expression, however, Robyn ran a hand down his face and the look disappeared as if he'd wiped it away with his palm. The wide, slightly mocking grin she knew so well appeared in its place and he started across the ballroom, his eyes fixed on her, his destination unmistakable.

Oh, no. He could keep his smile to himself, for she didn't want any part of him or his heart-stopping grin. She stiffened her spine and turned her back on him, intending to resume her study of Lady Sutton's turban, and nearly bumped right into Miss Thurston.

For the past two hours she'd stood not ten paces away from Miss Thurston, but that young lady acted as if Lily had just sprouted from the floor at their feet. "Oh, good evening, Miss Somerset. You're acquainted with Miss Darlington, I believe?"

Lily stared at Miss Thurston and Miss Darlington for a moment, confused. The two of them had whispered and gossiped about her all night, but neither of them had deigned to speak or even nod to her, so why . . .

Of course. They'd caught a delicious whiff of scandal when Robyn entered the room, and now they wanted to be right on hand for the feast. Once they'd stuffed themselves on gossip, they'd no doubt serve the banquet again to every one of their ravenous acquaintances.

Lily glanced around the ballroom and felt a hysterical urge to laugh. The entire company looked like marionettes, with their heads all jerking in Robyn's direction as he sauntered across the room. It looked as if invisible strings were attached to their chins.

"Miss Somerset." Miss Darlington sank into a polite curtsy, but Lily could see an avaricious gleam in her beady brown eyes.

They were as horrible as Mrs. Tittleton. Worse, even, for at least Mrs. Tittleton didn't pretend to be anything other than a spiteful gossip.

Lily felt her cheeks grow hot with anger, but she took a deep breath and forced herself to return Miss Darlington's curtsy with a stiff, proper one of her own. "Good evening, Miss Thurston. Miss Darlington. You are acquainted with Lady Sutherland?"

Robyn joined them as Lady Catherine murmured her greetings. "Good evening, Mother." He kissed her cheek.

There was no sign of Lord Pelkey, but Archie came straight to Lily and bowed over her hand. "Good evening, Miss Somerset. How lovely you look."

Lily returned his smile with a genuine one of her own. She'd never been so relieved to see anyone in her life as she was to see Archie. "Lord Archibald. I'm pleased to see you this evening."

Robyn turned to Lily then, his dark eyes alight with amusement. "Good evening, Miss Somerset. Aren't you pleased to see me, as well?"

He found this humorous, did he? Lily didn't approve of violence of any sort, yet at that moment she had the most intense fantasy of kicking Robyn in the shin.

She didn't deign to reply, but only nodded at him and turned her attention back to Archie. If Robyn tried to kiss *her* cheek, she *would* do him an injury. She'd hit him over the head with her fan.

He wasn't so easily discouraged, however. He took her hand and leaned toward her in an attempt to catch her eyes. "I'd be honored if you'd join me in a dance, Miss Somerset."

He addressed her with all propriety, but Lily began to fume nonetheless. Why had he bothered to come to Almack's at all? And how *dare* he look at her like a cat looks at a bowl of cream? He seemed not to have the slightest doubt she'd dance with him, which made Lily more determined than ever *not* to.

She withdrew her hand. "No, thank you, Mr. Sutherland. I don't intend to dance this evening."

Lady Catherine gave her a puzzled glance. "Oh, but Lily, I thought you wanted—"

"Of course you'll dance," Robyn interrupted. "That's why you're here, isn't it? To dance with eligible gentlemen?"

Miss Thurston hissed softly at this uncouth reply.

Lily's jaws ground together. *Why, the gall of him!* Oh, how she'd *love* to put Robyn in his place. A few well-chosen words . . .

No. She mustn't let him goad her into any behavior unworthy of her. A proper young lady never caused a scene in public, especially when the company near her was scrutinizing her every move with the avidity of a pack of hunting dogs waiting for a dead bird to drop out of the sky.

If there was ever a time to hold her tongue, it was now.

But Robyn Sutherland could drive a saint to sin. She was no saint, and despite her best intentions . . .

"It's so very *late* in the evening, and I'm *so* fatigued," she heard herself say. "I'd much rather talk than dance. Miss Thurston, Miss Darlington, and I were just discussing how pleasant Almack's is. Weren't we?" She beamed at them.

The two young ladies exchanged glances, but Lily knew

they'd never walk away now—not when their mouths watered for scandal. They'd agree to whatever she said if only they could linger long enough to savor the choicest tidbits. "Er, yes," Miss Thurston agreed. "We were."

"Mr. Sutherland confided to me just the other morning how much he enjoys the balls here," Lily said. "I'm certain he'd be interested in sharing his thoughts about Almack's. Do share, Mr. Sutherland."

Lily turned wide, innocent blue eyes on Robyn. She didn't know quite what to expect of him, but she hadn't thought to find him gazing right back at her with the look of a man who's just awoken from a nap. He did *not* look properly chastened. Instead his eyes lit with humor, and a hint of a mischievous smile twitched at the corner of his lips.

"Oh, we'd be delighted to hear Mr. Sutherland's thoughts," Miss Thurston breathed. "Wouldn't we, Beatrice?"

"Oh, *yes*," Miss Darlington cooed. "On any topic whatsoever."

Archie, who appeared far less interested in listening to Robyn hold forth on any topic whatsoever, held out his hand to Lady Catherine. "Will you dance, my lady?"

Lady Catherine gave her assent and they left to join the set.

Robyn favored Miss Thurston and Miss Darlington with his most charming smile. "Ladies, how amiable you are. You flatter me."

Miss Thurston was rendered momentarily mute by the smile, and Miss Darlington looked ready to swoon. They appeared to have quite forgotten Lily, but she was quite satisfied with them, for they didn't have a fine feature between them, and each was so dim-witted, Robyn couldn't possibly enjoy their conversation.

It was the perfect punishment, yet he didn't look in the least as though he were suffering. "Of course, any discussion about Almack's must begin with an observation on the fineness of the company," he began, with the air of a gentleman delivering a dissertation.

Miss Darlington clasped her hands together worshipfully, as if Robyn had solved the riddle of the Sphinx. "Oh, yes. Only the very best society is welcome."

Miss Thurston gave Lily a sidelong glance. "That's true, for the most part."

Robyn took no direct notice of this comment, but Lily thought she saw his jaw clench. "When you say the *best* company, Miss Darlington, of course you mean only the most intelligent, the most accomplished, and the *kindest* members of society are welcome at Almack's."

Miss Darlington didn't reply right away, but looked blankly at Robyn. "Kindest?" she repeated after a moment, as if she weren't quite sure of the definition of the word.

"Oh, yes. That's how *I* describe the *ton*. Kind. This room fairly overflows with kindness, generosity of spirit, and goodwill. Don't you agree?"

Robyn raised an eyebrow at her.

Oh, dear. Lily bit her lip to hold in either a grimace or a laugh. She hardly knew which. Robyn was like a fox with two dull-witted hens. She should never have set him loose on these ladies, and yet she couldn't deny it amused her to watch Miss Darlington struggle with a concept so utterly foreign to her.

"I, ah—that is, of course I do," Miss Darlington squeaked at last.

Robyn nodded as if he were satisfied with this tepid reply. "And the fashions! If I didn't know otherwise, I'd think we were in France rather than England, for the ladies here this evening rival even the most elegant of Parisian society. In fact, I'd venture to say I've never seen such fashions *in my life*."

He darted a droll look at Lily, which she pretended not to see.

"Oh, yes, I couldn't agree more, Mr. Sutherland. The

English ladies are always at the forefront of the fashions," blurted Miss Thurston, as if determined to leap into the conversation at all costs.

Lily hid a grin. Best to leap now, for Miss Thurston was better qualified to discuss fashion than kindness.

Marginally better qualified.

"Just so," Robyn agreed. "And who exemplifies a more *remarkable* taste in fashion than you, Miss Thurston? Your gown . . ." Robyn gestured with his hands, as though words failed him. "It's a very, ah, unusual shade of green. Most flattering."

Miss Thurston shot Lily a triumphant glance and fluffed the skirts of her gown.

"And Miss Darlington! What an astonishing plume that is. I noticed it even before I crossed the threshold."

Miss Darlington nodded graciously in acknowledgment of this compliment and the plume waved wildly atop her head. Robyn shot Lily another look, eyes wide, as if he were terrified to find the enormous plume bearing down on him.

Lily stared back at him, torn between horror at his behavior and hysterical laughter. What had come over her, to stand by while he teased them so mercilessly? But amazingly, neither of the ladies seemed to have the least idea he was mocking them. Ashamed as she was of her behavior, however, Lily was wild to hear what he'd say next.

"Of course, it goes without saying the company at Almack's is distinguished by superior manners," Robyn went on. "I'm sure I don't have to tell you, ladies, that by *manners*, I don't only refer to the exquisite art of conversation, but also to elegant dancing—"

Here Robyn broke off, as if a thought had just occurred to him. "Do you dance this evening, Miss Thurston?"

"Yes!" she shouted. "That is," she continued in more moderate tones, "I do intend to dance this evening, Mr. Sutherland." She batted stubby eyelashes eagerly at him.

But instead of asking her to dance, Robyn paused, and the pause went on just a shade past the moment when he should have extended the invitation. When he did speak again, he addressed Miss Darlington. "And you, Miss Darlington? Do you intend to dance this evening?"

"I long for a dance," Miss Darlington said, but just when Lily thought she'd grab Robyn and drag him forcibly to the dance floor, Miss Thurston interrupted her.

"Didn't you say, Beatrice, you never intended to dance tonight? I'm sure you said your new slippers pinched dreadfully and you couldn't dance in them."

"I said no such thing, Alice," Miss Darlington exclaimed. "It was *you* who said you didn't care to dance tonight. Why, not ten minutes ago you said it hardly mattered no one had invited you to dance, for you didn't wish to anyway."

The two ladies glared at each other, but just as Lily began to fear a brawl would erupt, Robyn interceded. "Just as I said," he drawled. "Superior manners. Delightful."

Lily stared at him, appalled.

Oh, no. He'd gone too far now, just as he always did. The two young ladies flushed angrily, and just like that, Robyn's spell dissolved like a puff of smoke in the air.

Lily felt a guilty wash of color surge into her face, for she was just as much at fault as he was. "Mr. Sutherland," she said, determined to put a stop to the conversation, if belatedly. "Perhaps you could fetch us some lemonade—"

But trying to contain Robyn now was like trying to hold cupped water in her hands. Once the water flowed through her fingers, there was no putting it back again. "But really," Robyn said as if Lily hadn't spoken. "The best thing about Almack's is the convenience of it."

Miss Darlington scowled at him. Even her plume quivered with indignation. "Convenience? Whatever do you mean?"

"Well, I suppose as you are young ladies, you wouldn't understand, as the convenience is more of an advantage for the gentlemen. For us, Almack's is rather like a shop."

Miss Thurston gave a haughty sniff. "I confess I don't see your point, Mr. Sutherland. Almack's is *nothing* like a shop."

Robyn shook his head. "I beg your pardon, Miss Thurston, but indeed it is. London during the season is a marriage mart, and gentlemen who wish to secure a wife shop for her at Almack's. The Wednesday ball provides a perfect opportunity to inspect the season's wares."

Miss Darlington and Miss Thurston both gasped in outrage, and Lily began to feel quite desperate. She laid a hand on his arm. "I don't think—"

Robyn took no notice of her. "I've often wondered, in fact, why the patronesses don't provide the debutantes with placards listing their attractions. You know, this young lady has a fine complexion but only a moderate fortune, or that young lady is an heiress, but she's dim-witted and a malicious gossip."

Placards? Oh, dear God. Why wouldn't he stop? Lily considered hitting him with her fan after all. It might startle him into silence, and it couldn't get any worse at this point, could it?

She was wrong. It did get worse. Much worse.

"That way a gentleman would know beforehand what he's getting," Robyn went on. "It would certainly be helpful, and then perhaps more gentlemen would turn up at these balls. For we won't come just for the lemonade, you know." He winked at Miss Darlington.

The color receded from her face. "Scandalous!"

"What, the lemonade? I quite agree. The cake, too. Stale, you know. I suppose the patronesses don't offer spirits in an effort to civilize the gentlemen, but savages that we are, we only get drunk before we arrive."

Lily closed her eyes in despair. It was too late. Even the fan couldn't help her. Nothing short of unconsciousness would stop Robyn now.

"I can well believe that of *you*," Miss Thurston spat. She took a deep breath and drew herself up like a headmistress about to deliver an ear boxing. "I vow you must be in your cups right now to speak to gently bred ladies in such a disgusting manner."

Miss Darlington's face had gone purple. "I do hope you don't imagine drunkenness excuses your behavior this evening, Mr. Sutherland. Arriving late, refusing to dance, talking about placards and drinking! And Lord Pelkey isn't wearing a cravat!"

This last point had nothing to do with Robyn, but the missing cravat seemed to have deeply offended Miss Darlington.

Robyn lifted an eyebrow at this outburst. "Pelkey's cravat? He lost it at an inn in Covent Garden. The Pirate's Peg Leg, I believe it was. We were playing a game, you see."

Lily could well imagine what kind of game they'd been playing. "Don't, Robyn."

But it was no use. "It's a splendid game. One gentleman holds a barmaid on his lap. She hikes her skirts to her knees and extends her leg and the other gentlemen take turns trying to wrap the cravat around her leg."

Miss Thurston swayed, as if she were about to faint.

Robyn gave her an encouraging smile. "The gentleman may only use his teeth at this point in the game, of course, for it wouldn't be challenging otherwise, and what fun is there in that?"

He addressed this question to Miss Darlington and paused, as if he expected her to answer, but only a choked whimper escaped her lips.

Robyn smiled brightly at them. "We left the Pirate in rather a hurry tonight, and Pelkey left his cravat wrapped around Molly's leg. Or was her name Mary? I can't remember, but no matter. That explains the cravat. Does that make you feel any better?"

Miss Thurston and Miss Darlington stared at him, both of them white-faced and speechless. They were still gaping when Archie and Lady Catherine returned from the dance.

Archie took one look at the ladies' stunned expressions and turned to Robyn. His face darkened with suspicion at Robyn's angelic smile. "Sutherland! What—"

Then Lily did something she never imagined she'd do. "The orchestra has just struck up a reel. Lord Archibald, will you be kind enough to partner me in a dance?"

Chapter Nine

"*She told me she didn't intend to dance tonight,*" *Robyn* said to no one in particular.

Silence greeted this statement. He looked around in surprise to find he stood alone. His mother had drifted off in the direction of the card room with Lady Sutton. Miss Darlington and Miss Thurston, both stiff with outrage, had retreated to the opposite side of the ballroom, as far away from Robyn as they could get.

That was another thing he despised about Almack's. Once a man had terrified all the virgins away, there wasn't a thing left to do.

He watched as Lily moved through the figures of the dance on Archie's arm. She didn't look fatigued to him. On the contrary, she looked quite lively, and Archie looked bloody pleased with himself, like a man who'd just won a fortune at a gaming hell.

Smug bastard.

It hadn't occurred to Robyn that Lily might not forgive him. Everyone always forgave him, for everything.

"She told *me* she didn't intend to dance tonight," Robyn repeated to no one at all.

"It's not a question of intent. It's one of opportunity. Or at least it was until Archie arrived. Whatever would we do without Archie, Robyn?"

Robyn whirled around to find Eleanor standing behind him. "I was just thinking the same thing. What if Archie weren't here at all?"

He expected Eleanor to scold him, but to his surprise, she laughed. "Ah, well, then I suppose you'd have to dance with Lily, and as you don't seem keen to do so, you owe Archie a debt of gratitude."

"Who says I don't want to dance with Lily? For God's sake, I asked her to dance as soon as I arrived and she refused me. She said she didn't intend to dance tonight."

He felt foolish repeating himself a third time, but it seemed imperative someone understand *he* was the wronged party here. Lily had *lied* to him. Surely Ellie could see none of this was his fault?

His sister didn't look at all sympathetic, however. "Perhaps she meant she didn't think she'd be invited to dance. She had good reason to think so. This is her first dance this evening, you know."

Impossible. Not tonight. Not in that gown. Not on any night in any gown, but especially not tonight. Not unless every gentleman in the ballroom was blind.

"What's happened to her convent garb?"

Lily had shed yesterday's dark lacy monstrosity in favor of a pale blue silk gown that waved and undulated around her curves. Her creamy bosom rose in perfect swells over the low-cut neckline. Her maid had gathered her hair into sleek waves at the back of her head, leaving her white neck exposed.

Ellie looked puzzled. "Her *what*?"

"Her convent garb." Robyn clutched at his neck with both hands. "The high-necked gowns. Look rather like lace-encrusted nooses? You know the ones."

"Oh, that. Charlotte refused to help Lily with Lord Atherton unless Lily left off wearing them in public, and you know what Charlotte's like when she puts her foot down."

Robyn moistened his lips with a dart of his tongue, his eyes fixed on Lily as she glided through the dance. His throat had gone dry, but he doubted Almack's weak lemonade would quench this particular thirst.

She looked delicious, like a body of cool, refreshing water on a sweltering day. He wanted to sip at her, dive into her, and he'd wager he wasn't the only one. "I don't believe this is her first dance this evening."

Ellie raised an eyebrow. "Oh, I assure you it is. You know how the *ton* loves their gossip, especially malicious gossip. The young ladies are jealous of Lily and only too thrilled to have a reason to snub her. Mrs. Tittleton gives them the perfect excuse to do so."

"But the gentlemen—"

Ellie cut him off. "The gentlemen are far worse than the ladies. Not one of them has even glanced at Lily this evening, unless you count Lord Atherton. When he asked Charlotte to dance, he looked at Lily as if she were an insect he'd flicked off his coat sleeve."

Robyn rolled his eyes. Of *course* Atherton had snubbed Lily. Eleanor should have known that would happen. Millicent Chase's offenses against the *ton* were legendary, and now Lily had been caught in a scandal herself. Atherton wasn't the type of man who forgave social offenses.

Or any offenses, really. Robyn scanned the ballroom for the man in question. Ah, there—dancing with Miss McEwan, a Scottish lass with a face like a woolly sheep, who was rumored to have more money than she did freckles.

Come to think on it, Atherton did spend a good deal of time sniffing around the heiresses—

"Nearly every person in this room has spent their day poring over the scandal sheet and calling on their acquaintances to dissect it in detail," Ellie said. "What did you expect, Robyn?"

He hadn't expected the *ton* to nip and scratch Lily to ribbons, but if he could judge by that spiteful cat Miss Thurston and her friend, they'd done just that—surrounded her like a pack of hissing felines toying with a defenseless mouse. "I expected the *ton* to bow at Almack's altar, as they always do. Lily has the voucher. It should be good enough to appease the gossips."

He *was* a bit of an expert when it came to scandal and the *ton*, as this most recent incident with Lily was by no means his first, or even his worst, offense against propriety. His scandals never amounted to much in the end. The marriage-minded mamas forgave him every offense because he was single and wealthy. No title, of course, but the Sutherlands were good *ton*. The gentlemen forgave him as well because he was a crack shot and could hold his drink. As for the widows and the bored, aristocratic wives . . .

They were the most forgiving of all. Sometimes they forgave him twice.

A few charming smiles, a touch of contrition, perhaps a dance with a debutante or two, and his sins were washed clean.

"I can't imagine how you got her the voucher to begin with," Ellie remarked, "especially given the reception she's received tonight."

Robyn wasn't about to tell his sister the details of *that* transaction. "That bad?"

Ellie shrugged. "Oh, no. Not as terrible as you imagine, I'm sure. No worse than having a tooth pulled, for example."

Robyn winced. As much as he'd prefer to believe Ellie

exaggerated, when he'd walked through the door tonight and seen Lily's face, he'd felt that unfamiliar twinge of conscience again. She'd looked miserable enough, but also resigned, as if she'd never expected him to show up tonight. As if she'd expected him to disappoint her. Wise of her really, and yet . . .

Damn it, she hadn't any right to look so forlorn, like a lost child.

"I never thought we'd see you at all tonight," Ellie said, as if she could read his mind. "What made you decide to come?"

Robyn gave her a sullen look. The last thing he wanted to do was hand over credit to Archie, but he'd still be at the Pirate right now, most likely with his head under some barmaid's skirts, if Archie hadn't started to natter on about Lily's bones being picked clean by the *ton*.

"Archie might have said something to make me reconsider," he muttered.

Eleanor nodded. "Ah. Archie does have a highly developed sense of right and wrong." She paused. "You do as well, Robyn."

Robyn snorted. "You're a fond sister, Eleanor, if you can say that with a straight face."

Ellie didn't laugh. "I *am* a fond sister, but it's perfectly true all the same. You're here, aren't you? If you had no conscience, you wouldn't be, no matter what Archie said."

Eleanor gave him far too much credit. Yes, he was here, but his reasons were more selfish than noble. He was bored with his usual debaucheries, so he'd come to amuse himself. Besides, the sooner Lily was back in the *ton*'s good graces, the sooner he'd be free of her.

He didn't say so, however. He merely raised a skeptical eyebrow. "Bloody inconvenient thing, a conscience."

"Did it ever occur to you, Robyn, if I believed you as callous as you wish to appear, I *wouldn't* be such a fond sister?"

He didn't have an answer for that, so he remained silent.

"Still," Ellie continued, as if she'd put a lot of thought into the matter. "One does wonder why, if you're going to do the right thing in the end, you don't just do it to begin with."

Robyn ran a finger under his cravat. Had the room grown warm? "What does that mean?"

Ellie touched his arm so he'd look at her. "It's easier to believe the worst of yourself, but you don't have to, you know. No one else does. Not everyone is like Father."

Robyn stared at her, stunned. Is that what Eleanor thought? That he cared one whit for what their bastard of a father had thought of him? That it *mattered* to him his dear papa hadn't expected him to amount to anything more than a selfish rogue? He'd learned at a young age not to give a bloody damn what the old man thought.

He shrugged and retreated behind his grin. "I'm aware of that, Eleanor."

His sister shook her head. "I don't think you are. Though I suppose it's easier for you if no one ever expects anything of you."

Robyn's grin stretched so tight across his face, he thought his lips would split. "Including me? That's what you'll say next, isn't it? You're quite the philosopher this evening, Eleanor."

Good Lord, women were foolish. Ellie had more sense than most, but it seemed even she couldn't resist the lure of the tragically scarred hero. Bloody Byron—it was his fault. He'd brought a plague down on the head of every gentleman in London.

The set ended just then, and both Ellie and Robyn turned to watch Archie escort Lily off the dance floor. They were both breathless from the dance, and Lily was laughing at some witticism of Archie's.

Ellie dug her fingers into Robyn's arm. "The evening isn't over yet, you know."

No. The evening wasn't over. Not yet. And he wouldn't let Lily slip through his fingers a second time.

"I thank you for the dance, Miss Somerset," Archie said as he delivered Lily to Robyn's side. He turned to Ellie with a bow. "Will you dance, Eleanor?"

Ellie took the hand he offered with a gracious smile. "Indeed I will." She glanced back over her shoulder at Robyn as Archie led her to the dance floor. "Do make the most of the rest of your evening, brother."

Lily hadn't time to catch her breath before Robyn slipped a firm hand under her elbow. "Will you dance with me, Lily?"

She tried to tug out of his grip. "No, thank you. I'm fatigued."

He gave her his most charming smile. "No, you're not. You've only danced once this evening."

Lily made an irritated noise in her throat and glared accusingly at Ellie's back. "It's not the *dance* I find fatiguing."

Robyn gave a negligent shrug. "I'm sure you don't mean to say you find my conversation fatiguing. So tell me, Lily. Are you having an enjoyable evening?"

She pinched her lips together, and when she spoke, her voice was pure ice and broken glass. "Oh, yes. Perfectly enjoyable."

Robyn's eyes narrowed. He knew very well she'd had a wretched evening, and the sooner she told him so and took him to task for his neglect, the sooner they could put this business behind them. "Ellie seems to think otherwise. Has Almack's somehow fallen short of your expectations?"

Go on. Say it, he urged her silently. *Say it isn't Almack's that's proved such a disappointment tonight.*

"Ellie is mistaken." She kept her eyes fixed on the dancers.

Oh, she was furious with him, all right. For one moment, before she'd looked away, he'd seen a black ocean tempest beneath the calm, placid blue eyes. "If you're angry with me, why don't you just say so?"

She spared him a brief glance, then turned back to the dancers. "What's the point? It's over now."

Robyn clenched his fists. He couldn't bear this smooth, expressionless Lily. With every one of her bland replies, he became more determined to have the truth out of her. He wanted to talk to the *real* Lily—the one who'd slapped him so hard, his ears vibrated. "You're still furious with me, so it isn't bloody over, is it?"

"Robyn!" She frowned at him.

"What? You don't like it when I curse? Then tell me so. You don't like it when I'm rude to your friends? Then say so, Lily."

She stiffened beside him. "Miss Thurston and Miss Darlington aren't my friends."

She had every right to be furious with him, and she *would* be, even if it killed him. "No? But they must be. Why else would you be so eager to put an end to my game? It was good sport, baiting those two harpies. I could have kept it up all night."

Lily glared at him. "That's precisely why I tried to put an end to it! Because you *would* have kept it up all night. What was I supposed to do? Hit you over the head with my fan to make you stop?"

Robyn couldn't help grinning at the idea that Lily might forget herself so completely, she'd batter him about the head with her fan. "A blow would have put just the right touch on the business, don't you think? Miss Thurston would have been gratified."

Lily wasn't amused. "For pity's sake! I hate to say it, but I agree with Miss Thurston. You can't speak of pirates and drunkenness and"—she glanced around and lowered her voice—"and exposed legs in front of well-bred young ladies."

The color in her cheeks deepened when she said the

words *exposed legs*. He'd never found a blush charming before, but on her . . .

He cleared his throat. "I beg your pardon. Clearly I *can* speak of such things, because I just *did*."

Lily pursed her lips. "Very well. If you wish to quibble over words, you *shouldn't* speak of such things to a lady."

Robyn dismissed this with a wave of his hand. "I never quibble, and anyway, you're only angry because I put them in their place when you were too proper to do it yourself. Whether or not those two are well bred is another matter."

Two bright spots of color bloomed on her cheeks. Ah, now they were getting somewhere. Robyn felt a surge of anticipation. What would it be like to see Lily in a temper? To see that ocean tempest released and all of Almack's patrons swept away in its sucking undertow?

Glorious, no doubt.

"Whether they're well bred or not isn't the point."

"Oh? I'd wager neither of them spoke to *you* with respect tonight. Why do they deserve my consideration, then? I hope you're not going to say it's because they're welcome at Almack's. This room is fit to burst with people who don't deserve any respect."

"Even Miss Thurston and her odious friend deserve to be spoken to with respect," Lily insisted.

"Why? You don't have any affection for either of them, or any genuine concern for their feelings. At one point I would have sworn you were delighted to see them put in their places."

Lily looked away—guiltily, he thought. "Because it isn't proper."

"Damn propriety. You're not truly angry because I teased them, so what's all the fuss about?"

Lily huffed out an exasperated breath. "Because it isn't *done*, and you know it as well as I do. They'll gossip about you. They'll say you're a wicked rogue, and that will pale in comparison to what they'll say about me."

Or what they'd already said. His voice gentled. "Weren't they already gossiping about you before I teased them?"

Lily dropped her eyes, but not before he saw a flash of pain there. He felt an echo of it in his chest. Damn it, he didn't want to hurt her, but it had become of the utmost importance, somehow, that she tell him the truth.

He touched her wrist. "This isn't about them at all, is it? You're hurt because I neglected to escort you to Almack's for no better reason than I was wrapping a cravat around a barmaid's exposed thigh with my teeth. Just say it, Lily."

At last her smooth façade splintered apart and the tempest began to surge through the cracks. "Fine," she hissed. "It isn't about them. It's about *you*. It doesn't matter what you were doing, or how many cravats you held between your teeth. You left me to face the *ton* alone."

Robyn let out a slow breath. There it was. He'd had to goad her into saying it, but there it was. He opened his mouth to beg her pardon when she muttered something that made the words freeze in his throat.

"Well, you needn't worry about escorting me anywhere from now on. I've asked Archie to take your place, and he's agreed to help me. You're free to go back to your cravats and your barmaids."

She'd asked Archie to take his place? Robyn stared at her, speechless. Whatever he'd expected her to say or do, he hadn't expected this. He tried to scrape together a rational response, but a cold, bitter fury swelled in his throat and blocked his words.

He hadn't any right be angry, for he'd forced her to take matters into her own hands. He couldn't imagine why he hadn't seen it coming, in fact, as such a reasonable, rational solution was exactly what he'd expect from Lily. It made perfect sense for her to ask Archie to . . . replace him, for God knew he was sure to disappoint her again.

He *was* a selfish rogue, just as his father said he'd be. How gratified the old earl would have been to see it. Hart

Sutherland had *so* loved to be right, especially when he predicted the worst possible outcome.

But Robyn didn't care if he'd just been handed the very thing he'd asked for—on a silver salver, no less. He didn't care that he was now free of any obligations to anyone; free to search under the skirts of every barmaid in London, with Lily's blessing. Never mind that he was acting with stunning perversity, like a child who shoves a toy away and then screams because he no longer has it.

He didn't care. *He'd changed his bloody mind, hadn't he?*

For a long moment neither of them said a word. They stood there and stared at each other, her gaze defiant, as if she dared him to protest.

They were still staring at each other when the dance ended. There was a flurry around them as couples moved off the floor and others took their places.

The music began to swell around them.

A waltz. *A waltz at Almack's.* And here he was, standing on the edge of the dance floor. With Lily.

Why, fate practically *begged* him to do it.

He studied her face. It would cause a scandal. *Another* scandal. Mrs. Tittleton would get wind of it. She'd gleefully report it to all of London, and the *ton* would as gleefully devour it.

And there wouldn't be a damn thing Archie could do about it.

One sin against propriety was bad enough, but two? No—a second sin, and with the same gentleman? That was far stickier, like trying to pull one's foot out of quicksand. Archie would never be able to extricate Lily from it.

She'd need *him* to get her out of this one.

He took hold of her arm. Before he could reconsider the wisdom of his actions, he led her onto the dance floor, laid one hand on her waist, and rested the other on her shoulder.

And swept her into the dance.

Chapter Ten

Robyn's fingers felt warm against the cool silk of her gown.
His other hand cradled the curve of her shoulder and the
tip of his gloved thumb just grazed the bare skin of her
collarbone. It was difficult to think of anything but the heat
of his hand, as if that one touch somehow had the power to
melt away her anger.

Or draw it out of her like a leech drew blood from the
diseased. Well, she'd been bled enough for one night, thank
you.

Lily struggled to steady her breath. She didn't want to
lose any more of herself to Robyn, but whenever she got
near him, the dizzying kiss they'd shared in Lord Barrow's
study rushed back at her the way the floor rushed up to
smack one in the face during a faint.

She'd spent the past few days trying to forget what it felt
like when he'd kissed her. It should have been easy enough
to do. She'd hardly seen him since then. He avoided the town
house, and now that she'd released him from his obligation

to her, he'd be off with Lord Pelkey, his mouth full of starched linen.

Or off with Lady Downes, his mouth full of . . . well. She didn't want to think about what his mouth would be full of then.

Robyn guided her into a turn. "How does Delia get on?"

It was an innocent enough question, but she didn't want to talk to Robyn any more than she wanted to touch him. He'd charm her right out of her satin slippers, and she'd be right back where she started—on his lap in Lord Barrow's study. Or worse.

Lily threw back her shoulders and stiffened her spine. "Fine."

"*Fine.* She's fine, and you're having an enjoyable evening. Damnation—doesn't all this *fine* and *enjoyable* exhaust you? Wouldn't it be easier to admit sometimes things are in a bloody mess?"

Lily sniffed. "Easier for you, perhaps, as chaos is your natural state."

He only grinned at that. "Come now, Lily. If Delia's fine, then why does Alec look as though he's been dragged behind a horse every time I see him?"

She sighed. No sooner had she decided she didn't care to talk than Robyn decided nothing would do but conversation.

Perverse man.

"Delia's ill a good deal of the time. Lady Catherine says there's no cause for worry, that illness is common for ladies who are increasing, but Alec worries for her nonetheless."

Robyn snorted. "Alec would worry if Delia stubbed a toe or had a sliver in her thumb."

Lily glared at him. "Well, what of it? A decent husband is concerned for his wife's well-being. It's just as it should be."

Robyn's tone was light, but his dark eyes glittered strangely. "It's so much easier when things are just as they should be. If only everyone would stay in their proper place."

You can't arrange your life like those dolls, Lily. You can't line people up neatly on your bed . . .

She missed a step and stumbled against him. The muscles in his arm flexed against her waist, keeping her upright, and Lily's toes curled inside her slippers. "As to that, I hardly remember when things were just as they should be."

She hoped her snappish tone would discourage him from further conversation. And further flexing.

It didn't work. "I'm sure you worry for Delia, as well."

"I don't like to see her ill, if that's what you mean."

"No, I imagine you don't. You're a devoted sister. As devoted a sister as Alec is a husband. It warms my heart, all this devotion."

He took pains to keep his voice casual, but Lily detected a subtle edge, hard and unmistakable. She darted a quick look at him under cover of her lashes and noticed a muscle twitching in his jaw. "Whatever is the matter with you, Robyn? You haven't any cause to be angry with me—"

Robyn widened his eyes at her. "Angry? Who says I'm angry with you? I'm *fine*. I'm having *such* an enjoyable evening."

Lily sealed her lips closed, determined not to notice his teasing. Since all Robyn ever did was tease, this conversation was over.

She couldn't imagine why the dance wasn't. It seemed interminable.

"What of your other sisters?" he persisted. "Alec says they'll arrive in London soon."

Lily's feet began to ache. Or was it her head? "They will, as soon as they can put things in order in Surrey and close up the cottage. We expect them in a month or so."

His inched his fingers around her waist to press them against her back. "I'm afraid you're tense, Lily. I can feel it right here." He stroked her lower back, his touch light, like the tip of a feather drifting down her spine. "It feels like a steel rod is laced into your corset."

Lily caught her breath. If she hadn't been tense before, she was *now*.

Panic began to creep up on her. She didn't want her skin to leap up to meet his fingers every time Robyn touched her. She didn't trust him. He'd proved himself as wicked as his sisters said he was. More so, even, with his black eye and his barmaids and his knowing, teasing fingers.

She tried to squirm away from him. "I'm not tense. Why should I be? I look forward to my sisters' arrival in London."

"Just what London needs—three more young ladies with the Somerset blue eyes. I can hear gentlemen's hearts break even as we speak."

Lily frowned. "My goodness. I hope not."

"Why not? It's what every young lady dreams of, isn't it? To come to London, become the belle of her season, and break every heart in the city?"

Perhaps every *foolish* young lady dreamed of such things. "No. I hope my sisters don't wish for that. I'd much rather each of them settle quietly with a respectable gentleman than tear around London like furies, causing upheaval wherever they go."

"A respectable gentleman like Lord Atherton, you mean?" He gave her a sly grin. "That sounds dull."

Lily's heart fluttered strangely in her chest at that grin. It wouldn't do, that flutter. She preferred dullness over heart palpitations. "Yes. He's just the type of man I'd wish for my younger sisters."

"And for yourself, of course. But there is only one Lord Atherton, and *you're* going to marry him, so whatever will your sisters do?"

"There *is* more than one respectable gentleman in London, though one might not know it from the company *you* keep."

He leaned toward her so his voice was a low rumble in her ear. "There's no help for it, you know. Your sisters *will* break hearts. One glance from those famous Somerset blue eyes and the gentlemen of London will fall to their knees."

Lily just prevented a shiver from the soft drift of his breath against her ear. She jerked her head back. "What nonsense."

After all, *she* had the Somerset blue eyes, and *Robyn's* heart appeared to be intact. Not that it mattered in the least to her. She didn't want his heart, or his lips at her ear, or his hand on her waist. She didn't want him to kiss her ever again, either.

"Wait and see," he murmured.

Lily said nothing. She didn't wish to discuss blue eyes and broken hearts with Robyn, and especially not gentlemen falling to their knees. How did he manage to make everything sound so wicked?

"Hyacinth is quite young still," he said after a moment. "She may feel overwhelmed at first. London is nothing like Surrey."

Lily nodded, relieved. This seemed a much safer topic of conversation. "No, indeed. I expect all three of them will feel as though they're lost in a maze."

Robyn frowned. "Maze? What maze?"

"Oh, never mind. It doesn't matter."

He didn't say anything for a while, then, "Is that how *you* feel? As if you're lost in a maze?"

Lily glanced up at him, surprised by his serious tone. "Rather, yes."

He appeared to consider this. "Do you mean in the sense that London is a grand adventure and you anticipate with joy the surprise around every corner?"

"No." But there wasn't any point in explaining it to him, for he'd never understand. No doubt he adored mazes, had probably chased his lady friends through dozens of them.

"It's more like tearing blindly down path after path, only to become more desperate for a way out with each step."

For pity's sake! Where had that explanation come from? Now he'd laugh at her.

But he didn't laugh. "That sounds awful."

"It *is* awful. I don't care for mazes. My family visited one when I was a child, and I suppose I've never recovered from it."

He raised an eyebrow. "You had to *recover* from a visit to a maze? I'm almost afraid to ask, but what happened?"

"I got lost."

This time he did laugh. "Isn't that the point?"

I was very young. I was lost for a long time. I was alone.

Lily opened her mouth, but she closed it again before the excuses could escape. She stared up at Robyn. Yes, being lost *was* rather the point, wasn't it? Odd, but she'd never thought of it quite that way before. She felt the ghost of a smile lift the corners of her mouth. She supposed it *was* rather funny.

He grinned back at her. "I remember visiting a maze when I was six or so. I got lost, too, and had a grand time of it. I climbed under the hedgerows or clambered over them until I got to the center of the maze."

"But that's against the rules!" she exclaimed. "You're not supposed to cut through the hedges."

He didn't look the least repentant. "No, but I did find my way to the heart of the maze. How old were you when you got lost?"

"Five, or thereabouts. I never did find my way out on my own. My father found me curled up under a stone bench near the middle, sobbing. I suppose I must have believed I was lost forever."

Robyn's smile faded, and his fingers tightened suddenly at her waist.

By the time her father had gathered her into his arms, she'd been beside herself. The worst part of that day, though, wasn't that she'd been lost. The worst part was that Delia, and even Iris, who was younger than Lily, had been delighted with the winding pathways and the clever animal topiaries. They'd spent the rest of that day talking excitedly about what fun they'd had in the maze.

Only she had detested it. Only she had been terrified.

Lily shrugged. "I'm sure my sisters will do very well in London, provided they avoid the notice of Mrs. Tittleton."

She glanced up at him to see how he took this set-down, but it seemed to amuse rather than annoy him. His smile returned as he looked down at her, and she felt her breath stop in her lungs again.

Blast him. Why must he be so very handsome, and at the same time such a hopeless rogue? It was the smile—the contrary man had the devil's own smile. At first just the merest quirk at one corner of his lips, and then, as if it were sneaking up on his mouth, the smile crept, oh so slowly, to the other corner until at last it took possession of his entire face and his eyes lit up with it.

Robyn's smile wasn't really a smile at all. It was an event.

A young lady didn't have a chance against that smile, and never mind the velvety dark eyes framed with lashes so thick and sooty, they seemed to weigh down his eyelids. A young lady who didn't know better could be mesmerized by those sleepy eyes, and she'd have to be blind not to see the way his thick dark hair waved across his forehead and curled against the bronze skin at the back of his neck.

Her fingers fairly itched to touch his hair, to stroke his neck. Oh, why were the respectable gentlemen never as devastating as the rogues?

"There you go again," Robyn murmured. "One mention of Mrs. Tittleton and you've gone as stiff as Lord Atherton's upper lip."

Lord Atherton's upper lip? Lily resisted the mad giggle that rose to her lips. "What an awful thing to say."

Robyn chuckled. "Awful, yes, but true nonetheless."

He swept her into a turn, and for a moment she thought her feet had left the floor altogether. Robyn danced beautifully, just as he did everything else. Once he made up his mind to do it, that is, which happened seldom enough.

"Forget about Mrs. Tittleton," he whispered. His lips were right next to her ear again, but this time she didn't pull away. "Relax."

Lily's rib cage expanded with a deep unsteady breath as he pulled her closer against him and wrapped his arm tighter around her. He rested his forearm at the curve of her waist and opened his hand on her lower back.

"Surely you've waltzed before, Lily?" His breath stirred the wavy tendrils at her temple.

"I—that is, yes, of course."

She'd waltzed a few times, but never like this. She and Robyn moved together like the springs and wheels and pins inside a grandfather clock, each tiny piece fitted precisely, balanced against its fellows, the tension finely calibrated, all clicking and whirring in perfect harmony.

They didn't dance so much as they floated across the floor.

She forgot about Mrs. Tittleton. She forgot about the ache in her feet and the terrified child lost in a maze. She forgot why she'd been in such a frenzy over Robyn's behavior. She forgot about Miss Thurston and Miss Darlington and Lord Atherton.

She forgot it all, and let the music flow into the open spaces in her mind where all those worries had been, until she could hear only the swell of the strings and could feel only Robyn's hand, warm and firm against her back.

"There. That's it. You're safe." His lips grazed the top of her head.

But she wasn't safe. No woman was safe with a man whose touch burned through the silk of her gown as if he held hot coals in his palm. She was more lost now than she'd ever been in that puzzle maze.

The thought drifted through the dimmest recesses of her mind, but it was there and gone so swiftly she wondered if she'd imagined it, and imagined the gentle press of his lips against the wisps of hair at her forehead.

She and Robyn spun into another turn and indistinct faces blurred in and out of her line of vision. The light shifted as it moved over the silk skirts of the lady next to her, a rich magenta, a flash of blood red, like a jewel. Lily noticed the startling whiteness of Robyn's shirt, his strong jaw above his cravat, the shadow of a beard just emerging, and felt the movement of his muscular arm under her gloved fingertips. She looked down at his hand, so much larger than hers, and saw the pale blue silk of her skirts brush against his black breeches.

She heard a soft gasp and realized it came from her.

When the last notes of music finally died away, neither she nor Robyn moved for a moment. The seconds ticked past, one after the other as they stood motionless on the floor. Lily felt the most overwhelming urge to rest her head against his chest.

At last Robyn took her hand. "Come." He placed her hand on his arm to escort her back to Lady Catherine.

Lily didn't notice the stares, the heads turning to follow their progress, or the young ladies with their lips pressed against their companion's ears.

"Lily," Lady Catherine said as they approached. Her hand fluttered nervously at her throat. "It grows late."

Lily looked from Lady Catherine to Ellie, who stared at Robyn, her mouth a thin, grim line.

Whatever was the matter?

Charlotte took a step toward Lily and caught her hand. "Oh, Lily. Didn't you know—"

Lady Catherine laid a warning hand on Charlotte's shoulder and gave an almost imperceptible shake of her head. Charlotte fell silent.

"I'm quite fatigued," Lady Catherine said in a faint voice.

"Yes. I am, as well." Ellie took Lily's arm and drew her away from Robyn. "It's time we went home."

Chapter Eleven

*Robyn opened the front door and peered with one blood-*shot eye through the crack he'd made, then leapt back, his hand flying up to shield his face.

Jesus. What business did the sun have to shine so insistently? He'd never known it to do so before. Then again, as he rarely saw London in the daytime, he wasn't one to judge. He opened the door a little wider and peered out, blinking and cursing at the continued assault on his retinas.

He glanced around, but no one was about. The street in front of the Mayfair town house was deserted. It was early yet. The *ton* wouldn't be caught dead rising at this hour. They'd still be asleep, or lounging in their beds with their chocolate in one hand and the scandals sheets in the other.

The scandal sheets—the very reason he was awake, upright, and outdoors at such an ungodly hour. Robyn continued to shield his eyes with a hand as he felt his way down the town house stairs and turned onto one of the quiet streets of Mayfair. He doubted he'd have to hunt for long before Mrs. Tittleton turned up.

Twenty minutes later he strolled back up to the town house with the scandal sheet tucked under his arm. He peered around the corner. The street was still deserted. He unfolded the sheet, but kept it close to his chest in case anyone crept up behind him and tried to read over his shoulder. He didn't know why he was behaving like a thief smuggling stolen goods past a Bow Street runner. In another few hours all of London would read the story for themselves.

Still, even a condemned man deserved a brief reprieve before the noose tightened around his neck.

He looked down at the scandal sheet and there it was, staring back at him, complete with an illustration of a couple engaged in a risqué waltz. The gentleman leered down at the lady's exposed bosom and one of his gloved hands squeezed her arse. Horrified aristocrats surrounded the scandalous couple, hands over their mouths, and more than one young lady had fallen into a faint.

Robyn had to admit the swooning debutantes were a nice touch.

My dear devoted readers:

It pains Mrs. Tittleton to be obliged to report yet another lapse in propriety so soon after the scandalous events that took place just a few short days ago at Lord and Lady B-----'s musical evening; events that so shocked Mrs. Tittleton's gentle readers. But alas, it seems Mr. R-b—t S—-r—d and Miss L—y S—r—t's passionate enthusiasm for each other's company resulted in another display of affection so improper, several innocent debutantes were carried out of Almack's ballroom in a swoon.

Mrs. Tittleton regrets extremely that fashionable young gentlemen will forget themselves so thoroughly

as to carry on in such a disgraceful manner at Al-
mack's, London's very temple of good breeding. This
is to say nothing of certain young ladies who disre-
gard, with casual insolence, Almack's stricture against
waltzing without express permission from our esteemed
hostesses.

More than one witness to the indecency reported see-
ing Mr. R-b—t S—-r—d press his lips against Miss L—y
S—r—t's golden curls. Mrs. Tittleton feels it incumbent
upon her to ask, on behalf of her faithful readers, and
with a deeply regretful sigh: What next, Mr. R-b—t
S—-r—d and Miss S—r—t? What next?

Robyn reached up to loosen his cravat, but his fingers met only bare skin. Right. He hadn't yet donned his cravat. The noose had tightened. The executioner was hoisting the rope. He needed to see to Lily at once, or he'd swing for sure.

To be fair, he *had* slipped the noose about his own neck.

He'd gone a bit fuzzy around the edges after Lily informed him he was dismissed from his post as escort, but he was reasonably sure he'd never squeezed her arse. He'd remember *that*, if he remembered nothing else.

Even without the arse squeeze, it was bad enough.

But devil take it, a man didn't like to be tossed aside like pair of worn-out Hessians. Surely Lily could understand he had his pride to consider? That was all it was, of course—pride.

Perhaps she wouldn't see it that way, though.

He glanced down at Mrs. Tittleton and thought of Lily's face when she'd told him about being lost in a maze as a child.

Damnation. Perhaps he'd made just the *tiniest* miscalculation this time.

He'd make it right. He'd be the very model of a perfect escort from now on. If he could just get to Lily before she found out about this on her own, he could explain. She'd forgive him. Everyone always did.

He folded the paper back under his arm and dashed up the town house stairs.

"Rylands!" He slammed the door shut behind him. "What time is it?"

Rylands, as usual, stood guard in the foyer. "Not yet eight o'clock, sir," the butler replied in a faintly accusing tone. "In the *morning*," he added, as if this point needed instant clarification.

"Yes, thank you, Rylands. I did notice quite a large, bright object in the sky. I assume it's the sun. Has my mother come down yet? Or either of my sisters?"

Rylands's left eyebrow rose infinitesimally, just enough to indicate disapproval without being insolent. Another person wouldn't have even noticed it, but Robyn had been on the receiving end of Rylands's eloquent eyebrow before.

"No, sir."

"Miss Somerset?"

Another barely discernible eyebrow quirk. "No, sir."

What had he done to set off the eyebrow this morning? Surely Rylands hadn't read Mrs. Tittleton?

"Good."

Robyn took the stairs two at a time. When he reached the landing on the third floor, he didn't turn left toward his own bedchamber, but instead glanced down over the railing and into the foyer below. He couldn't see Rylands from this angle, which meant Rylands couldn't see him, either.

Robyn turned right, toward the guest wing of the house.

He didn't intend to enter Lily's bedchamber, of course, but there could be no impropriety in waiting outside her door for her to emerge for breakfast, and unless Mrs. bloody Tittleton also lurked in the hallway outside Lily's room, no one had to know.

He came to a stop outside her bedchamber. Eight o'clock.

They'd arrived home from Almack's rather late. It could be ages before she emerged, so—

Thump.

Robyn pressed his ear to the door and heard a faint splash, the unmistakable sound of water being poured from a pitcher into a porcelain bowl.

Lily was awake. He could hear her footsteps as she moved about the room.

She may be awake, but experience had taught him that women could linger in their bedchamber for ages, even when they were in there alone.

Perhaps he'd just knock. No harm in knocking. He wouldn't enter her bedchamber, but would speak to her from the hallway.

Yes, he'd better knock and get this over with. He didn't have all day to stand around and wait for Lily to dress and come down for breakfast.

Well, actually, he *did* have all day, but that wasn't the point, was it? It wouldn't take but a minute to tell her about Mrs. Tittleton's latest assault, and another to reassure her that he'd help her out of the debacle. Then he could be on his way.

But wasn't there a chance Lily would be in dishabille when she answered the door? Or only partially dressed? If she were only partially dressed, it stood to reason she'd be partially undressed.

Lily. *Undressed*. Without her nun's garb. Perhaps in a sheer white night rail . . .

He swallowed. Try as he might, he couldn't think of any scenario in which it would be proper for him to see Lily undressed. Even so, his hand rose without his consent and his knuckles met the smooth wood of the door.

Surely she had a robe? Why, he wouldn't be able to see a thing through her robe. He wasn't going to enter her bedchamber in any case; he wouldn't be near enough for it to be at all improper.

"Yes? Come in," Lily called.

Come in? Well, since she insisted, it would be rude of him to refuse. It would be quieter in her room, and much more private, which was just as well, since it was a somewhat delicate matter they had to discuss. Yes, privacy was desirable.

Robyn took one guilty look behind him, but Mrs. Tittleton didn't leap from the shadows. No one did. The hallway was deserted.

He opened the door, stepped over the threshold, and closed it behind him.

And nearly fell to his knees.

He didn't see Lily, but he felt her here, everywhere at once, haunting every corner of the room. In a flash he was back in Lord Barrow's study with his face buried in her hair, inhaling that delicious scent of warm sun on meadow grasses, that this-is-what-daisies-would-smell-like-if-they-had-a-scent, scent.

Robyn looked about, but Lily didn't appear. He wandered across the room to her dressing table as if in a dream. There was none of the usual feminine clutter here; every bottle and jar was arranged in precise rows and Lily's ribbons and hair fripperies were stacked in a tidy pile in one corner. He retrieved a silver hairbrush, brought it to his nose, closed his eyes, and inhaled. An image rose in his mind of the brush moving slowly through Lily's silky, honey-colored waves.

Yes.

He stumbled toward the bed, still clutching her brush. The scent was here, too. It rose from the bedclothes and drifted toward him, so palpable it felt as if someone had brushed a daisy against his lips. He stared down at the still unmade bed and pictured Lily tangled in the sheets, her long hair falling in fair waves across the pillow. He reached toward the bed, surprised to see his hand shook, and trailed his fingertips across the silky white sheets.

He seemed always to touch Lily like this, in half measures, with one finger only, or only with the tips of his fingers. Odd, because he liked to fill his hands with the warm, willing flesh of women he desired.

His hands, and his mouth.

But Lily's flesh wasn't warm and willing, and she wasn't a woman he desired. He liked women with spirit. Lily was too stiff. Too tidy. Too proper. He'd already decided that . . .

Dear God. Her sheets were still warm.

He heard a shocked gasp behind him and whirled around. Lily had emerged from her dressing closet and stood in the middle of the room, white-faced and openmouthed.

She was *not* wearing a robe.

His sluggish brain ground into action and warned him to turn away, but Robyn's eyes had other ideas. They devoured the sight of her in her flimsy night rail. The sheer fabric billowed around her legs, too loose to reveal a thing, but the top of the gown skimmed over her upper body, and he could discern, oh so faintly, the pale pink tips of her breasts through the white gown.

Robyn stared, mesmerized, as those blush-colored peaks began to pearl right before his eyes.

He ran a shaking hand over his mouth.

What in God's name had possessed him to enter her bedchamber? It was a catastrophic mistake. He hadn't slept in days, not since those few stolen kisses in Lord Barrow's study, and now—*now* he'd been cursed with a glimpse of the rosiest, most mouthwatering nipples he'd ever seen.

Lily held a pink gown of some sort in her hands and she hastily jerked it in front of herself. Astonishment kept her from speaking for a moment. Her mouth worked and a few outraged squeaks emerged, but no words. She looked ready to strangle him with one of her warm, scented sheets.

When she did find her voice at last, it trembled with rage. "What do you think you're doing in here, Robyn? Leave my bedchamber at once!"

That was when Robyn made his second catastrophic mistake. "You *did* ask me to come in, Lily."

Her eyes widened with disbelief. "I didn't—you—*what?* Leave, instantly!"

Robyn held his hands up in front of him and tiptoed toward the door, as if she were a wild animal about to spring on him and tear him to bits with her claws. "I only want to talk to you. I'll stand here, right by the door. I promise I won't move."

Lily stamped her foot—actually stamped it. Robyn felt a helpless grin twist his lips. He tried to shove it back into his mouth, for he shuddered to think what Lily would do if he dared to *laugh* at her right now.

But she saw it, and what could only be described as a howl of rage tore from her throat. She hurled the pink gown at his head with all of her strength. Robyn grabbed it out of the air instinctively before it could hit his face.

Then they both stood there, staring at each other. Lily looked as though she wished she'd thought things through before she threw her gown at him, and Robyn tried with every fiber in his body *not* to look at her heaving breasts.

"Put your robe on," he choked at last. "Once we've had a talk, I'll leave."

Lily turned on her heel without another word and disappeared into her dressing room. She returned a few moments later with her robe cinched like a noose around her waist. She did look a bit more comfortable with the extra layer of protection.

She shouldn't. Robe or no robe, the image of her in her white gown, hair streaming down her back, was seared into his brain. He'd never forget it, not even if she were wearing her nun's habit. Or a suit of armor.

She folded her arms across her chest and glared at him, her lips tight. "Well? What's so earth-shattering you felt the need to charge into my bedchamber this morning?"

Robyn opened his mouth to say that after today he'd

happily charge into her bedchamber on the merest pretense, but for once his brain was one step ahead of his mouth. He held out the scandal sheet. "This."

She didn't take it. Instead she eyed it as though it were a pistol, cocked and loaded. "I don't understand. There's nothing for her to tattle about. Is there?"

She raised troubled blue eyes to his and just like that she was a little girl again, a sobbing five-year-old child lost in a maze.

Robyn felt a strange, empty sensation near his chest. "Well, there may be one very minor thing."

"What? Has she written about how I was a wallflower at my first Almack's ball?"

God, if only it were just that. What would she do when she found out it was so much worse? "Not exactly. Perhaps you'd better read it yourself."

He held the paper out and this time she took it. She scanned the first few sentences. "'Lapse in propriety'? What lapse?"

Robyn said nothing, just watched as she continued down the lines of text.

"'Passionate enthusiasm for each other's company'? I don't understand this."

He could tell to the very second when she began to suspect what had happened. "'Waltzing without express permission from our esteemed hostesses.'"

She folded the paper into neat thirds and balanced it carefully on the side of her dressing table. "Young ladies need permission to waltz at Almack's?" Her voice was quiet, as if she were whispering an obscenity in church.

Robyn took a deep breath. "Yes. But you're new to London, and you didn't know. No one can blame you for it."

Silence. Then, "But *you* knew. Didn't you, Robyn?"

If only she'd just fly into a rage. He could easily soothe an outraged woman. But she didn't. She simply gazed at him, her blue eyes filled with a hurt she didn't bother to hide.

Admit nothing. If ever there was a time to obey that rule, it was now. It would be so much easier if he just told her he hadn't known. He opened his mouth and the lie hovered on the edge of his tongue, but much to his horror, the truth slipped out. "Yes. I knew."

A small sound escaped her—something between a laugh and a sob. "I confess it never occurred to me you'd go out of your way to publicly humiliate me."

Robyn's mouth fell open. Is that what she thought? It wasn't as if he'd hatched some nefarious scheme to humiliate her. It had just . . . happened. "I didn't intend to humiliate you. I got angry when you told me you'd asked Archie to replace me as your escort, and . . ."

He trailed off, not sure how to finish that sentence. He hadn't thought it through, damn it. He'd reacted with pure instinct, much as he always did. He didn't *want* to be replaced, and he'd seized an opportunity to make sure it didn't happen.

"You were angry," she repeated in disbelief. "You never wanted to act as my escort this season to begin with. I arranged it so you didn't have to. That made you *angry*?"

He opened his mouth to explain—to charm and cajole and wheedle until her fury dissolved. "I wanted . . ."

What *had* he wanted? He hadn't any idea. He closed his mouth. He couldn't explain it to her because he didn't understand it himself.

Lily didn't even notice his hesitation. "You were so angry you've ruined any chance I might have had to redeem myself with the *ton*. So angry"—and now her voice had begun to shake—"you've seen to it I will never be accepted in society."

"Ruined your chances? No. That's not—"

But she appeared not to hear him. "You did it all with a single dance, as well. It's brilliant, actually. Machiavellian, even."

Robyn reached her in one stride. Lily's lips parted in a gasp as he grasped her shoulders.

His eyes dropped to her mouth and his body flooded with heat. "Stop it, Lily. I never wanted to ruin you, and you won't *be* ruined. It's nothing as hopeless as all that. I'll make it right."

She gave a brittle little laugh and tried to twist away from him. "I don't see how."

He held her fast, his fingers tight on her shoulders. "We'll go along with Ellie's plan. It will still work. It's only a waltz, for God's sake. I'll be the very model of the faithful escort, and the *ton* will forget all about this. We'll brazen it out, just as we discussed."

Lily stared at him for a moment, her eyes going darker with each breath. "No."

Her silk robe dragged against his palms as his hands slid down her shoulders. He closed his fingers around her upper arms and pulled her closer to him. "What do you mean, *no*? This is the only way. You haven't any other choice."

She jerked her chin up. "I do have a choice. I've asked Archie to escort me and he's agreed. I don't see any reason to change plans now."

Robyn stared at her smooth white throat and his breaths came harsher, quicker. "Don't you? Then you're a fool. Archie can't help you out of it—not when both scandals involve you and me. If you're seen with Archie all over London now, it will only make matters worse."

A flush rose from her throat into her cheeks. "Perhaps it will. But I'd rather have Archie, even so."

She'd rather have Archie.

Robyn felt the familiar fury begin to gather in his throat. It continued to swell until it threatened to choke him. He pulled air into his lungs and forced himself to calm. "You'd rather have Archie, would you? I hope you'd rather be ruined than marry Atherton, as well. I told you—Archie can't do a thing for you anymore."

She moistened her lips with her tongue and swallowed. "I don't care."

A deep, hot ache twisted inside him, low in his belly. He snatched her wrists and dragged her hands to his chest and held them there, forced her to feel his heart slam against her palms. His voice dropped to a hoarse whisper. "You need *me*."

Her eyes widened with shock, but she didn't pull away. She stilled, her hands flat against his chest.

Robyn held his breath. *Was there a chance, then?*

Her eyes never left his as she shook her head. "No. You're wrong. I'm not ever going to need you, Robyn."

He stared at her. The twisting ache turned hard and cold, a ball of ice in his stomach.

Last night, when they'd waltzed, he'd felt it the instant she gave in to him. For a few brief moments she'd ceased to worry and strategize and plan. She dropped it all into a haphazard pile at her feet and she'd gone soft, boneless. She'd melted against him, and for those brief moments she'd felt perfect in his arms.

He had only to look at her now to see she'd begun to gather the pieces together again. As soon as he left the room, she'd sit on the floor, pull them into her lap, and try to reassemble them, only this time she'd leave out a piece.

Him.

He forced himself to release her before he could give in to the urge to drag her against his body and hold her until she admitted she *did* need him, that Archie could never do for her what he could. He stepped back, away from her, feeling as though he'd been hit with one of Pelkey's enormous fists.

He opened the door. "We'll see."

Once he gained the hallway, he turned back to look at her, but she'd closed the door behind him.

Chapter Twelve

To think, she'd been worried the ton would label her a wallflower.

Casual insolence . . . indecent . . . what else had Mrs. Tittleton said? There had been something about an improper display of affection, hadn't there?

And that dreadful picture! The gentleman, with his hand on the lady's . . . and then the bodice of the lady's gown, with her . . . Lily's reflection in the mirror went scarlet.

It certainly put the term wallflower in perspective.

"Would you like the gold combs, Miss Lily?" Betsy asked.

Lily sat at her looking glass, her chin cradled in her hand. She felt as though she'd been sitting here for hours. Betsy stood behind her, surrounded by her artillery of beauty, wielding her combs and pins and pomades like an expert swordsman in her quest to beautify Lily for the Chatsworths' ball this evening.

Lily had done her best to pretend there was no ball

tonight, but here she was, in a sleek bronze-colored evening gown with Betsy piling her hair atop her head. As if any of the fuss would do the least good at all.

Her eyes jerked to the glass when she felt Betsy slide the first comb into her hair.

"Just here, miss," Betsy said as she coaxed one delicate comb into the smooth waves next to Lily's ear, just above the elegant mass of curls at the back of her head. Betsy had outdone herself tonight, and the maid's face shone with satisfaction.

Lily didn't have the heart to tell her all of her efforts were wasted. "It's a masterpiece, Betsy," she said without enthusiasm. "But I don't want the combs. Not tonight."

Betsy's face clouded with disappointment. A sharp little arrow of guilt pierced through Lily, but she kept her mouth closed. The filigree combs were designed to glitter like tiny jewels and draw attention to the wearer's hair, and they did their job admirably.

Lily didn't want them. The last thing she wanted was to draw more attention to herself. She'd give anything to be the wallflower she'd dreaded being last night, in fact. The irony was not lost on her, and neither was the absurdity of quibbling with Betsy over the combs. Whether she wore them or not, the *ton* would find her.

Had there been any way around it, she wouldn't even attend the ball, but Lady Catherine had insisted.

Not just Lady Catherine, but Ellie and Charlotte, as well. Even Delia had been called into the fray. She'd arrived in Mayfair right after breakfast with a copy of the scandal sheet in her reticule, and all five ladies had retired to Lady Catherine's private parlor with the gravity of soldiers about to embark on a military campaign.

Eleanor sank into the chair next to Lily's. "I can't think how we neglected to tell you the rules about waltzing at Almack's. I beg your pardon, Lily."

Charlotte turned to her sister impatiently. "*You* beg her

pardon? I'm sure it's *Robyn* who should beg Lily's pardon, for he knew very well she didn't have permission to waltz. Why would he do such a dreadful thing?"

Ellie shook her head. "I can't account for it, either. Robyn is careless, to be sure, but he's never been unkind before. It's not like him to be hurtful."

Lily looked down at her hands. *Hurtful.*

She'd been dizzy with the pleasure of being held in Robyn's arms last night. He'd told her she was safe. She'd believed him, and all the time he'd swept her across the dance floor he'd known she'd pay dearly for that dance. He'd exposed her to the ridicule of the *ton.* Again.

Hurtful seemed a pale word to describe what he'd done. *Betrayal* was more fitting.

"I've had concerns about Robyn's behavior for some months now, but this . . ." Lady Catherine looked so distressed, Charlotte took her arm and led her to a chair.

Delia followed and took the seat next to Eleanor. "Has he said anything to you, Lily?"

Lily tried to think. She'd been so shocked to find him in her bedchamber, and then so upset over Mrs. Tittleton, she hardly knew what he'd said. "Yes. I spoke to him this morning."

She didn't mention he'd invaded her bedchamber and she'd been wearing nothing but her night rail at the time.

Delia leaned forward in her chair. "Did he offer any explanation for his behavior?"

"Yes," Lily said, remembering now. "He said he was angry."

"*He* was angry!" Charlotte threw her hands into the air. "What in the world does he have to be angry about?"

Lily frowned as she tried to piece together what he'd said. "Now that I think on it, it was rather strange. He was angry because I'd replaced him with Lord Archibald."

Delia's eyes narrowed. "Replaced him? In what sense?"

"As my escort. When Robyn didn't turn up to escort me

to Almack's, I asked Archie to act as my escort for the remainder of the season, and he agreed. I told Robyn as much, right before he led me into the waltz. It was a clever plan, Ellie." She turned to her friend. "But Robyn never agreed to it, and it couldn't work without him."

Eleanor gave Delia a quick glance, then turned back to Lily. "No, I don't suppose it would, and so you released him from his obligation to you. Did he say anything else this morning?"

Lily hesitated. "He told me Lord Archibald couldn't help me, not after the incident at Almack's. He said if I were seen all over town with Archie now, it would only make things worse. Then he said . . ."

Lily felt her cheeks grow warm.

Now it was Lady Catherine's turn to lean forward in her chair. "Yes? He said what?"

"He said only he could restore my reputation, and he promised to be a faithful escort. He said I . . . *need* him now."

Charlotte made a disgusted noise. "I shudder to think how Robyn defines the phrase *faithful escort*."

Delia, Ellie, and Lady Catherine said nothing, but Lily saw them exchange glances.

"Perhaps Robyn's right," Delia ventured after a moment. "Bringing Lord Archibald into it now will only complicate things. If Robyn escorts you, then—"

"No." Lily's voice was quiet. Final.

Delia cleared her throat. "Do you refuse because you think it will hurt your chances with Lord Atherton?"

Lily gave a bitter laugh. "Chances? No, I've quite given up hope in that quarter. All I wish for now is to get through the season without any further disasters."

"Oh, my dear," Charlotte murmured sympathetically, but Lily noticed her friend didn't look altogether sorry to find she no longer held out any hope for Lord Atherton.

"Why not accept Robyn's escort, then?" Ellie asked.

"He's still your best chance to escape this mess with your reputation unscathed."

"*No.*"

They didn't understand, and she couldn't explain to them this whole mess was no longer about Lord Barrow's study or the illicit waltz. It wasn't about the scandal, or Lord Atherton, or Robyn's behavior, either, though all of those things were bad enough.

The worst of it wasn't even that she couldn't trust Robyn.

It was that she couldn't trust *herself.* Robyn turned her into someone she wasn't, and—

No. That wasn't true. Deep down, under her smooth sashes and rigid propriety, lurked another young lady—one she kept well hidden, especially from herself.

Robyn goaded and teased and persuaded until that other young lady came roaring to the surface, and oh, she was a dreadful sort, the kind of young lady Lily despised, one who laughed too easily, lost her temper, slapped gentlemen's faces, and caused scenes at Almack's. The kind who opened her lips when a rogue kissed her, and then couldn't stop thinking about that kiss. That young lady wasn't thoughtful, or careful, or even *proper.* She abandoned every caution so she could twirl on the dance floor in Robyn's arms and tempt him into kissing her again.

That young lady terrified her.

Lily didn't want to be her. *Couldn't* be her, for when the dance was over and the kiss had ended, there was nothing left but chaos and disappointment.

Her eyes met Delia's. "I'll have Lord Archibald, or I won't have an escort at all."

Lady Catherine must have seen something in Lily's face, for she intervened. "Let's put the question of an escort aside for the moment. What shall we do about the Chatsworths' ball? It's tomorrow night, and we've already accepted the invitation."

Oh, dear God. Dread dropped like a stone into the pit of

Lily's stomach. Surely they didn't expect her to attend the ball *now*? It would be even worse than Almack's, and she didn't think she could face another ball as London's most notorious scandal. "You can make my excuses, can't you?"

Ellie took her hand. "Certainly we can, dear, but then what? You only postpone the inevitable, and it will get more difficult if you put it off."

Lily looked at Delia hopefully. "Perhaps it's a good time for me to visit Surrey? I can help our sisters close up the cottage, and—"

But Delia was already shaking her head. "I don't think that's a good idea. Iris will enter society as soon as she arrives in London, and Violet right after her, and naturally you'll want to accompany them to parties and balls. You don't want this still hanging over your head then, do you?"

Lily's heart sank. She didn't want this hanging over her sisters' heads; that much was certain.

"I can't think of a better place to get it over with than the Chatsworths' ball," Lady Catherine said. "Miranda Chatsworth is a dear friend of mine, and Charlotte and Eleanor have known her daughter Lizzie for ages. They'll all support Lily if we ask them to, without question."

Eleanor nodded. "They will. Archie will be invited, as well—he and Tristan Chatsworth were friends at university. You'll have his support, too, without it appearing as if he escorted you."

"We need only stay for a short time," Charlotte said.

The knot in Lily's stomach pulled tighter. "What of Robyn? Hasn't he been invited to the ball, as well?"

Ellie nodded. "Yes, but he hates balls and rarely attends them. Even if he does attend, he'll arrive late, and he'll come straight from White's or some other entertainment. He's not likely to come with us."

Lily had made a few more halfhearted protests, but in the end she had little choice in the matter, so she'd agreed to accompany the party to the Chatsworths' ball.

She hadn't even left her room yet, and already she regretted her promise.

"Are you sure you won't have the combs, miss?"

Lily's eyes met Betsy's in the mirror. "I'm sure, Betsy. Thank you."

She might be obliged to go to the ball, but she'd do her best to make sure no one noticed her. She was tempted to request that Betsy do her hair over again in a plainer style, but she was afraid the maid would burst into tears if she asked.

As it was, Betsy didn't look pleased. She laid the combs on the side of the dressing table with a disapproving grumble. "They're meant to go with that gown—"

Before Betsy could launch into her objections, however, she was interrupted by a brisk knock on the door.

Lily tensed. Ever since Robyn burst into her bedchamber that morning, she'd been on guard for another invasion. But surely even Robyn, audacious as he was, wouldn't dare interrupt her while she dressed for the evening?

Then again, why wouldn't he? He'd interrupted her that morning, *before* she'd dressed. Why would he draw the line at interrupting her *during*? She picked one of the combs up from the dressing table and studied it while she drew one slow breath after another and willed her heart to cease its frantic pounding.

She'd been barely out of her bed this morning when he'd dared to enter her room. She'd been shocked speechless to find him there, his dark hair disheveled, in just his shirt-sleeves, towering over the bed as if he were some marauding pirate, filling the space with his long legs and wide shoulders.

When she'd come upon him, hadn't he been *fingering* her sheets? Or had she imagined it?

When he'd whirled around to face her, he'd had such a look on his face. She didn't know quite how to describe the look, except that it was . . . fierce. His eyes had darkened as they'd raked over her in her night rail, and she'd felt a thrill of awareness in her belly, and there'd been no air after that, but a breathlessness such as she'd never known before—

Another knock, louder this time. "Lily? Open the door. It's me."

Charlotte.

Lily dropped the comb as a wave of strong emotion swept through her. *Relief, of course.* She was overjoyed to find it wasn't Robyn at her door again. She hadn't seen him at all since that morning, not since their argument, and he'd be off to White's tonight, or to see his mistress, or mistresses, or wherever it was he went when he'd managed to slip the noose of obligation.

Except there was no noose. Not anymore. She'd never accept his escort now, no matter what he said, for he'd say something entirely different the very next moment, and then where would she be? Standing alone in the middle of some ballroom, no doubt, while everyone whispered about her. She'd be there anyway, but at least this way she knew to expect it and could prepare herself.

"Lily? For pity's sake! You can't hide in there all night."

Lily sighed. "Come in."

No doubt Charlotte had come to see if she'd dressed for the evening, and wasn't hiding under her bedcovers. Or under her bed.

Charlotte sailed through the door, a vision in rose satin, her glossy hair swept on top of her head. Dainty little satin roses were woven in among the dark strands. "Oh, splendid. You're dressed."

Lily raised an eyebrow. "I don't want to attend the ball, but I can't very well crawl out the window, Charlotte. Though it did occur to me."

Charlotte tossed her head. "Oh, nonsense. It never occurred to *me.* You're made of sterner stuff than that. I did wonder if you'd plead the headache, though."

"Oh, I do have the headache, but as my head is still

attached to my body, I don't imagine it will be sufficient to excuse me from the Chatsworths' ball."

"Mother was rather insistent, was she not? But she's right, you know. You can't hide in the town house for the rest of the season."

Lily turned back to the looking glass and frowned at her reflection. "I don't see why not."

Charlotte plopped herself down on the stool next to Lily. "Shove over." She wriggled her bottom until Lily made room. "You know perfectly well why not. Because everyone will assume you're guilty if you never show your face again."

"They'll assume it anyway," Lily shot back. "I'm surprised the Chatsworths didn't send over a footman to snatch the invitation right out of Lady Catherine's hand."

Charlotte snorted. "Oh, nonsense. I've known Lizzy Chatsworth since we were in pinafores. She'd never dream of uninviting me, or you, for that matter, as you are my friend. The Chatsworths are good *ton*, but they also happen to be lovely people, as well."

Lily met Charlotte's eyes in the mirror. "I've never heard of such a thing."

She and Charlotte stared at each other in the glass for a moment, then the corner of Charlotte's mouth turned up in a slow grin.

She has Robyn's smile.

The thought caused a strange pang at Lily's heart, and yet Charlotte's smile was just as contagious as his, and Lily couldn't help but grin back at her friend.

"It's lucky it's the Chatsworths tonight, you know. Everyone attends their ball. It's always a mad crush. We can slip in and then slip right back out again. Everyone will be so frantic to be seen themselves, they won't bother with us."

Lily laid her brush down on the dressing table with a sigh. "Safety in numbers is better than nothing, I suppose, though I'd prefer anonymity."

"Oh, you'll be safe enough. Archie's just sent round a note to say he'll meet us there." Charlotte scooted off the edge of the stool. "Wait," she added, pausing behind Lily, who still sat in front of the glass. "You forgot your combs."

She slid one gold comb into Lily's coiffure, then turned Lily's head to the other side to place the second one.

Betsy beamed.

Charlotte stepped back to study the effect. "Yes. Perfect. I suppose you think to fade into the wallpaper with that dark-colored gown, Lily, but it won't work, you know. It's too flattering. Low-cut, as well." She gave Charlotte an impish grin and swept out the door in a cloud of rose satin.

Lily trailed after her. Perhaps there was still time to change her gown? The yellow silk might be less conspicuous . . .

Once they'd reached the top of the stairs, however, every thought fled her head.

Robyn stood in the foyer below with Ellie and Lady Catherine. He was attired in black evening dress, his hair brushed back from his face, his white cravat gleaming against his bronze skin.

Lily caught her breath. Gold combs and low-cut gowns would be the least of her worries tonight.

Chapter Thirteen

Before she could reason it away, a feverish awareness flooded through her.

Goodness, he was handsome.

But no sooner had that thought crossed her mind than Lily wanted to rip it from her head and hurl it down the stairs. He *was* handsome, and charming. She'd never known a more seductive man. Or a more dangerous one.

What was he doing here? She caught Ellie's eye as she made her way down the stairs, but Ellie gave a helpless shrug, as if she couldn't account for Robyn's presence this evening any more than Lily could.

Was this all some sort of game for him, or some joke at her expense? A few nights ago when she'd have been thrilled to have his escort, he hadn't bothered to turn up. Now she wanted him only to leave her in peace and here he was, devastating in his evening dress. The perfect gentleman.

The perfect escort.

Perhaps he found it amusing to see the *ton* toss her about

like a fish at the market? Well, she couldn't stop him. What could she do? Pound her fists against the floor and wail until he agreed not to accompany his family to the Chatsworths' ball?

Ellie came forward to take her hand as Lily reached the bottom stair. "Well, I feel quite eclipsed by you." She gestured toward Lily's gown. "It fairly shimmers."

Lily forced a smile at that, for the idea that Ellie could be eclipsed by *anyone* was laughable. She opened her mouth to say so when Robyn's low voice interrupted her. "You're stunning, Lily."

He looked at her with a hint of that same ferocity she'd seen that morning in her bedchamber. Lily's heart hammered against her ribs. She needed more time to steel herself against him, and she wasn't prepared for either the look or the compliment.

Charlotte saved her from a reply, however. "Well? What about me?" She eyed her brother with mock petulance. "Don't I look stunning, too?"

Robyn laughed. "As ever, Charlotte. I won't be able to leave your side tonight, or the swains will carry you away."

"Will they, indeed? Well, let's be off, then, for I wouldn't want to miss *that*."

Lady Catherine raised a reproving eyebrow. "My goodness, Charlotte." She took her youngest child firmly by the arm to lead her to the carriage.

Ellie and Lily followed, but before Lily could reach the door, Robyn stopped her with a hand on her arm. "I won't leave *your* side tonight, either," he murmured, his lips far too close to her ear. "No matter how much you may wish me to."

Lily's heart kicked in her chest again. "I wish you to even now."

But the words, so firm, so final when she'd said them in her head, became low and breathy on her lips, an invitation instead of a warning.

He leaned closer still, so close his lips nearly touched her neck. He drew in a long, deep breath, and Lily had the oddest sensation he was sniffing her. "Yet here I will remain, all night, until you admit you need me. You *will* admit it, Lily."

Lily closed her eyes and tried to steady her breathing. "No. Archie will meet us at the ball. I don't need you, Robyn."

He drew back slightly, but his fingers still held her arm. He repeated his words from that morning, but this time they sounded like a promise. *Or a threat.* "We'll see."

It wasn't far to the Chatsworths' town house, but Lily's nerves were frayed to ribbons before they'd gone two blocks. She sat bolt upright in the carriage, her skirts tucked tightly around her legs, but even so, Robyn's hard thigh pressed against her hip, so close his pantaloons were awash in folds of bronze silk and she could smell the light, spicy scent of his shaving soap. By the time they reached their destination, her skin felt too tight for her body, a flock of wild birds seemed to have nested in her belly, and she was ready to leap out the carriage window.

"It's a crush," Ellie said as they waited in the carriage queue.

Charlotte glanced out the window and smiled with satisfaction. "Yes. Just as I imagined it would be. You see, Lily?"

Lily stared out the window. Coaches were lined up three- and four-deep on both sides of the street, and the *ton* crowded the stairs and doorway of the Chatsworths' town house, a school of resplendent, silk-clad fish attempting to swim upstream against the current.

Her throat closed. "However will we find Archie in such a mad crush?"

Robyn shifted closer to her to see out the window. "What, you mean to say you didn't make an arrangement beforehand?"

Lily tried to move away from his thigh, but she was

pressed against the side of the carriage as it was. Robyn's mouth twitched at her movement, and he leaned so far over her, Lily feared he'd crawl right into her lap. "You'll have the devil of a time finding him, if he gets inside at all."

He shook his head with regret, but his tone put Lily in mind of a child who'd stolen a sweet from his nurse's apron pocket. If she hadn't been certain even *he* couldn't pull off such a grand prank, she'd believe Robyn had arranged the entire scenario, right down to the squirming mass on the town house steps, all of whom were in a perfect position to gawk at her as she alighted from the carriage.

Lily's jaw set. The evening was bound to be a disaster anyway, so what did it matter if Archie was lost in the crowd, or if the misery she'd endured at Almack's paled to nothing in comparison to this? It didn't matter that Robyn's dizzying scent clung to her skin, or that his warm thigh felt like part of her body now, as if she'd grown a new appendage. She'd never admit she needed him.

Admit it? She'd never *need* him. Period.

She must not have looked as confident as she felt, however, for Lady Catherine leaned forward and touched her hand. "It's all right, dear. I'll alight first with Charlotte, and you and Eleanor will follow directly behind us. We'll clear a path through the crowd for you, and Robyn will come after us."

The carriage jerked forward, then stopped abruptly. Miraculously, a place had opened just at the foot of the town house stairs, and their coachman had slid neatly into it. Lily sagged against her seat. Even the heavens had conspired against her.

The driver leapt from his perch, set the stairs, and opened the door to hand out Lady Catherine. Charlotte followed, then Ellie. Lily slid across the seat toward the door, but froze when she saw her friends were being jostled forward by the crowd. Eleanor turned around as if to go back to the carriage, but the ocean of bodies swept her up in their undertow.

Lily saw a look of despair cross Ellie's face as the crowd swallowed her.

Nausea roiled in Lily's stomach as she stared out the carriage window at the glittering, chattering crowd. *Oh, dear God.* She'd have to walk through alone, unless—

Robyn's voice was soft. "Take my arm, Lily."

She felt his dark gaze on her, but she kept her eyes fixed on the open door of the carriage. She couldn't look at him; couldn't bear to see the triumph on his face.

Robyn's hand, warm even through his glove, settled on her neck. "Oh, no," he murmured. "You *will* look at me."

He slid his hand up her neck to her cheek to turn her head gently toward his, until she had no choice but to look at him. Lily's eyes slowly rose to meet his.

What she saw there, in those dark depths, stunned her.

There was no triumph—none of the gloating satisfaction she'd expected to see. His eyes burned with that same fierce heat she'd glimpsed in the morning. His gaze drifted over her face, lingered on her mouth, the perusal so intense it felt as though he'd run his fingers across her skin.

He lifted her gloved hand from where it rested on the seat and placed it on his arm, and then the street was beneath her feet.

It seemed as if the crowd on the stairs all turned as one to watch their approach. The faces blurred together, a tunnel of flashing jewels; open, leering mouths; and pointed teeth. *So many teeth.*

A woman laughed, high-pitched and brittle, and a shiver darted down Lily's spine as the dark maze yawned open before her. With every breath, she disappeared deeper into its depths, yet no matter how many steps she took, she got no closer to the center. Soon the hedges would grow so high, she'd not be able to see over them, and then the pointed teeth would devour her.

"Relax, Lily," Robyn murmured.

He'd said the very same thing during their waltz, and

she'd heeded him, as if she had no choice—as if she were fated to follow every one of Robyn's whispered commands. She'd done as he'd bade her, and with each turn of the dance she'd felt her worries whirl away from her. She'd got precious little else from that dance, but she'd had that one moment of perfect freedom.

What would it be like, to feel that free every day?

She looked up at Robyn, so tall and confident beside her. Several gentlemen called out greetings to him. He nodded casually back at them. His arm was relaxed beneath her fingertips, reassuringly solid, his gait loose and fluid, as if he hadn't a care in the world. As if the two of them weren't at this very moment being swallowed whole by a dark maze from which they might never emerge.

It dawned on her then, in a moment of extreme clarity, that Robyn *hadn't* a care in the world. The *ton* could believe every word of Mrs. Tittleton's slander. They could think him the worst kind of lecherous rake, and Robyn would never care enough to bat even one of his sinfully long eyelashes over it.

The realization came on an unexpected burst of admiration.

Oh, how glorious it must be, to care nothing for society's censure.

But then, on its heels came another, grimmer thought.

How terrible it must be, to care for nothing at all.

She'd ruined the sleeve of his coat.

Robyn glanced down at the crumpled folds of black superfine clutched in Lily's white fingers. Her face remained composed, her head high, but her eyes darted in every direction and her grip tightened with each step.

She did need him. He hadn't any idea why it mattered so much, but it did.

He braced his arm under her fingers, and for the first time

since their argument that morning, the hollow feeling in his chest began to ease.

When they reached the entrance to the town house, however, she dropped his arm and began to turn away from him.

He grasped her wrist before she could take another step.

Did she think to just walk away from him now? He'd said he'd take care of her tonight, and this time he damn well meant to keep his promise.

She turned back to face him. "Let go of me, Robyn."

"No. I don't think I will. I promised I'd stay by your side all night. What kind of man would I be if I didn't keep my promise?"

A shrill laugh prevented her from answering. A group of young ladies stood just at the entrance to the ballroom, watching them with wide eyes and ears perked like a pack of hounds tensed for the signal to begin the chase.

Lily glanced over at their spectators and bit her lip, as if she wasn't sure what to do next. Robyn watched her white teeth worry at her plump lower lip, and his good intentions vanished in an explosion of lust.

He should have spent more time on that lip in Lord Barrow's study. He should have run his tongue over it, then taken it into his mouth and sucked on it. He could spend hours tasting her lower lip, and hours more exploring the sweet bow of her upper lip. That bow maddened him. Try as he might, he couldn't forget how the sweet little dip had felt against his tongue.

"Stop this, Robyn." Lily's low, fierce voice jerked him back to the present.

He raised his eyes from her lips. "Stop what?"

She had trouble catching her breath. "Whatever game you're playing with me, stop it. Don't . . . look at me like that."

This last came out in a husky whisper.

Desire shot through his veins, hot and insistent. He'd gone as hard as steel for her the minute she appeared at the top of the stairs in her bronze silk gown, and for the entire carriage ride he could think of nothing but her hip pressed against his thigh.

Don't look at her? By the time they'd arrived at the Chatsworths' town house, he'd been ready to drag her across his lap until the insides of *both* her thighs pressed against him and he drowned in a deep pool of bronze silk.

One of the young ladies by the door laughed again.

Lily's shoulders tensed. "Charlotte's looking for us."

Robyn glanced behind her into the ballroom. It was a crush, but he spotted his sister's rose-colored gown at once. Charlotte craned her neck to see over the heads surrounding her, trying to find Lily.

"They can wait," he said.

"I will not keep Archie waiting. Not after he's been kind enough to help me."

Archie. Again.

Robyn dug his fingernails into his palms. "In case you hadn't noticed, *I'm* kind enough to help you, as well. Why won't you let me, Lily? It is really so difficult?"

"Yes." One word. No hesitation.

He forgot about the tittering chits at the doorway and stepped toward Lily. "Why?"

"You frighten me, Robyn."

Frightened her? An odd sense of dread clawed at his throat. "No."

"Yes," she whispered, so low he had to lean toward her to hear it. "Because you break your promises, and then you flash that irresistible grin and it's impossible not to forgive you. And once you're forgiven, you break your promises again."

Robyn searched her eyes for some hint she didn't mean it, but it was like looking into opaque blue glass.

"Perhaps you do wish to help me," Lily said. "Tonight. But what about tomorrow? You will have found something else to amuse you by then, and where will that leave me?"

Where, indeed?

It was all true, of course, and it wasn't the first time he'd heard it, but for some reason this time the words did more than scratch the surface. This time they pierced through layers of muscle and bone.

There wasn't much he could say, really. "I see."

Lily hesitated for a second, as if she wished to say something more, but she thought better of it and remained silent.

That was it, then. There was no reason to linger. He jerked his chin in the direction of the ballroom. "Archie awaits."

He turned away before she could say anything else. He wasn't sure why he'd come here in the first place. Lily made it more than clear that morning she didn't want him, and he wished to be free of her in any case. Well, now he was free, and just as well, as there were far more titillating diversions to be had tonight than the Chatsworths' ball.

Robyn rubbed a hand across his chest. Ridiculous that the hollow feeling should return now, when Lily had handed him just what he wanted.

He'd go off and find Pelkey. Surely some barmaid in London needed a cravat wrapped around her thigh.

Afterward, he couldn't have said what made him turn toward her again. Perhaps he hoped she'd call him back, or maybe he wanted one last glimpse of her in her bronze gown as she walked away from him.

Maybe he heard her gasp.

But turn he did. Lily stood at the entrance to the ballroom, frozen. Her back was to him, but he knew at once something was horribly wrong. She lifted one hand to her face, and he saw it was shaking.

He'd taken a hasty step back toward her before he noticed the other woman, also frozen, standing at the entrance to the ballroom, her gaze locked on Lily's face.

The woman was elderly, her body a victim of the ravages of time, but despite her shrunken frame and deeply lined face, she had a certain grand style still. Her plentiful white hair was piled on top of her head and her blue eyes glittered with a determined intelligence. She was frail with age, but even so she carried her wasted frame with a regal haughtiness. A female companion held her by one arm, and in the other she carried a black, silver-tipped walking stick.

Robyn froze as well, staring at the woman over Lily's shoulder. There was something wrong. He couldn't quite put his finger on what it was, but it had to do with the unusual blue color of the woman's eyes. She looked familiar, a bit like . . .

Lily. She looked like Lily.

But the older woman couldn't be a Somerset. Lily's mother had died last year, and there was no one else, except—

Realization slammed into him. The woman wasn't a Somerset. She was a Chase. Lady Anne Chase, Lily's maternal grandmother, the woman who'd washed her hands of Lily's mother when Millicent dared to defy her family's expectations and marry Lily's father, Henry Somerset.

This was the woman who'd turned her back on her only child.

The woman stared at Lily, her aged face rigid and pale. She raised her walking stick slowly and pointed it at Lily. "You—"

But she got no further, for Lily turned and fled.

Chapter Fourteen

Robyn reached out for her, but she flew past him as if she didn't see him.

But he saw her. He saw her face, and the numb despair there made the blood freeze in his veins.

The crowd on the steps stood gaping stupidly after Lily as she fled down the stairs, then closed ranks behind her. Their voices rose in an excited buzz.

"What's happened? Was that the Somerset girl?"

"Oh ho, another scandal! Well, like mother, like daughter, they say."

"What an entertaining season we're having. I do hope the younger girls are as exciting as the elder—"

Robyn shoved heedlessly against the silk-clad bodies. He tried to catch a glimpse of Lily ahead of him, but her dark gown disappeared against the brighter colors worn by the rest of the crowd.

His foot landed hard on the bottom step. She couldn't have gotten far . . .

There.

It felt as though he'd been at the Chatsworths' ball for hours, but it must have only been minutes, because the Sutherland carriage was still where they'd left it, caught in the crush near the stairs.

"Wait, Lily!"

It was too late. The driver saw her flying toward him. He scrambled down from the box, eyes wide, and threw open the door. Lily leapt into the dark interior and the driver slammed the door shut behind her.

Robyn's shoes rang against the cobbles as he charged after her. He could still catch her, if only—

Impossibly, the carriage began to thread its way through the tangled mass surrounding it.

Damn it. Now what? He glared after the carriage as it forced its way into the congested street. A second carriage shoved in behind it, poised to take advantage of the opening.

Archie's carriage.

"Carlson!" Robyn bellowed to the driver as he barreled through the last of the bodies lingering on the sidewalk.

Carlson looked over his shoulder, saw Robyn, and pulled the horses to a stop. Before he could descend from the box, Robyn yanked open the door and threw himself into the carriage. "My town house, and hurry, man. It's urgent."

"Yes, sir. Right away, Mr. Sutherland."

Carlson had missed his chance to escape the crush of carriages when he'd stopped to wait for Robyn, and by the time they were free of the labyrinth of wheels and hooves, the Sutherland carriage was nowhere in sight.

Robyn resisted the urge to pound his fist on the roof to hurry Carlson along. If Lily had fled to her room by the time he arrived, he'd damn well chase her right into her bedchamber.

Again.

Robyn had the carriage door open even before Carlson rolled to a stop in front of the town house. "Return to the

ball and find Lord Archibald. Tell him Miss Somerset has
been taken ill and I've escorted her home."

"Yes, sir."

Robyn ran up the front steps, slammed through the door,
and skidded to a halt in the foyer. "Lily."

She sat slumped on a stair in a puddle of bronze silk, her
head against the railing. She looked as if she'd tried to climb
the stairs but had given up before she could reach the top.

She raised her head when he entered and looked at him
dully. "I—I think my grandmother knows I'm in London."

"Yes. I think she does."

He climbed a few steps and held out his hand to her. To
his relief, she took it—not because she'd forgiven him, he
was sure, but because she was too exhausted to fight with
anyone anymore. He tugged her gently to her feet and led
her down the last few stairs and into the long hallway that
led to Alec's study.

The servants still came in here to dust, but they hadn't
laid a fire in this room since Alec and Delia moved to Grosvenor Street weeks before. Alec had offered Robyn the room
for his own use, but short of debauching a woman on the
wide desktop, Robyn couldn't think of a single use for a
study.

"It's a bit chilly, but it will do." He lit the lamp on the
desk then crossed to the sideboard and studied the decanters
arranged across the top. "Ah, here we are. Alec's left his
brandy, and a fine one it is, too."

Lily stood in the middle of the room, rubbing her hands
up and down her arms.

Robyn poured three fingers of brandy into a glass, handed
it to her, and gestured toward a plump leather sofa. He retrieved a blanket from the back of a chair and draped it
across Lily's shoulders before he joined her. "There. That's
better. Still cold? Drink your brandy."

She took an obedient sip and stared down into her glass.
For a long time neither of them said anything.

Finally Lily stirred. "Well." She looked at him and tried to smile. "At least there's no reason to worry about Mrs. Tittleton anymore."

He didn't pretend to misunderstand her. Mrs. Tittleton could print a full retraction, but if Lady Chase cut Lily and her sisters, it would end any chance they had of being accepted by the *ton*. If one could judge by Lady Chase's reaction when she saw Lily, it seemed more a question of *when* she'd cut them, than *if*.

Robyn took a long swallow of his bandy. "Have you ever met her? Lady Chase, I mean?"

"No. My mother wrote to her for several years after she and my father married, but Lady Chase never answered any of her letters. We didn't talk about her much when we were growing up. I've never even seen her before tonight, but I knew right away who she was."

No doubt. Millicent Somerset must have inherited her looks from her mother.

"It might not be as bad as you imagine," he said. "She may cut you, but the Sutherlands will back you. It's not over yet."

Lily pulled the blanket tighter around her shoulders. "It is for me. Perhaps it's just as well. I'm not destined for London society, it seems."

Robyn's fingers tightened on his glass. He couldn't deny she'd had a rough go of it, or that he was the cause of most of her problems. Blast it, how had it gotten to this point? He'd begun innocently enough, his only thought to tease her a little, perhaps have a little amusement—

You'll find something else to amuse you, and where will that leave me?

He thought of the look on Lily's face as she'd turned and fled tonight. Somewhere along the way, it had ceased to be amusing.

"Don't tell me you're going to let Lady Chase frighten you off."

"I don't see what choice I have. She can't be dismissed as easily as Mrs. Tittleton. She's a wealthy, influential countess, and the only family we have. If our own grandmother cuts us, and she will, the *ton* will take note of it and follow her lead."

Just when he'd decided she did have spirit, after all . . . "I never took you for such a coward, Lily."

He sat and waited for her to argue with him, to tell him she was no coward, but she said nothing. She kept her eyes on her glass, turning it around and around between her palms. "You don't understand," she whispered at last. "I can't get into a battle with Lady Chase."

She'd just give up, then? Robyn drained his glass in one angry swallow. He reached forward, snatched her glass from her, and dropped it on the table. The brandy sloshed over the side and splashed his hand. "Why the devil not? Because it wouldn't be *polite*? Because it's not *proper* to row with one's grandmother?"

She shook her head. "Not because of that, but because . . . because—didn't you see her, Robyn? Did you see her face? Her eyes?"

"I saw her. What of it? You're making excuses."

She lifted her hands to hide her face and Robyn saw they were shaking again.

What in God's name was wrong?

"Jesus. What is it? Did she say something to you?"

When she didn't answer, he slid across the sofa, took hold of her wrists, and pulled her hands away so he could see her face. He sucked in a breath at the despair he saw there. She'd had that same look when she'd fled past him tonight—a look he'd hoped never to see again.

He dropped her wrists and cradled her face in his hands. "Tell me."

Lily took a deep, shuddering breath. "She looks so much like my mother. Oh, she's much older, and I know it sounds foolish, but when I saw her I thought, just for one brief second, I hoped . . . I haven't seen my mother in so very long, and her eyes are the same . . ."

Her voice trailed off then, but Robyn heard what she couldn't say.

To see her grandmother standing there, as if she'd been conjured out of thin air . . . it must have been a terrible shock for her, and even Robyn had noticed the resemblance between Lady Chase and Lily, who was said to be the image of Millicent Somerset.

For the briefest moment, when she'd seen Lady Chase, Lily had hoped for the impossible. She'd hoped she was looking at her mother.

He stared into Lily's anguished face and something shifted painfully in his chest. He knew she'd lost both her parents in a carriage accident, had known it as long as he'd known her, but he'd never understood the depth of that loss until he saw it written on her face tonight.

Now that Lily had got those first words out, the rest poured from her as though a dam had given way. "Don't you see? My mother wouldn't want me to . . . hurt Lady Chase. For all my grandmother's faults, my mother loved her still. She deeply regretted the estrangement between them. Lady Chase might despise me and my sisters, but I can't despise her in return. I can't hurt her. She may be a miserable old lady, but she's all I have left of my mother, and—"

"Hush, Lily. It's all right. I understand."

But he didn't. How could he? He loved his family, of course, but selfish as he was, he never put their desires before his own. He never put anyone's desires before his own.

Oh, perhaps he had as a child, but that had been a long time ago. He hadn't the first notion how it felt to sacrifice anything for the people he loved anymore, much less to care for the feelings of someone he didn't even know.

But Lily did. Lady Chase would wrong her, would publicly repudiate her family, and yet still Lily wished to spare her grandmother pain.

Lily—he'd always thought her beautiful, and since their kiss in Lord Barrow's study he'd wanted her desperately, but even his desire for her was selfish. He wanted her for the same reason he wanted any beautiful thing. For his own amusement, his own gratification.

He closed his eyes to shut out the sight of Lily's face, still cradled in his hands, but he saw her, behind his eyelids, not as she was now, but as she might have been at age five, a small blond-haired child, lost in a puzzle maze.

He didn't want to see inside Lily's heart; he didn't want to see all she hid behind her tight lips and rigid propriety. He didn't want to know that her beauty was the least remarkable thing about her. He wished he hadn't seen any of it even now, even as her face still rested in his hands.

He felt a drop of wetness touch his thumb and opened his eyes to see tears caught in her lashes. Pain, hot and sharp as a blade, slashed through him. "Don't cry, love. Don't . . ."

He brushed his thumbs under her eyes to catch her tears, and then, somehow, his mouth was there. Her tears wet his lips, warm salt on his tongue. He pressed his lips to her eyelids, one at a time, and felt them flutter closed under his mouth.

Her lips were a breath away from his. *Just a few harmless kisses . . . nothing more.*

But even as the words echoed through him, he knew they were a lie. There was no such thing as harmless anymore, and there was no such thing as simple, either. Not when it came to Lily.

She gazed at him with soft blue eyes for a moment. Her silk skirts rustled faintly as she slid toward him across the leather sofa, closing the distance between them.

If she touched him now . . . "Don't."

Her gown brushed against his legs. Robyn closed his eyes and dredged up every drop of his control. "You're upset, Lily. You don't know what you're doing."

Her hands settled on his chest. One fist closed around a fold of his waistcoat.

He looked down at her parted lips and a strangled sound tore from his throat, either a groan or a sigh. He caught her around her waist, his fingers slippery against the bronze silk, and urged her forward until her hips were cradled between his thighs.

He touched her then, with one long finger, just the lightest caress against her bottom lip.

So gentle, the press of his thumb against her lip, just the slightest pressure, just enough to open her mouth the merest fraction. He stared at her, his hand cradling her chin, and eased his thumb down until it slipped inside her mouth to touch the wet warmth there.

A tremor shook him. "God, Lily."

Long waves of her hair had come loose during her flight, and he brushed them aside so he could press his lips to her ear. "Put your arms around me," he demanded in a whisper.

She slid her fingers into the hair at the back of his neck, and his body shook with the urge to roll her beneath him.

"Yes," he murmured. "Just like that. Now kiss me."

She hesitated for what felt like an eternity. He held his breath and waited for her to choose, every cell in his body aching for her kiss.

That first brush of her closed lips against his, so light, like the initial strokes of a brush upon a blank canvas. He remained motionless and let her learn the shape of his mouth with her lips and tongue, her shy kiss the sweetest torture he'd ever known.

He held back until he could stand it no more, then his lips opened and his tongue darted out to taste the bow of her upper lip.

She froze for a moment, then melted into his chest. "Robyn," she murmured. "Please . . ."

With that breathless plea, his control snapped. He took

her mouth hard, crushing her lips beneath his until she opened them. He thrust inside on the first stroke, tasting her deeply, desperate to feel the heat of her tongue against his. "Kiss me back."

She did, her tongue hesitant at first, then bolder, a hot stroke inside his mouth.

"*Oh*."

Her soft, wondering sigh undid him.

Time slid sideways and spun away as his lips explored hers. The kiss lasted only seconds; or was it hours? Long enough for her mouth to open eagerly under his.

He had to stop.

Even as the warning echoed in his head, he pressed his fingers into the arch of her back.

Not yet. Not yet.

He was fully, achingly aroused for her, and some feral, wild part of him wanted her to feel it. He wanted her to *know*.

He held her against him, groaning aloud at the feel of her warm body between his thighs, her soft belly cradling his hard cock. "This is what you do to me, Lily."

He half hoped she'd be shocked, that she'd slap him or at least scramble away from him and take the decision out of his hands. Instead she gasped and arched her body into his.

You can never have her.

He knew it, but she lay against him, trembling and eager, and he couldn't make himself stop.

Warm silk slid under his palms as he traced his hands up her back and cupped her face to still her and take her lips again, slowly this time. He tasted her bottom lip, tested the softness there, and tugged it gently between his own to suck on it.

Yes.

He let his hand skim down the front of her neck and his lips followed, lingering at the soft skin just under her chin before he moved to her neck. She shivered as his tongue traced that long line, and he shifted lower so he could press his lips to the place where her pulse beat against her throat.

"*Robyn* . . ."

Desire rushed through him at the sound of his name, so breathless on her lips. She wanted him. He could hear her desire in her short, panting breaths, but he heard uncertainty there, too.

"Shhh, love," he whispered against her throat. "Just let me . . ."

He hooked his fingers under her flimsy lace sleeves and slid them down just a little—enough to reveal the tops of her breasts only. His pulse leapt at the sight of her skin, so smooth and white and bared for him. Only him, for he knew no other man had ever seen her like this.

"Lily," he breathed. "You're so beautiful, love."

He spread his hands across her back and lifted her to him, nuzzling the soft, soft skin of her neck before he dragged his open mouth across her breasts, nipping at the lovely swells that rose from the bodice of her gown.

She gave a breathless whimper and clutched at his hair to hold him against her.

Oh, dear God—her scent was strongest here, between her breasts, over her heart. His tongue darted out to taste her there, but he knew—he knew, even before her skin met his mouth, what she'd taste like.

It maddened him, that scent of sweet green grass and sun; that taste of wild strawberries.

Pure, distilled innocence.

It would be so easy to snatch that innocence for himself. He never denied himself whatever, or whoever, he wanted.

But not this time. Not tonight.

He allowed his mouth to linger against her skin for a heartbeat before he set her away and retreated to the other side of the sofa. He sat, unmoving, his head tipped back, his breaths quick, harsh. "I think I've gone mad."

Lily put a hand to her lips, dazed. "Robyn? What—"

"Go to bed," he said hoarsely.

She didn't move.

He looked at her, hoping the shadows in the room hid his eyes. "This isn't the time or place, and you don't really want this."

The time and place for *this* didn't exist. Not for him and Lily. He'd disappoint her, just as he did his mother, and Alec and his sisters. Just as he'd disappointed his father. He wouldn't set out to do it, but it would happen nonetheless, and she deserved better than that. Better than him.

Her voice brushed against him, so soft. "I don't think you know what I want."

Robyn closed his eyes.

Wasn't it better to get it over with now? Before he really cocked it up?

He couldn't look at her when he said it. "Very well, then. *I* don't want this."

He didn't open his eyes. For a moment there was no sound, then he heard a soft rustle of skirts as Lily rose from the sofa, and felt the edge of the blanket fall over his leg as she let it drop.

His eyes were still closed when the door shut quietly behind her.

Chapter Fifteen

"I've got it." Eleanor *entered the drawing room waving a* scandal sheet over her head.

Charlotte looked up from her embroidery with a frown. "Well, that was quick. What, did one of the *ton* leave it on our doorstep? It's one way to make sure we see it."

"No." Ellie hesitated. "Actually, I had it from Robyn."

Charlotte dropped her embroidery into her lap. "Robyn! How strange. I wouldn't have imagined him even awake at this hour, much less in possession of Mrs. Tittleton's latest slander."

Eleanor took her seat. "Awake? It's nearly one o'clock, Charlotte. Still, his behavior was rather odd. Did you go straight to bed when you arrived home last night, Lily?"

Lily had sunk low in her seat the second Robyn's name was mentioned, but at this, her head snapped up.

Bed? How would she know anything about Robyn's bed? What in the world could Ellie mean by such a question—

"Ouch!" She looked down to see a drop of blood on the

tip of her finger where she'd driven her needle into the pad of flesh there. The blood welled, then dripped onto the white ground of her needlework.

Splendid. Blue violets in a straw basket on a bloody white background. If it was the only blood she shed today, she'd count herself lucky.

Ellie looked at her expectantly.

Lily's face grew warm. "I did lie down almost immediately upon my return home, yes." There. That would do. It wasn't a lie, after all. There was no need to mention she'd lain down *on top* of Robyn.

No need to mention it or even to think about it, and certainly no need to spend all day dwelling on each and every moment of it to the exclusion of every other thought in her head. It had amounted to nothing. Less than nothing.

"What's the matter with Robyn, then?" Lady Catherine set her work aside and chose a biscuit off the tray on the table in front of her. "You said his behavior is odd?"

Ellie tapped the scandal sheet against her knee. "Quite odd, yes. He's in a foul mood, for one thing. Rather bearish. He even looks bearish. A fright, really."

Charlotte snorted. "So far I haven't heard anything out of the ordinary."

"He says he fell asleep in Alec's study. Indeed, he told me he spent the night there."

Both Lady Catherine and Charlotte exclaimed at this.

"Now, that *is* odd," Charlotte said. "He has an aversion to studies and places of work of any kind. I've never known him to go anywhere near one if he could avoid it."

Lily kept her eyes on her embroidery and did her best to look uninterested in the discussion, but her brain began to churn. Robyn had been very much awake when she'd left the study. Had he fallen off to sleep after she left, like an innocent babe in arms?

She supposed she shouldn't be surprised to find their encounter had meant so little to him. Very likely he'd drifted off into a blissful sleep the moment she left the room, while she'd thrashed in her sheets and pummeled her pillow until dawn lit the sky outside her bedchamber window. She'd fallen into a fitful sleep at last, but even then she'd dreamed of him, his tongue tasting her lips, his hands on her back, pressing her against him—

Yet Robyn had similar encounters nearly every night, didn't he, and with a wide selection of eager partners. Lady Downes, for example, or any barmaid with a bare leg. Why should *she* be any different?

Yet she was different, wasn't she? Lily doubted he'd ever sent any of those other ladies away without . . . well, *without*. How he must have laughed at her awkward kisses and clumsy caresses as soon as the door closed behind her last night.

"Even odder," Ellie continued, "he's still dressed in his evening clothes, but I know he's been up for hours, for he told me he rose early to search out the scandal sheet."

"What's he been doing all morning, then?" Charlotte asked.

"Sitting in Alec's study." Ellie glanced at Lily, a strange look on her face. "I know he escorted you home last night, Lily. I hope you two didn't quarrel. Was he still downstairs when you retired?"

Lily looked down at the bloody violets in her lap to avoid Eleanor's penetrating gaze. "He was. What of Mrs. Tittleton, Ellie?"

She'd rather discuss Mrs. Tittleton than Robyn? *Dear God.* That was a bad sign, indeed.

Ellie looked down at the sheet still clutched in her fingers as if she'd forgotten it was there. "Oh, yes. Well, that's another odd thing."

"Oh, no," Charlotte groaned. "I suppose there's a lurid and greatly exaggerated account of the confrontation between Lily and Lady Chase?"

The color must have drained from Lily's face then, for

Ellie shot to her feet and hurried across the room to her. "I beg your pardon, Lily. I should have made myself clear. It's odd in the best possible way."

She held the paper out to Lily.

Lily reached for it as if she were afraid it would burst into flames in her hand. She ran her eyes quickly over the sheet, turned it over and glanced at the back, then looked up at Ellie. "There's nothing here."

"What, nothing?" Charlotte tossed away her embroidery and held out her hand for the paper.

Lily could hardly believe it herself. She rose to hand the paper to Charlotte, then paced over to the window, then to the fireplace, unable to sit still. She was relieved, of course—vastly so. It was the best possible outcome. She couldn't think of anything that could please her more, in fact. Not one thing. Yet her spirits still remained low, for reasons she didn't care to examine.

Why would Robyn send her away last night and then spend the night in the study?

Lily shook her head to clear the traitorous thought. It hardly mattered. Whatever Robyn chose to do with his lovers hadn't a thing to do with her—he'd made that clear last night. She had far more important things to worry about than where Robyn chose to spend his nights, or with whom he chose to spend them.

Or what he did with them. And *to* them.

Charlotte ran a careful eye over the sheet. "Why, how curious. What can it mean?"

"Perhaps the awful woman has at last developed a conscience," Lady Catherine said.

Lily doubted it. "I'm not certain this is good news."

What fresh torture might Mrs. Tittleton have in mind? It seemed too much to hope that the odious woman would overlook such a delicious scandal. Whatever it was, it was sure to be dreadful, like a series of columns on Lily's exploits with Robyn, followed by a detailed account of how Lady Anne Chase had cut her own granddaughters.

Dreadful, indeed. *So why didn't Lily care more?*

She glanced at Ellie. "What do you think, Eleanor?"

Ellie spread her hands wide in a helpless gesture. "I hardly know what to think. It could be that—"

She got no further, for at that moment a commotion broke out in the entryway. Lily couldn't quite make it out, but it sounded as if a visitor had come to call and Rylands had denied them entrance.

"Now what?" Lady Catherine muttered irritably. "Charlotte, be a dear and see what the trouble is, won't you?"

"Of course." Charlotte rose to do her mother's bidding, but before she could take a step toward the door, the argument in the entryway grew louder. Lily heard a woman's voice raised in anger.

"Stand aside, young man, for enter I will, despite your objections!"

"I'm afraid not, ma'am," a low voice drawled. "Miss Somerset is not at home to visitors."

Good God. It wasn't Rylands who refused entrance. It was Robyn.

Lily's first confused thought was that Mrs. Tittleton had come to call. Why, the audacity of the woman!

A loud rap sounded then, as if someone had stamped a foot.

"Don't you try and put *me* off, *thump*, you rapscallion, *thump*. Do you know who I am? *Thump*. I *will* see her." *Thump*.

"Oh, I know who you are, Lady Chase," Robyn replied, a thread of warning now underlying his polite tone.

Oh, *dear God.* Lily swayed as the room tilted crazily.

It wasn't Mrs. Tittleton, and the rap they'd heard wasn't a stamped foot. It was a cane being thumped repeatedly against the marble floor. Lily grasped the mantelpiece for support and pressed her hand to her stomach to forestall the sudden queasiness.

Lady Anne Chase had come to call. She stood in the entryway at this very moment, sounding as though she was about to strike Robyn with her cane.

All four ladies in the drawing room realized it at once. There was a brief silence as they exchanged stricken glances, then Charlotte moved to the door. "Don't worry, Lily. Robyn won't let her in." She placed a hand flat against the wood panel, as if she were prepared to tackle Lady Chase to the floor should the old woman manage to get past Robyn.

"And *I* know who *you* are." *Thump.* "Young Sutherland, is it? All of London knows who *you* are, you young scoundrel."

"I'm sorry my behavior has disappointed you, ma'am," Robyn said, sounding anything but sorry. "Scoundrel or no, I'm afraid I won't allow you to harass Miss Somerset."

A pool of warmth gathered in Lily's stomach at Robyn's words, and for the first time that day, her spirits lifted.

Which only proved beyond a doubt what a fool she was.

"Harass! Why, how *dare* you? I demand to see my granddaughter this instant!"

"Granddaughter?" Lady Catherine said. "*Granddaughter.* Come away from the door, Charlotte."

Charlotte's eyes widened. "But—"

"Do as I say." Lady Catherine's tone was mild, but she advanced to the door with determined steps. She stopped in front of it and turned to Lily. "I think you'd better see what Lady Chase has to say, my dear. May I let her in?"

Oh, please don't! Lily opened her mouth to say the words aloud, but then closed it again, surprised to find a part of her clamored to hear what her grandmother had to say. Whatever it was, Lady Chase would surely find a way to say it, and it was much better done here in the privacy of the drawing room than at a ball with every member of the *ton* gawking at them.

Lily loosened her grip on the mantel and raised her chin. She'd hear Lady Chase out, and she'd do it in a way that would have made her mother proud.

She returned Lady Catherine's steady gaze and nodded. "Very well."

Lady Catherine held her eyes for a moment, and her fond look made Lily's throat choke with emotion. Then she nodded, stepped to the door, and opened it. "Robyn, please show Lady Chase into the drawing room."

There was a brief, surprised silence from the other side of the door, then a sound of rustling skirts as Lady Chase sailed into the room, Robyn in her wake. He was silent now, but his dark eyes found Lily's as soon as he crossed the threshold.

Lady Chase, however, seemed not to notice Lily, but fixed a beady blue eye on Lady Catherine. "Well, Lady Catherine Sutherland. I believe we've met before. It's a pleasure to see you again, of course."

Lady Catherine curtsied. "You are very welcome in my home, my lady."

"Am I, indeed? I don't imagine that's true, given the reception I've received." She raised her cane and jabbed it in Robyn's direction. "*This* is your son, I believe?"

"Yes, my lady. This is my younger son, Mr. Robert Sutherland, and my two daughters, Charlotte and Eleanor Sutherland."

Both Charlotte and Ellie rose and curtsied politely to Lady Chase, but their expressions remained cold.

Lady Chase hardly spared them a glance, but she eyed Robyn as if she'd scraped him off the bottom of her shoe. "Humph."

Lady Catherine made a gesture toward Lily, who stood motionless by the fireplace, her face pale and set. "This, Lady Chase, is the second eldest of your five granddaughters. Miss Lily Somerset."

Lily watched as if in a dream as Lady Chase turned

slowly toward her. The old lady was every bit as imposing as she'd been last night, with her cane and her snow white hair, but this time Lily scarcely noticed her grandmother's severe grandeur. This time Lily found herself staring into those eyes, sunken in folds of wrinkled, powdered white flesh, but still so piercing, so blue.

So like her mother's blue eyes, except these eyes held a profound sadness deep in their depths. Lily hadn't noticed it last night; she'd been too far away and too shocked to notice anything, but looking at her grandmother now, a memory drifted into her consciousness.

Some years ago she'd attended an art exhibit and been fascinated with a collection of ancient Chinese vases. She'd been unable to take her eyes off them, so beautiful were they, and yet each one held a crack or a tiny chip or some other flaw that marred the surface. Lily found them more beautiful because of those imperfections. It amazed her, the way the minuscule flaws misled one into believing the vases were fragile, when each of them had remained whole for thousands of years.

Lady Chase was very like those vases, with her aged majesty and her flawed blue eyes.

For the first time that day, the old woman seemed to hesitate, but after a moment she held a hand out to Lily. "Come here, girl, and let me have a look at you."

Lily's eyes found Robyn's then. It would worry her later, how she'd instinctively sought him out, as if she couldn't stir a step toward her grandmother without seeing him first, as if his dark eyes were the only means by which her feet could move across the floor. He returned her gaze with a look so warm and encouraging, it was as if he'd taken her hand.

Lily straightened her spine, held her head high, and crossed the room to Lady Chase, who still stood with her hand extended. Lily took it and felt the gnarled fingers close tightly around hers.

"So like her," Lady Chase murmured, as if to herself. "The eyes, yes, and the hair, and yet there's some of Henry Somerset there, too. I see it."

Lily, shocked to hear her father's name on Lady Chase's lips, had a sudden urge to snatch her hand away, but she resisted it. She'd always thought her grandmother despised her father, but Lady Chase's voice was soft when she spoke of him, not angry or bitter.

Lily looked into her grandmother's eyes and saw they'd gone cloudy, as if Lady Chase were lost in her memories. "My lady?"

The old lady seemed to come to herself again when Lily spoke. She cleared her throat. "Well, well, child. You're the very image of your mother, as I'm sure you've been told many times."

"Yes, my lady," Lily replied, then added hesitantly, "My sisters and I all resemble her greatly, Lady Chase."

"Indeed, indeed. Five of you, are there? The new Lady Carlisle the eldest? I saw her once, you know, several weeks ago, shopping on Bond Street. Knew her right away as Millicent's daughter, just as I knew you last night."

"Yes, ma'am," Lily murmured, not sure what else to say.

"Why did you run away, child?"

Lady Chase's voice had gentled, and to her horror, Lily felt hot tears gather in her throat. She swallowed. "I—the scandal, my lady. There's been some unpleasantness, and I was afraid—"

"Ah. You mean that Tittleton creature, I assume?" Lady Chase waved an imperious hand. "There will be no more of *that*, I can assure you. The woman has been dealt with. She will not bother you again."

Lily's mouth dropped open. Had Lady Chase found a way to silence Mrs. Tittleton's gossiping tongue? It seemed too good to be true, but then Lily recalled there had been nothing in the paper this morning about last night, and they'd all been so sure there would be.

"I'm very appreciative—" Lily was about to express her gratitude when the greater implications of Lady Chase's actions struck her and rendered her mute.

Her grandmother had *protected* her from Mrs. Tittleton. It was the very last thing in the world Lily would have expected. What could it mean?

Lady Chase waved off her thanks. "Never mind, never mind. Now, I've come to call today to extend an invitation for tomorrow night. A small affair at my town house. Just a few intimate friends and the . . . family."

She stumbled a little over the last word, then went on. "Your family will attend as well, Lady Catherine, and Lord and Lady Carlisle. You are *all* welcome, I suppose," she added, casting a dubious eye in Robyn's direction.

The room plunged into silence as every eye in the room fixed on Lady Chase.

Lady Catherine recovered first. "That is very kind, my lady, but might I inquire—"

"If you are otherwise engaged, you will change your plans," Lady Chase ordered. "I insist upon it." A quick rap with the cane punctuated this statement.

Robyn had remained by the door throughout the whole of this exchange, but now he stepped farther into the room. "My mother means to inquire into your intentions toward Miss Somerset, Lady Chase."

Lady Chase turned and looked him up and down. "She does, eh? Do you," she asked, facing Lily again, "have questions in regards to my intentions as well, child?"

Lily took a deep breath. "Yes, Lady Chase."

The blue eyes softened a little. "I'm not Lady Chase to you, child. I'm your grandmother, and you are my deceased daughter's child. My intention is we all begin to behave as such. I have made a start today, and this is how I intend to go on. We've been too long estranged. Do you not agree?"

"I do," Lily whispered. "My mother deeply regretted the estrangement. My sisters and I have always regretted it as well, both for her sake and our own. But why, after all these years—"

"Your grandfather died last year," Lady Chase said abruptly. "Were you aware? He passed on not three months after the terrible accident that took your parents. I've always thought he died of . . . well, no matter what I thought."

Her voice trailed off. Lily remained silent, waiting.

"He was a hard man, your grandfather. A good man, but a hard one. Unforgiving. He paid dearly for it, too. Oh my, yes, he did."

Lily heard the slight break in her grandmother's voice and thought of the beautiful vases, made more so because of their distinctive cracks and flaws. She placed her hand over her grandmother's dry, thin one.

Lady Chase patted her hand. "There. It's settled. I shall see you all tomorrow evening."

With one final severe glance in Robyn's direction, Lady Chase swept out the door.

Chapter Sixteen

There wasn't enough wine in the world to get him through this evening.

A small fete, Lady Chase had said. Just a few intimate friends and the family. Robyn looked around at the fifty or so guests assembled in the ballroom. Either Lady Chase had a great many intimate friends, or the old dragon had lied.

She had provided quite a surfeit of drink, however, and he was doing everything in his power to do justice to it.

"Thirsty, are you?" Alec gestured to Robyn's empty glass.

Robyn watched in disgust as his brother took a judicious sip from his own full glass. "Or something. Christ, Alec. Delia could do a better job with that wine than you are."

"I could, indeed," Delia agreed.

Alec snorted. "For about half an hour, and then you'd see that wine again, and under far less appetizing circumstances."

Delia's mouth dropped open. "Alec!"

Robyn rolled his eyes and grabbed a glass from a passing tray. He looked at it with distaste. Wine would have to do until he managed to escape this hell, or ferret out where the late Lord Chase kept his whiskey.

Delia arched an eyebrow at her husband. "I'll have you know I feel quite well. Better than I have in weeks."

Alec gave her an appraising look. "You look fatigued, Lady Carlisle. I'll have the carriage brought round."

Delia frowned. "Certainly not. It's not every day one gains a new family member, is it? I could hardly believe it when Lily told me."

"I can hardly believe it *now*," Robyn muttered.

Delia turned to watch as Lord Atherton maneuvered Lily into another sweeping turn in the dance. "Lily appears to be enjoying herself."

Atherton. It had to be bloody Atherton.

Robyn emptied his wineglass with one swallow. "Yes, doesn't she?"

Lord Atherton hadn't spared Lily a glance during the Mrs. Tittleton debacle. He hadn't spoken a word to her at Almack's, and yet there she was in his arms, smiling up at him as if he were the most compelling man she'd ever met.

She had a bloody short memory.

Mere hours ago she'd been in Robyn's arms, pressed against him, pleading with him to—

Delia broke into his reverie. "You don't sound at all pleased about it, Robyn. You're happy for her, aren't you?"

Was he happy for her? He should be. He knew better than anyone it meant the world to Lily to be reunited with her grandmother. Lady Chase had made Mrs. Tittleton and her ugly scandal disappear, and by the most wondrous stroke of luck, Lady Chase and Lady Atherton were the oldest and dearest of friends.

Yes, wasn't that fortunate?

Robyn glanced over at those two worthy ladies, huddled together like a couple of cantankerous old sheep. The two dowagers commanded a view of the entire room from where they stood, and even from this distance, Robyn could see both their gazes fixed on Atherton and Lily.

Yes, the stars had finally aligned in Lily's favor, and if one could judge by Atherton's ridiculously satisfied expression, her plans were falling neatly into place at last.

Of course he was bloody happy for her. Ecstatic, even. He'd never been happier about anything in his life, damn it. If his stomach churned with bile and queasiness clutched at his throat, it was the fault of the watery wine he'd drunk. It hadn't a thing to do with Lily and Atherton.

Though he would have thought she'd at least have some difficulty transferring her affections to Atherton after she'd kissed *him* with such abandon. It was almost *impolite*, how completely she seemed to have forgotten him.

Without thinking, he raised his empty glass to his lips again, but lowered it when he noticed Delia and Alec looking at him expectantly. Delia had asked him a question, hadn't she? What the devil was it? Oh, yes—wasn't he happy for Lily?

He pasted a grim smile on his face. "Delighted."

Delia raised an eyebrow. "My goodness. *That's* delighted? You look as if a horse stepped on your foot."

"It's just that I can't imagine why Lily looks so amused," Robyn said. "Atherton's never said an entertaining word in his life. He's as dull as a page of Latin declensions. Isn't he, Alec?"

Alec shrugged. "He's a steady sort. I don't know if that means he's dull. Steadiness could be just what Lily needs."

Robyn glared at his brother. *Traitor.*

Delia mulled this over. "Perhaps," she said after a brief hesitation.

Robyn studied her. She didn't sound convinced. Could it be Delia thought Atherton wasn't right for Lily? *How interesting.*

He hadn't time to question her, however, for the dance concluded and Atherton led Lily back to Delia's side.

"My goodness, it's warm, isn't it?" Lily asked. Her cheeks were stained a fetching shade of pink and she was breathless from her exertions in the dance.

For some reason Robyn didn't care to probe into, her breathlessness annoyed him. "Not at all. Perhaps you've over-exerted yourself with excessive dancing, Miss Somerset?"

Lily gave him a cool look. "One dance is hardly excessive, Mr. Sutherland."

Robyn's jaw went so tight, a breath of air could have shattered it. "That depends on the dance."

Atherton cleared his throat. "May I fetch you some refreshment?" he asked, bowing to Lily.

Yes, do, Atherton. Take yourself off.

Before Lily could answer, Delia intervened. "It's lovely to see such color in your cheeks, Lily, but I'm afraid you look a little too flushed. Gentlemen, if you would excuse us?"

"Thank you for the dance, Miss Somerset." Atherton bowed again. "I hope you will honor me again this evening?"

"Of course," Lily murmured with a smile as she and Delia went off in search of the ladies' retiring room.

Silence descended as soon as Alec, Robyn, and Lord Atherton were left alone.

"How are you, Atherton?" Alec asked at last. "I hope your mother is well?"

"Yes, indeed. Very well, thank you, Carlisle. Your own mother is well?"

"Yes, very well, I thank you."

Another silence as they all stared blankly at each other.

"Miss Somerset is a charming young lady," Lord Atherton offered at last.

Alec snatched at it. "Yes—"

Before he could get a second word out, however, Robyn interrupted him. "She was charming last week as well,

Atherton. She's been charming since she arrived in London, weeks ago. Did you not happen to meet her during that time?"

Atherton turned a cold, speculative eye upon Robyn. "No, indeed. I have not had the pleasure of her acquaintance before this evening."

Lying bastard.

"No? How odd that you didn't meet her at Almack's last Wednesday, for I'm sure I saw you there. You danced with our sister Charlotte, I believe?"

Atherton shrugged. "I believe I did, yes—dance with Miss Sutherland, I mean. I was not introduced to Miss Somerset on that occasion, however."

Another lie.

"Curious, isn't it, that you never met before?"

Robyn noticed a faint flush rise above Atherton's collar, but his voice remained cool. "I confess I don't see what's so curious about it, Sutherland. London is a large city. I'd venture to say I haven't made the acquaintance of every young lady out this season."

"Certainly not those young ladies who don't matter anyway," Robyn said, his own voice deceptively casual.

Atherton's flush deepened. "What does that mean, sir?"

Robyn shrugged. "I simply find it interesting you never met Miss Somerset until Lady Chase publicly acknowledged her."

Atherton bared his teeth in a cold smile. "It sounds as though you accuse me of something, Sutherland, but I'm at a loss to determine what."

"We all have our vices, don't we?" Robyn asked.

"*You* certainly do," Atherton shot back.

"Indeed I do, and I'm man enough to own up to them. What could yours be, Atherton, that you've gone to such lengths to hide them?"

Atherton took a threatening step toward Robyn. "Now see here—"

Alec laid a hand on Atherton's arm. "What does it matter when Lily and Lord Atherton met?"

Robyn turned to find Alec looking at him as though he'd lost his wits. "I'll tell you why it matters—"

"I'm sure she's happy to have made your acquaintance at last," Alec said to Atherton, throwing a quelling look in Robyn's direction.

Atherton bowed to Alec. "You're too kind, Carlisle."

Atherton turned to Robyn then, his look so icy it could freeze fire. "I assure you she can't be as gratified to make my acquaintance as I am to make hers. Now, if you'll excuse me, gentlemen, I believe my mother is looking for me."

Alec nodded. "Of course."

Atherton gave Robyn a smug smile. "Oh, and, Sutherland? Now that I've had the pleasure of meeting Miss Somerset, you can be quite sure I won't overlook her again."

He held Robyn's eyes for a beat longer than necessary before he turned and disappeared into the crowd.

Robyn stared after him for a moment, then turned to face his brother. "I never thought I'd agree with Atherton, but you *are* too kind, Alec."

"Is that so?" Alec said, in the same tone he'd used when he'd caught ten-year-old Robyn hiding rotten eggs in his tutor's bedchamber. "Just what do you have against Atherton?"

Robyn drained his third glass of wine. "The man's an iceberg, Alec. The water appears still and blue on the surface, but the next thing you know, your boat has been shattered to pieces and you've drowned."

Alec laughed. "Such a dramatic analogy. But I think you credit Atherton with far more complexity of character than he has. Besides, I've never heard a word said against him."

The floor shifted a little under Robyn's feet. "No. No one has. But then no one ever breathed a word against our father, either."

He hadn't meant to say it. He didn't even realize he thought it until the words were out of his mouth, but it was true. There was something off about Atherton—something disturbing lurking under that smooth surface.

Robyn half expected his brother to be angry, but Alec only considered him for a moment, then said, "If you think so, we'll keep a close eye on him."

Robyn let go of the breath he'd been holding. "Good."

"But take care you don't have some other, more complicated reason to chase away Lily's suitors, Robyn."

Robyn opened his mouth to deny he had any reason whatsoever, but then closed it again. There wasn't any point trying to hide things from Alec—never had been, either. "It's damned inconvenient sometimes, having you as a brother."

Alec smirked. "Yes, I imagine it is."

"I'm off to pursue more worldly pleasures—promised Archie I'd meet him later, and it will please Lady Chase if I go. Took an instant dislike to me, she did. I can't imagine why."

"I can," Alec called after him as Robyn marched across the ballroom to pay his respects to his hostess.

He'd bid Lady Chase a good evening, and then as far as he was concerned, she could go to the devil, and Atherton along with her.

He hated routs, or fetes, or whatever this evening's entertainment was called, almost as much as he hated musical evenings. Why, he could be up to his knees in whiskey by now, or bedding that actress—what was her name? The one in the trousers. Louise Bannister. He could be up to his neck, or some other more sensitive part of his anatomy, in Louise Bannister.

Lily had hardly looked his way once this evening. She didn't need his escort now, or anyone's, come to that. Archie would be devastated to hear it, enamored as he was with her. He was under Lily's spell. Fascinated by her. Poor old

Archie was so besotted, he'd actually *wanted* to escort her to every dull entertainment of the season.

Robyn made a disgusted sound in his throat. Thank God he hadn't got his own foot caught in *that* trap.

It was past time to leave her to her well-laid plans and her suitors and the lavish attention of her aristocratic grandmother, and go back to his own pursuits. Like securing a mistress, for a start. He hadn't been half out of his clothes with desire for Louise Bannister, but she'd do in a pinch.

And it bloody pinched, all right. He'd been in a heightened state of arousal for weeks. *Lily's fault, as well.*

The desire he felt for her wouldn't last much longer, surely. The novelty of the prim seductress was bound to wear off soon, and who better to help it on its way than a practiced siren like Louise Bannister?

He drew to a halt before Lady Chase, fixed a bland smile on his face, and swept into an exaggerated bow. "My lady, I thank you for a pleasant evening. I have a prior engagement, and must bid you good night."

There, that should satisfy the old bird.

The old bird apparently was not satisfied, however, for she stopped him before he could make his escape.

"It looked to me as though you stood in a corner all night, drinking to excess and glowering at my granddaughter. Pleasant, was it?"

Robyn's mouth fell open. She'd seen all that from across the room? The old lady had better eyesight than he would have thought. "Ah, well, I wouldn't say glowering, exactly."

"Do you have designs on my granddaughter, Mr. Sutherland?"

Robyn had to make an effort to keep his mouth from dropping open again. "Designs?"

"Yes, designs, young man. Don't pretend you don't know what I mean. I don't care for the way you look at my granddaughter, sir, and I won't have you sniffing under her skirts for your next conquest."

Good Lord. Robyn wasn't sure whether to laugh or blush. "Sniffing under her skirts? What a vulgar thing to say, Lady Chase."

"It's a vulgar thing to *do*, as well. Lily is no longer a friendless orphan, Mr. Sutherland, so don't imagine you can get away with your roguish antics with her."

Robyn stared at her. So he was being warned away from Lily now, was he?

All at once he found himself coldly furious. He could have engaged in his roguish antics with Lily days ago, but he'd resisted. And when had Lily *ever* been as pathetic as her grandmother made her sound? "Lily has never been friendless, my lady. You don't give her enough credit. Lovely as she is, she makes friends wherever she goes."

Lady Chase's eyebrows shot up at this. "Well, I—"

Robyn wasn't finished. "The Sutherlands have been her friends these last months—her family, too, when her *own* family refused to acknowledge her."

Lady Chase flushed a dull red at that reminder. "I suppose you think that gives you some claim on her, don't you, young man? I don't approve of you, Mr. Sutherland, and I won't hesitate to make my sentiments known to my granddaughter."

"Indeed?" Robyn's voice was soft. "I imagine you had a similar conversation with your daughter, right before she ran off with Henry Somerset. Take care, Lady Chase. You wouldn't want history to repeat itself."

Now it was Lady Chase's turn to go openmouthed, but Robyn didn't wait to hear what she'd say. He gave her another stiff bow, turned on his heel, and strode to the door.

He'd had quite enough of this fete, or rout, or whatever the bloody hell it was. He'd had enough of watered-down wine. He'd had enough of Lord Atherton's smooth lies and Lady Chase's warnings.

And he'd had enough of Lily, with her absurdly soft skin

and huge blue eyes. He'd had enough of her innocent kisses and her fresh meadow scent, if it was really even her scent at all. Now he thought about it, that scent probably did come out of a bottle. It was too innocent to be real.

He'd had enough of—

Lily. She came toward him from the dim hallway. Alone. What unfortunate timing. *For her.*

Robyn's eyes narrowed and every muscle in his body pulled tight with anger, frustration, and thwarted desire.

He stopped in front of her, so close he heard her faint gasp. "My, such uncharacteristic carelessness, Lily. Have you forgotten what happened the last time you went to the ladies' retiring room alone? What have you done with Delia?"

She seemed to sense his dangerous mood, for she tried to slip past him. "She's resting. I'm on my way to fetch Alec to take her home."

He blocked her way, then moved forward to back her closer to the wall. "Ah. Well, you'd best hurry. I believe you promised to dance with Atherton again. I'm sure he's as patient as a saint, but you don't want to keep him waiting."

A flush rose on her cheeks. "No. I don't. Let me pass, if you please."

Robyn dragged a finger down her pink cheek, testing the heat there. "By all means, don't let me keep you, madam."

The blue eyes opened wide. "*Madam?*"

Savage triumph swept through him as her flush deepened and spread down her neck. He trailed his finger in its wake until he rested the tip at the base of her throat. "Oh, yes. I think it's better if we keep it formal from now on. I know Lady Chase will prefer it."

Lily's pulse leapt wildly against his fingertip. "L-Lady Chase? I don't know what you mean."

Robyn dipped his head to whisper in her ear. "Why don't you ask her? I'm sure she'll be pleased to tell you all about my wicked designs on you."

So deliciously wicked . . . and so impossible.

He needed to get out of there—he needed to find Pelkey, or Archie, or any bloody thing to take his mind off Lily.

He jerked his finger away from her throat and backed up so she could pass.

Lily hesitated, then edged past him, her shoulder brushing against his chest. "I *will* ask her."

Close . . . close enough that he could wrap an arm around her waist, ease her back against the wall and hold her there with his body, sink his face into her neck, and—

Robyn forced his arms to his sides. "You do that. I wish you a good night."

"You're leaving already? But . . . it's so early."

He gave her a low, mocking bow. "Early in the evening perhaps, but long, long overdue otherwise."

Lily followed Robyn down the hallway, heart tight in her chest, and watched as he walked out the front door of the town house and disappeared into the night.

Someone touched her elbow. "Miss Somerset?"

She turned to find Lord Atherton standing next to her. He bowed. "I believe you promised me this dance?"

Lily watched her hand reach forward, as if it were not a part of her body, to grasp Lord Atherton's arm.

"Yes, my lord," she murmured as he led her away. "I believe I did."

Chapter Seventeen

The entrance hall looked like a bloody conservatory. Lilies, of course. Trust Atherton to sacrifice the romantic to the literal. The man lacked imagination.

Robyn stomped down the last few steps into the foyer and glanced around. Rylands had disappeared on some errand, and if he could judge by the scrape of silverware against porcelain, the rest of the family was in the breakfast parlor. He was alone. Just him and the enormous display of lilies sitting on a hall table.

Yesterday's lilies had disappeared. Most likely Lily had taken them to her room. She'd probably placed them next to her bed so they were the last thing she saw before she fell asleep and the first when she awoke each morning.

Touching, that. Nearly brought a tear to his eye. Or maybe lilies just made his eyes water.

He hoped they made Lily's eyes water, too. In fact, he hoped she awoke every morning with a heavy head and burning eyes. Why should he be the only one? Never mind if his ailments were the result of whiskey, and entirely self-induced.

Robyn glanced around once more then sauntered over to the flowers, taking care to tread quietly. Ah. Lily must not have seen this arrangement yet, for the card was still here. He plucked it from the blooms.

To Lily. Affectionately, Francis.

Robyn snorted. *Affectionately?* Hardly a declaration of passionate love, was it? Either Atherton was no poet, or he'd mistaken Lily for his sister. Or his mother. The thought filled Robyn with a petulant sort of satisfaction.

Still. Francis, and Lily? They already called each other by their given names. A few weeks' worth of flowers and a few rides around Rotten Row was all it took to win her affections, it seemed. He'd have expected more from Lily.

What other intimacies did she permit?

Robyn stuffed the card back into the flower arrangement. What did it matter if Atherton kissed her hand, or her cheek, or her lips? Damn it, he didn't want to know—didn't want to think about it.

Yet here he was, thinking about it anyway. Good God, it had only been two weeks.

Two weeks. Fourteen days. Fourteen days in which he'd spoken hardly a single word to her.

He hadn't seen much of her, as he'd made it a point to be absent from the town house as often as possible. He went out every evening with Pelkey and Archie and spent his nights at Archie's bachelor's chambers in St. James's Place.

He wasn't sure why he was here now, really, except Archie insisted he make an appearance in Mayfair before his mother hired runners to drag the Thames in search of him.

Archie also had the nerve to hint Robyn should have a bath. *The bastard.*

He hadn't slept at all, but he'd bathed, and being a duti-ful son, he'd report for breakfast this morning. Then he'd disappear for another seven days. At least.

The breakfast room rang with feminine voices. A lively debate was under way, but the minute Robyn crossed the threshold, it trailed off into silence.

His mother wasn't even here, damn it. She'd probably left for Delia and Alec's house already. Let her drag the Thames, then, for he'd no intention of dining here tomorrow morning, as well.

"Oh, don't let me interrupt you." He gave his sisters a sarcastic wave of his hand. "I'll just have my coffee quietly in the corner. Pretend I'm not here."

"Good morning, Robyn," Ellie said, a little too cheer-fully. "We're just discussing the theater. Here, sit next to me." She patted the chair next to her.

A quick glance revealed the seat next to Ellie was directly across the table from Lily. He could hardly refuse to sit next to his sister, but . . .

He let his cup and saucer hit the table with a thud. He'd sit where he bloody well pleased, Lily be damned.

He plopped down in the chair next to Ellie, crossed his booted feet with as much noise and fuss as possible, and fixed his gaze on Lily.

And immediately regretted it.

She looked nothing less than edible in a peach-colored morning gown. He'd never fully appreciated the way such a gown could cling to a woman's curves before. Her hair looked a little damp, as if she'd just bathed. A few stray curls still clung to her neck, and his mouth watered to tickle those damp curls with his tongue.

Where was her nun's habit this morning? He supposed *that* wouldn't do anymore, now that Atherton was court-ing her.

He stared down at his breakfast plate. He'd lost his ap-petite for his eggs because Lily looked like a luscious, sweet peach tart in that gown, and now nothing would do for him but peach tarts.

Who did she think she was, ruining his breakfast?

She'd ruined a perfectly good season of debauchery, as well. He could hardly believe he'd been satisfied with a quick grab and tickle in the dark with Alicia Downes only weeks ago. Now he couldn't even enjoy *that* without wishing he could grab and tickle Lily instead.

"What about the theater?" he asked Ellie. His eyes never left Lily's face.

Ellie cleared her throat. "Lord Atherton suggested we see *Twelfth Night* this evening. We haven't used our box since we arrived in London, and I do love Shakespeare."

Lily's eyes darted toward him, albeit unwillingly. She turned as red as a peony when she found him staring at her, and became quite preoccupied with arranging her eggs neatly on one side of her plate with her fork.

For God's sake, not the blush again. He watched in helpless fascination as it drifted down her long throat to her—

"Did you see it?"

Robyn turned to Ellie. "I didn't see a blasted thing—oh, you mean *Twelfth Night*? I did see it. Part of it anyway."

"Well, what did you think?" Charlotte asked. "Did you enjoy it?"

"I enjoyed seeing Louise Bannister in breeches," he drawled.

He hadn't enjoyed it as much as he ought, which was bloody annoying enough.

Lily's fault.

"She plays Viola, you know," he added helpfully.

He watched Lily over the rim of his cup as he slurped rudely at his coffee. "She pretends to be Cesario in order to catch Orsino's eye, and I can assure you she's quite eye-catching in her breeches—"

"We're all familiar with the play," Lily snapped. She

flushed again when Ellie and Charlotte turned to her in surprise.

Robyn raised his eyebrows at her. *My, she sounds cross all of a sudden.* "Are you? I beg your pardon. I must have misunderstood Charlotte's question."

"Yes, well, I think we get the idea. Shall we all go, then?" Ellie asked.

Charlotte shrugged. "Oh, why not? I suppose one must go to the theater at some point during the season, mustn't one?"

Robyn gave Lily his best maddening grin and rose from his chair. "How right you are, Charlotte. I couldn't agree more. Perhaps Archie and I will accompany you. It will be a pleasure to see Miss Bannister—I mean, the play again. I didn't appreciate it from every angle the first time."

Charlotte blinked in surprise to find him in such vehement agreement with her. "We'd better use the Sutherland box, then. It's a large one. Do you think Lord Atherton will mind, Lily?"

Robyn's grin widened at Lily's scowl. "Atherton's not the sort who minds about much of anything at all. Is he, Lily?"

Her jaw tightened. "It will be fine, Charlotte."

Robyn tossed his napkin onto the table. Against all expectations, it had been quite a productive morning. "It's settled, then. I shall see you all tonight."

He whistled as he left the room.

Breeches, indeed.

Lily jerked at the handfuls of skirts that lay crumpled underneath her and arranged them to fall gracefully around her chair.

Blast. Either the skirts were too voluminous, or the chair was too small.

Perhaps breeches weren't such a ridiculous idea after all.

Though not on Louise Bannister, and not in *public*. Certainly not to encourage wicked behavior from rakes like Robyn Sutherland.

Two weeks. He hadn't spoken to her in two weeks, and when he finally did speak, the best he could do was wax poetic about Louise Bannister's breeches? Not that she cared that he hadn't spoken to her, of course. She'd been far too busy to even notice.

"You look lovely tonight." Lord Atherton said.

Rather perfunctorily, in Lily's opinion.

Francis. She must remember to call him Francis. He'd asked her to, and she'd agreed, but for some reason he remained Lord Atherton in her mind.

He waved his hand around in the air to indicate her gown. "What color did you say it was again? Blue?"

"Cobalt," Lily said, more pettishly than she'd intended. Honestly, though—anyone could see it was cobalt.

Two weeks. Lord Atherton had taken her for drives along Rotten Row in his phaeton, and showered her with flowers and compliments. The courtship was everything she wanted—proper, correct, polite, and from the very man she wanted it from.

It had been the dullest two weeks of her life.

Robyn's fault.

Oh, Lord Atherton was attentive enough, but their exchange about the color of her gown was the most interesting conversation they'd had this week. They had little to say to each other. So little, in fact, she'd gone from pondering whether she really wanted to marry *him* to wondering why in the world he'd want to marry *her*.

"Oh, here's Robyn and Archie," Charlotte said. "They should liven us up."

Oh, yes, indeed. Robyn did tend to keep things lively— too lively by half for any decent young lady. She glanced at Lord . . . *Francis*, who sat sedately beside her. Sedate was far better than lively. Of course it was. She very much preferred sedate to lively.

Why had Robyn insisted on coming tonight in the first place? Did he really intend to drool over Louise Bannister, right in front of her? Well, how fortunate for him Louise Bannister wasn't a decent young lady.

"Evening, Atherton."

A knot gathered in Lily's stomach. The low, amused voice came from directly behind her. She shivered, sure she could feel Robyn's hot breath against the back of her neck, left bare this evening by one of Betsy's more elaborate hair creations.

She wouldn't turn around, then. She would simply ignore him—

"Good evening, Miss Somerset."

As usual, Robyn refused to be ignored. He stepped forward, bowed, then took her gloved hand in his and raised it to his mouth. His eyes held hers as his lips lingered just a shade longer than was proper. Lord Atherton settled a proprietary hand on the back of her chair, but she couldn't tear her eyes away from Robyn.

The knot in her belly tightened. Drat it, he was so handsome in his black evening attire. No one would guess the heart of a rake beat under that proper dark silk waistcoat, or that his impeccable white gloves hid hands that could reduce a woman to a heap of quivering flesh.

Not unless they looked into his eyes, or noticed the too-wide cast of his lips. The lips and eyes gave him away for the wicked rogue he was. No woman could look into those eyes or endure that slow smile and not find herself going breathless.

What was it Lady Chase called him? Rapscallion? Young scoundrel?

Yes, either of those would do.

"How beautiful you look tonight," he murmured, not at

all perfunctorily. Lily's stomach bottomed out in a way it hadn't even considered doing when Francis complimented her five minutes ago. Then again, one of Robyn's most dangerous qualities was making her believe everything he said, regardless of whether she should or not.

Lady Chase appeared far less inclined to fall under Robyn's spell than Lily, however.

"Humph. Young Sutherland, is it?" She gave him a long, measuring look. "And who are *you*?" she barked, holding up her quizzing glass to peer at Archie, who'd followed Robyn into the box.

"This is Alistair Wroth, Lord Archibald, my lady," Robyn replied, bowing to Lady Chase.

Archie gave Lily a sly wink, then also bowed to Lady Chase. "It's a pleasure to meet you, my lady. My Aunt Bettina speaks highly of you."

Lady Chase looked from Robyn to Archie with her quizzing glass, then turned to Lady Catherine with her verdict. "Humph. Am I to understand I'm to suffer two young scoundrels now?"

"I'm afraid so, Lady Chase," Charlotte put in with an unrepentant grin. "Archie and Robyn go everywhere together."

"Indeed? Well, they can go to the back of the box together, then. The play has begun."

Robyn bowed again, and he and Archie made their way to the back of the box. Lord Atherton stiffened as Robyn took the seat just behind Lily's, and her own back went rigid with awareness. She became almost painfully conscious of the bare skin at the back of her neck, and the long tendrils of hair that brushed against her shoulders, also left mostly bare by her gown.

She brushed away the wisps of hair and touched the back of her neck with a gloved hand.

Behind her, a man drew in a sharp breath through his teeth.

She didn't suppose it was Archie.

Lily's hand dropped at once. She clenched them together in her lap and forced herself to focus on the stage, but it was no use. She could feel his eyes on her. She even imagined she could feel his breath on the back of her neck, little puffs of air like whispers in her ear.

It grew worse once Miss Bannister took the stage. She was prettier than Lily had expected her to be—petite, with dark hair, a saucy smile, and scandalously tight breeches. Lily found herself studying every line of Miss Bannister's figure in those breeches, trying to see her as a man must see her. As Robyn saw her.

It wasn't difficult to determine why he'd returned to the theater to study her from *every angle*. Lily fancied he grew quieter every time Miss Bannister was onstage, as if he concentrated only on her.

By the time the lights went up for intermission, Lily's back was so tense, she feared her spine would snap. Worse, she'd have to face Robyn again now, and speak with him as if she hadn't spent the last hour picturing him doing unspeakable things to Miss Bannister.

She drew a deep breath and prepared herself to withstand his teasing, but as soon as Robyn and Archie rose from their seats, they began making their bows to Lady Chase and Lady Catherine. "Our apologies, my lady, Mother, but Lord Archibald and I have some business to attend to. Will you excuse us?"

Lady Catherine smiled and nodded. "Of course."

Lady Chase was somewhat less benevolent. "Business, eh? I can well imagine what kind of business you two rascals have. Be off with you, then." She dismissed them with an imperious wave of her cane.

Both gentlemen turned and bowed to the ladies, and without another glance in Lily's direction, Robyn exited the box.

Charlotte sighed. "I don't suppose they'll be back. Pity." She glanced sideways at Lord Atherton and lowered her voice. "They were our only chance at an entertaining evening."

"Why shouldn't they be back?" Lily cringed at the shrill note in her voice.

"Oh, they have far more exciting amusements in mind for this evening," Ellie said. "Robyn sent off a note ten minutes before the curtain fell just now. Didn't you see?"

Charlotte snickered. "They've run off like two thieves in the night to see if the note has had the desired effect."

Lily's brows drew together. "A note? To whom? What desired effect?"

Ellie glanced at her mother, then whispered to Lily behind her fan. "To Miss Bannister. That's my guess anyway. What do you think, Charlotte?"

"Oh, yes, I think so, too. Well, it was bound to happen, wasn't it? I'm surprised Robyn didn't secure a mistress earlier in the season. It's been weeks. He must be in rather a . . . froth by now, and Louise Bannister looks lively enough for him. Perhaps I should buy some breeches."

"Mistress!" The word was out before Lily could stop it, and in a rather louder voice than she'd intended. She looked guiltily to either side of her, but Lord Atherton didn't appear to notice her outburst, and Lady Chase was a trifle hard of hearing. Neither of them paid her any mind.

"I wish he wouldn't chase actresses," Charlotte said. "They tend to encourage him in his wild antics. A nice widow is always better."

"I do prefer Miss Bannister to Lady Downes, though," Ellie put in. "That woman's a viper—a serpent in a silk gown. There's no telling what deviltry she'd lead Robyn into."

Mistress. Lily slumped in her chair, her limbs too weak all of a sudden to support her weight. Robyn would make Miss Bannister his mistress so he could admire her in her breeches in private. From every angle. At length. He'd slide his long-fingered hands up those plump, feminine thighs, and . . .

She was going to be sick.

"Miss Somerset, are you unwell?"

Lily supposed her face must have paled, for Francis had abandoned his study of the pit and now looked at her with mild concern.

"I have a slight headache, that's all."

Headache. Heartache. It amounted to the same thing, didn't it?

"Shall we leave, then?"

Lily supposed she couldn't fault his solicitousness.

She sat up straighter in her chair. She would *not* run out of the theater like a child, no matter how much she wanted to. What if Robyn heard of it? He'd think she'd run home because he'd gone off to feel Louise Bannister's thighs. She wouldn't have it.

She forced a smile. "No, of course not. I'm perfectly well."

Lady Chase laid her hand over Lily's then, and motioned for her to lean down.

"What do you think of Atherton, my dear?" The old lady gave a wheezing cackle and Lily resisted the urge to stuff her fingers into her ears. "He's a fine gentleman, isn't he? Respectable. Handsome. Just what a young man should be. Don't you agree?"

Lily glanced at Lord Atherton. He was respectable, yes, and even handsome, with his fair hair and bright blue eyes. She couldn't fault him on any account. A few weeks ago the idea of a faultless suitor would have thrilled her.

Before she'd discovered the flaws were what made a man fascinating. Beautiful, even. *The cracks in the glaze.*

Then again, a lady needed to distinguish between those flaws she could tolerate, and those that would shatter her.

"I've known his mother for ages, you know," Lady Chase went on, her dry lips nearly touching Lily's ear. "Known him since he was in short pants, too. A good lad he was, and he's grown into a fine man. He'll make a solid, reliable husband."

The lights began to dim then, and Lady Chase settled back into her seat.

Her grandmother wanted the match. What would she do if Lily refused? Disown her, as she'd disowned Lily's mother? If she did, where would that leave Lily's younger sisters? They'd go from having the brightest of prospects as Lady Chase's granddaughters to the center of the worst kind of vicious gossip, and it would be all Lily's fault.

She felt as if a stone had rolled onto her chest.

She glanced at Lord Atherton from the corner of her eye. He would make a fine husband. Not a passionate or a tender one. Not even a loving one perhaps, but he'd be a reliable one.

Francis. She must call him Francis now. It wouldn't do to call him Lord Atherton after they were wed.

Or worse—to think of him as Lord Atherton after he became her husband.

Chapter Eighteen

Louise Bannister's arse in breeches was a work of art.

Robyn staggered up the last step and paused on the landing. He swayed a little as he turned around to look behind him, a puzzled frown on his face. Why were there so many damn steps? He closed his eyes then opened them again, but the steps were all still there.

What the devil?

Someone had come into the town house and added more steps since he'd come down the staircase this morning.

He shook his head as he shuffled down the hall toward his bedchamber. Now, what had he been thinking about? Ah, yes. Louise Bannister's arse. Plump, round, generous— if an artist wanted to sculpt the perfect arse, he need look no farther than Louise Bannister in her breeches for his model.

Robyn was a great lover of art. Or was that a great lover of perfect arses? He couldn't quite recall, but it didn't really matter, for love it as he might, he hadn't laid one finger on any part of Louise Bannister tonight, including her arse.

He'd intended to lay a finger on it, or perhaps an entire hand. Two hands, even. He'd walked into the box tonight, he'd seen Lily seated there with Atherton's arm draped possessively over the back of her chair, and at that very moment he'd resolved on a good, long debauch with Louise Bannister.

Why not? There was nothing to stop him, and he'd been without a woman since he'd arrived in London. It was unheard of. Things were becoming rather, well, desperate. For the sake of his very health, he needed to secure a mistress.

But then Lily, damn her, had decided to wear her hair swept atop her head tonight. He'd been seated right behind her for the entire first act, riveted by the sight of her bare, delectable neck. The loose tendrils of hair brushing against her white skin drove him mad. Lily had known, too—she'd felt his stare and he'd felt her quiver in response, her nervous hand coming up to touch her neck. From that point on, he could think of nothing but sinking to his knees behind her chair and pressing his lips against that scented skin. The loose tendrils of her hair would brush against him as she reached behind her to wrap her arms around him—

Well. All thoughts of Louise Bannister's arse had flown out of his head, scattered like a flock of birds threatened by a hungry cat.

That was the trouble with art. You never knew when you were going to lose interest in it.

Fortunately for Miss Bannister, Archie proved a more steadfast admirer, and had remained behind in her dressing room to escort her home after the final curtain fell. It hadn't been clear whether they'd adjourn to Archie's chambers or Miss Bannister's, so Robyn had decided to keep away from St. James's Place tonight.

Far be it from him to interfere in a gentleman's study of fine art.

He took another unsteady step in the general direction of his chambers. Christ, he was sotted. He should never have let Pelkey talk him into a game of cravats in that last tavern, but he hadn't wanted to return home until he was sure Lily was safely tucked away in her bed, white sheets pulled neatly under her chin, dreaming the dreams of the chaste.

He doubted he'd be so fortunate. No, it would be another long, agonizing night filled with blue eyes, fair hair tangled in his hands, perfect white breasts heaving with passion, and a scent that left him hard and aching alone in his bed, near crazed with unsated lust.

He could hear the blood rush through his veins even now.

". . . a delightful evening. Thank you for your escort, my lord."

Oh, wait. That wasn't his blood. It was the front door opening. His mother and sisters filed into the entrance hall. Lily followed after them, her hand on Atherton's arm.

"Lady Sutherland. Miss Sutherland. Miss Charlotte." Atherton bowed to each in turn. "Thank you for a pleasurable evening."

Robyn nearly laughed aloud at Charlotte's expression. He knew that look. She hadn't found her evening pleasurable. Ellie curtsied politely, but Charlotte only tapped her foot impatiently.

Atherton cleared his throat and bowed again to Lady Catherine. "May I have a brief word with Miss Somerset before I take my leave?"

Robyn considered leaping over the railing to throw Atherton out the door himself, but his mother would never allow—

"One brief word only, my lord." Lady Catherine smiled indulgently. "Come along, girls."

Robyn's mouth fell open. *Christ, even his own mother*—

Robyn ducked into the dim hallway and pressed against the wall until his mother and sisters had mounted the stairs and turned in the direction of their own bedchambers, then he sneaked back to the landing and hung just far enough over the rail to see Lily and Atherton, but not so far they were likely to see him.

Atherton held her hands in his and looked down at her adoringly—that is, as adoringly as Atherton looked at anything. Bile burned Robyn's throat. He might have cast his accounts right then and there had he seen a similarly adoring look on Lily's face. Fortunately she had her back to him.

Atherton brought one of her hands to his lips, then the other. "I'd like to . . ."

Mumble, mumble, mumble.

Robyn leaned farther over the railing. *He'd like to what?* Trust Atherton to speak as if his mouth were stuffed full of marbles.

Speak up, man!

". . . see Lord Carlisle tomorrow . . . call on you in the afternoon?"

Robyn's entire body went so stiff, he feared he'd topple over the railing and shatter into a thousand pieces on the marble floor below.

Well, that was it, then. Atherton planned to speak to Alec tomorrow. Once he got Alec's permission, he'd make Lily a formal offer of marriage. She'd accept, of course, and whatever farce she'd been engaged in with Robyn would come to an abrupt halt so she could embark on her new farce with Atherton.

There was a brief silence, then Lily murmured something Robyn couldn't hear. Whatever it was, Atherton seemed pleased, for he leaned toward her. His mouth drew closer to hers, then closer still . . .

Robyn held his breath and waited for Lily to slap Atherton across his smug, marble-filled mouth, but her hands remained motionless at her sides and she stood docilely, as if she'd waited all night for Atherton's halfhearted kiss.

Maybe she had. Perhaps the entire time he'd been enthralled with the back of her neck, she'd been breathless with anticipation for the moment when Atherton would press his dry, closed lips to hers.

Robyn's hands clenched into fists as Atherton's lips met Lily's. It was quick—blessedly so. So quick Robyn couldn't decide whether to be outraged Atherton had kissed her at all, or offended the man had taken such poor advantage of such a promising opportunity.

Men like Atherton were a disgrace to the entire gender.

Alone with Lily, her luscious pink lips at his disposal, and the best Atherton could offer was a stiff little peck on her mouth, leaving all her eager passions untapped, thrashing and squirming in that delicious body. That she'd be wasted on a man who couldn't appreciate her sensuality made Robyn want to rip his hair still bloody from the roots.

Atherton didn't deserve her.

Neither do you.

Robyn backed away from the railing and retreated into the darkness of the hallway. No, he didn't deserve her, but then he'd made a life's habit of taking things he didn't deserve, and he didn't intend to change that habit tonight. Not when the woman he didn't deserve had mounted the staircase, was even now only steps from the second-floor landing.

The woman he wanted above all others.

"You call that a kiss?"

"Oh!" Lily whirled around at the sound of his voice. Her hand flew to her chest and patted it as if to calm her heart. "Robyn! What in the world are you doing, skulking back there like some common criminal?"

"You call that a kiss?" Robyn repeated. He leaned one hip against the railing.

This time the question registered. He saw incredulity slide over her face, then she drew herself up with dignity. "Were you *spying* on me?"

"Yes." What point was there in denial? Spying would be the least of his sins tonight.

Lily sputtered for a moment in outrage, but managed to spit out a sentence at last. "Why, how *dare* you?"

"You didn't answer my question. You call that a kiss?" He narrowed his eyes on her face. "You look just the same as ever. You're not flushed with passion, nor are you panting for breath."

"I—that's none of your business."

Robyn straightened and moved toward her. "Your lips aren't even pink. Not more so than usual, that is."

Something in his expression made her eyes go wide. "Don't come near me."

But she didn't back away.

He ignored her words, cupped her face in one hand, and brushed the tip of his bare thumb softly against her lower lip, as if testing its plumpness. "Not swollen, either. Atherton should be horsewhipped."

"He's—he's a gentleman."

A dark chuckle escaped Robyn's lips. "He's a bloody fool. It's as if he didn't kiss you at all. If I put my mouth on you, you'd damn well know it, and for days afterward. If I had such an opportunity, you'd not walk away from me until my tongue touched every inch of your mouth, inside and out."

Lily's mouth went soft and her lips opened, as if she imagined his tongue against her there.

Robyn suppressed a harsh groan and kept his voice soft and low. "I may not be a gentleman, but I'm no fool, either, to let such a chance escape me."

He hadn't planned to do it, but he also didn't hesitate. He grasped her arm, hurried her down the hall, through his bedchamber door, and shut the door behind her. "Well," he crooned, his lips close to her ear. "This certainly brings back fond memories, doesn't it?"

"You must be mad! Let me out of here this instant!"

He'd gone mad for certain.

"Hmmm . . . let me think about it. No. Not yet."

Lily pushed hard against his chest, to no effect. She

huffed out a breath. "You'd accost me, a guest in your own home? That's going a bit far even for *you*, Robyn."

"Someone has to accost you. You need to learn not to loiter in dark hallways."

"*Loiter?* I never—"

"I would think you'd know that already, but here you are again, at the mercy of, what did you call me last time? A conscienceless seducer? Or was it a lascivious rake?"

"What difference does it make?" Lily snapped. "Either one will do."

Robyn shifted to press her more firmly against the door and planted his hands on either side of her head. His mouth hovered near her neck, but he didn't kiss her. "Ah. I suppose I deserve that. Or I *will* deserve it by the time I let you leave this room."

He stood so close to her, he could see her throat work as she swallowed. "I don't understand you, Robyn. I thought we were friends."

Friends? Did she think to convince him, or herself? Or did she think she could reason him into releasing her? How like Lily not to see they'd gone far, far beyond reason.

His breath stirred the hair at her temple and he felt a shiver pass through her. "Oh, no. I don't kiss my friends, and I'd very much like to kiss you right now."

She made another halfhearted attempt to escape. "I suppose it matters not at all that *I* don't want to kiss *you*."

Robyn chuckled. "Don't you? But I'm afraid I don't believe you. Deny it all you like, but you do need me, Lily, just as I promised you would. I want to hear you say it. Then perhaps I might be persuaded to let you go."

"Is that what this is for you?" Her voice throbbed with pent-up emotion. "Another game to prove you were right all along?"

Robyn's passion-fogged brain worked sluggishly to produce a denial. "I don't care about being right. I care only about being satisfied."

"Don't you? But I'm afraid *I* don't believe *you*, for everything is a game to you. Very well. *I need you.* There. I've said it, and I congratulate you on your victory. Does that satisfy you?"

A dozen different emotions roiled through him, but satisfaction wasn't among them. He buried his face in the soft skin where her shoulder met her neck and inhaled. "Oh, believe me, sweet. I'm *far* from satisfied."

"Pity," she said. "Perhaps it's because even when I need you, I wish I didn't. Does that mean you don't win?"

That scent was Lily's. No perfume could be so intoxicating. For some reason the realization angered him. "That's the second time you've accused me of playing games with you, but I think you're the one who's playing games."

He felt her stiffen against him. "Me? That's absurd."

"Why?" He ran the backs of his fingers down her cheek. "Because the proper, demure Lily Somerset would never play games with a notorious rake like me? But you are, you know."

Lily gasped as his fingers stroked from her cheek over her jaw and trailed down the front of her throat. "I—I don't know what you mean."

Her soft gasp sent a shock of pure lust through him. He wanted to make her gasp again and again, to make her sigh, and to catch each breathless exhalation against his mouth. "Oh, I think you do. You've got Atherton arranged on one side of the chessboard and me on the other. I suppose he'd be the white pieces and I'd be the black. Isn't that right, Lily?"

She pulled a sharp, outraged breath into her lungs. "You flatter yourself. What makes you think you're on the board at all?"

Robyn traced the hollow at the base of her throat. He felt her pulse leap against the pad of his finger and laughed softly. "Oh, I'm there. You don't want me there, and you'll continue to deny it, but I'm there all the same. Shall I tell you how I know?"

"No," she said at once.

But Robyn heard the panic in her voice and realized on a surge of triumph that she already knew. He pressed his mouth against the base of her throat and let the tip of his tongue taste the hollow, just one stroke, as light as a breath.

"Your pulse jumps when I taste you here," he murmured against her throat. "That's how I know."

She shook her head even as her arms came up to circle his neck and her fingers sank into his hair.

"Do you deny it still?" Robyn planted brief, hot kisses against her neck and under her chin, stopping only when his mouth hovered over hers, so close, but not quite touching. "Your lips are open, and soft and wet. So wet, Lily. That's how I know."

She made a sound then, a whimper, a sob—he didn't know. He didn't care. He knew only that she wanted him as badly as he wanted her, and he'd prove it to her before he'd let her walk out the door.

He dragged his hands down her sides, closed them around her waist, and held them there so he could feel the heat of her skin through the cool silk of her gown, turning his palms to fire.

"Your skin is so hot, and when I move my hands here"— he slid his palms over her rib cage—"I feel your breath quicken against my fingers. I can feel you gasp, Lily. That's how I know."

She did gasp then. The sound of her quick breath in his ear made him want to sink to his knees. "Robyn, please . . ."

"Please what? Please kiss you? Or please let you go? You don't know yourself what you want, do you?"

But Robyn knew what he wanted, and if he didn't let her go immediately, he would take it. He'd take *her*, right against this door, her skirts hiked to her waist and her legs wrapped around him as he thrust inside her, thrust until he spent all the pent-up frustration of the past few weeks into her warm, writhing body.

Lily moaned, as if she knew what he was thinking. "I don't know—"

"You *don't* know, do you, love?" His tongue darted out to lick at her earlobe. "But if you know nothing else, know this. It's no game I'm playing with you. Not anymore." His hands drifted down her back until they closed around her lush, firm buttocks. He lifted her against him so she could feel how much he wanted her. "Does this feel like a game to you?"

Her fingers dug into his shoulders and he felt her arch against him. "It feels so . . ."

Control. Stay in control.

It took every ounce of his will to do it, but Robyn released her. His breath heaved in and out of his chest and his cock throbbed, so he stepped back, away from her, before the demands of his body urged him to pull her into his arms again.

"You told me the other night you wished you didn't need me. But your *body* needs mine, no matter how much your mind tries to deny it. Pursue your game with Atherton, then, Lily, but do it knowing you give up a great deal to have him, for he will never own your body the way I do."

Chapter Nineteen

"*No one owns me, Robyn. Not my body or any other part* of me."

His eyes glittered like dark ice. "Atherton will. Or have you forgotten the law makes you his property once you marry him? He can do whatever he wishes to you when you're his wife."

The idea seemed to infuriate him. Lily tried to step away from the rage she saw in his face, but the door was already at her back.

He advanced on her—so close, his coat brushed against her gown. "How pleased you must be to see things going your way at last. But before you congratulate yourself, you should consider whether you even want Atherton at all."

He'll never own your body the way I do.

"And if I decide I do want him?"

He paused, then shrugged, as if it mattered not in the least to him what she decided. "I'll be the first to wish you joy."

Lily let out the breath she'd been holding in a defeated rush. Just as she feared, this was no more than a game of tug-of-war to Robyn.

"Though I've no idea why you *would* want him."

A traitorous hope rose again in her breast at these words. "Why not? He's a trustworthy, virtuous man. He's just the kind of man any sensible young lady wants as a husband."

Robyn laughed, but he didn't look amused. "Trustworthy and virtuous—what a passionate endorsement. May I ask how you know he is either of these things?"

"Charlotte said—"

"Charlotte! You'd base your choice of husband on a whim of Charlotte's?"

It didn't seem the right time to mention Charlotte didn't approve of Lord Atherton, either, so Lily changed the subject. "He has an impeccable reputation, and—"

"Please," Robyn scoffed. "You must know you can't believe all of what you hear, or even what you *don't* hear. What of the lies Mrs. Tittleton told about you? Just because the *ton* whispers it all over London doesn't make it true."

"The gossip I heard about *you* proved to be true. Why should I imagine the *ton* is any less accurate about Lord Atherton?"

As soon as the words left her mouth, she wanted to reach into the air, grab them, and force them back behind her lips. He said nothing, but she couldn't mistake the look of surprised hurt on his face.

Oh, why had she said it? Shame and an odd sort of misery lodged in her chest like a shard of glass. She seemed to forever be saying words she never intended to say when she was with Robyn.

"What in the world do you have against Lord Atherton?" she rushed on, trying to distract them both from her hurtful words. "My goodness, do you even know the man?"

"Do *you*?"

Lily let her head tip back against the door. "Of course I know him."

He looked at her with skeptical dark eyes. "There's something . . . not right about him, Lily. There's something cold there."

"Don't be ridiculous," Lily replied, but his words made her uneasy.

She didn't know Lord Atherton well, it was true, but surely that didn't matter? She knew him as well as any young lady knows her prospective husband. Once she married him, she'd learn the feel of his hair and the beat of his heart and the press of his lips.

She shut her eyes, but she couldn't hide from the thought that burrowed into her brain and echoed inside her skull, awful in its raw truth.

She didn't want to know Lord Atherton the way she knew Robyn.

What would it be like never to again feel the soft, curling hair at the back of Robyn's neck, or his strong heartbeat against her cheek and the delicious pressure of his lips on hers? Never to feel that joyous exhilaration she'd felt when she'd danced with him at Almack's, as though her feet didn't touch the floor while she whirled dizzily in his arms, her belly jumping with an excited pleasure every time he looked at her.

His hands on her, burning through her silk gown.

When she danced with Lord Atherton, when he held her in his arms, she felt . . .

Nothing. Oh, perhaps she'd felt a lukewarm triumph to have secured his notice at last. She was gratified by his polite attentiveness, but with Lord Atherton, she was as she'd always been. Just Lily, the child who got lost in a maze and hid under a bench and sobbed until her father rescued her.

"Look at me."

She raised her eyes to Robyn's face. His lashes, so long

and dark they were almost feminine, and the rough prickles of black hair just visible along his jaw. His mouth, so serious now, but a mouth that could transform as quickly as a heartbeat into that wide, slightly crooked smile that made her knees collapse beneath her like a sandcastle swept away by the tide.

What a coward she was.

When Robyn kissed her or touched her, she felt like a doll caught in the palms of his hands, a doll whose limbs he arranged to suit his whim and pleasure. Maybe he did own her body then, as much as any man could ever own a woman. Maybe she *did* need him.

But as intent as he was to make her admit it, Robyn had never said a word about her heart.

Wasn't it just as well? Surely it was better if she kept her heart in her own possession? Much safer than turning it over to any man. Robyn might be distracted with it for a short time, but he'd abandon it for some other, far more exciting plaything eventually, and then where would she be? Her heart couldn't withstand another blow like the one it sustained when her parents died, and she didn't know if she could trust Robyn not to squeeze that tender organ until it stopped beating.

Perhaps Lord Atherton wasn't worthy of her. Perhaps she did deserve better, but she wasn't sure it mattered. If she married Lord Atherton, she'd have a peaceful life, her younger sisters' futures would be secure, and she didn't have to risk her heart for any of it.

She'd never desire Lord Atherton the way she desired Robyn. She'd never love him.

Wasn't that the way she wanted it?

Robyn leaned down to look into her face. "You don't want him, Lily. I'm not sure you ever did."

No, but then that had been the point all along. She hadn't wanted to admit it at first, but she'd chosen Lord Atherton because she knew she'd never feel any real passion for him, and she'd persisted in her choice even after she realized he believed the gossip about her. Even after he'd shown himself unworthy of her regard.

She gazed up into Robyn's face. He'd become so dear to her, it made her chest ache to look at him.

He'd never said a word about her heart.

"What do you want of me, Robyn? You don't want *me*. Not really. And you never did—not until you believed Lord Atherton might."

Robyn stared at her. "You think I don't want you?"

"Perhaps you want me in the same way you want Lady Downes, or any nameless barmaid who happens to be sitting on your knee. You don't want *me*."

His voice, quiet, disbelieving. "You think I don't want you."

No longer a question.

He slipped his finger under her chin and tilted her face up to his.

He was going to kiss her. He was going to kiss her, and she was going to let him.

It was inevitable, his hot mouth descending on hers, as inevitable as the tide drawing the sand in its wake as it receded. A tide of desire, low in her belly, it drew her, pulled her toward him and swept everything before it. She'd waited for this, she realized then; had known she'd be in Robyn's arms again, even as she'd sat straight-backed and rigid next to the man she planned to marry.

Robyn wrapped his hands around her waist, and his warm breath bathed her ear. "Go to your bed, Lily, before I take you to mine."

His bed. A fierce need pounded through her at the thought of Robyn laying her across his bed, his hands against her thighs, opening her, his body over hers, primed to ease the ache he'd made there, an ache only he could satisfy.

Perhaps she'd meant to push him away—to run away to her bedchamber like the coward she was, but instead her hands slipped inside his coat to skim over his lean waist and up his back to ease it from his shoulders. The coat dropped to the floor behind him as her fingers closed over the buttons of his waistcoat, pulling clumsily at them.

Robyn groaned and reached down to clasp her hips and gather her tightly against him. His tongue teased at her lips and she opened them at once, her own tongue coming forward to stroke against his.

"This is what a kiss should be, Lily," he whispered as his lips trailed across her jaw. His mouth stopped at her ear, and his teeth closed on her earlobe.

Lily shivered at the wet drag of his tongue as he moved to kiss her chin, her neck. He nibbled at her collarbone then settled at the sensitive flesh where her neck met her shoulder, left bare by her daring gown.

Her breath stopped in her lungs at the sensation of his teeth against her, then returned in a gasping sob. It was almost too much, the desire between them. It grew, a canopy of dark leaves over her, then around her, until she feared she'd be lost inside it. "Robyn, I can't . . ."

He made a choked noise low in his throat. "It's all right if you're afraid, love. I'll take care of you."

He was there, his warm body bracing hers, his knee against the blue silk of her skirts, between her legs.

"Please . . . yes, that's it, sweet," he murmured when he felt her legs open to take his body between them. He pressed closer into her and Lily felt him, hard and insistent against her.

His mouth closed over hers again, not as rough this time, but coaxing, soft, as he'd kissed her that first time in Lord Barrow's study—the same kiss she'd found so erotic, she'd been unable to keep her lips closed against his tongue.

She wasn't able to deny him now, either. She had no wish to, but opened her mouth eagerly to take his tongue inside, her own tongue stopping long enough to taste his bottom lip, to make him moan before she slipped inside to kiss him for what felt like forever.

Perhaps it was forever, or perhaps it was only minutes or seconds, but when he raised his mouth at last, she knew she was lost again, the branches thick above her head, each panicked breath more desperate than the last, her footsteps echoing in her ears as she fought to get back to a place she knew. Oh God, she was afraid . . .

But again he was there, his hands on her back, stroking her, steady and strong. "You're safe, Lily. I've got you. It's all right to take what you want."

"I—I want to touch you . . . *now*. Please, Robyn."

She began to struggle with his shirt, to rip at it in her haste to get to his skin underneath. It gave at last, baring a patch of his chest to her. She leaned forward to place her lips against the skin there, so smooth but for the dark hairs scattered across the bronzed skin, springy under her tongue.

"Ah, God, yes." He threw back his head, his hands going to where hers pulled frantically at the waist of his breeches, tearing the shirt away. He groaned again when her nails raked across his back.

He dragged down the rough lace of her sleeve and she shivered a little in his arms. Robyn laughed softly, the sound a dark promise. "I'm going to kiss you here."

"Oh. Oh, that's . . ." But the feel of his mouth against her bared shoulder stopped her words.

"Does that feel good, sweet?" he murmured, his voice low and wicked.

"*Yes*. So good."

"I need to touch you, Lily—to stroke your breasts. Will you let me, love?"

His hands moved slowly up her rib cage until his palms cupped her breasts. His thumb inched up to stroke against one nipple. He circled lightly, his eyes never leaving her face, then he began a rhythmic stroking, again and again over the hardened nub.

His eyes left her face to drop to her breast, and he seemed transfixed by the sight of her nipple peaked against his stroking fingers. "Tell me how it feels." His eyes dropped half closed as he continued to stroke her. "Don't be afraid of your own pleasure, Lily."

She jerked in his arms with each pass of his thumb across the tip of her breast. "It feels . . . it feels as if you're touching me everywhere."

He slipped her other sleeve down so both her shoulders were bare. "I want to touch you everywhere. Taste you everywhere."

Lily felt a rush of cool air across her heated flesh and looked down to find her breasts bare, his hand dark against her white skin, her nipples flushed pink and hard against his fingers, begging for his touch.

Robyn's breath left his lungs in a ragged sigh. "So beautiful. I knew you would be. I'm going to put my mouth on you here—it will feel so good, love. Don't be afraid. Just let me . . ."

His dark head bowed over her and his mouth closed over the tip of one of her breasts.

Lily felt her knees buckle under her, saw the latticework of leaves above her head, heard the distant laugh of a child as she ran along the twisting pathways. But it wasn't *her* laugh. It couldn't be, because she was afraid of the maze . . .

A panicked moan tore from her throat. "I don't . . . I don't know what to do."

He growled softly, and she felt the vibration of it against her breast. "Oh, love, you don't have to do a thing. Just let me touch you. Let me give you pleasure."

He held her, murmuring to her all the while in that low, hypnotic voice, describing how he would touch her. She tensed for his hands, his mouth, so desperate for him she forgot the towering hedges and the darkness and the terror and knew only Robyn, his voice both soothing and erotic, his body warm against hers.

Oh, it was so wicked, his hot tongue licking her nipple, rough and soft at once, and so wet against her flesh, his mouth sucking at her while his thumb continued to circle her other nipple lightly. She clasped his head, her fingers sinking into his hair to hold him tight against her.

Pleasure. Oh, God, he gave her pleasure, pleasure such as she'd never felt before, his mouth and tongue relentless, wet and insistent against her, darting over her swollen flesh then suckling her until she thought she'd scream with the pleasure.

Her core throbbed, as if her body were poised on the edge of something. Her center drew tighter and tighter as if straining toward some culmination. She didn't know what, but she drew closer to it with his every touch, the crushed stones hard against her feet, the heart of the maze just around the next turn, mere steps away . . .

Her fingers clutched at Robyn's hair and she whimpered in need.

He looked up at her then, his face flushed with a dark triumph. Without warning, he dropped to his knees before her. He laid his head against her belly for a moment, his breath sawing in and out of his chest. One strong arm wrapped around her thighs as he sank lower. His other hand reached under her skirts and closed around her ankle.

"What do you need, Lily?" His hand inched up her skirts. "Can you tell me?"

"I—I don't know." She panted as his warm hand moved up her calf and rested at the back of her knee.

"You *do* know. Tell me what you want. Ask me to touch you." His voice was low and thick with suppressed need.

Her hands fell to his shoulders and she gripped them hard to keep from sinking to the floor beside him. "I want you to touch me—"

She stopped on a choked cry as Robyn's hands drifted

up the backs of her legs to the curve of her buttocks, then moved to the insides of her thighs to press gently. "Open for me, love."

He meant for her to open her legs. Oh, God, could she do it? Could she trust him?

He brushed his thumbs against her, the faintest touch, barely teasing the curls between her thighs.

"*Oh.*" Her breath caught and her thighs parted.

Robyn nuzzled his cheek against her belly as he found the slit in her drawers. He probed there, separated her cleft with gentle fingers.

Lily dug her fingers hard into his shoulders as pleasure flooded through her.

"*Yes.* You want me right here. So wet for me, Lily." He stroked a finger between her parted folds, just once, then stopped and looked up at her, waiting for something.

Lily pushed against the hand between her legs. Oh, she was shameless, but she'd do anything, say anything, to feel him move against her again. "Robyn, *please* . . ."

His finger stroked again, once, twice, his eyes never leaving her face. "You want me to touch you here, don't you? Tell me."

"*Yes*, right there . . ."

Lily cried out as his finger drifted lightly over the tiny nub of flesh between her legs, then circled for the briefest of moments before he stopped again. She arched her back, and her hips began to move, seeking that delicious friction. "I want you . . . *harder*. Faster."

A harsh groan tore from his throat. His head fell forward and he opened his mouth against her belly. She felt his bite through the thin silk of her gown just as his fingers began to move again.

Lily's breath came in short, panting gasps as he circled her, *oh, so slowly still*—maddeningly slowly, but relentless now, harder, his clever fingers never leaving her wet, aching flesh and his mouth still working against her belly. He licked and nipped and sucked at her as if he tasted something far more delicious in his mouth than a damp fold of her gown.

Her gasps turned to whimpers and then pleas as his fingers began to circle more quickly. "Oh, please, oh *please* . . ."

His groan was muffled by a mouthful of silk. "Come for me, Lily. *Now.*"

The tight knot he'd drawn inside her body began to unravel. Lily's knees shook as wave after exquisite wave of pleasure swept her into a whirling vortex. Her body shuddered and convulsed in his arms, and he held her throughout the storm of sensation, one arm tight around her thighs. His fingers never ceased circling, but after a moment they grew gentler, slower.

Dear God.

She went limp in his arms. He lowered her to the floor and smoothed her skirts down over her legs. Lily laid her head on his chest and felt his heartbeat, strong under her ear, and an image drifted into her mind. Not a dream, and not a memory, but a moment that had never happened. A young child in a puzzle maze, lost but unafraid, the sun flashing on her fair hair, smiling as she wanders from one turn to the next, until at last the heart of the maze unfolds before her.

Robyn gazed down at her, his hand brushing the hair away from her forehead. He was whispering to her, she realized then, but she didn't try and make sense of his words. She let his voice flow over her, warm and low, and stared into dark eyes still hot with desire.

He hadn't . . . there was more, wasn't there? He hadn't taken his own pleasure.

Lily shifted closer to him and felt his heated length jerk against her. Oh, there was more. So much more.

She reached for him, laid her hand on his thigh. The muscle twitched under her touch and a groan tore from his chest.

Desperate to give him the same pleasure he'd given her,

she brought his ear close to her lips with a touch against his cheek and whispered, "Show me how to touch you."

Robyn hesitated, then shook his head. He caught the hand resting on his thigh and brought it to his lips. "No."

Disappointment pierced her. Didn't he want her to touch him? "But I want to . . ."

His breath snagged in his chest and he seemed to struggle with himself for a moment, but then he shook his head again. "No, Lily."

"But why?"

Robyn shifted away from her. Only a sliver of space opened between their bodies, but to Lily it felt like a chasm.

"Atherton will propose to you tomorrow," Robyn murmured. "I won't have you answer him with the memory of my body moving inside yours. For your sake, I also won't take what belongs to him. Tonight is about you, Lily. It's just for you."

Just for her. Lily felt a sob rise in her throat, but before it could break free, Robyn rose to his feet and held his hand down to her. She stared at him for a moment, then accepted his hand and rose up beside him.

He pressed his lips against her forehead. "Go to bed, before I change my mind."

He turned from her, walked to the window at the other end of the room, and spread his arms wide against the sill, his dark head bowed. He didn't move as Lily backed toward the door, then slipped into the hallway. The patter of her slippers echoed dully against the carpeted floor as she fled to her bedchamber.

Chapter Twenty

Breakfast the next morning was a quiet affair. Lily was rather late to the table, for she'd spent half the morning pacing from her bed to her dressing table, wondering how she could possibly face Robyn after the way he'd . . . and she'd . . . and they'd . . .

Every time she recalled the way she'd trembled in his arms and pleaded with him to touch her, her entire body exploded in heat and set her face aflame with embarrassment and longing. Then back across her room she'd go, hoping to cool her cheeks and put a halt to her lurid imagination.

For imagine she did—her mind worked feverishly to conjure an answer for every question left unanswered after Robyn had sent her back to her room the night before.

She needn't have worried about meeting him at the breakfast table. He didn't appear at all that morning. Lily was ready to jump from her skin every time she heard a noise in the hallway outside the breakfast room until at last

Ellie informed her, far too casually, that Robyn had left the house earlier that morning.

Ellie had fallen into a rather morose silence after that announcement, though Lily noticed her friend's sharp eyes on her more than once.

Charlotte wasn't in a much better state than Eleanor. She seemed to be more agitated even than Lily. "Oh, Lily, I meant to ask you if Lord Atherton . . ." she began, but lapsed into silence without finishing her sentence.

Lily was in no mood to endure one of Charlotte's interrogations, but she tried to arrange her face into an encouraging attitude. "Yes?"

Charlotte tried again, but whatever it was she wanted to say appeared to be lodged in her throat. "I wanted to say that I don't think you should . . ."

Lily tried to hide her impatience when Charlotte trailed off again. "If you think what it is, Charlotte, I'll be in my bedchamber writing letters."

She laid her napkin down on her untouched plate and made her way to her bedchamber. She did have letters to write, to each of her sisters, so she settled onto a settee and picked up Iris's latest missive, which had arrived nearly a week ago.

Iris wasn't a patient correspondent, and Lily imagined her sister was nearly wild for a response by this point, but she'd avoided this task for days for the simple reason that she had no idea what to say.

Iris's letter was filled with questions about the London entertainments, eager inquiries about ladies' fashions, and repeated demands that Lily describe, in breathless detail, each of her encounters with her London beaux. Her sister seemed to be under the impression there were scores of them. She'd have been shocked to find there were only two.

Two beaux, but only one who mattered, and that one not really a beau at all.

What was Lily to say to her sister?

Dearest Iris,

*The entertainments are sufficient to entertain, the la-
dies' fashions are sufficient to cover the ladies (with a
few notable and shocking exceptions), and just last night
the rogue I've fallen madly in love with, the wickedest
gentleman in London, used his talented mouth and fingers to bring me to screaming, shaking pleasure.*

She set Iris's letter aside. No. It wouldn't do, would it?

There was a knock on the door. Charlotte, most likely,
ready to begin her interrogation. Lily braced herself for the
inevitable and went to admit her friend.

But it wasn't Charlotte. Instead, Delia stood on the
threshold.

She ran a shrewd eye over Lily's face. "Well, for a young
lady who's had her every wish granted, you look remarkably
sober."

"Delia! My goodness. What are you doing here so early?
You shouldn't have come. You'll tire yourself and worry
Alec."

Delia entered the room and peeled her gloves off, one
finger at a time. "I'm not the only one who rose early this
morning. Lord Atherton is in Alec's study at this very moment, asking for your hand. I suppose you already know that,
however."

Lily closed the door behind Delia. "Will Alec refuse
him?"

She tried and failed to hide her hopeful tone.

Perhaps Alec would refuse, and then . . .

Delia took a seat on the sofa, laid her gloves carefully in
her lap, and folded her hands on top of them. "Of course
not. Why would he? He asked me if you'd settled on Atherton and I told him I believed you had, for you did say so,
Lily. Have you changed your mind?"

Lily thought she detected a hopeful note in Delia's voice, as well.

She rose and began to pace her room again, then paused in front of the mirror to study her reflection. One of her curls had escaped its pins. She tugged at the errant lock to wrestle it back into submission, but her hands faltered in midmotion before she could subdue it. She stared at her reflection for a moment, then loosed her grip on the curl and let it spring back into place outside its pin.

She turned back to Delia. "I do wonder why you keep asking me that question, Delia."

Delia shifted onto her side on the settee. "I don't like him."

Lily gave a forlorn little laugh. "I think pregnancy has made you far too blunt."

Delia shrugged. "Perhaps it has. I'm too exhausted to meander about the point. In any case, it hardly matters what I think. Only your opinion matters, but as I said before, you look quite somber for a young lady who's finally caught her desired gentleman's eye, so I thought perhaps you'd changed your mind."

"I can't change my mind, even if I wished it. I've encouraged his attentions. He has every right to expect me to accept his proposals. It wouldn't be proper to refuse him now."

"Proper?" Delia's gave an incredulous laugh. "You'd marry a man because it's not *proper* to refuse him? My goodness, Lily, you'll pay a pretty price for that propriety. A marriage devoid of any kind of tender feeling will be a cold one, indeed."

"He's not devoid of tender feeling entirely, Delia," Lily began, though even to her own ears her protest sounded halfhearted.

"My dear, I refer to *your* feelings for *him*."

Lily supposed she could deny it, but there didn't seem to be much point. Delia already saw the truth, just as she always did.

"I know you said you wish for a quiet, peaceful life,"

Delia went on, "but be careful you don't find yourself with far more quiet and peace than you ever wanted."

Lily took a seat on the chair across from the settee. "Lady Chase—that is, our grandmother wants the match."

Delia shrugged. "Yes, I expect she does. She and Lady Atherton have been friends for ages."

"Her patronage means a great deal to Iris, Violet, and Hyacinth."

"It means a great deal to you, as well, as I'm sure you noticed at Lady Chase's fete the other night. That was the first time Lord Atherton ever danced with you, wasn't it?"

"Yes," Lily admitted, "but that's not the point. To refuse Lord Atherton at this stage might anger Lady Chase, and if she becomes angry . . ."

"I beg your pardon, but it is very much worth noting that Lord Atherton hadn't a kind word for you before Lady Chase acknowledged you. As for our sisters, well, it would be unfortunate if our grandmother withdrew her patronage, but you can hardly plan your future based on every whim of Lady Chase's, can you? Our mother certainly didn't."

Lily's throat closed at the mention of their mother, but Delia didn't flinch. She continued to regard Lily with steady, serious blue eyes.

Lily's voice came out in a whisper. "It will cause another scandal . . ."

To her surprise, Delia smiled. "Oh, my yes. Well, what would the *ton* do for entertainment if the Somerset family ceased to cause scandals? Think how dull London would be then."

Lily smiled back at her sister despite herself. "They'd all have to retire to the country."

"Yes, well, I do hope someone will warn the country first."

"Indeed."

They gazed at each other for a moment, then both of them broke into helpless giggles.

Delia kicked off her slippers and reclined on the settee. "Speaking of Lady Chase's fete, how does Robyn get on?"

Lily felt her face grow hot at mention of Robyn, then hotter still when Delia noticed and raised an enquiring eyebrow. "Robyn? I—what do you mean? He gets on just fine. I think. That is, how would I know how he gets on?"

Delia's eyebrow rose another notch at Lily's fumbling reply. "I thought he seemed a bit out of sorts the other night. I don't suppose you have any notion what's troubling him?"

"No," Lily said too quickly.

Delia tapped her finger against her chin. "Hmmm. He seems . . . angry. No, no, that's not it. He seems melancholy."

Melancholy. The word caused Lily a pang, but a lie rose to her lips nonetheless. "He seems just the same as ever to me."

Delia looked at her for a moment, but Lily continued to avoid her sister's eyes. Finally Delia sank back against the settee with a disappointed sigh. She stayed for another hour to help Lily finish a letter to Iris, but she didn't bring up either Lord Atherton or Robyn again.

Lily lingered in her bedchamber after Delia took her leave, her stomach a mass of writhing nerves. Lord Atherton would arrive soon. Indeed, he could even now be on his way to Mayfair, with every expectation of an acceptance of his proposal.

She should be doing something to prepare. Rehearsing a proper acknowledgment of the honor he did her, practicing her words of acceptance, perhaps, or at the very least perfecting her toilette? Did she really want to accept Lord Atherton with a defiant curl bouncing on top of her head, scorning its proper place under its pins?

She wandered over to sit before the looking glass and tried to smooth the rebellious curl back in place.

It's all right if you're afraid, love. I'll take care of you.

Lily stared at her reflection in the glass. The night of the Chatsworths' ball she'd sat in this very chair as Betsy arranged her hair, cursing Robyn for the trick he'd played her at Almack's. Cursing his selfishness.

Yet that night it was Robyn who'd come after her when she fled from Lady Chase, and Robyn who'd taken her into the study and draped a blanket over her shoulders. Robyn had dried her tears and held her in his arms and kissed her so tenderly, and then sent her off to her room, untouched. Well, mostly untouched.

He *had* taken care of her, just as he said he would. Not just the night of the ball, but last night, too, when he'd sent her away from him a second time, even as his body had been shaking with his desire for her.

Tonight is about you, Lily—it's just for you.

A sob rose in her throat. Was he melancholy, as Delia said? She couldn't bear it if he was. Just the possibility caused her heart to spasm with pain.

She closed her eyes and thought of the pleasure he'd given her last night—such pleasure she'd trembled in his arms, begged him to touch her, then cried out for him in the final moments, when it became so intense her entire body shuddered with it.

Oh, love, you don't have to do a thing . . . just let me give you pleasure.

He'd gloried in her pleasure, and he'd taken nothing for himself.

Before Robyn, she'd never known such pleasure existed, but that wasn't even the most precious of the gifts he'd given her.

She'd denied her own voice for so long, she'd forgotten she could still speak. Since her parents' deaths she'd been locked inside herself, trapped in the darkest corner of the maze, certain that if she only stayed quiet, if she only behaved, nothing awful could ever touch her again.

She'd become so fearful, she'd nearly lost the ability to speak altogether; had forgotten the power of words.

Tell me what you want. Ask me to touch you.

With every stroke of his hand and every touch of his mouth against her skin, Robyn had made her ask for what she wanted, and oh, how wonderful it had been, to be in his arms, and to tell him how good he made her feel. To tell him how desperately she wanted his hands on her.

To speak the truth to him. To speak the truth to *herself.*

A soft knock sounded on the door. Lily opened her eyes. "Yes?"

Lady Catherine entered the room. "Lily? Lord Atherton is downstairs. He's asked for a private word with you."

Lily took one last look in the glass, then rose from the bench.

"My dear Lily." Lady Catherine took both of Lily's hands in hers.

Lily looked into her face, the face of the woman who'd become a second mother to her. Lady Catherine's eyes were shadowed with doubt, and her smooth skin was marred by worry lines.

"Before you go downstairs, dear, I want to say something to you."

Lily nodded. She didn't trust herself to speak.

Lady Catherine's fingers tightened. "Nothing has yet been done that can't be undone. Do you understand?"

Lily squeezed the fingers that held hers and nodded again.

"When Lord Atherton asks for your hand, Lily, I hope you will remember your only obligation is to yourself."

"Yes, my lady. I'll remember," Lily whispered.

Lady Catherine leaned forward and kissed her cheek. "Good."

Lord Atherton waited for her in the drawing room. He turned away from the window when Lily entered, crossed the room to her, and took her hands in his. "Miss Somerset . . . Lily. How lovely you look this afternoon. I thank you for seeing me."

Lily studied him, searching inside her breast for any rush

of pleasure at the sight of him, any weakening of the knees or hitch in her breath that might hint at attraction, but aside from a detached appreciation for his handsomeness—and he *was* handsome, by any lady's reckoning—she felt nothing.

What's more, she sensed he felt little for her in return, for all his apparent tenderness as he gazed down at her.

"You can't be at a loss to understand why I'm here, my dear." He dropped to one knee and raised her bare hand to his lips. "As I'm sure you realize, I'm sensible of your superior attractions."

Lily felt her eyes widen. Her superior attractions? It was hardly the passionate adoration a young lady longed for from her betrothed.

So beautiful. I knew you would be, Lily.

"From the moment I first laid eyes on you, I determined I must make you my wife."

Indeed? It hadn't been *quite* the first moment he'd laid eyes on her, though, had it? She remembered their introduction well, and she did not recall now that she'd been overwhelmed by any signs of warm regard on his part.

Quite the opposite.

"I've come directly from a visit to Lord Carlisle, and he's granted me permission to request you do me the inestimable honor of becoming my wife."

It was the perfect proposal—utterly correct, neatly and economically done. Two weeks ago Lily would have swooned. Not with love or passion, but with satisfaction. Two weeks ago, Lord Atherton on bended knee before her, asking with the utmost propriety for her hand, would have been all Lily could have asked for.

It's all right to take what you want.

Robyn's words from last night echoed inside her head. But was it really all right to take what she wanted?

Oh, it was too late! For weeks she'd led Lord Atherton on, had given him every reason to believe his proposal would be accepted. She'd toyed with him, a respectable gentleman.

She'd schemed and plotted to snare him, and now that he'd come up to scratch at last . . .

She wouldn't be a labeled a jilt if she refused him, but it was a near thing. Lady Atherton would be furious, and Lady Chase, as well. She'd accused Robyn of being selfish, but wasn't it the pinnacle of selfishness for her to refuse Lord Atherton, when she knew it might damage her sisters' prospects?

But to marry a man she didn't love—what could be more unfair to him, more selfish than that?

She looked down at him, on one knee before her, his bright blue eyes fixed on her face. She believed he was a good man; a virtuous man. He'd give her a peaceful, quiet life, and he'd take care of her.

Don't be afraid. I'll take care of you.

Lily drew in a deep breath. "My lord, I thank you for the great honor you do me . . ."

Bright morning light had flooded the drawing room when Lord Atherton arrived, but it had long since faded to twilight. Lily hadn't lit the lamps. Shadows played across the yellow-papered walls as the sun moved westward across the sky, but still she sat, watching the fire burn down to embers.

She'd been here for hours. She hadn't moved since she'd heard the front door close behind Lord Atherton.

Francis. He'd asked her to call him Francis.

He'd made a formal offer for her hand, and she'd given him her answer. Even now, hours later, Lily couldn't quite believe her own reply. She'd known precisely what she'd say to him when he proposed, right up to the point when he'd actually uttered the words. She'd felt vaguely surprised when she heard her answer leave her lips, as if someone else had replied for her in a language she couldn't understand.

She'd expected Charlotte to descend on her as soon as Lord Atherton left, but strangely, Charlotte hadn't come. No one had, not even a servant. She'd been left alone in the silent room to ponder whether she'd just made the most grievous error of her life.

There was nothing to do now but wait.

Her heart crashed against her ribs with wild hope one moment, then sank into her slippers in despair the next. The knots in her belly grew tighter with every minute that passed, and there was but one reason for it.

She watched the light until it disappeared entirely and dark gathered in the corners of the drawing room. Still, she didn't light the lamps, but sat quietly, hands folded in her lap, and waited for Robyn to come home.

Chapter Twenty-one

As far as the ladies at the Slippery Eel went, she was one of the prettier ones. Dark hair. Clear white skin. Eyes? Robyn hadn't any idea, but it didn't matter. She had all the requisite parts—large breasts overflowing a flimsy gown, full lips, and from what he could tell by the feel of her against his lap, a shapely arse.

She'd do as well as the next for what he had in mind. A quick servicing; necessary, yes, but about as satisfying as cleaning one's teeth or polishing one's boots. He looked forward to it with about as much enthusiasm.

"You don't look happy, Sutherland." Archie poured a few fingers of whiskey into a glass and held it out to Robyn. "Perhaps you need another drink."

Robyn didn't reach for the glass. "What would you have me do, Archie? Dance a jig? I'm happy enough."

Archie raised his glass to the doxy. "Not nearly as happy as you should be for a man with such a lovely and accommodating lady in his lap."

The woman giggled, then leaned across Robyn, snatched the glass from Archie, and held it playfully against Robyn's lips. "Here you are, pet. Have a little nip. This'll cheer you up."

Robyn jerked his head aside, ignoring the woman's pout. "No, thank you. I don't want any."

Archie took the glass from the girl and placed it carefully on the table. "Ah. Here's the question of the season, Sutherland. What the hell *do* you want?"

I want to touch you . . . now. Please, Robyn.

"What difference does it make? I can't have it, so there's an end to the discussion."

To Robyn's irritation, Archie laughed. "You sound like you did when we were lads, teasing Alec for some toy or treat. You've not been thwarted in your desires much since then. Good for you, isn't it, to want something you can't have?"

If only it were a toy or a treat, or something equally meaningless. If only it were as simple a matter as *want* and *desire*, but neither word did justice to what he felt for Lily. He'd need an entirely new language to describe this want, so deep it had become a part of him.

It wasn't just her body he wanted, though God knew he burned for her with a desire so intense, it scorched him. No, he wanted *her*. In the cruelest bit of irony imaginable, he wanted her so much, he'd been unable to take her last night.

Robyn Sutherland, the wickedest rake in London, unable to take a women who'd lain under him, trembling with desire. A woman he wanted more than any other. The *only* woman he wanted. She'd cried out for him, and he'd sent her off to bed as pure as he'd found her.

Or nearly so.

It was awful, this new kind of want. It had nothing to do with him and everything to do with Lily. He wanted her to be happy—to have whatever she wanted, even if what she wanted was Atherton.

Even if what she wanted wasn't him.

Archie swallowed the whiskey he'd poured for Robyn. "Can't imagine what it is you want that's proved so elusive."

She'd be engaged by the time he saw her again. Was doubtless engaged even now, and the whole family celebrating the betrothal.

Robyn picked up the empty glass and held it out to Archie. He wouldn't be going home anytime soon, so he may as well get sotted. "No, I don't suppose you can."

Archie poured some whiskey in the glass and handed it back to the doxy. She took it, and this time when she held it to Robyn's lips, he drank obediently. "There you go, pet—drink up."

"You can have your pick of the ladies here at the Eel." Archie spread his arms wide and whiskey sloshed over his glass onto the carpet. "You could have had Miss Bannister, as well. She wanted *you*—she only settled for me after you wandered off."

"Is she everything I thought she'd be, then?" Robyn asked without interest, hoping to change the subject.

Archie grinned. "And more. Very satisfactory, indeed, which leads me to ask once again, what is it you want, Sutherland? You don't want Louise Bannister, and you don't appear to want this charming young thing on your lap." Archie tilted his glass toward the doxy in another sloppy toast. "So what, or *whom*, do you want?"

Lily's arms twined around his neck, her breathless sighs; her hot mouth pressed against his bare chest, white breasts tipped with the sweetest nipples he'd ever seen, hard and eager under his tongue . . .

I want you. Harder. Faster. Show me how to touch you.

"Oooh!" the doxy squealed. She shifted on his lap to fit her generous arse more tightly against his burgeoning erection. "He *does* want me, don't you, pet? Come on, then, love—take me upstairs."

Robyn hadn't the heart to tell her the promising swell she felt had nothing to do with her, but neither did he want to join her in one of the private chambers upstairs. He couldn't tup some doxy whose name he didn't recall when he could still feel Lily arching against him—could still hear her cries as she came on his hand.

Dear God. Was he to become a monk, then? He didn't relish that prospect, but for the first time in his life, he couldn't simply replace one woman with another.

How many nights had he spent in the Slippery Eel with a glass of whiskey on the table before him and a doxy in his lap? He looked from one end of the room to the other. The scene was utterly familiar. The same red tufted settees with the same half-clad women draped over them, the same eager gentlemen and the same drunken laughter. He'd spent count-less nights in this room, each of them indistinguishable from the last.

But it wasn't the same, because *he* wasn't the same, and he couldn't stand to sit here another minute as if tonight were just like any other night he'd spent at the Slippery Eel. Everything had changed. To try and go back to how it had been before was impossible, like trying to put spilt whiskey back into a glass.

He had to get out of here.

Robyn tried to disentangle the doxy's arms from around his neck. "I don't think so. Not tonight."

Archie gave a wise nod. "I think, my dear, our friend here has been crossed in love."

The doxy resisted Robyn's efforts to free himself from her grip. She clung to him like an octopus, her tentacles wrapped with determination around his neck. "Aww, come on then, pet. A fine young handsome buck like you? I'll do you right."

Robyn rose from the settee with the doxy still in his arms.

She gave an excited squeal. "That's it, pet—you won't even remember her name after Nellie's done with you."

If brute force couldn't get her off his lap, perhaps gravity could. Robyn walked around the table, leaned over Archie, who was still seated on the settee, and dumped the woman into his lap.

The doxy's squeal of anticipation turned to a shrill protest, and Archie didn't look any happier than she did. "Sutherland, what the *devil*—"

Robyn didn't linger to hear the rest of Archie's harangue. He was out the door before the doxy regained her feet, but once he stood alone on the street outside, he realized he hadn't anywhere to go. He couldn't go home yet.

He'd try to be happy for Lily tomorrow. But not tonight.

The door to the Eel slammed behind him and Archie joined him on the street. "Bloody hell, Sutherland—" he began, but the look on Robyn's face must have surprised him into reconsidering his words, for he paused, cleared his throat, and then asked easily, "Where to, then?"

Robyn shrugged. "No idea."

"Shall we just walk until an amusement presents itself?"

Robyn shrugged again. He didn't care much what they did, as long as they avoided Mayfair. If he saw Atherton, he'd likely slam his fist into the man's smug face. "I suppose."

They hadn't made it more than four blocks when a commotion outside one of the gaming hells caught their attention.

"Ah," said Archie. "I do love London. Always a brawl or some other amusement to be had." He jerked his chin in the direction of the hell across the street, where a riotous crowd of aristocrats and common rabble stood together, all drunk, shouting and laughing over some antics taking place within. "Shall we?"

In Robyn's current mood, a riot seemed just the thing. "By all means."

They crossed the street and stopped at the entrance to the hell. A rough-looking man with a hat pulled low over his face leaned against the door.

"What's all the fuss, my good man?" Archie asked him.

The man spat on the ground at his feet. "Some bleedin'

cove inside losing all his blunt at the tables. Foxed, he is. Other coves is tryin' to drag 'im away afore he's cleaned out."

"Sounds like a typical night in Merry Old London. You don't suppose it's Pelkey?" Archie asked, turning to Robyn.

"Wouldn't be the first time, would it?"

Archie began to push his way good-naturedly through the crowd. "Step aside, gents."

Robyn shoved a few sweaty, gin-soaked revelers to the side and made his way into the hell. He half hoped one of them might shove him back, but even the more dangerous-looking patrons seemed to prefer to steer clear of him tonight.

Archie pointed at a crowd of men around the hazard table. "There."

Robyn watched as the dice tumbled down the baize and hit the wall, followed by a roar of either glee or commiseration from the onlookers. He couldn't see who threw the dice, but they continued to roll at an alarming rate, as if the man who tossed them was determined to lose a fortune.

"I doubt it's Pelkey," Robyn said. "He doesn't do anything that quickly."

Archie grinned. "No. Let's see who it is, then. Perhaps we can help his friends get the poor bastard out the door."

They set to pushing and shoving at bodies again until they cleared a space at the end of the hazard table. The man who threw the dice had his head down as he watched them skitter across the baize. Robyn caught a glimpse of fair hair, then the dice hit the wall, the man raised his head, and Robyn's eyes locked on his face.

He froze. *Jesus* . . .

Next to him Archie drew a sharp breath, "Good Lord! Isn't that . . ."

Atherton.

Robyn stared, speechless. Questions buzzed through his brain like a swarm of insects, each indistinguishable from the next, except for one.

If Atherton was here, then where in the world was Lily?

Archie stood stuttering beside him, still trying to piece it together. "Atherton! But—but he doesn't gamble. Does he? I thought the man was a model of restraint and rectitude."

Robyn hadn't thought so—he'd known there had to be *something* unsavory about Atherton. But gaming? He'd never heard even a breath of gossip about Atherton having a fondness for the tables. Though if the man stayed away from the fashionable gaming houses and only frequented the hells, he could hide it easily enough, at least for a time.

He watched Atherton gather the dice tightly into his fist to prepare for another throw, but Robyn didn't intend to stand by and watch while Atherton lost his family's fortune at hazard. He turned away before the dice could hit the table.

He needed to get to Lily. *Now.*

He heard an angry shout behind him. He paid it no mind, but shoved back through the mass of sticky male bodies. He'd gained the street when he heard another shout, Archie this time, a warning, but before Robyn could turn, a heavy weight slammed into his back. He pitched forward and his forehead met the street with a hard crack. He tried to move, to rise to his knees, but whatever had hit him remained on top of him, preventing him. Hard fingers clawed into his hair and jerked his head back, but before his attacker could slam his skull into the street a second time, the heavy weight was jerked off Robyn's back.

"Bleedin' 'ell. That's not right, that's not," said a disgusted voice.

A second later Robyn was able to rise to his knees. Something warm trickled into his eyes. He reached up to brush it away, then looked down in astonishment to find his hand covered in blood.

An explosion of vile curses erupted next to his ear, then Robyn felt a hand slide under his arm to help him back to his feet.

Archie.

"Robyn. Christ, that looks bad," Archie said in an un-steady voice. He pulled a handkerchief from his pocket and pressed it into Robyn's hand. "Hold it against the gash."

Gash? What gash?

He hadn't time to ask before Archie rounded furiously on someone who stood behind them. "What the *bloody hell* do you think you're doing?"

"I'll tells you what he did," said the same disgusted voice Robyn had heard before. It was the man with the cap he and Archie had spoken to before they entered the hell. "He knocked this swell to the ground when 'is back was turned, he did. I thought you nobs fought gentleman-like, but that weren't sporting, were it?"

"Not sporting at all," Archie replied in a dangerous voice.

Robyn, still dazed from the blow to his head, turned to see whom Archie was glaring at.

Atherton stood on the street, his chest heaving. His blue eyes, filled with rage, were fixed on Robyn.

Atherton had knocked him to the ground?

"You're behind it, aren't you, Sutherland?" Atherton snarled. He lunged toward Robyn again but his two friends held him back, each with a hand on his arm. Robyn didn't recognize one of them, but the other was Adrian Brougham, Lord Stafford, a friend of Atherton's and a decent enough fellow.

"Stafford?" Robyn bit out.

The young man shook his head. "Apologies, Sutherland. He's . . . not on form tonight. Can you just let it go?"

Robyn could. Not out of any consideration for Atherton, but because he'd now become desperate to get to Lily, and he didn't want to be delayed by Atherton's temper tantrum.

Before he could assure Stafford he'd forget the whole matter, however, Atherton wrenched free of his friends' grip and lunged for Robyn again. "I had her right where I wanted her, and then you got to her, didn't you, Sutherland? You made her change her mind!"

He grabbed Robyn by the throat, but this time Robyn saw him coming and he was ready. He slammed his fists under Atherton's elbows and Atherton's hands dropped away from his neck. Before he could recover, Robyn smashed a fist into his face. Blood spurted from Atherton's nose and splattered all over Robyn's white cravat.

Damn, it was satisfying to feel Atherton's nose crumple under his fist.

The blow should have laid Atherton flat, but he was like a man possessed. He swung a fist at Robyn, aiming for his eye, but he missed and the blow glanced off Robyn's jaw.

Archie, Stafford, and Atherton's other friend stood by, but none of them tried to stop it now, for it had gone from a brawl to a matter of honor. Most of the men who'd gathered to watch Atherton lose his fortune had followed him out of the hell, now eager to see him lose a tooth, or worse.

"He's a big 'un, that one," said one of them, nodding at Robyn. "Looks a bit dicked in the nob, too. I'll take a wager on 'im."

A shout went up as men scrambled to lay wagers on the outcome of the fight. The noise swelled to life around him, but Robyn paid no attention. The blood from the gash on his head flowed steadily into his eyes now, obscuring his vision, but he ignored it, his gaze focused on Atherton.

Atherton circled, waiting for an opening. "You said something to her, Sutherland. I know you did. I saw the way you looked at her. You said something to her to make her refuse me."

Robyn dropped his fists in astonishment. "She *refused* you?"

Right there, in the midst of a brawl, blood streaming down his face, Robyn smiled.

That smile seemed to infuriate Atherton, who took immediate advantage of Robyn's inattention and landed a blow to his ribs that made Robyn's breath seize in his lungs. "You know damn well she did, for you talked her into it. Want her money for yourself, no doubt."

Robyn coughed some air into his abused lungs and let out a wheezing laugh. "Atherton, you bloody fool. She doesn't have two farthings to rub together."

Atherton took a wild swing at Robyn's face, but his fist flew wide. "You're the fool, Sutherland. Do you imagine Lady Chase hasn't dowered her precious granddaughter? Who do you think will inherit all the Chase money when she dies, if not Miss Somerset and her sisters?"

All the blood rushed to Robyn's head then. His ears roared with it. He thought of Lily, so beautiful in every way. Atherton had come so close to having that perfect creature for his own, and all this time he'd wanted Lily *for her money*?

When Robyn thought how close she'd come to marrying the bastard, he wanted to pummel Atherton to the ground and keep pummeling him until he became indistinguishable from the street under their feet.

Archie appeared equally incensed. "You greedy bastard. What need have you for any woman's money? Isn't your own fortune enough for you?"

"It's gone," Stafford said quietly. "His entire fortune's been lost at the hazard table."

The heiresses . . . it made such perfect sense, Robyn was stunned he hadn't worked it out before now. Atherton had spent most of the season on the heels of one heiress after another because he'd emptied the family coffers.

The roar in Robyn's ears became deafening. "You'd have dragged her into disgrace along with you, wouldn't you, Atherton? Thank God she came to her senses before she agreed to marry you. She deserves far, far better."

"Better? What, Millicent Chase's daughter? I think not. Why else would I choose to court her? She'd be lucky to have me, penniless or not. Though she is delicious, I'll grant you that. I confess I regret I won't get the chance to toss up her skirts."

A red haze clouded Robyn's vision. *He was going to kill Atherton.*

He lunged forward with a snarl and seized the neck of Atherton's coat. "Don't *ever* talk about touching her again."

Robyn's voice had gone soft and deadly, but Atherton was too incensed to hear the menace there. Instead of heeding it, he plunged forward. "Perhaps it's just as well she *did* refuse me, for you've no doubt already had her."

Robyn froze. "*What did you say?*"

Too late, Atherton realized his danger, but even then he refused to back down. Fueled by drink and fury, he spat, "Only that I've no wish to raise a Sutherland bastard in my house."

Robyn didn't remember much after that apart from a confused series of sounds: the crack of his fist as it crashed into Atherton's jaw, the man's wheezing cough as he took another blow to the stomach, and finally a hollow grunt and the thud of a body as it hit the street.

When Robyn came to himself again, he stood over Atherton, who lay in a bloody heap on the ground. The men surrounding them shouted in victory or groaned in defeat according to the wagers they'd made, but when Robyn spoke, they all fell silent at once.

"Send round word of your second, Atherton. My man will call on yours tomorrow."

Chapter Twenty-two

The fire burned down to cinders in the grate, and still Robyn didn't come home. Lily wrapped her arms around her body to generate some warmth, but the chill of the room had sunk into her bones.

What could keep Robyn out to such a late hour? Visions of Louise Bannister's tight breeches filled Lily's head. She shivered again, but not from the chill in the room this time.

Perhaps she'd best go to bed.

She rose and tried to shake some feeling back into limbs gone numb from sitting so long in the same attitude. She winced as blood rushed back into her feet, then tingled and burned up her legs.

Could a heart grow numb if it languished too long in one's chest?

Lily emerged from the drawing room into the still, dark entryway. Even Rylands, who apparently knew better than to wait up for Robyn, had gone off to bed hours ago. Her legs continued to twitch in protest as she began to mount the stairs.

She'd reached the fourth step when she heard the door open quietly behind her.

Her heart had not yet gone numb, for it lurched in her chest as she turned, then dropped like a stone into the pit of her stomach.

Robyn stood in the entryway, covered in blood. Lily watched, horror-struck, as a few dark red drops trickled from his battered knuckles to drip onto the white marble floor.

For a moment she couldn't move; she could only stand, her hand over her mouth, frozen with shock. "Oh, dear God. *Robyn*."

She did move then—she must have, for she felt each stair slap the bottom of her slippers as she dashed back down into the entryway.

Robyn held his hands up in front of him. "It's not as bad as it looks. Most of the blood isn't even mine."

"Not yours?" Blood seeped steadily from a gash on his forehead. A bruise that put his earlier black eye to shame bloomed on his jaw, and his white cravat was so splattered with red, it looked as if he'd spent his evening in a slaughterhouse. "Is that someone else's blood seeping from the wound on your head, then?"

"Well, no, I suppose *that* is mine, but the blood on my cravat isn't."

Goodness, men were foolish. What difference did it make which blood was *his*? "Never mind. It's sufficient that at least some of it is yours. Come with me."

Robyn raised an eyebrow at her imperious tone, but he didn't offer any resistance. "Yes, ma'am."

Lily took his arm, intending to lead him to the stillroom to get a closer look at the gash on his forehead, but they'd taken only a step when Robyn's soft gasp of pain brought her to an immediate halt. "Robyn?"

He pressed one of his hands against the left side of his body, over his ribs. "It's nothing to fret over. It's just a bruised rib. Or perhaps it's cracked. It's difficult to tell."

A cracked rib? That was far more serious than a cut on the forehead. Lily's heart kicked hard, threatening to crack her own ribs.

She slipped her arm as gently as she could around his waist and urged him to lean against her. "The stillroom won't do for a cracked rib. You need to lie down at once. Lean on me, and I'll help you up the stairs to your bedchamber."

He tried to disentangle himself from her arm. "Don't be absurd. I'll send you tumbling down the stairs if I lean on you."

Lily ignored this and eased him toward the stairs. Robyn fussed and protested the entire way, but at length she managed to get him up the stairs, down the hallway, and into his bedchamber.

Once they'd entered, however, she drew to a halt. "Where's your bed?"

Robyn grinned. "Ah. I've had dreams where you demand to be taken to my bed. Of course, in the dreams I can actually move without assistance."

"Only you could manage to flirt while suffering a cracked rib," Lily said, even as she felt a warm rush of pleasure at his words. "Your bed, sir?"

He gestured toward an open door on the right. "Through there."

It seemed to Lily as though Robyn leaned more heavily on her now, and his breathing became labored, so she moved forward as quickly as his injury would allow. He sat on the edge of the bed while she propped up his pillows, then she eased him back against them and helped him lift his feet up. He lay back with a sigh and closed his eyes.

She stood over him, not sure what to do next. His forehead needed tending, and the cuts on his knuckles, as well. Perhaps she'd better call a servant . . .

"Don't you dare call a servant to tend me," Robyn said, as if he'd read her mind. "The last thing I need is some footman prodding at me with his cold hands."

"Well, I can't very well leave you here like this!"

He opened one eye. "Why not? I'm fine."

His dark hair was matted with blood from the cut on his forehead, his jaw had turned an ominous shade of purple, and his knuckles had started to bleed again. "You're *not* fine. You look a perfect disaster. Please don't tell me Lord Pelkey did this to you?"

He opened the other eye. "A disaster? What an unkind thing to say. And no, Pelkey had nothing to do with it."

Lily crossed her arms over her chest. "How, then?"

He hesitated. "A brawl outside one of the gaming hells."

Oh, for pity's sake. He deserved a cracked rib for being foolish enough to brawl. Still, she couldn't simply leave him here with blood trickling into his eyes. She sighed. "I'll help you. Do you have any water?"

Robyn raised himself up on his elbows, but the movement seemed to cost him some effort. "Are your hands cold?"

"Freezing," she snapped. "Now, the water, if you would?"

He jerked his head in the direction of the window then collapsed onto the pillows again. "Over there. This is *not* how it went in my dream, by the way."

Lily found the water and a towel on the washstand. She set the bowl down on a table near the bed, then stood over him, her hands on her hips. "Can you sit forward a little? I think you'd feel better if I removed your coat."

Robyn heaved himself off the pillows with a pained groan. "If I recall, in my dream we *did* tear off our clothes."

Lily grasped the sleeve of his coat and pulled carefully until his arm came loose, then she leaned closer to slide it across his back and off his other arm. "There. That's much better."

When she'd finished, he fell back against the pillows again, as if the effort had exhausted him. "Now that I think on it, it was *me* who tore off *your* clothes. I believe I prefer it that way."

"I suppose you think I'll remove my clothing to accommodate you?"

Lily felt herself flush as soon as the words left her mouth. Goodness—was *she* flirting with *him* now?

Robyn's eyes gleamed. "Well, I am *very badly* injured." That dangerous grin lifted one corner of his mouth. "It might distract me from the *terrible, awful* pain I suffer."

Lily reached for the basin and sat on the edge of the bed. "You told me you were fine not five minutes ago."

"Yes, well, I'm in far more pain now than I was then, though *that* has little enough to do with my injuries."

He winced when she touched the wet cloth to the gash on his head.

Lily dabbed at it, then leaned forward to get a closer look. It was an ugly gash, but she didn't think it would need to be sewn closed. She brushed the towel over his forehead until it was reasonably clean, then dipped it in the water again and began to clear some of the blood out of his hair.

She worked steadily for some minutes before she realized Robyn had gone still and quiet. She glanced down at him, half expecting he'd fallen asleep, but his dark eyes were open, watching her.

Lily's breath caught at the look he gave her. "I'm sorry. Am I hurting you?"

He nodded once. His gaze never left her face. "Yes."

She jerked her hand away, but he caught her by the wrist and pressed her fingers against his cheek. "Don't stop."

Lily swallowed. "You have cuts on your hand."

He didn't release her, but moved their joined hands away from his face so he could see. His knuckles were no longer oozing, but they were caked in dried blood. "So I do."

She withdrew her hand, dipped the towel in the water, and stroked the wet cloth over his knuckles. Robyn closed his eyes again and drew in a deep, slow breath.

Lily studied his face, at once both familiar and utterly new to her. She'd always thought him heartbreakingly handsome, and he was so now, with his long, dark lashes curled on his cheekbones.

She leaned close—she'd never noticed the tiny white scar on his bottom lip.

The tiny imperfections. The cracks in the glaze.

Perhaps that's what love was, then. To see those scars, those imperfections, and to know they were what made a person beautiful.

She loved him. Bruised, battered, and bloody as he was, she thought him beautiful.

Why didn't he touch her? Did he think her afraid still? She wasn't, not anymore—

No. That was a lie. She was afraid.

Robyn might care for her, but he'd made her no promises, and yet she, the prim and proper Lily Somerset, had rejected a proposal from the most respectable gentleman in London, only to give her virtue to the wickedest one instead.

This was what she wanted—she knew that now.

Robyn hadn't revealed his heart to her, but he'd helped her to see what lay inside her own, and once she had, everything changed. Giving her heart into his keeping had been the truly terrifying part, but it was done. It felt like a lie to hold back her body when he already held her heart.

She wanted to give him everything.

She was afraid, but she wasn't a coward anymore.

Lily brought his damaged hand to her mouth and touched her lips to his knuckles. His eyes fluttered under his lids, but he closed them tighter, and she sensed a reluctance in him, as if he believed he dreamed her touch and didn't want to wake.

She kissed each of his fingers in turn. His lips parted, but his eyes remained closed. He let out a faint groan when she slipped one of his fingers into her mouth. His body shifted restlessly on the bed, but still he didn't open his eyes.

"You refused Atherton?" His voice was hoarse.

It didn't occur to her to wonder how he knew. "Yes."

He opened his eyes at last, and the look that burned in their depths stole her breath. He said nothing more—just watched her with his hot, dark eyes as she loosed the buttons on his waistcoat and spread the silk wide so she could get to the shirt beneath.

His breathing quickened as her fingers fisted in the linen to pull it free of his breeches. She slid one hand against the bare skin of his belly and felt the hard muscles under his smooth skin jump under her fingers.

"Your hands aren't cold," he murmured. He arched his body just a little, as if seeking her touch.

She teased a finger around his bellybutton. "Well, not anymore."

Robyn gasped a little at the sensation, but then he caught her hand and moved it away from his body. "This isn't a good idea, Lily."

Lily sat back and regarded him. Did he think to refuse her? Perhaps he didn't want her anymore . . .

Oh, no. He did. She had only to look at his parted lips and flushed skin to see it. Had he decided to be noble, then? It would be just like Robyn to refuse to take her virtue the very moment she'd made up her mind to give it to him.

She placed her hand on his chest to feel his heartbeat. It pounded under her palm, and she could see his pulse leap in his neck.

He caught his breath at her touch. "Are you trying to drive me mad?"

Drive him mad? Well, it was one way to overcome his uncharacteristic fit of virtuousness.

Perhaps she did want to drive him just the tiniest bit mad. *Could she?*

She gave him an affronted look. "Certainly not, Mr. Sutherland. I'm simply checking you for further injuries."

She ran her gaze over him. The shirt posed somewhat of

a problem, as she couldn't remove it entirely unless he sat up. Yet she didn't want him to move . . . there was something wicked about having him lie here, stilled for her hands, only half divested of his clothing.

She hiked her skirts to her knees, crawled onto the bed, and lay down on her side, propped up on her elbow next to him.

Robyn gaped at her, shocked. "What in the blazes do you think you're doing?"

Lily had to press her lips together to keep from laughing. "I told you. I'm checking you for injuries. Now, here's a bad one . . ."

She trailed light fingers against his jaw, then pressed her mouth where her fingers had been. She kissed him lightly, then dipped lower to lick his neck. A faint trace of salt and spicy soap met her tongue. She nipped at him with her teeth and felt a deep shudder pass through his body. "Oh, dear. Is it tender there?"

His voice was choked. "This is highly improper."

"Improper? I'm sure I don't know what you mean," Lily whispered into his ear. Her teeth closed over his earlobe. "Think of me as your nurse. Nothing more."

She traced her tongue over the whorls of his ear and he hissed in a sharp breath. Curious, she dipped her tongue into his ear and was thrilled when a gasp escaped him.

"Nurses don't often climb into bed with their patients."

"I'm very thorough." She squirmed closer to him, then leaned over to place her mouth on his forehead, where he'd been cut. If her breasts just happened to press against his chest? Well, it was all in the name of medicine. "This cut on your head is rather deep."

"Deep?" He sounded dazed.

She teased her lips over his face. "I'm afraid so. And there's a little injury right here, on your bottom lip." She darted her tongue at the tiny scar.

His body surged under hers and his hands gripped her waist. "That's an old scar," he managed.

Lily pulled a little away from him so she could look down into his face. His cheekbones were flushed with color, and his lids had gone heavy over dark, burning eyes.

She leaned down again and hovered her lips over his. "I'm the nurse, so I'll be the judge of that. Now if you'll just lie still like a docile patient, Mr. Sutherland . . ."

She loved his lips, especially the full lower one, just a shade too wide for perfection. She cupped a hand around his cheek and took that lip into her mouth. She sucked it inside and teased at it with her tongue.

It was as if flame had been set to dry tinder. Robyn groaned and opened his mouth ravenously under hers. His tongue thrust into her wet warmth. She curled her tongue around his and matched each of his maddening strokes, urging her mouth against his with a breathless gasp.

Oh, yes. This was what she wanted.

Robyn gripped the back of her neck and strained up from his pillows to press his mouth harder against hers, but she evaded him, then tore her mouth from his with an effort. She wasn't quite done yet.

He fell back with a groan. "What now?"

He sounded so pitiful, she almost sympathized with him. Not enough to stop, though. "I'm not quite done with my examination. A cracked rib, I believe?"

He was panting now. "You can't mean to—"

"What kind of nurse would I be if I didn't?"

He stared straight up at the canopy above them, his body rigid, as if he were afraid of what she might do next.

She lay a hand on his chest. "You needn't look as if I'm about to torture you, Robyn. Are you afraid I'll hurt you?"

He jerked his head once, still not looking at her. "No. I'm afraid I'll leap on you and crack my other ribs."

Leap on her? My goodness. What would that be like?

"You're injured. Leaping is discouraged in such situations, I believe."

He drew her hand to his mouth and kissed the tip of her finger. "I'm injured. Not *dead*."

"Indeed? Not from lack of trying."

But she didn't want to argue with him about the brawl. Not at the moment anyway. She eased away from him and shimmied lower on the bed so she was flush with his torso.

A tantalizing bit of skin remained visible from when she'd pulled his shirt up earlier, but now Lily dragged the linen up as far as it would go. "*Oh, my.*"

She couldn't help the breathless exclamation. His chest was not quite exposed because the shirt wouldn't go that far, but his belly . . . oh, she could make do with his belly. Hard, ridged muscle; smooth, golden skin; and a few fascinating hairs that thickened before they vanished into his breeches. She trailed a finger over that crisp hair and saw Robyn's hands fist on the coverlet in response.

She slid her hand up, under his shirt, and laid it flat against the center of his chest. She paused, watching him, then ran one finger around his nipple, just once, hardly a touch at all.

A low moan broke from his chest. Fascinated, she did it again, and again, then slipped both hands under his shirt to tease his nipples. He gasped and writhed under her hands despite the pain in his ribs, as if he were helpless to stop himself.

Oh, dear God. Her entire body flushed with heat and she grew damp between her legs. She'd thought to tease him a little, but she never imagined *she* could become so aroused from watching him, still half clothed, writhing in an agony of lust.

She wanted to taste him. She wanted . . . without conscious thought she brought her mouth to his stomach. Hungry for him, she licked and nipped at him, her wet tongue dragging dangerously close to the fall of his breeches.

Robyn sank his fingers into her hair. Pins scattered everywhere, and a long lock came loose and brushed against his stomach. He arched convulsively, as if he'd die if he couldn't get more of his flesh into her mouth. "Lily, my *God*."

She knew just how to touch him then, as if she'd done this dozens of times before. She could feel him, hot and hard under her hand, as she clawed at the buttons of his falls. When they came free at last, she pushed desperately at the cloth to get to . . .

His swollen shaft rose from the tangle of fabric now bunched at his hips, and he was, *oh*, he was magnificent as he rose proudly from his crumpled clothing. She had to touch him, *would* touch him . . .

"Ah, God, *yes* . . ."

His skin felt like satin under her stroking fingers. She stared, fascinated by the sight of her own white hand stroking his flesh, and then her lips were on him again, low on his belly, biting and licking him there as her hand slicked over him.

Robyn's hips arched off the bed. "So good, sweet. Ah, yes, *so good*."

His groans and gasps made her feel wicked—*he* made her wicked, and oh, she was *so* wicked, because she wanted to put her mouth on him, *there*, where her hand was, and slide her lips . . .

He cried out when her mouth closed over him. "No! Don't . . . ah, ah, please, stop . . ."

But even as he said no, his hand tightened in her hair. He fisted the thick curls while his hips thrust upward once, then again. She closed her lips tight around his hard flesh and drew on him until he began to beg her, to beg her *not* to stop.

Yes. Lily's core flooded with wet heat as she sucked him deeper into her mouth.

This—*this* was what she wanted.

Chapter Twenty-three

He was going to come. He hadn't even made love to Lily yet, and he was about to come in her mouth. She was still a virgin. For God's sake, she was still *dressed*.

He was a savage, lustful, rutting animal.

Robyn called on every decent, pure, virtuous thing he could think of. *Puppies. Flowers. Sunrises. Cooing babies*, and drew his aching flesh free of Lily's hot mouth before he utterly disgraced himself.

He lay still for a few moments on the bed, gasping for breath as he tried to reason with his cock. Lily drew herself up onto her knees beside him, her face a picture of distress. "Didn't you like . . . that?"

Like it? He may never be able to breathe again.

How had he let it get so far? One minute she'd been kissing him, and the next she'd been on her knees between his thighs.

His cock twitched painfully, and yet he couldn't prevent a grin. His proper, prim Lily, so ladylike and demure, had been on the verge of bringing him to ecstasy with her mouth. She'd seemed to know just what to do. How to touch him, how to please him.

His shook his head, his grin widening. The heart of a vixen beat under those decorous gowns.

His vixen, and he was wild for her.

He'd make love to her. Tonight. He might draw the line at reaching pleasure in her mouth, but his virtue extended only so far. He *would* make her his.

First things first, however. He raised himself to a sitting position and shed his waistcoat and shirt, breeches and drawers, his ribs screaming in protest at the movement. He lay back on the covers, naked, and held his arms out to Lily.

She went to him without question. When she was stretched out next to him, her head on his chest and his arms wrapped around her, he answered her question. "I love what you did to me, so much I almost couldn't stop."

She ran her hand over his chest. "Then why did you stop me? Don't you want me?"

He shivered as she brushed her fingers over one of his nipples. She seemed to be fascinated with that part of his body. "Never think I don't want you, Lily. I want you desperately— more than I've ever wanted anyone."

Her body melted against his. He pressed his lips to her temple, and the scent of daisies and warm grass made him dizzy. "You're an innocent. As much as I love your mouth on me, I want to make love to you first. I want to watch you—to see your face when I bring you to pleasure."

"Oh." She was quiet for a moment, then, "Do you think you might want to do that tonight?"

Robyn chuckled. *Oh, God, how he loved her.*

For answer, he began to pull the remaining pins from her hair. When it tumbled about her shoulders, he gathered fist-fuls of the heavy, honey-colored locks in his hands and brought them to his lips to kiss them. "So beautiful, like spun gold."

She blushed with pleasure and he had an overwhelming urge to taste that blush, to follow that wash of pink from her face to her neck and under the neckline of her gown. He ran his lips over her cheeks, then dropped lower to caress her jawline. She shivered against him as his tongue found her neck. He opened his mouth against her to kiss and nibble at her for a moment before he slid down, his mouth dragging over every inch of bare skin he could reach.

He stopped when he arrived at the neckline of her gown. "Lily." He reached behind her to free her buttons. "You have too many clothes on."

She gave a shaky little laugh. "Do I?"

The laugh turned to a gasp when he tugged the dress down and brought his hands up to cup her breasts.

He watched her face. "Do you like it when I touch you here, sweetheart?"

He brushed his palms over her nipples, and she had to catch her breath to answer. "Y-yes. You like it when I touch you there, too."

Robyn grinned. She had no idea. He'd take her touch anywhere he could get it. His nose. His big toe. He'd go as hard as stone for her if she even grazed his elbow.

Robyn slipped a finger down her chest, then hooked it into the fabric of her bodice and pulled it down farther, baring her. He stared at her nipples, peaked under the thin material of her shift.

Oh, God, her sweet, pink nipples made him crazy.

He tore her gown off with a few quick tugs and eased her back on the bed. With a low groan, he settled on top of her.

His mouth closed over one of her nipples, licking and sucking it until the dusky pink nub rose hard and firm against the damp material. He drew back to look at her and his eyes darkened at the sight of the inflamed tip, easily visible through the wet white shift. He brushed his thumb over the straining peak, then pinched it lightly between his finger and thumb.

His eyes shot to her face when she cried out. "So tender. Someday I'll make you come just by suckling you."

He placed his hands firmly against her shoulders to still her and closed his lips over her other nipple. He drew hard on it, then laved at the tip with his tongue. Lily dug her fingers into his hair and arched against his mouth, then gasped as his tongue lashed at her. "Ah, Robyn, please, *please . . ."*

Her half-broken pleas drove him wild. He devoured her, nipping at her with his teeth. He darted his tongue over the peaks to soothe them, then sucked them into his hot, wet mouth again.

He'd didn't realize he'd begun to grind mindlessly against the sweet spot between her legs until she made a sound, half plea, half question. Oh, God, he'd lost control of himself again. He wanted her so badly, was desperate to sink into her wet heat, and yet . . . he drew back and looked down at her.

She gazed back at him, her eyes so blue, so trusting. "Robyn?"

This was *Lily.* Not one of his mistresses. Not Lady Downes, and not some doxy whose name he couldn't recall. This wasn't some casual fuck. He loved her. *Loved her.*

Robyn drew in a deep breath and forced himself to slow. He brushed her hair back from her face with both hands and dropped a kiss on her forehead. "Ah, sweetheart. I'm sorry. I just want you so much."

She caressed his cheek. "I want you, too."

Robyn closed his eyes and prayed for control. "Are you sure, Lily? You can tell me no, love—*should* tell me no."

He could still stop—would stop. He buried his face in her neck, his breath held. *If she said no, he'd stop . . .*

She closed her fingers in the hair at the back of his neck and pulled his head up gently, so he had to look into her eyes. "I've never been surer of anything in my life."

No hesitation, no doubt. Just deep blue eyes, soft with

desire, gazing up at him with a look that made his breath stop. He leaned over and took her lips, the kiss soft, tender. A promise.

He gathered the hem of her shift in his hand and eased it up her body and over her head. "I'll take care of you, love. I'll make it so sweet for you."

He splayed his hands over her hips and eased her drawers down so she lay before him, naked, her skin flushed pink with desire.

Robyn's mouth went dry as he looked at her. "So beautiful, Lily. No, love," he said when she shyly raised her arms to cover her breasts. "I want to see you. Never hide yourself from me."

She let her arms fall open. Robyn took her wrists in his hands and raised them over her head so she lay open to his gaze. "Yes," he whispered. "That's it, love." He nudged her legs open wider and shifted closer to her so she cradled his cock between her thighs. "Now open for me . . . *yes*."

He couldn't prevent a groan when he felt her soft thatch of dark blond hair against his cock. The urge to bury himself deep inside her rose again, a beast clawing at him, but he ruthlessly tamped down his desire and eased a hand between her thighs to stroke the damp curls there.

He touched her softly with the tips of his fingers, just the barest hint of a caress, watching her. Only when a flush rose to her cheeks and he felt her body move restlessly under his did he deepen his caress, his fingers opening her to brush lightly against her tender bud.

"*Ah*." Lily's head began to thrash from side to side as he stroked her, his fingers moving just a little faster each time he circled.

He watched, all his attention on her, his eyes fixed on her flushed face. God, she was beautiful, and so uninhibited in her passion, Robyn felt sure he could come just watching her, just listening to her pant and moan as he brought her closer to the edge with each careful brush of his fingers.

"Yes," he groaned when her body began to arch. "Yes, Lily, just like that. Do you want more, sweetheart?"

"Oh, God, Robyn . . ."

That was a *yes*. He eased one finger into her tight sheath. She cried out and bowed off the bed. Robyn's cock clenched, desperate to be inside her, but he held back, thrusting his finger slowly, so slowly inside her, watching her and listening to her cries.

Waiting.

When she began to beg him, he'd know.

"Oh, oh, oh. Please. Robyn, I want . . . *please.*"

He sank a second finger into her, still thrusting, a little harder now, a little faster, just hard and fast enough to drive her wild, but not enough to make her come.

"You're so wet, Lily—so wet for me," he hissed, his eyes riveted on her writhing body. "Tell me what you want." He'd begun to stroke himself now, his other hand moving up and down his stiff cock.

He needed to get inside her or he'd come right now, on her soft belly . . .

He withdrew his fingers. Lily whimpered at the loss and her hips surged off the bed, desperate for their return.

Robyn held on to his control by the merest thread. "Tell me what you want."

"You." Lily arched her hips again. "I want you, Robyn. *Now.*"

Oh, thank God. Robyn pushed her knees wider apart, placed the head of his cock at her wet entrance, and nudged part of the way inside her. A harsh groan tore from his throat and he closed his eyes against the intense pleasure of her warm, eager body surrounding him.

Lily wrapped a leg around his hip and pushed frantically against him.

"No, no." He pinned her back to the bed with his weight. "Let me do it, sweetheart. I don't want to hurt you."

He *would* hurt her, but there was no help for it. He drew

back, then surged forward, thrusting all the way inside with one powerful stroke. She gave a faint cry as he tore through the thin barrier inside her body.

A savage triumph swept through him. She was his now—*his*. He alone would know how it felt to have her spread underneath him, his body buried deep inside hers. Every one of his animal instincts urged him to thrust savagely into her, to take her hard so she understood she belonged only to him now.

Sweat beaded on his brow and his arms shook under him, but Robyn forced himself to remain motionless. He pressed a tender kiss on her lips. "Ah, love. I'm sorry."

Lily had frozen underneath him at the sharp pain, but after a moment her body began to relax. Robyn reached down between her legs to find the center of her pleasure and stroke her there, his touch slow and gentle, until she began to melt around him again.

She sighed and her lips grazed his throat. She urged herself against him. "Don't stop. Please, Robyn."

A raw groan tore from his chest. He wrapped her leg back over his hip and began to move. He forced himself to thrust slowly, his rhythm easy, steady. Lily arched upward to meet each of his strokes. Robyn had never felt anything more seductive in his life than her arms around his neck, her body clasped around him as she moved with him, eager and innocent.

His body screamed for release, but he held back until Lily's quick breaths turned to sighs and whimpers and she began to bring herself harder against him.

Robyn put his mouth to the hollow of her throat to lick and suck at her. "Yes, sweetheart, move with me. You feel so good, Lily . . . so sweet around me."

His words seemed to excite her. She wrapped her other leg around his hip and surged hard against him, again and again, her sighs breathless exhalations against his ear.

He was lost, lost, drowning in her, his hips jerking, never

losing contact with her body, his desperate pleas buried in the damp skin of her throat. "Ah, God, Lily, *now*, please, love."

Lily's head tipped back against the pillows with a sound-less cry as she reached her climax in a rush of wet heat. Her body clenched around his thrusting cock, her passion sweet, so sweet, Robyn thought he'd die of the pleasure, her nails raking hard across his back as she gripped his shaft once, again, and again.

His back bowed with the delicious pressure. He cupped her face in his hands in the last moments to tell her—to tell her how beautiful she was to him, how much pleasure she gave him—but his own release took him then. He re-membered very little after that but his hoarse cry and his body shuddering over hers as he drove into her, became part of her.

Robyn drifted back to consciousness the way one breaks the surface of the water after a long, deep swim, in a kalei-doscope of sensations: his ragged breath, Lily's palm pressed to his back, both his hands fisted in her curls, her soft limbs wrapped around him and his body still buried in hers. She'd gone quiet and still beneath him, her only movement the soft stroke of her fingers against his back.

A wave of panic washed over him. He'd gone mindless at the end, delirious with pleasure when she'd clenched around him. Had he been too rough? Had he—*dear God*, had he hurt her?

"Lily? Did I hurt you? I'm sorry—"

Her fingers touched his lips to quiet him. "I'm not."

He gazed down at her. Her hair was a mass of wild tan-gles against the pillow and a dreamy half smile curled her mouth. She traced his lips with her finger for a moment, then laid her hand against his cheek.

Robyn's breath left his lungs in a deep, relieved sigh. *Thank God.* For once, he'd managed to do something right.

"We'll have to sneak you back to your bedchamber, you

know." He shifted off her so as not to crush her with his weight, then gathered her into his arms and dropped a kiss on the top of her head. "Not yet, though. Not yet."

She threw an arm over his chest and snuggled closer to his side. "Good, because I'm not certain I can move."

Robyn smiled. It occurred to him that he should be ashamed of himself for making love to an innocent with such unbridled enthusiasm, but he felt only fierce satisfaction. "If I had my way, you wouldn't move from my bed for weeks."

She giggled. "That would suit me." To emphasize her point, she pressed a light kiss against his nipple.

He moaned faintly and his cock twitched in anticipation. Good Lord. He'd had the most earth-shattering climax of his life just now, had been buried deep inside her mere minutes ago, and with one kiss, just like that, he wanted her again.

But even he wasn't such a beast as to take an innocent twice in one night.

"Lily," he choked out, but to his horror the word was less like the warning he'd intended, and more like a plea.

She seemed to hear it as one. She lingered over his nipple for a moment, then pressed a kiss to his chest and began to work her way down his body, her mouth hot against his now fevered flesh.

He reached down to stop her—*Jesus, he hoped it was to stop her*—when she gave a distressed cry. "Oh, no. Oh, Robyn."

He sat up. She was hunched over his torso, looking as if she wanted to cry. His heart lurched in his chest. "What? Lily, for God's sake, what is it?"

She pointed a shaking finger and he looked down to find an ugly black bruise the size of a dinner plate covering his ribs where he'd taken the blow from Atherton.

"It's all right, love. Oh, no—don't *cry*, Lily."

Too late. Her blue eyes filled with tears.

"It doesn't hurt a bit," he lied, desperate to make her stop.

It did, of course. It hurt like hell, more so now after their enthusiastic lovemaking, but he wasn't about to confess that to Lily, especially as the pleasure had far exceeded the pain.

"*It doesn't hurt?* I don't believe you!" She leaned over his torso and her lips drifted across the bruise in the lightest, gentlest of kisses.

Robyn's heart swelled in his chest at the tenderness of the gesture. "Come here, sweetheart. It's all right. I'd have expected more stoicism from my nurse, you know."

She settled back into his open arms, careful not to jostle his ribs. "It must have been a very ugly brawl, indeed. Oh, Robyn, why would you endanger yourself like that? Promise me you'll never fight again."

Her voice was tense with anxiety, and she'd gone rigid in his arms. Robyn pulled her close, stroked her hair, and murmured soothing promises to her until he felt the tension drain from her body. "I won't do so again."

He wouldn't tell her he'd brawled with Atherton, or why, and he certainly wouldn't tell her about the duel. She wouldn't hear of it from his sisters or his mother, for they didn't know about it themselves. He planned to ask Alec to be his second, but he could trust his brother not to breathe a word to Delia. Archie could be trusted to keep silent, as well.

There was no need for her to know. It would only terrify her. The whole thing would be over before two days had passed and, God willing, he'd still be in one piece when it was.

She stirred against him. "Promise me, Robyn."

"I do, love. I promise."

He continued to stroke her hair until she fell asleep.

Chapter Twenty-four

"Well, you look quite pleased with yourself this morning, Lily," Charlotte said with the air of someone rendering a verdict.

Lily fluffed her skirts out across the carriage seat and gave Charlotte a demure smile. "Do I? I can't imagine why."

Pleased. Such a pale word to describe how she felt this morning.

They were on their way to pay a morning call to Lady Chase. Even at this early hour the carriage labored through the congested London streets, but to Lily, it felt as if they floated on a cloud.

"Oh, I can," Charlotte said. "Indeed, I *know* why."

Lily's gaze shot to her friend's face. Had Charlotte seen her with Robyn last night?

She hadn't returned to her bedchamber until the wee hours of the morning. The house had been so silent and still, Lily was certain they'd escaped unobserved, but if Charlotte *had* seen them, one glance would have been enough for her to see what they'd been up to.

Robyn had worn only a robe, and Lily had been clutching her gaping dress to her breasts, not having bothered with the buttons. Once they'd reached her door, he'd kissed her, then kissed her again, and she'd clasped her arms around his neck to pull him closer. . .

It hadn't been a quick good night.

Lily cleared a lump of panic from her throat. "You *know*? Whatever do you mean, Charlotte? What do you know?"

Charlotte waved a hand through the air. "You've refused Lord Atherton, and so you're able to sleep again. Wonderful, isn't it, the salutary effects of a restful night? I can't think of anything more satisfying than a pleasant sleep."

I can.

Heat rushed to Lily's face at the thought, but Charlotte had turned to the window and didn't notice. "We're here."

The carriage rolled to a stop, and Charlotte gathered her gloves and reticule from the seat. "I do hope Lady Chase isn't irritated with us for coming so early. Why couldn't we wait for the proper time to call?"

Lily smoothed her gloves over her suddenly damp palms. "I wanted to get it over with as soon as possible."

She didn't look forward to this errand. She must tell Lady Chase she'd refused Lord Atherton, and when she did, she and Charlotte might well find themselves back in the carriage and on their way home in short order.

Charlotte's face softened and she reached across the carriage to take Lily's hand. "It will be all right, you know, one way or another."

Lily squeezed her fingers. "You're a dear to come with me, Charlotte. It may prove to be an unpleasant errand, indeed. I do hope there isn't a scene."

Charlotte shrugged. "For my part, I adore a shocking scene every now and again, but I daresay we won't have one this morning. For all your fretting, it's bound to be deadly dull."

Lady Chase received them with every appearance of pleasure, despite the early hour. She waved away Lily's apology. "Never mind that, child. No need to stand on ceremony with your grandmamma, you know."

Lily gave her grandmother what she hoped was a confident smile. "That's kind of you, ma'am."

"Well, Miss Sutherland." The old lady gave Charlotte a brisk nod. "You're welcome, as well. Shall we have some tea? Yes? The parlor, then, Eddesley."

Once they were settled and a maid had brought the tea, Lady Chase turned her shrewd blue eyes on Lily. "What brings you two young ladies out so early, then? Not very fashionable, is it?"

Lily's teacup rattled as she replaced it in the saucer. "I, ah, that is, I have something I wish to discuss with you, Grandmother, and I feel it cannot wait."

Charlotte rose from her seat and retreated to the window, as if she found something terribly interesting in Lady Chase's front garden.

"Is that so? Pray, what might that be, child?"

Lady Chase's calm, steady regard flustered Lily even more. "I've made a decision I fear will displease you."

Lady Chase retrieved her tea and took a tiny sip. "Have you, now? I suppose you refer to your rejection of Lord Atherton's suit."

Lily's stomach dropped right into her slippers. How could her grandmother know already? Why, she'd only told Lord Atherton last night!

"I—I, well, yes, but how—how did you—"

"My dear child, I've known Lady Atherton for more years than I care to count. Naturally she told me as soon as Atherton informed her. I'm sorry to say she was *not* pleased. Neither was Atherton, I gather."

Lily tried to gather her wits. "No, he was not. Not at all,

I'm afraid." He'd been downright angry, in fact, so much so he'd bordered on ungentlemanly, but Lily saw no reason to inform Lady Chase of this.

"I suppose you . . ." Lily faltered for a moment, then forced the rest of the sentence past numb lips. "I suppose you're not pleased, either, ma'am? It's my understanding you favored the match."

"Oh, yes, I did. A splendid match for you. Why did you refuse him?"

Lily stared at her grandmother, taken aback by the question. She hadn't thought her motives would interest Lady Chase. She hesitated again, but then opted for the truth. "I don't love him."

Lady Chase nodded, for all the world as if Lily had asked for more sugar in her tea. "Love, is it? Well, well. I suppose you do love that shameless rogue, don't you? Young Sutherland?"

The room tilted sideways, like the deck of a ship careening down the side of an enormous wave. Lily grasped a handful of the slippery yellow silk settee to keep from sliding to the floor in a heap.

She shot a panicked glance at Charlotte, who still stood at the window. *Oh, no*—had Charlotte overheard Lady Chase's question?

Even more to the point, how was Lily to answer? Charlotte might be listening even now, and then there was Lady Chase to consider. Dear God, she was trapped, a defenseless mouse caught between two birds of prey.

Lady Chase had evidently run out of patience, for she answered the question herself. "Now see here, miss. I know very well you *do* love Sutherland, scoundrel that he is. He's altogether undeserving of your regard, you know."

"Indeed, he is not!" Lily cried. "He's the best of men, my lady, so kind, and—"

"Yes, yes. Kind, generous, and clever, I'm sure. Handsome, too—let's not overlook handsome, for all the kindness in the world won't push a young chit's heart toward love as quickly as a pair of handsome eyes. Young Sutherland has fine, dark ones, I believe? Like his sister's, I think." She nodded toward Charlotte.

"Yes. Dark. Very fine, indeed." Despite herself, Lily felt a smile hover at the edges of her lips.

Lady Chase scowled at her. "Humph. Just as I thought."

Lily's smile faded. Before she could stop them, words began to tumble from her lips. "I'm sorry you don't approve, my lady, but I hope your displeasure won't extend to my younger sisters, for they are faultless in this, and I couldn't bear for them to—"

Lady Chase held up her hand for silence. Lily stared at the deep veins under the papery white skin, the glare of a large diamond on one of the long, spindly fingers, and despair clutched at her heart. Her sisters were to be punished for her selfishness. She'd known it would come to this—

"I'm deeply offended, child."

Oh, no. Here it was. Lily closed her eyes and prepared for Eddesley to toss them into the street on Lady Chase's orders.

"I'm deeply offended you think I'd disavow your sisters because you've rejected Lord Atherton."

Lily opened her eyes to stare at Lady Chase. Her mouth opened, then closed again before she could utter a word.

Lady Chase rapped her cane on the floor for emphasis. "I'm as offended you believe I'd disown *you* for the same reason."

Lily started to speak, but again the be-ringed hand shot into the air to prevent her. "Oh, I realize there's precedent for such belief. That business with your mother . . ."

Lady Chase's voice trailed off. Lily felt the old woman's eyes touch every part of her face—her chin, her cheekbones, her eyebrows—and she knew her grandmother saw her estranged daughter, Millicent, in every feature. A spasm of pain flashed across the old lady's face, there and gone as quickly as a diamond's flash.

The old lady reached forward and grasped Lily's hand between her own. "Well, girl, Sutherland's a foolish choice, but if he *is* your choice, I suppose I'll learn to live with it. Your grandfather and I lost a daughter because of his pride. It's too late for Lord Chase, but I've learned my lesson, and I won't lose my granddaughters, too."

Lily's heart twisted in her chest. Such pain—the grand old lady had paid a high price for her folly, and yet she'd triumphed over it in the end. Lily curled her fingers around her grandmother's hand and brought it to her lips, tenderness overwhelming her. "We don't want to lose you, either, Grandmother."

The old lady's eyes misted. She cleared her throat and gave a great sniff. "Well, now, there's no need for all that nonsense, girl. Let's just hope Sutherland doesn't make you regret your choice."

"Yes, ma'am," Lily said, hiding a grin at the old lady's gruffness.

"Miss Sutherland," Lady Chase called. "You may stop pretending to admire the view from my window now and join us."

"Of course, my lady." Charlotte turned from the window. On her way back to the settee, she shot Lily a look that said more clearly than words she *had* overheard Lady Chase's comments about Robyn, and the carriage ride home would be a merciless inquisition.

Lady Chase settled back against the settee. "Well, now we've got that foolish business out of the way, you must tell me what you think of this other foolish business."

Lily, who pretended not to see Charlotte's knowing smile, turned her attention back to her grandmother. "I beg your pardon, my lady. What foolish business?"

"Why, the duel, of course."

Charlotte and Lily gave each other blank looks. "Duel? What duel is that, ma'am?" Charlotte asked.

Lady Chase pursed her lips with disapproval. "Such a lot of foolishness if you ask me, but then, men are fools, aren't they? I suppose he said something he ought not to have said, and that hotheaded scoundrel took offense."

A dim, nameless fear began to sink sharp claws into Lily's heart. "Who said something he oughtn't? Who took offense?"

"Why, Lord Atherton, of course. He said something ungentlemanly, and young Sutherland took offense and issued a challenge. Don't tell me you didn't know?"

Lily's hand crept to her throat, and a sense of unreality swept over her. She turned and saw every drop of color drain from Charlotte's face.

No. It couldn't be. She wouldn't let it. "Robyn?" she whispered.

But she knew—even before Lady Chase nodded, she knew.

"Yes. Your Sutherland and Lord Atherton meet tomorrow at dawn, and we can only hope one or both of them don't pay for their recklessness with their lives."

"Swords or pistols?"

Robyn leaned back in his chair. They were in Alec's study with the doors closed.

"Pistols. Lucky thing, too. I've seen Atherton with a sword—Pelkey and I often stop in to watch at Angelo's after a bout at Gentleman Jackson's."

Alec considered this. "No such worry with pistols, though."

Robyn raised an eyebrow. "Why? Have you seen Atherton shoot?"

Alec grinned. "No. I've seen *you* shoot."

Robyn returned the grin, pleased by the compliment.

Alec couldn't have given him a better opening, and yet still he hesitated. Archie would act as his second if he asked, without question. Alec had responsibilities now, including a wife he adored who was several months gone with child. Perhaps he'd better ask Archie, after all—

"You're here to ask me to be your second?"

Robyn's gaze shot to Alec's face. "I thought to, yes, but perhaps Archie—"

"No." Alec looked at him, his eyes calm, and slowly shook his head. "I'll do it."

"But Delia—"

"I'll do it, Robyn."

Once Alec used that stubborn tone, argument was futile. Robyn nodded. "Very well."

He said no more, but he didn't need to say much. He held his brother's eyes, and a silent understanding passed between them.

"Who is Atherton's second?" Alec asked after a moment.

"Stafford. He sent a note round this morning to say he awaits your pleasure."

"I'll go around directly, then. Will you accept Atherton's apology, should he choose to offer one?"

"No. He knocked me to the ground when my back was turned, and that's the least of it."

Alec studied the gash on Robyn's head, the bruise on his jaw, and a faint smile rose to his lips. "Yes, I imagine it is. I hope he looks as bad as you do."

Robyn's lip curled. "He looks far worse."

Alec opened the top drawer of his desk and retrieved a key. "Since it's gone too far for an apology to suffice, I suppose I'd best lend you these."

He slid open the bottom drawer of the desk and drew out a wooden case. He fit the key into the brass lock, opened the case, and pushed it across the desk toward Robyn.

Inside was a pair of handsome dueling pistols. Robyn turned the box around and ran a finger over the green felt lining, then inspected the engraved crest affixed to the top inside cover of the box.

He raised his eyes to Alec's. "Manton's."

Alec nodded. "Yes. Walnut, with platinum and silver fittings. See the engraving here?"

Robyn whistled. "Very fine set. Have you ever fired them?"

"A few times at Manton's. Never in a duel, of course."

Robyn grinned. "What, never had to defend Delia's honor, then?"

He meant it as a jest, but instead of laughing, Alec's eyes narrowed. "You said the brawl with Atherton was the least of it. Do you defend your own honor, or someone else's? Some young lady's perhaps?"

Not *some* young lady. The *only* young lady.

Lily, her honey gold hair spread across his pillow, her soft hands on his chest, on his body, her blue eyes heavy-lidded with desire. She'd gasped when he entered her, and she clung so sweetly to him as he took her, her mouth hot against his flesh, her whimpers in his ears.

Given the chance, Atherton would have used her. He'd have stolen everything from her, squandered all that was fine about her. He'd have broken her.

Robyn drew in a slow, deep breath as boiling rage swept through him. His face heated with it. His pulse pounded with it.

He was going to kill Atherton.

"Ah. It's like that, is it?" Alec murmured. "Don't you think you owe me the whole story? Indeed, I demand it as your second."

Robyn eyed his brother. He'd never thought to hide the truth from Alec—had planned to confess it all. After the duel, that is, since he'd rather his own second didn't shoot him. The time of reckoning had come, however, so he faced it head on.

"Lily. Atherton insulted Lily."

Alec's face darkened. "What could Atherton possibly have to say against Lily?"

Robyn shifted restlessly in his chair. "She's refused him."

This didn't appease Alec. He merely shrugged. "I thought she might. Just as well. I don't see them as a match. Surely Atherton wouldn't be so ungentlemanly as to publicly insult her?"

"The devil he wouldn't. He's lost his entire fortune at the hazard tables, Alec. He wanted Lily for her money." Robyn almost spat the words. His brought his fist down hard on Alec's desk.

Alec picked up his quill to move it out of Robyn's way. "Money? What bloody money?"

"It seems Lady Chase plans to settle something on her— on all her granddaughters. She likely told Lady Atherton her plans, and then Atherton had it from his mother."

Alec's fingers tightened on the quill. "Jesus."

"That's not the worst of it. He said . . ." Robyn forced the words past stiff lips. "He had the gall to suggest any man who did marry Lily would be obliged to raise a Sutherland bastard."

Alec snapped the quill between his fingers. "I'll kill him myself."

Robyn gulped air into his lungs to try and calm himself. "Not if I get there first."

Alec paused for a moment and looked at Robyn, assessing. "So Mrs. Tittleton had the right of it, did she?"

Robyn sucked in another quick breath. *Christ.* Alec knew about Mrs. Tittleton? Lily had said—

"No need to look so shocked. Good Lord, you're as bad as Delia. Impending fatherhood or not, I'm not so distracted I could fail to hear *that* piece of gossip. Bloody everywhere, it was. So it's true, then?"

Robyn stared at him. Alec seemed to be taking this remarkably well. "Not all of it, no. At least, not at the start."

Alec leaned across the desk. "And now?"

Robyn eyed the pistols and wondered whether they were loaded. "It's all true now."

Alec relaxed back against his chair. "Ah. I don't suppose I need to ask your intentions toward her, then?"

Robyn's body went rigid. "I intend to kill any man who lays a finger on her, or any man who even *thinks* to lay a finger on her, or questions her honor in any way. She's *mine*, Alec. I love her, and I won't give her up, no matter who—"

Alec held up his hands to stop the barrage of words. "Who said anything about you giving her up?"

If Robyn hadn't known better, he'd have said his brother was amused. "She's too good for me," he muttered. "I know you think so, too—"

Alec's amusement faded. "*No.* I think nothing of the sort. It's *you* who thinks it, Robyn, not I."

Robyn was surprised into silence for a moment. He did think it. He knew he wasn't nearly good enough for Lily. He simply assumed everyone else would think so, as well. "Well, it's the truth, isn't it?"

Alec shook his head. "No. It's *never* been true that you're lacking somehow—that you're not good enough. Why do you think I didn't put a stop to this affair with Lily? I've known about it since the start, despite everyone's efforts to hide it."

Robyn rubbed a hand across the back of his neck. "Why *didn't* you put a stop to it?"

"Because I knew you wouldn't trifle with Lily," Alec said simply. "I thought you deserved the chance to prove it, if only to yourself. Despite what you may think, I never once doubted your preoccupation with her meant you were in love with her. Christ—I probably knew it even before you did."

Robyn's mouth dropped open. It was astounding that Alec had so much faith in him. And Ellie, too—something she'd said at Almack's came back to him then—something about his having a conscience.

If I believed you as callous as you wish to appear, I wouldn't be such a fond sister.

Damn. If that wasn't just like Ellie. If Alec was a step ahead of him, then Ellie was a step ahead of all of them.

Alec rubbed his fingers over his forehead. "I can see you're shocked." His face looked weary all of a sudden. "Sometimes I wish Father were still alive, so he could see the damage he's done."

"Father? What's he got to do with it?"

Alec gave a bitter laugh. "You still don't see it, do you, Robyn?" He tossed the broken quill across his desk. "Do you remember your second year at Eton? One of your tutors sent a note home to Father that first term about your extraordinary aptitude with numbers. Near-genius level, I believe he said."

Robyn frowned. "No. I recall I never excelled in maths at Eton, though, or any other subject, unless you count drinking to excess and brawling."

Alec's face went tight. "Do you recall what Father did to you, that first holiday you came home in your second year?"

Something cold lodged in Robyn's chest. "He thrashed me."

"Do you remember why?"

Robyn nodded. He didn't remember the maths tutor, but he remembered his father had thrashed him until he'd nearly lost consciousness. "I'd fought with the Earl of Huntington's son, and the earl barred Father from the Whip Club."

Alec's face twisted. "He thrashed you until you could barely walk. He never said a word about the tutor's note. You failed maths the following term."

Robyn put a hand to his forehead, as if he could pull the memory out with his fingers. *Jesus.* How could he have forgotten everything but the thrashing?

"Nothing you did was ever good enough for Father," Alec said. "You held out for years, trying your best, but at some point you just . . . gave up. Where do you suppose you got the idea you're such a disappointment to us all?"

Robyn stared at his brother. "I—I never thought about it. It's just always been there."

Alec looked him straight in the eyes. "It's time it wasn't anymore. It's time it disappeared. Don't you agree?"

Robyn tipped his head back against his chair and closed his eyes. He thought of Alec's words, and warmth began to spread through his chest. His throat worked as he struggled to allow it to wash over him, to believe he might deserve his brother's faith in him.

When he did open his eyes, he was able to face Alec without flinching. "I think it will have to, won't it? I can't allow Lily to marry a selfish, debauched rogue, after all."

Alec let out a long, slow sigh, but he kept his voice light. "It wouldn't be gentlemanly to do so, no. Speaking of gentlemanly . . ." He paused, as if not sure how to continue. "You have, ah, anticipated your wedding vows?"

Robyn had the grace to flush. He hesitated, then faced his brother again—the brother who'd always been more of a father to him, despite the closeness in their ages. "I suppose you're ashamed of me. I'm ashamed of myself."

Alec's eyebrows shot up. "Ashamed? I'm not such a hypocrite as that. More than one high stickler will be counting off the months as soon as my heir makes his appearance. Or *her* appearance. Besides." He gave Robyn a wink. "I well know the witchery the Somerset women weave. No mortal man can resist their allure. I think it's the blue eyes."

Lily's eyes. Such a deep blue they put the ocean to shame. Robyn grinned at Alec. "Once you've drowned, there seems little point in resistance."

Alec laughed and rose to his feet. "I'm off for Stafford's, then. Will you await my return?"

Robyn nodded. "Oh, and Alec? You can't tell Delia anything about this."

Alec's brow furrowed. "I can't promise that. I think my wife will wonder when I disappear from our bed before dawn tomorrow."

Robyn hadn't thought of that. "Will she swear not to tell Lily, then? I don't want Lily to know until after the duel. She'll go mad with worry when there's no need for it."

Alec searched his brother's face, his own expression serious. "See that there isn't any need, Robyn, and I'll see what I can do to secure Delia's promise."

Chapter Twenty-five

Lord Stafford offered a formal apology on Lord Atherton's behalf, an apology which Alec, acting on Robyn's behalf, just as formally refused. Robyn would meet Lord Atherton at Wimbledon Common at dawn the following day.

Tomorrow. It would come soon enough.

He had tonight, and he'd spend it with Lily in his arms. It had been hours since he'd last held her.

It felt like years. Decades.

Robyn glanced around the empty foyer. He'd hoped to find her waiting for him, but there was no sign of her in the entryway. The entire house seemed deserted, strangely silent, as if the occupants were in mourning.

Robyn felt a prickle of warning at the back of his neck as he walked down the hallway toward the parlor. He could hear muted voices within. He pushed open the door, entered, and wished at once he hadn't.

The despair in the room knocked him back a step. Three pairs of dark eyes turned toward him.

Eleanor and Charlotte sat by the fire with his mother. His sisters' eyes were red from crying.

"Robyn." His mother's voice trembled over the word. She walked across the room to fold him in her arms, but her embrace felt desperate—the embrace of a mother fearful she'd soon lose her child.

They knew. Somehow they'd found out about the duel.

If his sisters and mother knew, then Lily knew, as well. It didn't matter how they'd discovered it. All that mattered was to find Lily and try and explain it to her as best he could.

"Lily. Where is she?"

Lady Catherine looked stricken. "She's in her bedchamber with Delia. She's inconsolable, Robyn."

Ellie rose to her feet and clutched the back of her chair for support. "Is there . . . is there no other way?"

Robyn felt his face go hard and tight. "No. The offense is unforgivable."

Charlotte buried her face in her hands. "When?"

"Dawn, tomorrow. Alec will act as my second." He hesitated. "I'm sorry to put you through this."

He turned away as he said it, for he couldn't bear to see his sisters and mother in such anguish. He'd done this to them. Grief welled in his throat at the thought, but Atherton had gone too far. Robyn had no other choice than to demand satisfaction.

Lady Catherine put her hand on his shoulder and drew him a little away from his sisters. "Go to Lily. Try to make her understand. It won't be easy, I warn you. Make it right with her, Robyn, before the . . ." Lady Catherine's breath caught on a sob. "Before tomorrow morning. Make her understand, and ask her to forgive you."

Robyn took the stairs at a dead run, and within seconds he stood outside Lily's door. All was silent within. He knocked, and the door opened at once.

Delia stood there, her face pale. "It's very bad," she said without preamble. "She's—"

"I know. Will you leave us alone for a few minutes? Please, Delia."

Delia let out a long breath. "Yes, of course. If Lily asks, tell her I've gone downstairs to check on Lady Catherine."

She squeezed his arm as she passed. "Robyn? You will take the utmost care of yourself tomorrow? You won't do anything foolish?"

Robyn caught her hand and squeezed back. "I promise you. I'll see Alec remains safe, as well."

He closed the door behind her and entered the room to find Lily lying on her side on the bed, her knees drawn up to her chest. A fist gripped Robyn's heart and squeezed until every breath choked him. He wanted to fall to his knees before her, to beg her, but how did one beg for forgiveness for causing such pain?

"Oh, love. Please don't . . ." he began, but he stopped when he realized he hadn't any idea what to say, or how to comfort her.

She watched him cross the room but didn't raise her head from the pillow. He stretched out beside her on the bed and shifted her gently so her head fell onto his chest. She didn't resist him, but she remained limp and motionless beside him, a rag doll.

He ran his hands over her hair, her back, and whispered an endless stream of words into her ear: how much he loved her, how sorry he was. She didn't move or speak. He couldn't be sure she even registered his words, but he kept on just the same.

She'd understand—he'd make her understand.

At last she drew a long, unsteady breath. "You lied to me. You promised you'd never fight again."

Robyn pulled her close against him. "Yes."

She grasped a fold of his shirt tight in her fingers, a punishment, not a caress. "You broke your promise. How can I believe anything you say after this?"

He pressed his lips hard against her temple. *He had to touch her*—had to show her somehow. "I need you to trust me, Lily."

Her body tensed against his. "No. There's only one way I can trust you now."

He couldn't let her pull away from him. If she did, he knew in the deepest depths of his heart he might never hold her in his arms again. "How? I'll do anything I can, love."

She looked up into his face. "Keep the promise you made me. Don't duel with Lord Atherton. Then there is no lie. No broken promise."

Robyn closed his eyes. She asked him for the one thing he couldn't give her. If Atherton were permitted to insult Lily so grievously, what would stop others from doing the same? She was the most precious thing he'd ever had—she'd chosen him, and he was already a better man for it. Would he repay her by allowing her name to be sullied? No. He wouldn't stand by and see her hurt like that.

"I can't do that, Lily."

She twisted away from him, just as he feared she would, and rose from the bed. "You could if you wished to. Why not say the truth? It isn't that you can't. You *won't*."

Robyn sat up, every bone in his body aching with weariness. "I can't. I won't. It amounts to the same thing."

She began to pace from one side of the bedchamber to the other. "What is so unforgivable you'd risk your life over it? In what way has he offended you?"

He dragged himself to his feet and stepped in front of her to force her to halt, to look at him. If she only looked at him, perhaps she'd see . . .

"I will not repeat what he said. Ever. I can only ask you to believe me when I tell you it's unpardonable. I cannot, or will not, let it pass unchallenged."

He thought she might touch him then, but she wrapped her arms around herself instead. "But I *don't* believe you,

Robyn, because you break your promises—to your family, and now to me. I never can believe you again, about anything."

Robyn's shoulders sagged. "You don't mean that, Lily."

Her chin shot up. "I do mean it. I can never trust such a selfish man."

He said nothing. He couldn't speak.

Lily's control seemed to slip farther away with every word she uttered. "You'd continue these games with Lord Atherton, even with your very life at stake? Haven't you a care for your mother and sisters? For Alec?"

He gripped her hard by the shoulders. "Of course I care for them. Listen to me—"

"Haven't you a care for . . . me?" Her voice broke on the last word, and tears flooded her eyes.

Robyn sank to his knees and wrapped his arms around her waist. "Lily, please. You know I care for you. I love you. I *am* selfish, but I love you more than I love myself."

"Then do this for me," she whispered. "I—I can't watch you die, Robyn."

Her hands were on him, her fingers sliding into his hair to pull his head up and force him to look at her, but he couldn't bear it. Couldn't bear to see the despair there.

He pressed his face against her soft belly. "I can't. Don't—don't ask it of me, Lily."

She remained still and silent. His heartbeat thundered in his ears as he waited, a dull thud, a death knell.

Her hands slid away from him. When she spoke, it was as if she did so from a great distance. "I leave tonight. I'll stay with Delia and Alec until they go to Bellwood next week, and then I'll go with them." She reached around to grasp his wrists and pull his arms away from her waist. "You won't see me again for some time, Robyn."

His arms fell away from her, but he stayed on his knees. Perhaps he'd never rise. Perhaps he'd never have the strength to rise again. He heard the soft rustle of Lily's silk gown, then the sound of the door as it opened and closed, but he didn't raise his head.

"Lily? Lily, wake up!"

Her lungs ached and burned with each of her panicked breaths. Her gasps echoed inside her head—her gasps and the frantic pounding of her feet on the gravel pathway. She ran as fast as she could, but the tunnel of trees narrowed around her, closed in. The end of the tunnel blurred and receded with every step until the weak light she'd glimpsed ahead grew dim, and dimmer still, then vanished into the dark mist. *No way out.* She fell to the ground with a sickening thud and the leaves slithered over her, first her body, then her face. Her eyes. She tried to scream but the leaves crept into her mouth; they gagged her, choked her, suffocated her . . .

"Wake up, Lily! You're having a nightmare."

Delia's voice. A hand shook her shoulder. Hard. Lily opened her eyes.

Delia hovered over the bed, her face white. She brushed the damp, tangled hair from Lily's eyes. "It's all right— you're awake now. It was only a bad dream, Lily."

Lily rolled over onto her back and threw an arm over her eyes. *A bad dream.* Delia had snatched her from one nightmare into another one.

Except this one was real.

Delia drew the covers back, took Lily's hand, and led her to the chairs by the fire. "Come. There's no point in trying to sleep."

Lily glanced at the window, her breath trapped in her lungs. No—it was not yet dawn, but the eastern sky showed the barest hint of light. An hour. Perhaps two. No more than that.

What had she said to Robyn before she'd left him there on his knees, alone in her bedchamber? *You won't see me for some time.*

Strange—a strange thing to say to a man who might not live past the dawn.

"Oh, my dear," Delia murmured as Lily fell to her own knees and let her head fall into her sister's lap.

"I dreamed of the maze." Lily's words were muffled against Delia's nightdress.

Delia began a soothing caress over Lily's hair. "It's been some time since you had that nightmare, hasn't it?"

"Weeks. Not since we arrived in London."

Delia continued her rhythmic stroking. "I used to dream about the carriage accident, as if I'd been there with Father and Mother. I could feel it as it happened. Hear it, even. It was . . . quite awful."

A tremor passed through Delia at the memory.

Lily wrapped an arm around her sister's knee. "But you don't have the dream anymore?"

"No. It stopped when I fell in love with Alec."

Lily stiffened. She knew her sister well, and she knew what Delia was about to say. "It's not the same thing. You trust Alec. I can't trust Robyn. Not anymore."

"I don't believe that, Lily."

Lil turned her face away. "He lied to me."

Delia never ceased her slow caress. "Why do you suppose he lied?"

Lily remained quiet for a while and concentrated only on Delia's gentle hands, then replied, "To escape the consequences. He knew I'd never forgive him."

But even as the words left her mouth, she knew them for a lie. He hadn't lied to save his skin. He'd lied because—

"No, Lily," Delia murmured. "Perhaps he ought not to have lied—perhaps he should have told you the truth right away, but he did it to protect you, not to hurt you. His lie came from love, not selfishness."

A lie of love. Was there such a thing?

Delia's hand stilled. "In any case, the lie is not the reason you won't forgive him, and it's not because you don't trust him, either."

Lily jerked her head out from under Delia's hand. "What do you mean? Of course it is."

Delia shook her head. "No. You may choose to leave Robyn over this, but don't lie to yourself about the reason."

Thank God they hadn't lit the lamps. Lily was suddenly grateful Delia couldn't see her. But even with the darkness to hide her, she pressed her face against Delia's white muslin night rail. She burned with shame, but she didn't know why.

"You wanted Lord Atherton because you don't love him—could never love him." Delia twisted a lock of Lily's hair in her fingers. "Isn't that true?"

Lily hesitated, then nodded her head against Delia's leg. She'd admitted as much to herself already.

"You do love Robyn. One need only look at you to see that. But with great love comes risk, and you, Lily, have never made your peace with risk."

Lily's breath hitched in her throat. "You believe I left Robyn out of cowardice?"

How many times had she accused herself of the same thing? Too many to count, but the accusations always ended with an excuse. So be it. Cowards don't get . . .

Hurt. Cowards don't get hurt.

Then why did she feel as if her heart were being ripped from her chest when she thought of Robyn with his head bowed, on his knees in her bedchamber?

"Not cowardice," Delia said. "Fear. You're terrified, and with good reason, for you've seen far too much tragedy this past year."

Lily raised her head from Delia's lap and rose to her knees. Fear. Cowardice. Weren't they the same thing? Didn't a fearful person behave like a coward?

No. One was a coward only when they allowed their fears to crush them. She thought she'd overcome her cowardice, had told herself she had . . .

Delia reached a hand down to help her onto the sofa. "What you need to decide, my dear, is how much you're willing to give up to be safe."

Lily stared down at her lap.

"Look at me, Lily." Delia put a hand on her knee. "You've already done the brave thing. You chose Robyn over Lord Atherton. Will you truly give him up now, when he needs you the most?"

Lily pressed her palms into her eyes. Oh, she didn't know! Robyn would always be unpredictable. He'd always challenge her. But wasn't that part of what she loved about him?

Wasn't safety an illusion, in any case? A thing of smoke and mirrors? If she'd learned one thing since she came to London, it was that they were all balanced on the head of a pin. No one had any real control over their fate. The best she could do was try and find her way out of the maze instead of crumpling to the ground and giving up.

Robyn had taught her that.

Yet to court danger, to taunt death as Robyn would today—that was something else. Something worse.

Lily shook her head. "But to fight a duel, Delia—isn't that the very heart of selfishness? His mother and sisters are in agony, and what of Alec, who's obliged to second him? For pity's sake, Delia, what of you?"

"Don't you mean, what of *you*? You accuse him of selfishness, and yet he does this for you."

Delia sighed when Lily didn't answer. "Robyn is Alec's younger brother, Lily. Alec insisted on being his second. And Robyn has no choice in this. The offense is too grave. He could not overlook it without loss of honor."

Lily gave a short, bitter laugh. "Honor? No, I don't believe that. What insult could Lord Atherton have dealt Robyn that demands such a sacrifice?"

Delia stared at her. "You think Lord Atherton insulted Robyn?"

Lily cleared her throat, but nothing could remove the lump lodged there. "Didn't he?"

Delia shook her head. "I promised Alec I'd say nothing of this to you, but it seems wrong . . . Robyn didn't tell you anything?"

Tell her what? "No. He refused to repeat what Lord Atherton said."

"I didn't imagine he'd repeat it, but I thought he'd at least tell you—"

An awful suspicion took hold of Lily. "Tell me what? Delia, for pity's sake, don't keep anything from me."

Delia hesitated, then took Lily's hand. "Lord Atherton didn't insult Robyn, Lily. He insulted *you*."

Lily swayed as all the blood rushed from her head at once.

She covered her face with her hands. How could she not have realized it?

She'd called Robyn selfish. She'd told him she'd never trust him again. *Dear God*—she'd told him she was *leaving* him. Everything she'd accused him of, everything she'd reproached him for, he'd done for her.

At dawn he'd stand motionless while Lord Atherton shot at him, and he'd do it believing she didn't care for him anymore. If Atherton's bullet found his head, his heart, he would draw his last breath believing she didn't love him enough to take a risk for him, even as he risked everything for her.

Lily's eyes darted to the window. Fingers of new light streaked across the sky. Dawn, or nearly so. She reached out a trembling hand to clutch Delia's arm.

"Take me to him."

Chapter Twenty-six

"It's not too late to accept his apology."

Robyn turned away from the window. Alec lounged against the carriage seat with every appearance of ease, but Robyn could see a muscle twitching in his brother's jaw. The wooden box with the dueling pistols sat beside him on the seat.

Alec was right, of course. He could accept Atherton's apology and leave the dueling field with nary a shot fired. He could go back to Alec's house and throw himself at Lily's feet. He could tell her truthfully he didn't break his promise, he hadn't lied to her. He could beg her to forgive him.

Such a small, simple thing, to accept an apology. So easy. *So impossible.* "No."

"No. I didn't suppose you would." Alec twisted his mouth in a pained half smile.

"Would you, given the circumstances?"

Alec drummed his fingers on the box at his side. "No."

Robyn turned back to the window. "No. I didn't suppose you would."

Both men fell silent. The carriage wheels rattled over the London streets, southwest toward Wimbledon Common. After a while the sound of the wheels became quieter, muffled. They'd passed onto the softer ground of the park.

Not long now.

"Alec, if the worst should happen . . ."

Robyn's voice trailed off into silence. He should say things, shouldn't he? Give instructions of some sort. Something. He cleared his throat. "I've left a letter for Lily. If the worst should happen, you'll see she gets it?"

He'd remained awake long into the night, writing the letter, trying to find the words to tell Lily everything he hadn't had a chance to say, and everything he'd already said, but not enough times. When he at last retired to his bed, he hadn't slept. He'd lain awake the rest of the night, inhaling the scent of sun, warm grass, and daisies that still lingered on his sheets.

"Give it to her yourself when we get home." Alec gave a casual shrug, but the gesture looked forced.

"Atherton's already here, as arranged, and Stafford with him," Alec said a few moments later. "Archie's here as well, with the surgeon."

The carriage drew to a halt. It was time.

Robyn opened the door and stepped down onto the ground. He looked into the sky to see streaks of pale pink light filtering through the smog. Would it be one of those rare London days when the air became soft and the coal smoke inexplicably cleared and one could see the sky? What would Lily do with such a fine day? He hoped she'd go outdoors, feel the warm air on her skin, and raise her face to the blue above.

Archie came around the side of the carriage and lay a warning hand on Robyn's shoulder. "Atherton's a wreck. I think he's still half-sotted from last night. Stafford wants to step in for him, but Atherton won't have it."

"Christ." Alec descended from the carriage after Robyn. "He's more dangerous in that condition than he would be otherwise. He may not be able to aim, but he'll be damned unpredictable. He could shoot wild before you ever reach your mark, Robyn."

Robyn gave Alec a grim smile. "I'll take my chances."

"Damn it, Robyn," Alec began, but Robyn turned away. He rounded the carriages and walked over to Atherton and Stafford. "Gentlemen." He gave them a formal bow. "I await your pleasure."

Stafford returned the bow, all correct politeness, but there were white lines of strain around his mouth. Atherton, who looked rather unsteady on his feet, said nothing, but he did sway forward in what Robyn took to be an attempt at a bow.

Alec and Archie followed behind Robyn. Stafford exchanged bows with them both. "Your weapon, if you please." He held out his hand.

Alec retrieved one of the Manton pistols from the box and handed it over to Stafford.

"Very fine," Stafford murmured, balancing the weapon in his hand. "The weapons are comparable." He handed a pistol to Alec for inspection.

"One of Purdey's," Alec murmured to Archie and Robyn. "Also very fine. May I have your word of honor you've loaded in accordance with the agreement?" Alec asked, addressing Stafford.

"You have my word of honor, and I ask for your word in return."

"You have my word. Single shot, smooth."

Stafford nodded, then turned to Atherton, who watched the proceedings with an odd smirk, but had yet to say a word. Stafford spoke to him in low, urgent tones.

Atherton glanced over Stafford's shoulder and locked

eyes with Robyn. He gave an ugly sneer, then turned back to Stafford and jerked his head. Whatever Stafford asked of him, Atherton had refused.

Stafford hesitated, then pressed the pistol into Atherton's hand. Atherton looked down at it as if he wasn't quite sure why it was there.

Jesus. Atherton was nearly incoherent. Robyn didn't care to fire on a man who looked as if he could barely hold a pistol, but if the sneer was any indication, Atherton was still filled with rage. Every time Lily's name came up in company, Robyn knew that same sneer would appear on Atherton's face.

Alec handed the pistol to Robyn. "He looks as though he's about to fall over."

"Can he stand his mark?"

Alec glanced back at Stafford and Atherton, then shook his head. "Difficult to say. What a bloody mess. I'd hate to be Stafford right now. It's like sending a man to the gallows."

Robyn felt his face go stiff. "A guilty man deserves the gallows."

"Gentlemen," Stafford called before Alec could answer. "Fifteen paces?"

Robyn glanced at Alec, then frowned. "I believe we agreed on ten, my lord."

Stafford gave a curt bow. "You're a marksman, Mr. Sutherland."

And Atherton is in no shape to duel. Stafford didn't say this, but he didn't need to.

Robyn returned the bow. "Very well. Fifteen paces."

Robyn and Atherton moved into position, back to back, and counted off their paces. When Robyn turned, he found Atherton facing him, his pistol aimed at Robyn's heart.

Robyn raised his arm, took aim, and then held, waiting for the signal.

"One shot only, gentlemen, simultaneous," Stafford called. He held a white handkerchief aloft. Robyn fixed his eyes on Atherton, his arm steady, every muscle in his body tensed, and waited for the white linen to flutter to the ground.

Lord Stafford raised his arm, but before the cloth could leave his fingers, a deafening crack thundered inside Robyn's skull. He dimly registered a high-pitched, terrified scream; not Alec or Archie—a woman's scream. The smell of burnt powder stung his nostrils as clouds of acrid smoke issued from the end of Atherton's pistol.

"We're too late, Delia."

Lily sat with her face pressed to the carriage window, panic choking her. The sun continued to rise, and Lily's despair grew with every inch it crept closer and closer to the horizon.

Delia sat across from her, her hands in her lap, knuckles white. "We can't be far behind. I thought perhaps we'd over-take the carriage . . ."

But they hadn't overtaken the carriage. They'd entered Wimbledon Commons some minutes ago, but Delia knew only that the duel was to be fought here. Alec, never dream-ing they'd follow, hadn't told her precisely where, and no doubt he'd taken care to choose an obscure spot.

The carriage rolled aimlessly over the grounds. They were no closer than they'd been when they'd entered the Commons.

Lily darted a look out the window. "We'll not make it. It's dawn even now."

Dawn. Robyn could be stretched on his back on Wimble-don Commons even now, lifeless, the dark eyes she loved so well staring sightlessly up at a sky he'd never see again.

Lily bit down hard on her cheek, and her mouth filled with blood, sharp metal on her tongue.

It seemed incredible it was only weeks ago she'd worried the *ton* would gossip about her. She'd thought it the worst calamity to be called a wallflower, or have Mrs. Tittleton sneer at her. Now Robyn would pay, perhaps with his life, to defend a reputation she no longer cared a thing about. What did it matter what Lord Atherton said of her? What anyone said of her?

Nothing mattered anymore—nothing but Robyn.

She pressed her lips together to keep a hysterical little laugh from escaping. What a fitting punishment for her folly, and what a bloody taste it had, that bitter irony.

"Lily!"

Lily jumped, startled by Delia's gasp, but just then, without warning, the carriage made a sudden, hard turn to the right and Lily slid across the seat and crashed into the opposite door.

When she righted herself, she found Delia, who'd managed to hang on, pointing a shaking finger out the window. "There! The driver's seen them as well. Oh, *thank God*."

Lily scrambled back across the seat to get to the window. Just ahead, through a gap in a grove of tall trees, she could see the first pale shafts of sunlight flash off the roof of a black carriage.

Please, please don't let us be too late.

The driver flew over the grounds at a speed that would have terrified her in any other situation, and yet it felt as if the distant carriage roof only receded, just as the end of the maze had in her nightmare. It drifted farther away with every thump of their horses' hooves.

She could close her eyes. She could collapse to the floor of the carriage so she didn't have to watch . . .

Lily threw her shoulders back and set her jaw. *No.* Not this time. She wasn't a child lost in a maze anymore. She *would* reach Robyn in time, and if she didn't . . . if she didn't . . .

She *would*, because any other outcome was unthinkable.

Delia pressed her palms to the window. "I see Alec and Archie, but I don't see . . . oh! Oh, *no*. Robyn and Lord

Atherton have walked their paces. Oh, *hurry*!" She slammed her fist against the roof of the carriage.

Lily rose to her knees on the carriage seat. She craned her neck and saw Alec, Archie, and a man she didn't recognize standing off to the side of a clear patch of ground. One of the men turned at the sound of the carriage as it approached, shock on his face.

Robyn. Where was Robyn?

Another man stood at the edge of the clearing, a bit of white cloth in his hand. Just beyond him, in the center of the clearing—there!

Robyn and Atherton faced each other, their arms extended, pistols gripped in their hands. At this moment, he was still alive. There was still hope. Dear God, *please, please . . .*

The carriage screeched to a halt. Lily clawed at the door, Delia right behind her. They wrenched it open and fell to the ground.

Crack! A sound, a whip slicing through the air, but louder, deafening. Lily had a confused impression of smoke, a burning smell, and then Delia's voice, shrill, hysterical. "He's anticipated the signal! Lord Atherton—he's shot too soon!"

Lily didn't hear her own scream. She didn't feel the dust under her knees as she fell to the ground.

Robyn's knees shook and a trickle of sweat inched down his face. The air near his left shoulder shifted as the bullet passed.

Atherton's shot had gone wide.

Christ. It had been close—far closer than he'd have thought a man in Atherton's condition could aim.

But not close enough.

Robyn narrowed his eyes on his target and forced his arm to steady. His aim was dead on—he could feel it in every inch of his body. He stroked the trigger with his finger, and yet . . .

He hesitated. More sweat gathered in the small of his back.

Atherton had knocked him down, and now he'd disgraced himself by shooting ahead of the signal. It didn't matter whether it was done by design or accident. Either way, Robyn needed no further justification to lodge a bullet right between Atherton's eyes.

Atherton had insulted Lily—grievously insulted her. Robyn tightened his finger on the trigger, and yet still he hesitated as an image rose in his mind.

Lily, her face white, begging him not to duel with Atherton.

If he killed Atherton, he wouldn't be the only one to carry the burden of the man's death. Lily would carry it, too. Could he do that to her? Justified or not, this was murder, pure and simple. How could he ever deserve Lily if he had Atherton's blood on his hands?

Even if he never held her again, he wanted to deserve her.

Mere seconds had passed since Atherton had taken his shot. Was that all it took, then? Seconds? It seemed a pitifully brief amount of time for a life's worth of mistakes and regrets to drift through his mind.

Yet it was enough.

Robyn knew what he had to do, and he'd no longer hesitate.

He pulled his spine straight and focused on Atherton's left eye, his touch on the trigger so light, delicate, no more than a whisper, but enough, just enough . . .

Crack! The sound ripped through the quiet morning, but Robyn didn't hear it. The pistol kicked hard in his hand, but he didn't feel it. He focused only on his opponent. Atherton's head jerked back with the force of the bullet. He looked stunned as his knees gave out from under him and he toppled forward.

His face hit the ground.

Robyn let his arm fall to his side. He held the pistol loosely in his fingers. Stafford and the surgeon leapt toward Atherton, then hovered over the prone body.

Robyn waited. It was a long time before Stafford stood. When he did, he turned to Robyn, an unmistakable look of admiration on his face.

Then he and the doctor helped Atherton to his feet.

"You missed," Atherton hissed when Robyn drew close enough to hear him.

Robyn stepped forward until his face was inches from Atherton's. He flicked a dispassionate eye over the bloody wound where his bullet had grazed Atherton's cheekbone.

"I never miss," he said, his voice soft, deadly. "That's going to leave a nasty scar, Atherton. Let it be a reminder to you, and a warning. If I ever hear you breathe a word against Miss Somerset, I'll challenge you again. I won't miss then, either."

Atherton's face drained of color.

Satisfied, Robyn turned to walk back to Archie and Alec. That's when he saw her.

Lily, on her knees on the ground, face in her hands, her shoulders shaking. Without a word, he strode over to her, lifted her in his arms, and carried her to the carriage.

Alec did not look happy. He stood next to the carriage, shaking with a combination of rage and fear.

"What in the devil possessed you to . . . a dueling field, Delia? One of the most dangerous stunts . . . damned foolish . . . and with my child, no less!"

Alec was so incensed, he could hardly string a sentence together, but Delia seemed to understand him easily enough. She placed her hands on her hips. "I couldn't very well leave your child behind, could I?"

Alec gaped at her, then stomped forward and snatched

open the carriage door. "Get in. We'll discuss this—" He seemed surprised to see Lily and Robyn already seated in the carriage. "What the devil—"

Delia took her husband's arm with a heavy sigh. "We'll travel in yours, my lord." She dragged him toward the carriage he and Robyn had arrived in. "Archie, you'll meet us at Lady Catherine's? She'll be frantic until she sees Robyn with her own eyes."

Robyn reached forward and slammed the carriage door closed. "Lily." He wrapped his arms around her and pulled her into his lap. "What are you doing here?"

He rubbed his hands over her back. So many conflicting emotions washed over him at once, he couldn't tell how to disentangle one from another. Anger, yes, because she'd so carelessly risked her safety, but gratitude, as well. She was here—*she'd come here for him.* Joy, so profound it stole his breath, but also a paralyzing doubt. She was in his arms now, but how long would she stay there?

She wrapped her arms around his neck and pressed her face against his throat.

Hope.

"I made a terrible mistake," she gasped against him. "I'm so sorry, Robyn, so—"

He eased her backward on his lap and tipped her face up to his with gentle fingers under her chin. "Take a deep breath, sweetheart. Yes, that's it. Now tell me."

She pressed her palms to either side of his face. "I made a terrible mistake. When you told me of the duel I . . . all I could think was I'd lose you, and I couldn't bear it, and I said terrible things. I do trust you, Robyn, with my life, even, and—"

She wasn't finished, but Robyn couldn't keep from kissing her then. She kissed him back with a hunger that made him shake, but before he could coax her mouth to open under his, she pulled away.

"I can't think when you kiss me," she said. "I have to say

this. I made Delia bring me because I couldn't let you get hurt . . . I couldn't let you . . ."

Her voice shook and he knew she was thinking he could have died today. He brushed the hair back from her face. "Shh, love. Hush. It's all right now. It's all right."

She grabbed his wrist. "No, please let me say this. I behaved like a coward, Robyn. I was so afraid I'd lose you, I pushed you away, and I know I hurt you terribly. If you'd died today believing I'd left you, believing I didn't care for you, I could never have forgiven myself."

She pressed kisses against his eyes, his cheeks, and his chin, then slid her fingers into his hair and leaned forward to kiss his forehead.

Robyn's throat closed at the sweetness of it. "Do you care for me, Lily? Do you forgive me?"

She pulled back to look into his eyes. "Forgive you? All the way here I prayed to have a chance to beg you to forgive *me*. I love you, Robyn, so, so much. Please forgive me."

Robyn groaned. He closed his hands hard around her waist and let his face fall into her hair. Warm grass, sunshine, and daisies. He'd spend his entire life learning every nuance of her scent. "Ah, my Lily. I love you, too. So much it hurts."

"No more hurt, Robyn, not for either of us."

Robyn took her mouth then and let his kiss speak for him, telling her without words of the love and passion he felt for her.

No more hurt, and no more need for forgiveness.

Epilogue

Alexander Robert Henry Sutherland, heir to the Carlisle earldom, was born on a Tuesday, at 4:43 a.m., exactly 8 months and 27 days after Delia and Alec's wedding.

Robyn leaned his head back against a stack of pillows and swung his legs up on the bed. "Well, that should force more than one high stickler to bite her wagging tongue."

Lily stuck her head out of her dressing closet. "Oh, they quieted some time ago. They quite lost hope after Delia passed her eighth month."

Robyn tugged at his cravat. "Odd-looking child, don't you think? Poor thing looks like Alec."

Lily had disappeared back into her dressing closet, but at this, she stuck her head out again for a scold. "Robyn! What an awful thing to say!"

Robyn tossed his cravat to the floor, quickly followed by his coat. "Don't tell me you didn't notice how red and wrinkled he is."

"All babies are red and wrinkled. He's a beautiful child.

In fact, I heard your mother say he looks just like you did when you were born."

Robyn paused in the process of unbuttoning his waistcoat. "Good Lord."

Lily poked her head around the corner of the dressing closet again, but she kept her body out of sight. "He may be red and wrinkled now, but I think he stands a fair chance of growing up to be as devastatingly handsome as his uncle."

"If I'm so devastatingly handsome, why are you hiding back there? I don't care for these large apartments. How can I ever get my hands on you if you've got so many places to hide?"

After their wedding, Lady Catherine had insisted they take the master's apartments at the Mayfair town house until the renovations were complete on their own new home in Berkeley Square. Lily had protested the extravagance of purchasing the house, but her grandmother had insisted upon it, arguing that if Lily was obliged to live with "that scoundrel, young Sutherland," she at least deserved a lovely home.

"You had your hands on me all morning," Lily reminded him.

Robyn's waistcoat hit the floor and he began on his shirt. "That was ages ago, Mrs. Sutherland. Now either you come out, or I'll come in there and fetch you myself."

He rose from the bed and advanced on her dressing closet with a growl.

Lily ducked back behind the corner with a little squeal. "I have a surprise for you."

Robyn stopped, his shirt hanging loose. "Do you? I'm intrigued. What sort of surprise?"

"The kind of surprise you love most. Now, go and lie down on the bed and close your eyes, and if I catch you peeking, I promise you I'll dash back into the closet."

Robyn decided any movement toward the bed was a step

in the right direction, so he did as he was told. "All right. My eyes are closed."

He heard Lily creep across the floor. It sounded as though her feet were bare. He hoped the rest of her was, as well.

"Open your eyes."

He opened them to find Lily standing at the foot of the bed in her wrapper. "Are you naked under there?"

Lily giggled. "Not quite."

Robyn leaned up on his elbows. "I don't care for surprises that don't involve you being naked."

Lily began to untie the sash at her waist. "Indeed? What a shame. I suppose I'll have to save these for another gentleman, then."

The knot on the sash fell open, and Lily let the silk wrapper slither to the floor.

Robyn's jaw went slack. "Are those . . . breeches?"

Lily gave a little wiggle of her hips. "Yes. Do you like them?"

She stood before him clad only in a pair of tight-fitting breeches.

He ran a hand across his mouth. "Like them?"

He lunged for her, but Lily skipped away before he could catch her in his arms and drag her onto the bed. "Is that a yes? Or dear me, is it a no? You must not like them, for you seem quite anxious to get them off me."

Robyn came to his knees on the bed, prepared to lunge for her a second time. "Where—where did you get them?" He groaned when Lily turned with another little wiggle to show him the back view.

She smiled flirtatiously at him over her bare shoulder. "I had them made a while ago. I've been waiting for the right time to show them to you."

Robyn shook his head as if to clear it, then he began to creep toward the end of the bed, still on his knees. "Is there a . . . *wrong* time?"

Lily, who was more than ready to be caught, pretended not to notice him preparing to pounce on her. "No wrong time? Well, then, perhaps I'll wear them to the theater tomorrow night."

Robyn launched himself at her, grabbed her around the waist, and tossed her onto the bed. He was on top of her in a flash, pinning her with his body. Lily shrieked and laughed and pretended to struggle against him.

"The theater? Oh, I don't think so, my love." He ran his hands up her thighs and across her hips. "It would cause a riot, you know, because then every man in London would want what's mine."

Lily arched against him as his hands slid from her hips to her bottom. He filled his palms with a generous handful of her curves and pulled her hard against him. She moaned as she felt his other hand tear at the buttons of her breeches.

He caught her moan in his mouth. His tongue teased at her lips, then he pressed his mouth against her ear. "You wouldn't want to cause a scandal, would you, Mrs. Sutherland?"

Lily slid her hands inside his open shirt to caress his chest. "Scandal? I care nothing for scandal. It's far too late for that, I'm afraid. I've already married the wickedest gentleman in London."

Author's Note

There is some discrepancy in the scholarship regarding the year the waltz was first danced at Almack's. While some date it as early as 1813, others argue the waltz was not danced at Almack's until much later—closer to 1815. Some scholars credit Lady Jersey with bringing the waltz to Almack's hallowed halls, whereas others credit Countess Dorothea von Lieven with having introduced the scandalous dance to Almack's esteemed guests sometime in 1814.

For the purposes of Lily and Robyn's story, the author asks the indulgence of the reader for taking artistic license and assuming that by 1814 the waltz would have been known at Almack's and also to English society, yet still considered risqué enough that young ladies who were not yet "out" (had not yet been presented at Court) were prohibited by the Almack's patronesses from participating in the dance. To dance the waltz without permission was considered a deadly social transgression, one from which Lily's reputation would not have recovered.

Almack's patronesses were well known among London society for their strict adherence to the rules of propriety. In Chapter 7, Eleanor mentions to Lily and Lady Catherine that the Duke of Wellington himself would not be permitted to cross Almack's threshold should he arrive later than 11 p.m. This is a reference to a rumor circulating in London in 1814 that the duke was refused entrance to Almack's, either because he arrived late or because he was wearing trousers rather than the requisite knee breeches considered the proper attire at Almack's.

One hopes the duke might have had better luck had he made this attempt after his defeat of Napoleon at Waterloo in 1815, but considering the rigid propriety observed by Almack's patronesses, this is by no means certain.